David Milsted lives in Skye with his wife, writer Jan Holt, and four children. He claims that at 6′3″, he is probably the tallest living writer of humorous prose fiction in Scotland. Born in Sussex in 1954, he trained as a schoolteacher in Newcastle, and has lived in Carlisle, Orkney and Islay.

By the same author

The Chronicles of Craigfieth

DAVID MILSTED

Market Forces

GRAFTON BOOKS

A Division of the Collins Publishing Group

LONDON GLASGOW
TORONTO SYDNEY AUCKLAND

Grafton Books
A Division of the Collins Publishing Group
8 Grafton Street, London W1X 3LA

Published by Grafton Books 1990

First published in Great Britain by
Mainstream Publishing Company (Edinburgh) Ltd 1989

Copyright © David Milsted 1989

ISBN 0-586-20950-6

Printed and bound in Great Britain by
Collins, Glasgow

Set in Times

This book is for
JOHN D. I. MACDONALD LLB DipLP NP
and the good ghosts of Islay

CAUTION
Market Forces is a work of fiction and all the characters in it are fictitious, especially the nasty ones.

Prologue

It is a bright early spring morning some time in the near future in the small Scottish town of Craigfieth. Cold, but with just a hint of June's drowsy splendour; calm, though with that restive, febrile sort of stillness that goes with change, with beginnings. Clear, too – you can see for miles this morning, and the miles seem short – as if all visible creation has been assembled for a prologue, and is impatient for the swelling act to get on with it.

Mrs Spurtle, widow and tea-shop proprietrix, thinks of swelling acts as she glares at her blackly raked summer bulb border. Come on up, she thinks, come on up, and let me get at you. Spring, with all its unpleasant associations, is not Mrs Spurtle's favourite time of year; neither, for that matter, is winter, with all its false and grasping bonhomie, nor summer, which is decadent, if good for trade. She prefers autumn, season of blighted hopes and dying falls.

Her friend and helper Miss Phemister, however, already at work in the Bide-a-Wee kitchen and up to her pachydermic elbows in hot suds, senses its delicious unease and twitters softly. A soapy hand ventures to undo a cardigan button; then, trembling slightly, a second. Lascivious tongues of steam caress the broken pane above the sink. She starts to sing.

Mrs Spurtle spies out all the season's tell-tale signs as she pounds along the street. In the window of Glencairn's the baker's little mains-operated promotional mannikin – a santa just a few short winter weeks ago – has been got up as an especially revolting Easter Bunny; in one hand it carries a handwritten card urging her to ORDER YOU'RE HOT X BUN'S 'NOW'! So much, thinks Mrs Spurtle, for education. Madame's has twenty per cent off thermal socks and fleecy mittens; Haq's a display of boxed and quilted Mother's Day cards, all equally nauseating. Mr Meiklejohn is clearing his hot water bottles at three for the price of two and Grace Ganglion would have a nerve to be giving away brussels sprouts in that condition, never mind selling them. At least old Smellie, Mrs Ganglion's predecessor, had the decency to put the really yellow ones to the bottom. Even the Post Office is not immune: its latest selection of Special Commemoratives features lambs, chicks, and other emblems of pagan fecundity.

Miss Phemister has put daffodils in all the vases and is singing, 'For I'm to be Queen of the May, Mother, I'm to be – '

Mrs Spurtle hurls the door open. 'Stop squawking, woman!' she growls. 'It isn't May yet!'

Miss Phemister drops a plate. 'No, dear,' she bleats.'No, of course not. Silly of me.' Furtively, she refastens her buttons.

It is the near future. The townsfolk of Craigfieth have suffered a thousand million tiny siftings of life's grim riddle since the net curtain was last plucked aside. Some have fallen through; most are hanging on.

Mr McMurtry, now completely bald, cuddles his nest-egg at the Scottish Amiable and Providential Bank, resists the offers from head office to take early retirement on increasingly advantageous terms and pretends not to notice the obvious resentment of his investment manager, Mr Kirk, who drives a fast car and looks as though he shaves three times a week, and is often to be seen these days in the company of young Sayeed Haq. Sayeed has been away for his Management Studies degree and returned to help his younger sister Benazir look after their father's Universal Emporium during his parliamentary absences: yes, Mahommed Haq is Councillor Haq no longer, but the Honourable Member for Central Perthshire, Mahommed Haq, MP. Rumour has it that Ministerial responsibilities may shortly call him away from Scottish affairs, that the Prime Minister is keen to see the government's new Immigration Bill delivered by a safer pair of hands than those of its current caucasian midwife. If this is true, then Mr McMurtry may be among the first to know: the MP and he are on warm surname terms.

Mr Kirkpatrick has gone, having achieved by his marriage to Lord Margoyle's daughter (in Dunbroath Abbey, by the youthful Episcopalian bishop) an unlikely union of the unspeakable with the unimaginable. They were last heard of running a design consultancy in an improving area of south-east London where Davinia has many contacts eager to avail themselves of Wayne's talents as a co-ordinator of domestic fittings. His DIY Centre, once the cutting edge of the town's entrepreneurial revolution, has meanwhile severed its last remaining link with the antediluvian era of tiny brass screws, tarry string, and four-inch nails by the quarter-pound. It was bought by a company calling itself InnerSpace (Scotland) Ltd, rechristened The Ministry of the Interior, and filled with gaunt examples of what the older residents of Craigfieth recognize as once-commonplace items of household furniture. It is hardly ever open, though its window display appears to indicate a brisk turnover. It seems to enjoy a brisk turnover in managers, too.

Old Mr Fingal's Rod and Gun shop became the Fly Bite Restaurant. It is regularly mentioned in the programmes of the Dunbroath Festival Theatre, and has been patronized by Clement Freud and Roy Hattersley though not, fortunately, at the same time. *Les patrons* are Hamilton Fingal (Hammy, to his intimates) and his wife Amanda. 'My forebears stuffed animals,' quips Hammy in his publicity handout. 'Mandy and I prefer to stuff humans.' It is a jest which only those who have sampled the extreme end of the Fly Bite's *cuisine minceur* can fully appreciate. Mr Fingal senior enjoys the use of a bedsit at the rear of the premises in return for doing the washing-up and keeping otherwise out of sight. It is better than the Eventide, he tells himself.

Grace and Hamish Ganglion, that pair of star-crossed shopkeepers, are doing well; though it sometimes occurs to them (Grace in particular) that they do not see much of each other, they see enough to have produced two children: Ashley Oswald, who is now at school under the firm tutelage of the same Miss Pleat in whose classroom his father suffered a quarter of a century ago, and young Wally. Ashley Oswald shows aptitude for tactile expression and manipulative skill-building, according to his first report card, a fact which Grace puts down to long infant hours spent playing with the stock while she was establishing the Scottish Produce Centre as Mid Lummock's premier fruit and vegetable outlet. Young Wally, however (it is, according to his paternal grandfather, a family name), is more of a daddy's boy. Sometimes he sits and stares, and sometimes he just sits. 'He takes a lot in,' says Grace, adding proudly that he slept right through the night from the age of five weeks. He is large for his age, and very tractable. As Grace points out, you can put him anywhere and not worry.

Old Ganglion, Hamish's father, and Oswald Ochilree, fellow escapees from the semi-benevolent tyranny of the Craigfieth Eventide Home, still live in Rose Cottage, the latter's little pink-washed but and ben in the Lummock Hills. They have taken to signing their Christmas cards with the inscription, 'Still not dead yet – watch this space'. Lady Lazarus, their beloved Austin FX3 ex-London taxi-cab, has succumbed at last to the rusty scythe of the grim reaper, and is now presumably ferrying her maximum permitted number of shady passengers between the banks of Lethe. Her mortal remains serve as an early-cropping marijuana plantation (driver's cab, with the seat removed). Unenlightened visitors assume them to be fruitless tomatoes, and tactfully refrain from comment. The two old companions now drive a 2CV which on visits to Craigfieth is always parked outside the Fly Bite, 'to keep up its yuppie image'. They describe themselves as Gedoffs: short for Geriatric, Deathwardly Mobile Old Farts. They find this very funny. The final punchline, says Ganglion, will have to be something pretty bloody good if it's going to catch *them* short of a riposte. They have grown to resemble each other, in the mysterious way certain married couples do, and it is hard – especially for them – to think of one without the other: so they try not to and, on the whole, they succeed.

God is served in the Kirk by the Rev. Gilleasbuig MacAndrew and in the Gospel Hall by the evangelist, Clyde Bilt, a young man of obvious charm and rectitude who arrived on an open-ended free transfer from the United World Redemption Church of Christ the Communicator (Detroit) Inc, via the Scottish offices of Hosanna International ('Say HI! to Jesus'), newly franchized proprietors of HI! Vision, one of the nation's many deregulated TV channels. To hear Mr Bilt proclaim, at the beginning of his induction rally, 'My dear new fra-yunds and brethren, Ah truly declare before Gard that Ah was born again before my first diaper change,' was indeed a great relief all round; besides – foreby he had a beautiful wife and two exquisite children whose combined smile wattage might save a fortune in Hydro bills – he scarcely looked old enough to have *had* a past, far less strayed in it.

'Ah thank my Lord and Saviour Jesus Christ,' he declared (really it was surprising how nice some American accents could be) 'that my dear wife Chylblayne and myself and our darling littles ones, Fawn and Hall, have been spared temptation's evil influence but we must nat fergit, my friends, nat ever must we fergit, that each and every sin can be a durrway for each and every sinner to enner the glorious Kengdom of Gard. *Leddus nat slayem thet durr!*' Amen, they breathed, and humbly thanked Gard in their hearts that it wasn't their door any more.

'First it was policemen,' sighed the Rev. MacAndrew, that memorable evening. 'Now it's Gospel preachers. At least my congregation makes me feel young!'

'Never mind, dear,' said his wife. 'I never wanted you to have a portrait in the attic anyway.'

Later that night she surprised him with a second embrace just as he was dozing off. 'Gilleasbuig!' she whispered.

'Mmm?'

'Promise me something!'

'What?'

'You won't start jogging, will you?'

'Good heavens, no! Absolutely not.'

'Oh good,' she murmured. 'We'll see about your day-glo dentures in the morning then, dear.' Then she turned over in a wiggly sort of way that suggested to the Rev. MacAndrew that she might be offering him the chance to prove a point and, finding his suspicions confirmed, he proved it.

Clyde Bilt has quickly become a settled part of Craigfieth's social pattern, as familiar in the High Street as he is on the town's TV screens.

* * *

12

The passing years have seen a diminution – almost to vanishing point – in the number of Taiwanese wares imported, via a trading company in South Croydon, to the retail premises of the Craft Corner. Not only has Mrs Audrey Pitt-Holyoake increased her output of water-coloured landscapes – she finds the action of the paint-roller very therapeutic for her arthritis – but most of her remaining stock is now obtained from the workshops of the Highland Craft Centre, just twenty miles or so up the road in Blairlummock, Scotland's premier Visitor Village. Though aesthetically indistinguishable, for the most part, from the sweated produce of the Republic of China, these geegaws are entitled to that supreme cachet of ethnocultural authenticity, the Craft Made Label – and this, after all, is principally what the visitors are looking for. Mrs Pitt-Holyoake is doing quite nicely, and Dante Cottage, Mrs Pitt-Holyoake's cosy little nest, has been extensively re-chintzed, and is shortly (she hopes) to feature in the 'Byeways of Design' section of *Scottish Country Matters*.

What else is there to say? Nothing much, really: the Victorian mass that once housed the Craigfieth Museum is now the Sunnyvale Nursing Home, a privately run repository for the affluent aged, so little evident change there, except that the original skeletal remains have gone (no one is quite sure where) and the two prize exhibits – the Pictish Symbol Stone and the old Mercat Cross – have been put into storage by the Archaeological Service Department of Eastern Region, pending a decision on their final placement. After the splendid fight over the fate of these treasures a few years before, there was surprisingly little fuss made about this closure and removal; the new MP in particular counselled acquiescence in the matter, and most people were happy enough to accept his advice. The Sunnyvale has even fewer visitors than the museum had; most of the new relics are from outwith the burgh.

Mrs Spurtle opens the Bide-a-Wee's morning mail: it is a leaflet from the Gala Committee, intimating the preliminary arrangements for this year's festivities. Innovation, it seems, is in the air! Mr Bilt has promised a Carnival of Youth For Jesus in place of the usual offering from the Gospel choir; suggestions are invited for the Gala Queen's transport now that the Glenlummock Visitor Centre donkey is no more, and the Grand Opening Ceremony is to be performed not by one person but by two, viz Mince'n'Tatties (a.k.a. Norman Foffarty and Angus Thrums), the Well-Known Comedy Duo, As Seen On TV. The theme for this year's Best Dressed Shop Window competition is to be 'Our Heritage of Enterprise'; Mavis Thrush ('The Lummock Linnet') will read a selection of her own poems in the Community Centre, accompanied by her daughter Archibaldina on the Celtic harp, with assistance from the Scottish Arts Council. All this will, of course, be additional to all the familiar events that have become so much a tradition in the years since 1947 and as if to prove the point, the leaflet (S. Chisholm, Printer, Craigfieth) contains three glaring literals, including a particularly unfortunate transposition in the word 'stewardship'.

Mrs Spurtle sighs heavily. '*Plus ça change,*' she says.

'Oh yes, dear,' says Miss Phemister, 'but things still stay the same, really, don't they? Ay'm sorry,' she adds, 'isn't that what you meant?'

And yet . . . and yet . . . It is not just the mysteriousness of the Ministry of the Interior, with its invisible clientèle and its bewildering variety of managers; it is not just the translation of Cyril Bullock into Clyde Bilt, or of the

14

museum into the Sunnyvale, or of Haq into the Hon. Member for Central Perthshire. It is not even the inexplicable emptiness of certain houses in the High Street, houses that have certainly been bought by somebody, but which are still unoccupied, months afterwards. It is none of these things, nor yet is it the sum of them. It is a Something, just out of reach, just beyond perception, but there . . . somewhere, all the same, like the promise of the autumn fruit in the green bud of March. And, there – it's gone.

For the moment.

Chapter One

'Hamish!'

Grace's call came at an awkward moment. Hamish was about to negotiate the bend on the stairs, carrying a leaden Wally on one arm and a sit'n'ride lion, two cushions and a nylon shirt sleeve, Wally's comforter, in the other.

'Pear,' said Wally.

'Stair, yes,' said Hamish. 'What?'

'Hamish!'

'Pie,' said Wally.

'Shush!' said Hamish. 'What?'

'PIE!' said Wally.

'Oh, help! Sky, okay, right!'

Wally was essentially a creature of habit. One of his little morning routines was to launch himself backwards at this stage of the descent, gripping only his father's left ear for support, in order to look up at the skylight in the roof directly above them.

'Pie,' said Wally.

'Yeah, sky,' said Hamish. 'What is it, Grace?'

'Pow,' said Wally.

'Hamish!'

'What?'

'Pow!'

'No, no clouds. Blue sky.'

'HAMISH!'

'POW!'

'Oh all right, clouds, have it your own way. What?'

'QUICKLY!'

'Oh God!' Hamish dumped his inanimate burdens on the stair, retrieved his ear from little Wally's clenched fist, and began to reascend.

'Hamish!'

'Yeah, coming!'

'Leeve, Daddy!'

'What's the matter? Augh!'

'LEEVE, DADDY!' The furious infant reinforced his request with a vicious rabbit punch to Hamish's throat. Groaning, the beleaguered parent turned, stooped painfully to pick up the scrap of grubby nylon, and handed it over. Wally grabbed it, stuck a thumb in his mouth, and frowned contentedly.

Hamish found the bedroom deserted. 'Where are you?'

'Here!' called Grace.

'Where?'

'*Here!* In the airing cupboard.'

'Pubber,' said Wally. 'Mummy pubber!'

'Yeah, so it seems. What's Mummy doing in the pubber though, eh?'

'Mummy pubber,' Wally repeated, awarding Hamish a look of withering contempt. They found Grace emerging into the bathroom with an armful of bedlinen.

'What's up?'

'Look at these,' said Grace.

'What about them?'

'Feel them!'

Hamish adjusted Wally's sagging bottom into a slightly less uncomfortable position, and gave the offered sheet a perfunctory squeeze with his free hand. 'A bit damp?' he suggested.

'Amp,' said Wally, unplugging his thumb and making the sheet rather more so.

'It's absolutely soaking!' Grace corrected.

'Well, not absolutely, pet, it's kind of on the – '

'It's wringing wet, Hamish! It all is, look!' She seized half a dozen assorted purple towels, a wedding present from her aunt in Dalwhinnie, and let them thud to the floor. 'Saturated!' she said. 'And feel this wall, go on.'

'Pee a waw, Daddy!'

Hamish put a hand against the wall. A small piece of clammy plaster came away with it.

'Wet,' said Wally.

'Bloody hell!'

'Bad Daddy!'

'There, what did I tell you?'

'Well, it's not the cold tank,' said Hamish carefully. He indicated the pipes running up from the boiler through two holes in the dry boards above. 'It'd be coming through there, if it was. Besides, we'd hear the tank filling all the time if it was leaking.'

'So what is it then?' asked Grace, disgustedly hauling a stack of limp pillow-cases off the shelf.

'Wet,' said Wally.

'Rain?' suggested Hamish.

'We haven't had any rain for days.'

'It could take time to work through, though. If it was a loose slate, say, letting the wet in.'

'Wet in,' said Wally.

Grace said nothing.

'I'll have a look then, shall I?'

Hamish's inspection of the loft confirmed the blamelessness of the cold tank, which sat smugly on its wooden pier encased in unblemished polystyrene. The roof looked all right, as far as Hamish could see, whereas at ceiling level the undressed stone of the gable wall glistened a little in the rays of Ashley Oswald's Postman Pat pocket torch and four-colour ballpoint, suggesting the adjoining property as the source of the inundation. Hamish, who hated ladders, decided he had seen enough. Steadying himself firmly with both hands he clenched his elder son's torch between his teeth and lowered the trap-door gently on the top of his head.

His grateful sigh of relief as he rejoined Grace and Wally on terra firma was not simply that of the acrophobe; there was something of the relieved property owner in it as well.

'It's next door,' he said. 'It's coming through the wall low down.'

'Oh,' said Grace, not sounding terribly reassured. 'What are you going to do?'

'Well, I can't do anything right now, can I? Wally'll want his breakfast, won't you, Wally . . .?'

'No,' said Wally.

'And I'll have to get off to the shop. I'll try ringing from there.'

'Who?' Grace asked.

Hamish shrugged. 'Someone.'

'Wet,' said Wally. 'Wet leeve, Daddy!'

'Ugh!'

'He wiped the wall with it,' Grace explained.

'Pipe waw,' said Wally. 'Wet.'

It was a sign of the times, they decided as they bolted a hasty breakfast and coaxed Wally into eating some of his, that such a hitherto simple matter as alerting one's next-door neighbour to the possibility of malfunctioning plumbing should be so fraught with difficulty. The fact was that next door, one of a number of private properties between Sounds Good and Borden's Family Butchers, was unoccupied, and locked, and had been for the best part of a year past. The Ganglions, no less keen than any Craigfiethans to enquire after their neighbours, had been quite unable to discover the identity of the new owner. Even Angus Monzie was puzzled. Since the last folk, the Cummingses – he had been a milkman before the Bullocks sold up to Contragate Dairies of Dunbroath, who quickly rationalized the business's point-of-sale marketing interface – had moved away, not a single item of addressed mail had the postman delivered. 'It's gey curious,' Angus admitted, not bothering to conceal his disappointment in being denied his vocation as the town's leading intelligencer. Indeed, his displeasure was evidenced by the brutality with which he stuffed items of junk mail – prize draw vouchers, money-off coupons, election addresses, newspaper bingo cards, Regional Council newsletters and the like – through Number 31's sadly tarnished brass letterbox. He was the first to seize upon the Register of Electors when it came out: nothing. Angus Monzie's High Street round remained punctuated by gaps, irregular disquieting pauses like missed beats in a faltering pulse, and Number 31 was one of them. Something, it was agreed (especially at committee meetings of the Brighter Gardens and Neater Wynds Action Group), should be done about it, though what and by whom was beyond the power even of Mrs Spurtle to suggest.

'You could try the solicitors,' said Grace. 'Can you mind on who they were?'

'Something and Something,' Hamish replied, pausing to lick the honey off his knife (an irritating habit, and a bad example to the boys, but Grace had so far been unable to break him of it). 'They put a sticker on the For Sale notice, acquired for clients by . . . two names together, like Cain and Abel, Bang and Olufsen, horse and cart, something like that. I dunno. Not local anyway.'

'Fancy buying a house and then not going near it,' Grace tut-tutted. 'It's not right!'

'I saw a man there,' said Ashley Oswald. 'He got his breeks wet.'

'Where? Away with you, you don't know what we're talking about!'

'I do so!' Ashley Oswald protested. 'I saw him go through the back gate, and he got his breeks wet in the dockens. He had a key.'

'You mean he went in the back?' asked Hamish.

Ashley Oswald shrugged. 'He got his breeks wet.'

'When was this?' Grace frowned.

'Last weekend,' said Ashley Oswald. 'Not yesterday weekend but the weekend before yesterday. I was playing in the back lane with Tammy Sproat,' he added, anticipating the next question.'He had a car, Dad.'

'What sort?'

'A Ford Siesta GT Turbo Hacienda Special,' the boy replied promptly. 'With low profile tyres and stripes on.'

'Why didn't you tell us before, son?'

Ashley Oswald concentrated hard on getting the last Rice Krispie on to the end of his spoon. Tammy Sproat and he had waited until the man went away, and Tammy had said he was probably a drug smuggler, that was why he hadn't gone in the front door, and Tammy knew a way of getting windows open from the outside so's you could find where he'd stashed it all and get a reward. Tammy's secret way of getting windows open had bust the frame and a whole pane of glass had fallen out and smashed and Tammy had done a runner, leaving Ashley Oswald to hide in the coal bunker for half an hour before sneaking home to wash his knees before Mam saw them, that was why.

'I'll be late for school,' he said. 'I've got my school-bag, my reading book, my gym stuff, my dinner money and my milk money and Miss Pleat said we'd all to take something for the rabbits so I took a lettuce from the shop 'cos you were both busy when I minded on to ask and then when you weren't I forgot. Is that all right, Mam? Wally's put his breakfast in his ear.'

'Hold on,' said Hamish before the other half of his son

could disappear round the kitchen door. 'What did he look like, this man?'

'Old,' shouted Ashley Oswald from the hall. ''Bout your age, Dad. Bye.'

'Cheek!' said Hamish.

'I don't think it was Something and Something,' said Grace. 'I think it was Something Something, like Bugsy Malone or Marshall Ward, or something like that. Only we'll have to do something before it spoils our wallpaper.'

'Wawpaeiaeiar!' said Wally.

Hamish stopped, on his way to work, to cup his hands round his face and peer through the grimy front room-window of Number 31. The Cummingses had left their old net curtains behind – they were now an unattractive kippery colour – so it was difficult to tell if that mark on the party wall was a damp stain or merely the ghost of a piece of furniture. Though surely that dark patch on the floor –

'See onnything?'

Hamish started guiltily, banging his nose on the window.

'See onnything, son?' Angus Monzie said again.

'Oh, aye, erm, no,' said Hamish. Then he explained about the airing cupboard.

The postman sucked his teeth. 'Aye,' he said. 'Ye'll hauf tae do somethin' aboot that, right enough. That's no' right at all,' he added, stuffing a leaflet through the door. 'Ye'll be needin' tae get oan tae Clinch McKittrick, in my opinion.'

'Who?'

'Clinch McKittrick. The solly-icitors. They've just bowt Mrs Quaich's next tae the Bide-a-Wee, there's a . . .'

The postman's words were lost in the noise of a performance engine. They watched a car roar up the street, jink round the mini-roundabout where the Mercat

23

Cross used to be, and disappear on the Dunbroath road. Hamish, like Ashley Oswald, recognized it as a Siesta GT Turbo Hacienda Special, with low profile tyres. It had passed too quickly to be sure about the stripes.

Lurking behind a street light (Mrs Quaich had been second only to the dalek-like Miss Pleat as a source of terror in his early schooldays) Hamish squinted at the discreet black and white sticker on the bay window of the former headmistress: 'Acquired for Clients by Clinch McKittrick' it said; under that, in a mixture of upper and lower case, roman, san serif and italic, '*d*e*V*e*lop*M*e*N*t *t*H*ro*U*g*H *e*N*te*R*P*ri*S*e'.

Hamish repressed an anarchic giggle as he wondered what Mrs Quaich was making of it. It was the sort of thing he'd have had a week's sore knuckles for, if he'd done it.

An audio-visual retailer since late puberty, Hamish rarely found himself wondering, these days, what jargon really meant, if it meant anything at all. Still he could not help musing, as he went up the street to open the portals of Sounds Good (formerly the Bonaventure Wireless Shop) on the word 'development'. Development into what? And for whom? And – in view of Grace's airing cupboard – when?

Neville, latest in a long line of youth trainees, was waiting outside the shop, pointedly scrutinizing his pocket-watch. Hamish was not really sure what to make of Neville; though barely ten years younger than his employer, he seemed to belong to a different age – sometimes even a different planet – and within his first week at Sounds Good had contrived, somehow, to take what Hamish regarded as a fairly easy-going employer-employee relationship and stand it completely on its head. Despite, or because of his disconcerting habit of addressing Hamish as 'sir', there was something about him so unlike the usual, reliable sloppy run of scheme-fodder that Hamish found himself feeling quite nervous in the youth's presence.

'Sorry I'm late,' he muttered, fumbling for the shop key.

Neville composed his irritatingly bronzed features in a slow half-smile. 'That's quite all right, sir,' he said. 'I hadn't been waiting too long.'

'Oh good.' Bastard, thought Hamish, holding the door open. Neville was wearing the sort of smartly casual executive-look distressed co-ordinates he saw modelled by the androids in Grace's catalogues; twice a year, Hamish thanked his hazy conception of the Deity that having two kids and a mortgage meant he couldn't afford to buy them. As it was, he reflected bitterly, the second-hand value of Neville's trainers would probably clothe his employer from head to foot. Where young people – or some of them, at any rate – got their money from these days was a mystery to him. Sometimes he felt as old as Ashley Oswald thought he looked. Checking his socks to make sure they matched, he bent down to pick up the post Neville had so thoughtfully stepped over.

'Erm,' he began, 'what are we on this week? Customer environment enhancement, is it?'

'I don't think so, sir,' Neville replied with supercilious woodenness. 'I did the tidying and the dusting last week. I fancy we are on to day-to-day accounting techniques this morning, sir.'

'Eh? Oh, aye, them. Right, er, well I've got one or two phone calls to make, actually . . .'

'I quite understand, sir.'

'What? Oh, yeah. Well, p'raps you could check the list of weekend video rentals, then make sure they all come back. The book's over there, down the side of the till.'

'Of course,' said Neville. 'You mean this one, sir, the

25

one with "Eastern Region Education Committee, A.O. Ganglion droring bok" written on it?'

Hamish watched him put his briefcase – what the hell did he think he wanted that for? – on the counter and snap it arrogantly open. It wasn't a briefcase. 'What's that?' he boggled.

'Mmm? Oh this, sir? It's rather – ha-ha – antiquated I'm afraid, as laptop PCs go, but it serves my current needs. You keep all your video rentals in this – in this?'

'Yeah,' Hamish replied weakly, biting his tongue before he could add, 'I'm afraid so.' He shrugged. 'I'll be in the back, then.'

Neville nodded imperceptibly, already intent on his keyboard. The next few weeks, Hamish decided, were going to seem very long indeed. A spiteful thought occurred to him, and he put his head back round the office door. 'When you've done that,' he said, 'you can check the post and put the coffee on, all right?' And, he thought gleefully, go to Glencairn's for the rolls, ye poncy wee nyaff.

He hauled out the directory from under the telephone. (How he'd fought the old man to have that put in! In fact, he wasn't sure if it hadn't been during one of those arguments that his father had first uttered the phrase, 'I might as well be in the bleedin' Eventide.') It was odd, really, that those Clinch McKittrick people hadn't put an address or anything on their sticker; you'd think they'd want folk to know. Moreover, he quickly discovered, they weren't in the Eastern Region telephone directory either, which was even odder. Perhaps they'd only just got going.

He picked the receiver up, dialled 192, and amused himself by drawing a post-modernist multi-storey office block into the view of Pittenweem on the cover while the number rang. 'Directory Enquiries,' said a metallic voice. 'Which town?'

'Oh,' said Hamish, and put the receiver back. Stumped.

Grace was having a difficult morning: first, because Miss Pleat had instituted a No More Lending policy and sent Ashley Oswald straight home for his pencil case; second, because when she had sent Ashley Oswald off again with instructions to hurry or he'd miss school, Wally had echoed her instruction with a loud cry of 'Piss pool!' and then decided to make it his phrase for the day and repeat it to all the customers; third, because Babette, the new temporary assistant, had been released by the High School into an unsuspecting universe with no useful understanding of the words 'pound' and 'ounce' and an apparent inability to add up in her inelegantly coiffured head; and fourth, because the wholesalers were late and Mrs Quaich was giving some very black looks to Grace's lettuces, from which Ashley Oswald had evidently selected the only edible specimen. Hamish was not alone in passing into adulthood with an abiding fear of the retired headmistress: Mrs Quaich, for her part, would carry to the grave the air of a person permanently on playground duty.

'I'm awfy sorry,' Grace stammered, 'we're waiting on a delivery.'

Mrs Quaich beamed alarmingly. 'That's all right, my dear, I'll get something in Dunbroath this afternoon.' She billowed across to the counter, sending wafts of hair fixative ahead of her. 'I'm going to book myself a nice wee holiday, to celebrate!'

'Oh!' said Grace. 'Celebrate what?' The three other ladies in the shop ceased their disaffected mutterings among the carrots to attend to the conversation.

'I've sold my house!'

'Oh! Gosh, I'd only just heard you were thinking about – I mean, someone said, you know, that you'd mentioned, er . . .'

'That's quite right, I *did* mention it to Mr Monzie the other day, which is as good as putting it on the nine o'clock news of course! And do you know, I had ever such a nice young man – very well-mannered he was, not like the majority of young persons nowadays – come to the house on Saturday, which just goes to show, doesn't it, working on a Saturday. You don't catch many young folk at that if they can help it, and – well – I don't mind telling you, Grace dear' (here her three fellow customers fell to scrutinizing the appalling scene in the onion rack) 'he made me a very good offer indeed, *much* better than those silly old fuddy-duddies at Tummock and Tummle had led me to expect, and so . . .' she tossed her carefully varnished perm '. . . I took it! And now I'm going to have a nice wee cruise!'

'Lovely,' Grace agreed. 'And will you be leaving us then, Mrs Quaich?'

'Yes, but I'm not going far away, dear. Funnily enough the same people that nice young man came from, Clinch McKittrick – you know, they're very well thought of generally – have just, now then, what's the word my young man used? . . . expedited, that's it, just expedited a very select little development for retired persons in Dalglumph. In fact,' she dropped her voice to a piercing whisper, 'I got a little off the price! I can drive quite a hard bargain when I want to, you know!'

'Yes, I'm sure,' Grace said.

'Yes! And now perhaps your new girl – Babette, isn't it? Still blowing that nose, dear? Good! Perhaps you'd be so good as to give me half a stone of your Pentland Squires.'

'Uh?' said Babette.

'Persons who leave their mouths open,' snapped Mrs Quaich, reverting to her old self, 'let flies in.'

Grace intervened hastily. 'I'm afraid we've only got

pre-washed Romanos at the moment, Mrs Quaich. And they're in two-kilo packs, will that do? They're twenty-seven pence, Babette. That's fifty-four altogether. No – excuse me, Mrs Quaich – no, Babette, fifty-four from one pound leaves forty-six . . . *forty*-six, that's right. Sorry about that, Mrs Quaich.'

'"On whom my pains,"' quoted Mrs Quaich grimly, '"humanely taken, all, all lost, quite lost." You remember my saying that, do you, Grace?'

'Oh yes, Mrs Quaich,' Grace mumbled. 'Often.'

'We didn't do mental at High School,' Babette whined. 'They gave us calculators.'

'Pah!' said Mrs Quaich. 'There doesn't seem to be much to buy this morning, ladies,' she added for the benefit of the three scrutineers. 'Something to do with a delivery lorry not being here, a sign of the times no doubt. Good morning to you!'

'Good morning, Mrs Quaich,' droned everyone under the age of forty-two.

'When's coffee break?' asked Babette.

'Now, Neville,' said Hamish. 'Oh, and I've changed my mind about the rolls. We'll have some cakes from the Bide-a-Wee instead.' A dose of the Spurtles, Hamish thought, would be good for him.

'Any particular sort?'

'Eh? Aw, no, just get a selection, they're all pretty much the same. And ask for a receipt.'

'Very well, sir. Perhaps you'd care to scan my break-down, if you can spare the time while I'm away.'

Hamish flushed. 'Are you tryin' to take a rise out of me?'

Neville assumed a perfect mask of incredulity. 'No, sir!'

'No? Good. Well . . . just don't, all right?'

'Whatever you say, sir, of course. I've sorted the post:

bills on the left, reminders in the middle, final reminders on the right. And there's a promotional leaflet you might care to look at, and a letter from your bank, so I didn't open it. I hope I've not anticipated next week's course in clerical organization?'

'If you put the kettle on now,' gritted Hamish, pretending to study a wholesale price-list of DIN-BS adapter modules, 'it'll just have boiled by the time you get back.'

The leaflet was from a Dunbroath-based firm calling itself Eastern Sight'n'Sound and gave advance warning of an advertising campaign in the local press, followed by the delivery of a free, full-colour catalogue ('to every street in YOUR town, and every house in YOUR street') which would bring long-awaited good news ('especially to YOUR family'). The gospel according to Eastern Sight'n-'Sound (a division of the HI! (Scotland) Corporation) was that the very latest in state-of-the-art audio-visual technology, at unbeatable rock-bottom prices ('no-quibble-double-the-difference refunds GUARANTEED') would shortly be available ('delivered to YOUR door') simply by perusing the catalogue and making ONE *FREE* PHONE CALL! 'Think,' Hamish read, 'what this will mean for YOU!'

Hamish thought. Then, by way of compounding his gloom, he idly opened one of the final reminders.

The telephone rang.

'Hi!' Clyde Bilt switched on his most illuminating smile and raised both arms in Messianic salute. 'Just the very person Ah was looking for!'

Neville returned the evangelist's dental greeting with a subdued replica. 'How can I help you, Mr Bilt?'

'Hey, hey! None of this stuffy English "Mister Bilt", huh? All my brothers and sisters call me Clyde. And it's not "how can you help me", but how you *have* helped all of us in the UWR triple C in our unceasing mission to bring Our Lord Jesus Cry-est to the community!'

'Oh, well.' Neville blushed becomingly under his Apollonian tan. 'It was really just a rough idea, nothing more.'

'Ah know, mah frayund, Ah know it is just a rough idea – to you! But believe me, Ah know men and women who would be proud, Ah say, *proud*, to hold up your rough idea as the achievement of a lifetime's labour in the service of Our Lord Jesus Cry-est, truly and sincerely Ah do! Ah may tell you, mah frayund, that your "rough idea" for exponentially broadening the witness base, whaddidya call it agin?'

'"Earn-As-You-Save".'

'Exactly so, your idea has gone all the way up to Level Three at UWR triple C HQ! And believe me, mah frayund, you simply cannot git much haar than Level Three! And the feedback on the campaign, uh . . .'

'"Rocket To Redemption".'

'Yeah, that's it, real snappy and, uh, devotionally marketable. The feedback on that, in a single word, Neville, is – they like it! Ah mean,' Bilt continued before Neville could make another modest interjection, 'we're talking UK execkertive vahce-presidencies here, y'unnerstan'? We must rap on this one, mah frayund, rap and resolve.'

'I'll look forward to that, Clyde. Unfortunately at this moment in time I'm committed to my employer – '

'Oh, yeah, sure, the gramophone man. Whadde do, run outa sharp needles?'

'Actually, I'm going to the tea-rooms to get him some cakes. It's all part of the training.' He smiled ruefully.

'Your manifestly unassuming Christian humility does you great credit,' the evangelist replied, clasping Neville warmly by the left hand and the right shoulder. 'But never fail to be sure for one instant that you are made for haar thengs than retail phonographics, y'hear? Ah mean, you and me, we're lookin' at the future, y'follow me? The future.'

'I follow,' said Neville, giving Bilt's hand a brief manly squeeze. 'Rap and resolve.'

'Tomorrow belongs to us!' The evangelist's voice was low and fervent. 'And to the Lord Jesus Cry-est!'

'Amen,' said Neville.

'But that's ridiculous!' protested Hamish, his knuckles whitening on the handset. 'I sent it back to you over a fortnight ago; it can't take that long to replace, can it? I mean, you're not telling me that Gunn and Graham's engineers are still trying to take the back off, are you?'

'I couldn't tell you what Gunn and Graham's engineers are doing. We're not Gunn and Graham.'

'Eh? Since when?'

'Since we became part of Euro-Kay Electronics plc, last Thursday.'

'Oh. Okay, so you've changed your name, so what?'

'So, Mr Goitre – '

'Ganglion.'

'As you please. So, we have revised certain practices which the new management have identified as achieving an unacceptably low cost-return quotient.'

'Like fixing things, you mean?'

'No, Mr Gumboil, and I must say I find your attitude rather self-eliminating if I may say so. What I am referring to, *if* you'll allow me to get a word in edgeways, is the perfectly normal business practice of imposing a five per cent lower limit on returns for repair from our retail clients.'

'Oh? And what does all that lot mean when it's at home?'

'You have received our latest trade publication, I take it?'

'I dunno . . . wait a sec, you mean that big glossy thing with a fuzzy photo of a girl in a waterfall on the front?'

'That might be one way of describing it, yes. I take it this document is in your possession? My screen's telling me Sounds Good was activated in the mailshot.'

'Yeah, well.' Hamish swallowed. 'Yes and no. Mostly no by now. I gave it to my wee boy to play with.'

'Really, Mr . . . do you think that was an advisable thing to do?'

'Yeah, don't see why not, she did have a bikini on.'

The telephone sighed. 'For your benefit, then, I shall tell you that the rule, as its name fairly obviously implies, is a practice whereby the number of units accepted for repair must represent at least five per cent of your total stock situation in re that particular item as such, otherwise it's obviously not viable for us to accept them.'

'Why not?' asked Hamish.

The telephone sighed again. 'If it isn't obvious to you, Mr Gangrene, I really don't see how I can explain it.'

'Oh?' said Hamish. 'Why? No, hang on, we are talking about the KXV-3347F Series Two, aren't we? Okay, well, you sent me five, I've sent one back, that's more than five per cent, isn't it?'

'Not of a minimum stock of eighty, no.'

'*Eighty?*'

'We find,' purred the telephone, 'that our preferred clients regard eighty as a bare minimum for their normal stock requirements.'

'Oh yeah? Oh really? Well how come in that case, as a "preferred client", whatever that is . . .' Hamish swapped hands from left to right in order to throttle the handset more effectively, '. . . how come as a "preferred client" for over twenty years, counting my father, how come you only sent me five in the first place, eh?!'

'We didn't, Mr Ganglion. Gunn and Graham did.'

'Aw, help ma . . . So if I'm not about to change myself into F.W. Woolworth, what am I supposed to do now?'

'That really isn't for me to say, friend. You are of course free at any time to collect the item at your own expense and find an alternative dealer.'

'Oh, great! Triffic! Thanks a bunch, pal!'

'You're welcome,' said the telephone.

A weasel of steam slunk through the doorway and along the ceiling. The telephone rang again.

'What a nayce young man!' Miss Phemister piped as the Bide-a-Wee cowbells clonked behind the departing customer. 'Don't you think so, Joan dear?'

'You think all males under the age of thirty are nice,' Mrs Spurtle pointed out, 'so long as they haven't got two heads.'

'Oh really, Joan dear, Ay do think you can be a little unfair at taimes! Ay mean, he was so well dressed, and so polayte! And he had lovely blond hair and blue eyes, really quayte . . . quayte . . . well, you know!'

'Mmphm. Well at least his sort made the trains run on time. I will say that for them.'

Seeing Haq's empty of customers, Neville looked in on his way back up the street.

'Check?'

'Check,' said Sayeed Haq.

'Our clients in Enterprise City are doing their stuff,' said Neville.

Young Haq nodded and held up an Eastern Sight'n-'Sound leaflet. 'So I see. And your end?'

'Give me a week. No show on Noah yet. Can't be long.'

34

'No. How's Operation Aspirin?'

'My lady's still checking it out. A day, maybe two. She's seen the books and passed it on. They'll be well briefed. As for the actual – '

'We know nothing about that,' said Sayeed Haq.

'About what?' They slapped each other's hands in amusement at this one.

'Anything else?' Haq asked. He was a busy young man.

'A question: prime site seven. State of intelligence?'

'Sketchy. A difficult area. You are aware of the obstruction?'

Neville smiled tightly. 'Just been assessing it.' He held up his paper bag. 'I think I see a way round it, though.'

'A bonus if you do.'

Neville smiled again. 'You're giving me green for go on this one?'

'If you can handle it,' said Sayeed.

Neville grinned. 'Piece of cake!' he said. They found this very funny indeed.

'Mungo!' said Hamish, shoving the door shut with his foot. 'Long time no, you know.'

'Yeah,' said Mungo. 'Likewise.'

'How're you goin'? Still truckin'?'

'Completely trucked, old pal.'

'Eh?'

'Trucked. As in, "Ta fae aw the hard work, laddie, now truck off and collect your cards at the door on your way oot."'

Hamish blinked. 'You mean . . . you're not editor any more? Christ! How come?'

'Bought and sold, pal, bought and sold. By Mrs McConkie, sole prop since 1954 and a senile old bat, to Universal Regionals plc. Which is how I get to speak to you on a person-to-person line from the jannie's extension in the boiler-room. I just got here ahead of the rest of the editorial staff, correction, ex-editorial staff. So I thought to myself, who could I phone up and moan about it to without having to listen to all their problems as well, and naturally I thought of you.'

'Thanks,' said Hamish. 'What makes you think I've no' got any?'

'Oh? What's up?'

'Aw, just jokin' really. Nothing much.'

'No, go on, tell't me! It might cheer me up.'

'Aw, well, we've got a leak in the airing cupboard wall, an' – '

'What? Jesus, hold the front page! Book the satellite, man!'

'Yeah, well, like I said, it's no' much. Mind, it's kindo peculiar, cos we reckon it's coming through fae next door, an' next door's been empty ever since it was bought by some outfit called Clinch McKittrick that nobody seems to have heard of, an' – '

'Did I hear you say Clinch McKittrick?'

'Yeah. Why? Have you heard o' – '

'Hamish old pal, you know I think I might just pay you a visit.'

'Yeah, fine, but I mean it's just a leak in the loft somewhere, that's all.'

'Hey, whatever happened to our beautiful relationship, then? Besides, I'm freelance now, pal, gotta earn a living. And – What? . . . oh, yeah, yeah, yeah, okay, I'm finished . . . holding up the queue, pal, see you later, okay.'

Opening the office door, Hamish had time to register that everything above knee-height had disappeared before the telephone rang again. Business came first, he reminded himself, shutting the door again. Besides it was Neville's job.

'Sounds Good.'

'Hamish, it's me, Grace.'

'Oh, hi – '

'Hamish, you've got to do something. There's water coming in the shop and I can't find Babette to see to things while I . . . and the wholesalers haven't come and the shop's full of people wanting, and if it hadn't been for Wally I'd never have, because it was when he kept saying "wet" and Mrs Pulteney, you know what she's like, well I was just, and Wally kept on, and she said, you know that way she has of, and she said, "Oh dear, have we soaked through our nappy?" and so I said, "Of course not, Mrs Pulteney," trying to sound nice, I said, "I've only just this minute – " and then she said and I can just hear her, that way she has of, "Oh, but I think so because I think we can see a wee puddle, don't you, little man?" So of course I looked and of course it wasn't, it was . . . and then I couldn't find Babette anywhere and so I just went upstairs and oh, Hamish, one whole wall of the dining room and it's coming out of the socket in the hall as well and the carpets, and there's a shop full of people and I can't . . . and Babette's . . . and I'm going to phone the fire brigade because I can't, and Wally's . . . and the wholesalers haven't . . . and Babette's . . . and so you've got to *do* something, Hamish!'

'Yeah,' said Hamish. 'Right. Oh,' he added, simultaneously wishing he hadn't, 'Mungo's coming to see us.'

He bumped into something squashy by the Scottish music carousel, made a swift deduction and then, feeling his way forward, confirmed it. 'Look after the shop, Neville,' he bellowed through the fog. 'My house is flooding.' There was a muffled explosion at the back of the shop. 'That'll be the kettle,' he explained. 'White, two sugars.' He burst through the doorway and into the street like a pantomime demon, wreathed in infernal vapour.

He passed a puzzled Rev. MacAndrew, heard the clamant note of the Craigfieth Retained Station fire engine hard at his heels, and resolved to beat it to its destination. He had reached the front steps of Number 31, the source of his present discontent, before he realized he had won the race by default. The shiny red machine, its tyres gleaming with layers of bull and black shoe polish, had drawn to a splendid halt outside the billowing door of Sounds Good (formerly the Bonaventure Wireless Shop) and half a dozen of Mid Lummock's finest were even now preparing to storm the premises armed with axes, breathing apparatus and a snaking length of pink hose-reel.

'Aaauurgh!' said Hamish. 'No!' he shouted. 'No, no!'

'Hauv ye no insurance, laddie?' enquired Angus Monzie, suddenly at his elbow with shining eyes and a slack mouth moist with anticipation.

'Aaauurghhh!' said Hamish, and careered off up the street.

'Ach, my, my,' observed the postman, gobbling thoughtfully at a handy storm drain. 'That's just terrible!' And he set off to break the news at the Post Office.

Afterwards, in his quiet reflective moments (of which there were few), Hamish was to recall with deep contentment the spectacle of Neville, his hair and clothes drenched, his bronzer running, eyes bright with visceral terror, hands raised in a caricature of surrender as he appeared in the shop doorway before the retreating figure, glinting axe and spraying hose of Leading Fireman Lockerbie. But he had no time to be amused by it just at that moment.

'Not here,' he gasped, 'there. My house. Shop. Flood. Through from next door.'

'Urgh?' Leading Fireman Lockerbie swung round to face him, forgetting to turn his hose off first.

'No fire,' said Hamish, wiping his face with a dripping sleeve. 'Steam. Kettle.'

Leading Fireman Lockerbie looked at his hose. 'I'll no' be needin' this, then?' He had not gained his promotion for nothing.

'Not unless it sucks, no.'

'Make up, lads!' barked the Leading Fireman. 'We're wanted doon the street, seemingly.'

Hamish sank wearily on the rear platform of the fire engine, his arms clamped round the two valve outlets for support. He was still slumped there when the vehicle pulled away. His frantic fingers clutched at the valves, releasing four hundred gallons of water in two solid arcs as the machine executed a pretty U-turn in the road, and thoroughly putting out the many bystanders on the pavement. Angus Monzie came out of the Post Office. 'My goad,' he croaked, and went back in again.

It began to rain.

Grace was waiting for them, and conversing urgently with Sergeant MacEachran, who looked worried. He held up one hand as the first firemen approached, stirrup pump at the ready. 'Not in here, boys,' he said. 'Next door.'

They tried next door. 'It's locked, Donald,' said Leading Fireman Lockerbie.

'Aye,' replied Sergeant MacEachran, 'I ken.'

'Hamish!' said Grace, seizing him firmly by the lapels. 'The sergeant says they can't get in because it's breaking and entering and he'll have to get a warrant and I keep telling him there's water coming in and it's not us and they've got to do something, Hamish!'

'You do appreciate ma problem, Mr Ganglion,' said the sergeant.

Hamish thought. 'No,' he said as Grace tightened her grip. 'Not really.'

'It's no' a fireman's duty tae go breakin' intae other folk's hooses,' said Leading Fireman Lockerbie sadly.

'Then what is a fireman's duty?' screamed Grace.

Fireman Duff, a young recruit on his first call-out, sprang to attention. His helmet slid over his eyes; they hadn't got round to measuring him yet. 'A fireman's duty,' he parroted, 'is to save lives, save property, and render humanitarian assistance!'

'Aye,' agreed Leading Fireman Lockerbie, checking the answer off on his fingers. 'That's right.'

'Then what about my wallpaper?' Grace enquired, releasing Hamish to hammer on the man's chest with her fists.

'I reckon,' he replied hastily, 'we could mebbe call that humanitarian assistance, right enough.'

'What way are you going to do that?' asked Sergeant MacEachran. 'I have to warn you, Davie boy, that it will be my duty – '

'Nah, nah, Donald.' A glint of crafty intelligence appeared in the humanitarian's eye as he took the policeman to one side. 'What I reckon tae this one is, ye see, if we wiz jist tae put a ladder up at yon windae, for tae tak' a look insides mebbes, an' if the ladder wiz tae accidently put the windae in, why then we'd be duty bound tae tak' a bitty more look, jist tae ensure there wiznae ony further damage done, ye ken?'

'Ah!' said Sergeant MacEachran. 'Well, accidents will happen, Davie.'

'Aye, Donald, so they say right enough. Okay, Mr Ganglion . . . Mr Ganglion?'

But Hamish had gone. The fireman shrugged. 'Ach, well. Okay, boys, get tae work!'

Hamish had gone. Though not exactly a man of action he was less a man of debate, and his recent altercation with Euro-Kay Electronics had more than sufficed in that respect. Passing quickly through the shop, and paddling through the kitchen, he made his way up the garden to the back lane and so to the rear gate of Number 31 which, as Ashley Oswald had reported, offered a fine prospect of couch grass, ground elder, groundsel, dandelion, ragwort and nettles as well as dockens. He didn't notice the wet, of course. He did notice that a pane of glass in the back porch was conveniently missing.

The atmosphere inside the house was threatening, oppressive, as in the prelude to a thunderstorm. The electricity had been turned off and the rear of the building was ill-served for light. The air was dank. Ascending the uncarpeted staircase, Hamish could hear tell-tale thudding plops on the boards above. From higher up came the continuous rumbling of a filling cistern. There was another noise too, unidentifiable: a sound as of an elephant turning over on a badly sprung bed.

A strip of wallpaper on the first-floor landing had peeled back, revealing an expanse of leprous plaster that seemed to shift, as he watched it, under the film of water that made its way to the room below. His heart thudding, his hands moist, Hamish tackled the last two flights, stopping half-way up the second to look above him.

'Jesus Christ!' he whispered.

'*Jesus Christ!*'

Leading Fireman Lockerbie, footing the ladder, gazed up the leg of Fireman Duff's yellow oilskins. 'What is it, boy?'

Fireman Duff began a rapid descent, his overlarge boots slipping clumsily on the metal rungs. 'The whole fuckin' . . .'

The remainder of Fireman Duff's intelligence was drowned in a giant rumbling roar from within. The front door was flung inwards; an instant later a white-haired and whey-faced Hamish, his lower half gaudily plastered

41

with soggy junk mail, was expelled on a flood-tide of laths and plaster that tumbled over the steps, choked the storm drain and bubbled filthily away down the street. There was a second crash, and a wall of rubbishy water caught him behind the knees. He sat down heavily and was borne along a few feet then left, stranded, on what remained of the second-floor ceiling of Number 31, High Street, Craigfieth.

There followed some pregnant moments of refreshing silence, disturbed only by the playful plash of clean cascading water from inside the ruined house. An election leaflet drifted by, face upwards. Hamish watched as Mr Haq's smiling countenance disappeared under a parked car outside Melmotte's Bank.

A small figure crawled out from between Grace's legs.

'Daddy wet,' said Wally.

Chapter Two

There were many things about Mungo Beauly that Grace tried very hard to like. He was clean. He had a proper job. He drove a car. He managed his own washing. And there was, if she was honest, no one particular thing about him which could reasonably be identified as giving cause for offence. It wasn't his fault, particularly, if sometimes he said things Grace couldn't quite understand, or thought she might understand but wouldn't like if she did. He couldn't help being clever. And she could hardly blame him, even at his age – he was Hamish's senior by a year – for remaining single. It wasn't as if he was one of those . . . people who were entitled to sympathy because they couldn't help it and it takes all sorts. He'd had girlfriends, and there'd been nothing wrong with them either, really, considering. In fact, it was probably very responsible of him not to get married just yet. It wasn't as if he could offer, as she and Hamish could, the sort of secure and settled life that children really needed.

There was no good reason then – despite the fact that he didn't have a proper job any more and was driving a car that might not strictly speaking be his – why Mungo's presence in her lounge should make Grace feel edgy and irritable, like it always did. He was Hamish's friend, after all: his oldest and best friend, in fact. His relationship with Hamish pre-dated hers and was in many ways quite separate from it, of course. It wasn't, she told herself, as if she didn't have friends of her own – more than Hamish had, if she thought about it – girls who had been in her class at school, for instance, and who still lived in the town. She would see them at playgroup, or at the clinic, and have a good natter. Hamish had always been more of a loner; which was natural enough, when she thought of him and his father living the way they did, and the skin trouble he'd had through his teens. Perhaps her anxiety was traceable to Hamish's weakness – she had to acknowledge it – for being easily led. That year's difference must have meant a great deal when he and Mungo were at school, and sometimes she wondered whether Hamish had ever really shaken it off. And the things they'd done together, from the little she had learned of them, did not seem to her to be at all like the Hamish she knew: that rock group they were supposed to have had, for instance, or rather that Mungo had had, with Hamish as manager or something. As far as she could see, he'd allowed himself to be taken advantage of over that; there was all that business over the "hire" of amplification equipment from Hamish's shop that had never been properly explained. And Hamish going off places whenever Mungo felt like it, as if all he had to do was snap his fingers and Hamish would do whatever he wanted him to do. That wasn't how it was according to Hamish, of course, but then she knew Hamish, didn't she? Better than Hamish knew himself, over some things.

And she was sure, without needing to examine the reasons for being sure, that Mungo knew that she knew that Hamish was different, not really like himself, when Mungo was around. And even if she could not put a name to what the differences actually were, she spotted them nonetheless and her reaction to them, and Mungo's awareness (she was sure of this as well) of her reaction, and his reaction to that, all contributed to the prickling unease with which she welcomed him under her roof; with which, indeed, she responded to the mere mention of his name. There were times when the phone would ring and

44

she would be absolutely certain it was him, and be right, and be upset about being right (because she knew it was wrong of her, really, to feel the way she did) and then be upset about being upset, and blame Mungo for it.

And then feel guilty and unsettled about that, too, of course.

Mungo was an unsettling sort of person, there were no two ways about it. And it was typical of him to have turned up (and how long for? That was another thing) on a day like this. Not, she half-heartedly chastised herself, that he hadn't tried to help. It had been his idea to close the shop for the afternoon (she was bound to admit there seemed little point in keeping it open, flood or no flood) so that Grace could concentrate on mopping-up operations in the house, assisted by Wally, who derived intense pleasure from drawing her attention to new areas of dampness at floor level. By half past three she had worked her way to the lounge and was contemplating a quiet cup of tea before Ashley Oswald came home from school when Mungo came in with a tray.

'Thought we could do with a break,' he said, setting the tray down on the pouffe. 'And I found some biscuits for Wally,' he added, handing the delighted infant one of Grace's best side-plates and an assortment guaranteed to ruin his appetite for proper food. 'Sugar?'

Grace nodded, flinching a little as Mungo plonked the mug down on her best – and matless – occasional table.

He threw himself cheerfully into an armchair, flung one leg over the side of it (disarranging the loose cover on the arm) and blew his cheeks out. 'Phworr, bloody hell!' he said. 'I'm knackered!'

'Bad Daddy,' mumbled Wally through two and a half chocolate digestives. Grace gave a little start and spilt some tea; luckily, it went in her lap.

Mungo appeared, rather tellingly she thought, not to

notice any of this. 'I've squeegeed up the worst of it,' he went on, 'and hooshed all the bits into the street since there's so much gutter out there already, and I've covered the floor with some *Gazettes* I brought with me. You should be honoured,' he grinned. 'It's the last issue under my editorship. Very absorbent reading.'

'That's very kind of you,' Grace said tightly. Then added more amicably, 'It's true then, what Hamish said. You're, I mean, you've been . . .'

'Shaken out? Yeah, that's right, sister. Along with most of the rest of the people who write the rag every week. Ought to bring the newsprint bill down, wouldn't you say?'

Grace was genuinely shocked. 'They can't just do that, can they? I mean, you hadn't been . . . you know . . . had you?'

Mungo laughed. 'Dipping our fingers in the till, you mean? Siphoning off the small ads money, fiddling our expenses, some hope? No, it's all right, Grace, no need to count the knives and forks. The paper's under new ownership, that's all, and I dare say we'll all get redundancy money too, some day. And I don't suppose many people'll notice the difference this Thursday anyway.'

'But I thought you said most of the people who wrote the paper had been . . . like you? How are they going to manage without them? No, Wally darling, I think you've – oh, all right then, but just one more, mind!' Wally aborted his scream of protest and crammed in a jaffa cake instead.

Mungo inexpertly poured them another cup each, dribbling tea on the carpet. 'Depends what you mean by writing,' he said, setting the pot down. 'You see, you can pretty well run a local rag without reporters at all, if you want to. If a local paper digs up a real story and starts reporting it, ten to one it's because they've got an eye on

46

being picked up by the nationals and copied; if the rag's owned by a consortium that includes nationals anyway, it's that much less likely to happen. Or, to put it another way,' he continued, seeing that Grace didn't seem to be following him and honestly wanting her to understand, 'what do you buy the *Gazette* for, Grace? Go on, be honest.'

'Well,' she began. 'Well I don't, I mean . . .'

'Okay, rephrase it: which bit do you read first, when you get it?'

Grace blushed a little. 'The Sheriff Court,' she said.

'Fine, so do most people. It's the best bit, you meet all your friends there. And then?'

'Well, the letters of course, just to see if there's anyone I know writing in, and then there's the adverts, um, and . . . and, well, I look to see if there's anything about Craigfieth, I suppose.'

'Fine!' said Mungo. 'Splendid! A typical reader. So tell me, what was last week's lead story?'

'Erm,' said Grace. 'Like, on the front page, you mean?'

'Yup,' said Mungo. 'The big important news of the week, selected by yours truly for a splash headline. What was it?'

Grace's blush deepened. 'I don't know, I'm afraid.'

Mungo cackled alarmingly. 'Course you don't. And neither does anyone else, I shouldn't think. Well, I'll tell you: it was "Region Unveils Strategy Plan – Service Economy The Key, Says Convener". Gripping stuff, eh? Just the thing to get the punters dozing off before they get to the first crosshead – which, by the way, was "Consolidate" – wouldn't you say? Now, let's take the bits that you, like ninety-nine per cent of all known normal human beings, do actually read. One, Sheriff Court. No problem. Put a reasonably good shorthand writer – doesn't even need to be a reporter if you've got the NUJ under control, a secretary'll do – in the court, and you've enough for a whole page if you want it. Very cost effective! Then the letters page: even better. Costs nothing at all. We get hundreds every week, most of them boring, many of them incomprehensible, some of them stark staring bonkers. And I'll make you a prediction: this week's edition'll have a whole goddam page of readers' letters, under the heading "The new-look *Gazette* – now it's really *your* paper" or some such crap like that. Fine, where've we got to? Oh, yes, bits with your town in. Well, that's easy too – print everything you get sent, every WRI report, Lifeboat Ladies, Kirk Guild, Community Council, you name it. Costs peanuts, no editorial staff involved. Plus all the weddings and funerals, of course, and most of that comes free as well. Photographers and undertakers do it for you and bung it on their bill. And then of course there's photos of Mr and Mrs McThingummy's daughter who's just got a diploma in Applied Cosmetics or whatever, and all those boring old farts like Lad O' The Lummocks and Country Wife, who send their appalling drivel in batches of four in case they fall ill and can't write it. And then, if you're still stuck, run an advertising feature. That's not just free – the paper gets paid for it! Bet you a fiver there's one of those in this week's, too; with summer coming on I expect it'll be solid fuel merchants and domestic heating oil suppliers, all got up to look like a page of news with "advertising feature" in tiny wee letters at the top. Throw in a few pages of small ads, the usual full-pager for Mega-Messages, all the sports reports the clubs can be bothered to send you, and that just leaves the front page, which is taken care of by council handouts and politicians' press releases and which nobody bothers to read anyway, and you're home and dry! Reporters? Who needs 'em!'

'Oh,' said Grace. 'But you had some?'

'Ah!' exclaimed Mungo. 'My God, lassie, ye mean you noticed? Och aye, ma dearr,' he continued, lapsing into his repertoire of not-very-good *Dr Finlay's Casebook*-voices normally reserved for office parties, 'noo ye're taakin', Jaaanet! They're the optional extra, ye ken. People who go out looking for news: scandals, scams, fear and loathing in Duncruddie Mains, filth and corruption in Ballydull! And sometimes, just occasionally, after a lot of sniffing and digging, they find it: gutter journalism or an honourable public service, take your pick. Trouble is, sometimes, the object of all this grubbing about turns out to be someone sensitive, like a family friend or business colleague of the proprietor, or the landlord of your key informant, or – worst of all – a regular and valued advertiser, life-blood of the paper and all that, *then* what d'ye do, eh?'

'What?' asked Grace.

'Dunno,' said Mungo. 'I never quite got the chance to find out.'

The front doorbell rang. 'I'll go,' said Mungo helpfully. 'You scrape the European cocoa mountain off young Wally here. I've a vague idea who it might be.'

Ashley Oswald ran all the way home as soon as Miss Pleat finished snarling her valedictory prayer. Jungle drums in school playgrounds are tuned to a higher pitch than in the world outside, and news of the events at Number 31 had travelled, via the cycle shed and the climbing frame, to the dustbins where Ashley Oswald and his peers were wont to beguile their time, within eleven minutes of his father's precipitous exit from the front door. During the last fifty-eight seconds of its transmission the story under-went a strange and fabulous sea-change, maturing from a news agency report through various stages of journalistic embellishment until it became a fully fledged colour piece and, in the last breathless moment between the climbing frame and the dustbins, a modern legend with every right to take its place alongside King Canute and the Massacre of Tonypandy in the mainstream tradition of oral folklore, and just the right degree of the supernatural and the necrophilious. Nor had Ashley Oswald been able to demystify the tale with hard prosaic information about such things as airing cupboard walls and damp sheets: the origins of the sensation, like so many of the minor matters on which grown-ups seemed to waste their time, had simply passed him by. He had basked all afternoon in a most satisfactory glow of unspoken awe and admiration emanating from his class-mates. Even Miss Pleat had made a passing, sarcastic reference to 'the celebrity in our midst', and this had merely served to burnish the glow more highly still. Although made in terms of the celebrity's need to bend his mind to his Reader, and to the lesson in road safety that Tufty Fluffytail was about to give his Furryfolk Friends, any personal remark from Miss Pleat that was not immediately followed by some cruel and unusual punishment was distinctly a point in its recipient's favour. He made a sincere effort after that to concentrate on the telling-off Bobby Brown Rabbit was about to get from Mr Policeman Badger for running out into the road and making the custodian of the law crash into the Furryfolk Town letter-box. He wondered if Mr Policeman Badger would swear in Gaelic, like Sergeant MacEachran did.

Tammy Sproat, who had wondered the same thing out loud, was kept in at four o'clock, so Ashley Oswald savoured his initial disappointment on his own. The unhappy fact was that Number 31 looked just the same as it had seven and a half hours before. Far from being reduced to a heap of splintered wood, the front door was intact, and shut. The windows, unbroken, regarded the street with the same opaque indifference as before, and the puddles on the pavement outside looked no more floodlike than the puddles in the school playground. The area had not been sealed off by Murder Squad detectives. People did not cross themselves – or even the street – as they walked past. He encountered no posse of reporters and cameramen eager to record every detail of how he might be feeling about it all.

An irregular patch of whitish wet stuff in the road – witness to the council workmen's clearing-up operations – was the only evidence that anything remotely unpredictable had occurred in the vicinity.

The shop was shut, however, and that was something. Rather than risk being jeered at by his schoolmates for ringing his own front doorbell, Ashley Oswald mooched on down the street, turned up the back lane, down his own garden path – glancing guiltily at next door's broken window – and in through the unlocked rear door, and up the stairs. Mam wasn't in the kitchen, and the missing teapot and opened packet of best biscuits could mean only one thing: visitors. His spirits, already somewhat suppressed, sank lower. Ashley Oswald did not like visitors. They were usually female, usually old, like his mam, and usually asked him how he was getting on at school as a pretext for telling each other how their own children were getting on, which for some reason always seemed to be better than he was. He slunk through to the hall and heard voices – though not female voices – from the first-floor lounge.

While noting with approval that one of the voices was his Uncle Mungo's (he liked his Uncle Mungo, who had given him a copy of the *Gazette* with ASHLEY OSWALD PICKED FOR WORLD CUP SQUAD! as the headline for his last birthday), his finely honed instincts told him that what was going on in the lounge was a grown-up gathering at which his presence would not be welcomed. He crept along the landing, therefore, and listened outside the door instead.

'Are you related to the lady by any chance? Or acting for her in any way professionally?'

'No,' Mungo admitted.

'Then my advice to you, sir, is to stay well out of it. Look,' the man continued, 'I'll say it again, shall I? I haven't come here to threaten anybody, quite the reverse. I'm just advising you and your hubbie to watch your step, all right? Though I mean, obviously, if our friend here's going to insist on pushing his oar in where it's not wanted then fine, okay, I'll just let myself out and it'll be out of my hands altogether. I mean I'm not doing myself any favours being here, don't think that, whatever you do.'

'But I don't understand,' said Grace thickly. 'I mean there's the damage to our things, there's all the redecorations we'll have to do and the carpets, and we'll have to get someone to come for the upstairs I suppose, it's so . . . I mean, it's almost as if you're accusing us of deliberately, I don't know, ruining our own things on purpose or something, and I mean that's just stupid, isn't it!'

'Now, now, now! No one's accusing anyone of anything, Mrs Ganglion, at least I for one should hope not! Forgive me but I thought I'd made that quite clear! At least, not at this stage and let's just hope it doesn't go a stage further, eh? Mind you,' the man added, winking knowingly at his hostess, 'there's some who'll say there's no smoke without fire, you know the sort I mean? Not that I'm saying for one moment of course that that's necessarily the view that will be taken, that would all depend on various legal factors which are beyond my own immediate control, naturally, which is why I'm suggesting to you and your husband if he was here that it might well be better all round if we just left the insurance side out of it altogether. I'm trying to put myself in your position, aren't I, and I'm sure the last thing *I'd* want to do is bring the courts into it.'

'I suppose so,' Grace mumbled. 'Yes, thank you.'

Mungo took a deep breath. 'Yes, thank you very much, Mr . . .?'

The man rose, smiling understandingly at Grace. 'Like I told our friend here at the beginning of our little chat, all this is purely informal, Mrs Ganglion, you understand, being as I'm not here in any official capacity as such at this moment in time. Best leave all that sort of thing to solicitors, wouldn't you say, and hope in this case that won't be necessary.'

Mungo stood up too. 'And who would they be? These solicitors you mention?'

The man sighed. 'I must say, Mrs Ganglion, if I were you I really shouldn't want your friend here, if he is your friend – far be it for me to make any embarrassing enquiries in that respect of course, it's a free country – to bring in all these unpleasant formalities.' He squared up to face Mungo. 'However, since you insist on spoiling the atmosphere, sir, I take it you may have heard of Kenge and Carboys? They're not your ordinary everyday sort of High Street house agents, of course; I understand they specialize in liquidations, among other things, writs of sequestration and so on. You know what liquidation is, do you?'

'Oh yes,' said Mungo levelly. 'Taking over a firm's assets to clear a debt it can't pay.'

'More or less, more or less,' said the man. 'A bit like the business equivalent of putting the bailiffs in, Mrs Ganglion, or the poinders as I believe you call them north of the Border. Still, as I say, it probably won't come to that, will it? Not if we're sensible and play our cards right.'

Grace struggled groggily to her feet as the man began to open the door, understanding beginning to dawn on her with hideous clarity. 'You don't mean. . . ?' she began.

The man turned, braced the half-open door against his knee and waited, smiling interrogatively.

'You can't mean *we* . . . did it? Can you? That we caused the flooding, and made next door's ceiling . . . and everything? How are we supposed to have done that?'

'I don't mean anything, Mrs Ganglion. Only all I *am* saying is, all I'm trying to warn you about is, well, put yourself in my place; I mean I'm bound to wonder what they'll make of it higher up, aren't I? Well . . . I mean, purely off the top of my head, of course, I reckon they might say, there's your husband trying to blow up his shop one minute, and the next thing you know is, there he is running into the arms of a sergeant of police after bursting out of our client's house, which upon later inspection is discovered to have suffered, ooh, ten, twenty thousand pounds' worth of damage, maybe more, who can tell? And no prizes for guessing how he got in because although the back door's locked there's a smashed window right next to it, right? Plus of course, and don't forget, there's a joint on the cold water pipe shows clear signs of having been tampered with, right? And while of course it's no business of ours to say why anyone should take it into his head to go and do a thing like that, or precisely when he did it, the fact remains we don't know of anyone else who's been breaking and entering the premises, do we? So you see, there's all sorts of unpleasantness that could arise. Not to mention expense. Still, like I say, we'll just have to hope and pray it doesn't come to that, won't we? I'll see myself out.'

* * *

Feet going down the stair; the click and sigh of the draught excluder as the front door opened; the latch clicking as it shut. Ashley Oswald waited a full minute for something else to happen in his thin slice of vision, then pushed the door of his mam's hoover cupboard fully open and tiptoed out, taking care not to catch his feet in the cable that Mam always coiled so carefully the wrong way, so that it writhed all over the place as soon as she put the hoover away and let go. He stood for some moments in pounding silence, then for some moments more before he realized that the noise breaking in on his own special misery was his mam, crying, behind the closed lounge door. Silently, blindly, his hand on the banister serving in place of eyes, he found his way upstairs to his own bedroom, knelt on the bed without bothering to take off his school-bag or his shoes, and thought.

Petty and tedious as grown-up talk usually was – as Grace always said when she was telling him off, it all just washed through and out the other side – the last part of what he had heard, after the door had opened and he'd been nearly caught standing outside it, had been both clear and unforgettable. And he knew who the man was, of course; trust Tammy Sproat to get it wrong. And now Mam was crying, and Dad was in trouble, and if something terrible was going to happen, if all sorts of terrible things were going to happen, terrible grown-up things, and if it was all going to be his fault, well his and Tammy Sproat's, then he had better do something about it. He *and* Tammy Sproat. He felt a bit better after that.

Mungo's futile attempts at comfort and reassurance were interrupted, mercifully for both of them, by the rumble of a diesel engine, the hiss of air brakes, and another ring at the door.

'That'll be the delivery,' sniffled Grace. She blew her

nose in one of the tissues she had been cleaning the unusually silent Wally with. 'I'd better go and see to it,' she said, and stumbled heavily out.

Mungo grinned weakly at Wally, who seemed to take up the whole floor just by sitting on it. 'What d'ye think of it so far, then, Wally old pal?' he said.

'Man bad,' said Wally.

'Yeah,' said Mungo. 'I'll drink to that.'

'Jink!' said Wally. 'Maw biggie!'

'Go on, then,' said Mungo, tossing him the last of the jaffa cakes. 'And if anyone asks, say I ate it.'

McCrindle's had two regular drivers, one a peach-fuzzed, silent youth whose sole communication at the end of each delivery was a whispered 'thanks' when Grace signed the receipt, the other a gnarled and bandy-legged Fifer who talked all the time and would have had a toothy grin if he'd had any teeth left to grin with.

This man, who stood a foot taller than Grace and whose boiler suit was figure-eighted between the buttons down the front, with his grubby vest showing through, was neither. He shifted his feet impatiently and pushed a clipboard at her. 'Sign here,' he said, indicating with a black fingernail a small rectangle half occupied by a thick pencil cross.

'What for?' Grace heard herself say.

'Delivery,' he grunted, shuffling his feet again and looking away from her, up the street. The lorry, half as big again as McCrindle's and the wrong colour, loomed threateningly above her, a quivering wall of riveted steel.

Grace addressed herself to the man's ear, cratered and fleshy above the heavy rolls of neck. 'What of?'

'Your order,' he said, not moving. Then he tore his eyes away from the fascinations of the mini-roundabout. 'Look, lassie, d'ye want they veg're not?'

She saw now, peering round his bulk, that there were perhaps two dozen crates and an indeterminate number of bulging paper sacks at the furthest end of the transporter. 'Oh,' she said, 'I didn't know you were McCrindle's.'

It was the man's turn to look confused. 'Wha'?' he said.

'I said, I'm sorry I didn't realize you were McCrindle's. You're . . . I mean your lorry's different.'

'I don't know anythin' about no McCrindle's.' He seemed offended. 'I'm just told tae deliver they veg tae this address an' I just dae what I'm told, that's all I know. An' ye're tae sign for them, else I have tae tak' them back, an' I'm no' allowed tae dae that, reggle-asians, see?'

'Oh,' said Grace.

'Like it says here.' He slid an oily forefinger across the form, smudging the X. 'Excepting,' she read, 'that the packing has been bored, burst, broken or otherwise broached in transit, Semtex Transport are not responsible for the condition of goods upon delivery. This does not affect your statutory rights.'

'Ye see?' he said. 'An' it's gettin' late,' he added heavily.

Grace bridled a little. 'I know that! I normally get my delivery at nine o'clock in the morning, you know.'

'*Wha*'?' He took a melodramatic step backwards. '*Nine o'clock*, did you say? Nine-o'-effin'-cl . . . Haw, that's a good one, that is! Wait till I get this right! Nine o'clock! An' am I expected tae drive all night, then, eh, is that it, tae get here at nine o'clock, is that it, eh? Eh?'

'Well, no, b – '

'An' leave out aw the hypers an' supers till last, I suppose?'

'The wh – ?'

'I see. I see! Never mind there's a dozen hypers an'

57

supers on ma route, I'm supposed tae miss aw they out, am I? Eh?'

'Look, I – '

'An' unload aw their stuff tae get at yours, an' then load it aw back on again I suppose?'

'I don't kn – '

'An' never mind what way it was packed in the first place as per docket I suppose?'

'B – '

'I see! Oh, aye! I get the picture now! I'm tae gae tae heid office, I suppose, an' say, never mind aw yer hypers an' yer supers, forget aw them, they're no' important, I'm tae be at a wifie's in Craigfieth for nine o'clock! In the *mornin'!* Eh? Is that what you're sayin' I'm supposed tae say, is it?'

'No!'

'Aw well! Aw *well!* Tha's all right then, is it no'? I beg your pardon! Only, for a moment there, I thought I heard you say you was expectin' me at nine A.M., see?'

'Sorry,' said Grace.

'Right, now then.' He held out the clipboard again. 'Are you signin' this or am I tae phone heid office an' book intae a hotel? I mean,' he continued, as Grace tried to make the pen work on the greasy surface. 'It's only fair an' equitable, at the end o' the day, tae prioritize the hypers an' the supers, is it no'? I mean, in this day an' age, like, that's what it all comes down tae, daein' the hypers an' the supers first an' leavin' the smaller outlets tae the end o' the day, like, am I no' right?'

'Erm . . .'

'I mean, don't get me wrong, like, I'm no' a bosses' man, not in any way, shape or form, I wouldnae want you tae imagine I am, but in this day'nage, like, y'know what I mean? I mean, at the end o' the day I'm a Semtex driver, y'know what I mean?'

'Oh, yes,' said Grace. 'Yes, I do see that.'

'Aye,' said the man. 'Right then, so ye'll manage aw they veg aff the truck by yersel' awright, then, will ye?'

'Well . . .' Grace began, then realized it was not a question.

'I'm a transporter,' the man called over his shoulder, 'no' an unloader, at the end o' the day. Nothin' tae dae wi' me.'

'Grace?' Mungo was hovering in the doorway. 'Um, I think Wally's been sick.'

Mungo essayed a suggestion. Grace did not find it helpful. 'There isn't any better stuff to put the bad stuff at the bottom *of*!' she pointed out. 'I wish I'd never signed for it,' she added. 'I might have known I couldn't trust him.'

'Oh,' said Mungo.

Hamish coughed. 'Food's ready,' he said.

It was past seven o'clock. Wally and Ashley Oswald were both in bed, both supperless: Wally because, as Grace had predicted, he was stuffed to the gills with best biscuits and Ashley Oswald because, unaccountably, he simply hadn't wanted any and Grace, too tired and preoccupied to try accounting for it, had simply let him have his way. A bad day at school, she supposed, and let it go at that. There had been days when Miss Pleat had been more than enough to kill her own appetite, she remembered.

Hamish's arrival from work, festooned with print-outs from Neville's little electronic marvel, had heralded a concerted assault, punctuated by mutual debriefing on all the day's disasters, on the depredations wrought by next door's plumbing, followed by Hamish volunteering to knock something up for them all in the frying pan while Grace and Mungo sorted out the shop.

The discovery of the indifferent quality of the fruit and

vegetables had come as no great surprise to Grace, though she was sorely shocked by it all the same. She had finally got round to opening her morning mail during a respite from mopping up on the second landing. Conditioned by experience, rather than by authority, to regard all change – at least until it provided unimpeachable evidence to the contrary – as being change for the worse, she had greeted the news that the firm of J and J McCrindle (Wholesale Fruit and Vegetables) Ltd, Est. 1911, had been acquired by International Retail Supplies plc, Britain's fastest-growing disseminator of consumer perishables, with a despair leavened only by cynicism. She had taken over Smellie's determined to rid her nostrils for ever of the rancid tang of organic decomposition that had clung to the shop, and to its tweed-suited owner, for as long as she had worked there, and had spent long hours travelling from farm to farm in search of local produce while at the same time creating and satisfying a demand for green-grocerly exotica with weekly visits to the market in Dunbroath.

Within a few months the old Smellie system, of random deliveries of questionable stuff which often bore little resemblance to what had been ordered, was but an uneasy memory. The arrival of Ashley Oswald – not that she could blame him, of course – had seen the beginning of a deterioration in the stock of the Scottish Produce Centre (the new demand on her time and the obduracy of the garden having forced her to drop the suffix, 'And Herb Garden'). The plain fact was that other people – naturally enough, she supposed – were not as solicitous of the Scottish Produce Centre's welfare as she was; the difference in quality between the best that she could choose for herself and 'the best' as defined by those who now chose on her behalf had been directly proportional to the increase in the price demanded of her for the privilege of buying it. Reform of the European Community's Agricultural Policy, after a series of deadlocked summit conferences that had briefly revived media interest in 'the Falklands spirit', had led most of her farm suppliers to the unavoidable conclusion that they could earn more from their honest labour by directing it towards the end of growing things that people didn't want than they could by raising crops that people were willing and able to buy. The few who held out against this elegant economic reality had then combined into a co-operative which, run as it was by people wilfully ignorant of what was good for their short-to-medium-term welfare, soon had its credit withdrawn and went bust. McCrindle's bought it because they had been advised by their marketing consultants, Wyvern, Libbard and Thrip, that a homoeopathic dose of organic philanthropy might not, in the prevailing climate of health-conscious consumerism, come amiss. Grace thus found herself tied to a sole supplier – an event which, coincident with the arrival of her second child, she was content to regard as fortuitous. McCrindle's was, after all, an old-established family business. The acquisition of the failed co-op had, in fact, been the work of Innes McCrindle, grandson of the founder; he had raised the necessary capital by issuing shares in his inheritance and a majority of these, it now transpired, had been acquired by International Retail Supplies plc, high fliers on Britain's economic upswing and owners both of Semtex Transport, their sole distributor, and of Wyvern, Libbard and Thrip, marketing consultants. Innes McCrindle was given a seat on the board, to allay possible fears of monopolistic abuse. Their subsequent acquisition of Royal Mail Parcels had been hailed by the financial press as nothing short of good business sense. Dunbroath's fruit market had, meantime, become a business park.

'"Co-ordination of our retail distribution network,"'

Grace quoted from her letter, '"is computer-controlled at Semtex HQ in Droitwich." Huh! No wonder, then!'

'Where's Droitwich?' asked Hamish.

'Near Birmingham somewhere,' said Mungo.

'Exactly,' said Grace. 'Like I say, no wonder.'

'I hate computers,' said Hamish, thinking of Neville.

'I'll drink to that,' said Mungo, thinking of his replacement at the *Gazette* and pouring them all another cup of tea.

The three victims of the market economy finished their bacon and egg in silence.

'Leave the washing-up,' said Grace as Mungo made a belated move to deal with it. 'For the moment, anyway,' she added, not wanting to thwart his good intentions. 'Tell us what you were going to say this afternoon, before . . . you know.'

'Before this guy came round accusing me of demolishing next door, you mean?' asked Hamish.

'Yes,' said Grace.

'Yeah,' said Mungo. 'Right. Well.' He downed his tea. 'First thing is, you don't need to worry about that. The guy wouldn't give his name, talked a lot of rubbish, and made a few empty threats. Also, you'll find the name of his "organization's" solicitors in *Bleak House* by Charles Dickens, as studied by yours truly when he scraped through his Higher English. I don't know if what he said about the pipe being tampered with is true – '

'Oh yeah, true enough. Dave Lockerbie told me this afternoon. The compression joint'd been slackened off, with pliers he reckoned, judging by the scratches on the nut. He should know, I suppose, being a plumber for thingie's.'

'Thingie's?'

'Poulson's that was,' Grace translated. 'But you couldn't have done that, could you, Hamish? I mean, not in the time, and in any case it was leaking through to us for ages before you went in!'

'Yeah, well, like I say, empty threats, okay? Forget 'em. Without forgetting they've been made, mind you.'

'More likely it was the guy the bairn saw, weekend before last,' Hamish offered.

'Oh?' said Mungo.

Grace explained.

'Now that *is* interesting,' Mungo agreed. 'Especially in view of the car; can't be many like that around here.'

'No,' said Hamish. 'Mind you, it's no good asking him what the man looked like; he could've been bright green with three legs and the bairn wouldn't've noticed.'

'I'm not sure,' said Mungo thoughtfully, 'that I could tell you what our friend this afternoon looked like, if it comes to that. I'd recognize him again, but that's different, of course. What about you, Grace?'

She flushed. 'Sort of average,' she said. 'Darkish hair. With a jacket. Cold eyes, like a fish. He gave me the creeps.' She shivered illustratively.

'Yeah, well, there you are. You could arrest half the City of London on that description, and mine wouldn't be much better. Anyway, forget him for the moment, okay? No, what brought me hot-foot from my appointment at the dole office was you saying those two tragic words, Hamish old pal.'

'Clinch McKittrick?'

'The very same.'

'So who are they then?'

'Ah,' said Mungo. 'I was rather hoping you might tell me that.'

Neville, meanwhile, was paying his weekly visit to a number of houses in Logie Baird Avenue and Fleming

Way, his elegantly scuffed briefcase growing imperceptibly heavier with each call. At the last house he interrupted his business with a little unscheduled pleasantry.

'Hey,' he said, holding the little wad of notes over his open briefcase. 'Like to earn half this back?'

'Half?' said the girl.

'Yup. You have a brother, don't you?'

'That's a statement?'

'That's a statement. We like to look after our tenants.'

'Generous of you. Okay, so I have a brother.'

'Get him to ring me at eight forty. I'll be doing my workout till then and imputting after nine.'

'Hey! Twenty whole minutes off!'

'Five. But it's long enough for what I want to ask him. If he wants the other half, he can say yes.'

'Do I get to ask what it's about?'

'You want the money?'

'And that's my answer, huh? Okay, I'll pass it on.'

'Good. Oh.' He paused at the door. 'He's not known around here, is he?'

The girl grinned. 'You mean we don't all look the same, honky boy?'

'Sorry,' said Neville. 'I don't know what you're talking about.' He shut the door.

'What?' said Grace.

'But I thought you'd heard of them already,' said Hamish. 'On the phone this morning, I mean, you said – '

'Oh yes, I've heard of them. Um . . .' Mungo seemed suddenly disinclined to continue. 'I . . . suppose that you thought that's why I was coming over? To tell you, I mean?'

'We did hope, yes,' said Grace, not trying terribly hard

64

to conquer her instinctive anti-Beaulyism. 'Didn't we, Hamish?'

'Yeah-er,' Hamish replied, hoping this might allow him to keep a foot in each camp. 'I mean, being the editor of the *Gazette* and all that, we thought – '

'Ex-editor,' said Mungo. 'Also, ex-tenant of 21a, Corbie Buildings, Dunbroath. As from a fortnight ago when I found a certain nasty little sticker on the wall outside the main entrance.'

'Not – '

'Yes.'

'Oh, Mungo!' Grace exclaimed. 'But surely they can't – '

'Oh, yes they can. And they have, certain nasty little sticker being followed in short order by an even nastier little Recorded Delivery letter. All part of the housing reforms, you see, freeing us from the tentacles of dependency. Amen.'

'Hell fire,' said Hamish. 'First that, then . . .'

'Yeah, right. I wonder what number three's going to be? So you see, the fact is that I'd barely got started on finding out who these friendly wee enterprising developers are from my powerbase in Medialand when I found I hadn't got a powerbase any more. Not,' he added, holding up a hand, 'that I'm saying that was cause and effect, necessarily. I'm not that paranoid just yet. Only the point is that from what I *have* been able to find out it seems that Clinch McKittrick simply doesn't exist at all, which of course can't be true. And that's why I jumped down your throat when you mentioned the name, you see.'

'Oh,' said Hamish.

'Well, you'll stay the night anyway,' said Grace.

'Yes,' said Mungo. 'I mean, thanks. Thanks, Grace.'

'And then I suppose you'll be wanting to . . . ?'

'Ah,' said Mungo. 'Well of course I'd like to, but . . . um.'

Grace gave him a look which she hoped would come out as one of concern.

'Well – thing is, Grace – you were right. All along. About me. About me being a sponger and a bum, especially.'

'Oh, I –'

'No, no, really. You see, to say I didn't really save much out of my earnings would be a wee bit of an understatement. Or should that be overstatement? Anyway – not that I get, got, paid much, mind, but that's no excuse – what with being in a sort of negative cashflow situation as you might say, and Universal Regionals having something of a reputation as being a little slow, like say six months late, with their redundancy payments, I'm kind of, er, financially challenged just at the moment.'

'Like broke,' said Hamish.

'Broke would be quite a good way of putting it, yes. And, as such, a fully unpaid-up member of the Untouchables, the British *harijans*. Meaning they can't discriminate against you any more for being Irish, or black, or female, or all three at once – not officially, anyway – but being poor is another matter. You'd be amazed how many landlords operate a No Claimants policy. Like all the ones I've tried, for instance.

'Which is quite a lot,' he added. 'Thirty-two, I think, at the last count.'

'What about . . .' Grace began. 'I mean, you must have . . .'

'Contacts. Acquaintances. Ex-colleagues. All living in one-bedroom flats with no sofas and expecting the builders in any day. Et cetera.'

'You certainly find out who your friends are,' said Grace unthinkingly.

'That's what I was hoping,' said Mungo, not liking himself very much for saying it. 'I mean, if it works out okay – and that'd be up to you, of course – I would have an address for housing benefit. I mean, I will pay. And I know,' he went on, not giving Grace the chance to say something she might regret afterwards, 'I know you have your problems too – I mean, I've seen them, some of them. Only, I could help, maybe, or try anyway. Starting with Clinch McKittrick.'

Grace looked at Hamish.

Hamish said, 'Be funny if it turned out they were all the same people as, what-d'ye-call-'em, Euro-Kay, and Sight'n'Sound, and thingie, this outfit that's dumped all that garbage on Grace's shop, wouldn't it? All in it together. I mean, like, funny not funny.'

'That's silly, Hamish,' said Grace. 'Who'd want to gang up like that on us?'

'Yeah, right,' said Mungo. 'Or not. Look, tea's great for drowning in but I've got most of a bottle of hospitality whisky in the car, ex-editor's perks. Fancy a dram? No bribery intended.'

'Just a small one then,' said Grace automatically.

Mungo fetched the whisky, judging this to be an opportune moment to smuggle in his cases as well. The town this March evening seemed its usual well-regulated self, the velvet-dark main street pranked with soft pearly pools of light from the old standards, functional relics of pre-sodium days. The intermittent hum of sober traffic came from the Dunbroath road at one end; the faint, curiously tinny sound of evangelical witness from the Gospel Hall at the other. In between, a convoy of leading citizens, led by Mr Glencairn senior, passed like a dark, well-freighted fleet along the opposite pavement as it made its way from a meeting of the Kirk Session at the manse to the installation of an Initiate into the Mystical

Order of Stags in the rear function suite of the Ben Almond Hotel. It moved from pool to pool, its shadow looming and receding before it, past shop windows unlit and unbarred, past houses snugly, unfearfully curtained against the chill night air and nothing else.

'Evening,' came a signal from the fleet.

'Evening,' replied Mungo, closing the car door extra quietly so as not to give offence.

'A fine night.'

'Aye, so it is,' said Mungo. He turned for the house, remembering how much he had once loathed the place and thinking that he must be growing old, or mature, or something like that, and then wondering if perhaps Grace might take him on as a sort of temporary part-time replacement for Babette in return for his lodging, until he sorted something out.

She was waiting for him on the first landing. 'I've made up the spare bed,' she said, taking one of the cases. 'It's just a duvet, I'm afraid, because of the sheets. I didn't get time to dry them today.'

'Fine,' said Mungo. 'Grace?'

'Yes?'

'Thanks.'

Hamish poured the whisky while Grace got out five mats – idealized scenes of Mid Lummock, a wedding gift from Mrs Pitt-Holyoake – one each for their glasses, one for the bottle and one for the water jug.

'Well – ' began Mungo raising his glass. There was a soft rumbling sound, swelling like a drum roll then subsiding into heavy silence. 'What was that?'

'Next door's other ceiling, I should think,' said Hamish drily.

Grace took her small one off in a single swallow. 'What are we going to do?'

Mungo smiled, swirling his dram and staring into it. 'Business as usual, I hope.' He refilled Grace's glass.

'*Slàinte*, anyway. Don't let the bastards grind ye down. Now then, where's that washing-up?'

The following night, Tuesday night, saw a fire in the unoccupied premises at Number 11, High Street, next door to Sounds Good (formerly the Bonaventure Wireless Shop).

It was a very small fire. The cause, it was afterwards supposed, was an electrical fault, electrical faults being the Craigfieth Brigade's wonted explanation for conflagrations that did not involve chimneys or chip pans. Stripped as it had been of furniture, fittings, curtains and carpets, Number 11 – sold some months before by the executors of the late Thomasina Pitcairn, Craigfieth's first lady burgh councillor – contained little of a combustible nature. It was singularly unfortunate, therefore, that the electrical fault in question appeared to have its focus in the meter cupboard under the stairs, and that the open trap-door to the second landing should have allowed the flames free access to the roof timbers. Not, as Station Officer Heddle observed afterwards to Leading Fireman Lockerbie, but that it hadn't been kind of handy to have the hole in the roof already made for them to put the water in through, right enough.

The blaze was not visible for miles around, and certainly not from the third best house on the Lunie Estate. The estate, running right round the little town like a lairdly noose, boasted three fine houses. The first, Lunie Castle, was the occasional residence of the Laird himself, Lord Margoyle, and was empty for most of the year. The second was reserved for the exclusive use of his daughter, once the Hon. Davinia Moither, now the far from plain Mrs Wayne Kirkpatrick. It was always empty. The third was the residence of his Lordship's factor, trouble-shooter and general dogsbody Mr Snotter. Mr Snotter was this night bending his mind to the framing of a circular letter for his daughter and amanuensis, Belladonna, to type and send to certain unsuspecting persons resident in the Margoyle fiefdom. It was to be a very simple letter, one whose contents were not likely to cause its author any particular pang, yet he felt strangely loath to write it.

Although its purpose was to put into effect a threat that Mr Snotter had for many years cuddled to his breast – nursing it when it was sick through want of exercise, fondly allowing it to flash a claw or two when occasion and the Lunie interest demanded – he acknowledged himself more than a little piqued that its final and terrible execution should now be outwith his own control. He felt his importance – the reflected splendour of the Sun of Margoyle – diminished, albeit in his eyes only. Yet there on his desk were the instructions from MaxProf Associates, his Lordship's commercial managers in whose trust the continuing viability of the little kingdom had been placed, and there also was the curtly oleaginous note from Mr Dumbarton-Oakes, senior partner in the splendid legal firm of Broody's, Writers to the Signet, intimating that he, too, was in place below the trap and ready to slide the bolt. Mr Snotter's rôle was, in consequence, a somewhat supernumerary one and although the ignorant victims of the affair – the Great Unwashed, as he liked to call them – would be entirely unaware of this, still he resented it. But he was sufficient of a realist to know the letter must be written nonetheless, lest anyone should form a mistaken idea of the importance of factoring or the potency of one factor in particular. Indeed, now he came to consider it, the task of literary creation which now lay before him was made significant largely by its potential to spare him any tiresome contact with the addressees. There was no legal, practical or – he groped for the word – moral reason why such a warning should be issued at all, except as a means of forestalling the sort of whingeing nuisance which might otherwise occur once Messrs Broody's had played their part. Belladonna would sort out all the fiddly bits at the top of each letter – there must be no loopholes there, of course, for mischief-makers to wriggle through later on – so all he had to do was compose the one or two standard paragraphs above his own elegantly rubberstamped signature.

He tried a few practice sentences on the notepad he'd filched from his hotel bedroom at the last Annual General Meeting of ALAS, the Absentee Landowners' Association of Scotland. 'I have to inform you that, as a matter of estate policy . . .' No: that would not do. It sounded as though he was being compelled to write it, and that was altogether too near the truth. 'As part of a continuing review of estate policy, I am writing to inform you that . . .' No again: far too personal, too familiar; besides, he wasn't actually writing it as part of a continuing review. He sighed, cudgelling the syntax in the hope that it would eventually lie down and behave itself. 'The estate has been carrying out a review of its management, as a result of which it has been decided to . . .' He looked again at the last bit, decided he was not quite sure what the 'it' referred to, tore the whole sheet off, screwed it up and flung it away. The Great Unwashed, he decided, had no claim on his leisure hours, and would just have to wait. He would get Belladonna to help him with it in the morning. He switched the light off and went to bed to reread Norman Tebbit's memoirs.

Chapter Three

Thursday's dawn blushed through the roseate bedroom curtains of Dante Cottage and gently fingered the sleeping form of Mrs Audrey Pitt-Holyoake, decorously unconscious beneath her William Morris swansdown quilt. Forbearing to yawn, Craigfieth's leading craftswoman slipped out of bed and into her Laura Ashley dressing-gown and slippers, then pulled the tasselled cord to bare the thirty-six miniature leaded panes of her bedroom windows. A low spring sun broke like a blood orange over a distant drystane dyke and spilled itself in morning glory over the intervening fields of . . . whatever it was they'd been planted with this year. Canary seed? No, that couldn't be right . . . canary something, though, and fodder radish; such a peculiar crop, she thought, imagining the poor cattle having to eat some sort of rude salad in the winter; oh yes and mustard, fancy that! Canary *grass*, yes, that was it. Whatever that might be. She sighed perplexedly. Not so many years ago it had all been barley, and dear Godfrey – God rest his soul, she breathed automatically to herself – had begun every morning reciting that dear old Scots poem about Bold John Barley-corn. Who on earth, she wondered, would ever make a ballad out of fodder radish? Still, she supposed the growing of it gave employment to the people so she must not disparage it; must instead be content to hope it might turn out to be an improvement on the oilseed rape of recent years, whose horrid chrome yellow had clashed so distressingly with Dante Cottage's exterior.

She remembered poor Godfrey again as she ran her

morning bath, thinking of all the odd things farmers grew these days and of her late husband's own unfortunate – no, Audrey, she told herself, tipping in the salts, not unfortunate; disastrous – Nigerian experience. She had thought at the time – without saying so, of course – that it was one thing to emulate one's Sovereign's regard for the Commonwealth, but quite another to sink all one's newly redeemed War Bonds in a groundnut scheme. Her Majesty, after all, had not allowed her vision of a post-colonial rôle in Africa to impair her financial judgement; not, at any rate, to the extent that poor Godfrey had. She sighed again, rubbing in the almond oil. What cruel Providence was it, she asked herself, that could look on while her poor husband beggared them both with peanuts in Africa but could now allow her landlord to prosper with canary grass in Scotland?

This would not do! Buck up, Audrey! She seized the loofah and applied it vigorously to knees and elbows. This was no way to start the day! There was simply no such thing, after all, as a cloud without a silver lining. Why, but for that unfortunate peanut business she might never have thought of the Craft Corner as a means of livelihood. And without the Craft Corner, where would she be now? Not, surely, in her own lovely Dante Cottage! And not, certainly, in a position to surround herself with art and beauty or anoint herself with gentlewomanly balms and unguents! These thoughts bucked her up no end, as they always did, even to the extent of persuading her to treat herself to five minutes longer, and a little extra hot water. She turned the tap. It belched, coughed, hissed despairingly, then fell drily silent. Bother it! That made three times this year already, and summer was ages away yet. She would have to speak to Mr Snotter about it, right away. It wasn't as if she paid the estate any less for her

private supply than other householders did for the reliability of the public main – and imagine the fuss if *that* kept
failing! One was not a tenant of many years' standing for
nothing! She made a naughty resolution to telephone the
factor from the shop, for tax reasons, then stepped out of
the cooling bath. She caught sight of herself in the long
mirror, decided she didn't look a day over fifty-five,
especially when she breathed in, and went back to the
bedroom to do her callisthenics.

For once, the naked splendour of Mrs Pitt-Holyoake at
her open window did not distract Scrymgeour, head
keeper of the Lunie Estate, from his morning prowl of his
Lordship's policies. His binoculars lay beside him among
the sprouting mustard; the energetic nudist of Dante
Cottage exercised unregarded. The last thing Scrymgeour
wanted, while engaged in the delicate task of injecting
addled pheasants' eggs with mevinphos, was a trembling
hand.

Breakfasted and glowing, Mrs Pitt-Holyoake loaded her
latest canvases – six in a never-ending series of Lummock
views knocked off the night before while the TV was
temporarily on the blink – into the back of her beloved
Morris Traveller, shutting the doors (or, as she fondly
thought of them, casements) very gently so as not to
disturb the rust. She patted the old vehicle on the roof.
'If only you could talk,' she murmured affectionately.
'The things I've had in the back of you, old girl!' A few
green paint flakes drifted off as if by way of reply.
   Then began the complicated but thus far effectual
morning routine of coaxing the dear old bus into life.
Strictly, speaking, the ritual properly began the evening
before with the reversing of the car to a point where the
driver's right leg, bent to an angle not greater than ninety

degrees, could reach the telegraph pole at the top of the driveway. This was so Mrs Pitt-Holyoake could, as she put it, 'punt off' in the morning. The self-starter – never a sensible innovation, in her opinion – had long ceased to function beyond the production of a petulant, grizzling sort of noise from under the bonnet, and she firmly eschewed the use of all the various aerosol nostrums which, quite apart from the environmental havoc they might wreak, all required to be squirted up an air hose while the engine was turning over, an impossible feat for anyone with arms less than four and a half feet long. Mrs Pitt-Holyoake's system, then, was to switch on the ignition, depress the clutch, find first gear and 'punt off'. Inclement weather could make this last operation a disagreeable one; fortunately Dante Cottage was not overlooked (save by the unseen and lurking Scrymgeour) so the game septuagenarian felt no compunction whatever in hoisting up her skirt to save it getting wet. Sensible shoes, of course, had to be worn at all times but this was hardly a burden; Mrs Pitt-Holyoake was in any case very much a brown brogue person.

Once set in freewheel motion there were then five opportunities for the car's clutch to be let out and for the cycle of internal combustion to begin: two on the drive (the Rowan Tree and the MacMillan Stone, so called because aeons of erosion had worn one face to a drooping, lugubrious likeness of the last great Conservative premier) and three on the road itself. There was the Big Gorse Bush (some distance, this, from the junction with her drive but one needed that to make up for having to stop in case of traffic), the Tarry Patch (no matter how often the council resurfaced – which was hardly ever – it always reappeared) and the Dangerous Bend Sign right at the bottom of the hill; a tricky place, true, but she had only been obliged to use it once so far, thank goodness. This morning she sensed that the old lady would rejoice with the triumphant spring sun, and she was right: the Traveller fired first time, at the Rowan Tree, and – with a little careful jiggling and shoogling of the choke – was almost purring by the time Mrs Pitt-Holyoake slowed down for the junction. With the Dangerous Bend receding in her rear-view mirror she was able to free her mind from such trivial pursuits as mechanics and navigation and concentrate instead on loftier and more exciting thoughts.

First, there was the shop, the good old Craft Corner. Her Highland Crafts order was due any day now, a large order and her most ambitious and expensive to date, and it would be absolutely splendid if it should arrive today, early closing day. She could take the whole afternoon, with a clear conscience, to unpack, arrange and price it. Pricing was an exceptionally thrilling business. Audrey Pitt-Holyoake was not a greedy woman, nor a person disposed to exceed by very much the standard one hundred per cent mark-up, but she really thought that with one or two of the larger or more obviously artistic items – the sterling silver 'Stone Circle' wine coolers, for instance, or those rather fussily pointillistic samplers from the Dalglumph Women's Fabric Collective – she could afford to go a bit higher, if only to make the bargains in her end-of-season sale appear more attractive still. Her accumulated stock of watercolours ought to last her well into June, even with the publicity that might accrue from the article in *Scottish Country Matters*, so with a bit of luck she could look forward to at least ten weeks with nothing to do except sell, sell, sell! What bliss! It made the winter seem quite worthwhile after all. She coaxed the Traveller gently up to forty mph to celebrate the thought.

There was no doubt the Highland Craft Centre in Blairlummock was a boon and a blessing to her, if only because, by monopolizing the onward marketing of every craftsperson within a fifty-mile radius, it had made the retailer's task of choosing and ordering so much simpler and more straightforward. Gone were those endless days of searching round kilns and studios, of climbing stairs or battling up brambly tracks to remote and crumbling hovels in search of this or that petulant potter or dilettantish *daubiste*; of persuading the wretched creatures out of their foolish and fanciful notions of selling direct to the public, of talking them instead into supplying her; of begging and pleading, when a particular line of wares had proved popular with the visitors, that its creator should put sound commercial sense before half-baked notions of 'artistic integrity' and go on producing the same stuff, without variation; and then, when all was done and the aforesaid wretched creatures had been coaxed out of their ivory towers and into the marketplace, of plying them with threats and entreaties to prevent them supplying some other, larger, more avaricious retail outlet – which they almost always did, in the end – thus forcing her to start her searching all over again. It had all been a most fretful and tedious business and Mrs Pitt-Holyoake had not, in truth, been very good at it: hence her increasing reliance on Taiwan.

Thank goodness, the Highland Craft Centre had put a stop to all that. The focal point of Blairlummock (itself renowned, of course, as the region's first Visitor Village) the Centre provided both a retail marketplace and a wholesale distribution network for all the region's potters, painters, sketchers, sculptors, weavers, spinners, knitters, jewellers and allied knick-knack manufacturers, as well as mass-producing its own souvenirs at the lower end of the market. It imposed, in exchange for this unparalleled service, one simple rule: any errant art-and-craftists who took it on themselves to send their wares elsewhere would find they were instantly and irrevocably excommunicated from the Centre's charmed and lucrative circle. Brutal, perhaps, but it worked, and Mrs Pitt Holyoake approved of it. It wasn't just that it was so convenient – though the relief of being able to send one order by post instead of pursuing several dozen across country in the poor old Traveller was enormous – it was also, she assured herself, good for the business community as a whole. It could tell the visiting public, quite truthfully, that the crafts displayed for sale in its region were available nowhere else in Scotland. That cachet – and the exponential growth in tourism that went with it – was immense.

It occurred to Mrs Pitt-Holyoake, as she slowed to allow three sheep to cross pointlessly from one side of the single-track road to the other, that when the time came for her to sell the Craft Corner she might herself supply the Centre with the fruits of her paint-roller: what though she might, say, get fifty pounds per view instead of a hundred? She would have that much more time to produce them! The thought of ease and comfort in her eighth decade – not that the seventh was turning out at all badly, so far – was a very warming one. Two of the sheep decided to cross back again, but she managed to keep the engine running nonetheless – it had a tendency to die on her if she neglected it – and stayed firmly in second gear to negotiate the double bend that led down to the main Craigfieth road. The third sheep, appalled perhaps at its sudden individualism, made to rejoin its companions as the Traveller puttered off down the hill. It stood vacuously in the middle of the road, chewing slowly and watching the vehicle out of sight round the first bend. Then a dead crow fell on it.

For Mrs Joan Spurtle at the Bide-a-Wee Tearooms, the cost of Tuesday night's fire at Number 11 was counted in

78

the number of salad rolls purchased at Glencairn's and consumed on the hoof by persons who preferred watching the scaffolding activities of Homes-U-Like to snacking at their leisure at her establishment.

Ten thirty A.M. on early closing day, normally a relatively busy time for the two ladies, saw only two people in the tearooms – four, if one counted the brats whose demand for straws with their glasses of lurid Lummockade had been met by the adamantine Mrs Spurtle with the massive contempt it deserved. Straws in the Bide-a-Wee, indeed! They would be asking next, she supposed, for feeder cups and plastic bibs. She might have hoped – indeed, she hissed as much to her partner, quivering by the microwave – that the discreet but legible notice, 'No Haversacks, Buggies or Doggies *Please!*' would be sufficient indication to any but the most wilfully dim-witted of the kind of ambience to be found within, but there was of course no accounting for the congenital stupidity of some people. Miss Phemister agreed, of course, that it should be and that there wasn't, though secretly she felt a little sorry for the couple. They bore the unmistakable mark – a sort of moth-eaten, plaintive fatalism, as of those who have come to terms with their duty always to fall just a little short of meeting life's joyous challenges – of a family on holiday, in B and B accommodation, in Lummock View, Craigfieth, in March. The parents droned wearily at their offspring, and their offspring, poised, as Mrs Spurtle could see from her station behind the serving hatch, to smear and stuff jammy scone in the interstices of the basket chairs they sat in, whined wearily back. Miss Phemister, something of an expert in this narrow field of human psychology after many decades of genteel catering, deduced at once that the husband (whose thinning hair just failed to cover a pate the colour of underdone salmon) would have liked nothing better than an incompetent leisurely round on the golf course but supposed he would be in the doghouse if he did, while the wife (who somehow lacked the matronly maturity to match her choice of dress or, indeed, husband) was thinking, as she mechanically mopped and wiped and nagged, that there were only eleven more days to go, and feeling guilty for thinking it. The children, too young to yearn for alternatives to their lot, were frankly bored, and showing it. A copy of the *Tourist Guide to the Lummocks* lay open, unregarded, on the table. The talk, punctuated as it was by parental moanings was of the possibilities for their evening meal, eight grey and fractious hours away. Miss Phemister, then, felt sorry for them – sorry, and just a little envious – though of course she agreed with Joan about the straws.

'Time-wasters!' Mrs Spurtle snorted as she turned from the hatch.

'Yes, dear,' sighed Miss Phemister.

The Bide-a-Wee's loss of custom was not, however, Mrs Spurtle's only reason for disapproving of Tuesday night's fire. She had, over the previous year or so, been incubating a theory – one which was regularly taken out and tested on the inadequate but nonetheless captive critical faculties of Miss Honoria Phemister – and the fire had been just what she needed to cap it off.

'This town,' she said, 'is going to the dogs, Phemister.'

'Yes dear, Ay agree.'

'Something's got to be done about it!'

'Oh Ay know, dear, absolutely, yes.'

'So I'll just have to do it!'

'Oh!'

'What?'

'Ay mean, yes, dear, of course you must, if that's what you want – if you think that's best, Ay mean.'

'It is not a question,' said Mrs Spurtle softly, half

80

closing her eyes and tilting her nostrils as if to lift them clear of all the noisome traffickings of the world below, 'of what I want, or even of what I think. It is simply a question of duty.'

'Oh, yes, Ay wasn't forgetting that. Duty, yes of course, dear, only – '

'And of principle.'

'Yes, dear, that as well of course, only – '

'And, above all, of morality!'

'Oh!' Miss Phemister jumped, twitched and gulped. 'Yes, yes, quayte, although – '

'And service.'

Miss Phemister bleated quietly to herself.

'I have tried, Phemmy, God knows I have tried – '

'Oh yes, dear, Ay know you have, and – '

' – for many years, both on the Community Council and as chairwoman of the Brighter Gardens and Neater Wynds Action Group, to nurture and to inform, and to . . . to *lead*, yes, I don't mind admitting it, to lead, in my quiet way, this town's affairs. You know that.'

'Oh yes, dear, Ay do indeed!'

'It won't do.'

Miss Phemister struggled valiantly to come up with an acceptable response. 'Well, Ay . . . Ay mean, Ay don't know, Ay . . . Ay don't know about that, Joan dear! Ay mean, there was all that bunting the Community Council got the grant for, for the Gala and things like that, that was all your doing really, wasn't it, dear? Your idea, Ay mean. And look at all the taymes we've won Scotland in Bloom. Ay don't think you should belittle yourself, dear.'

'Tcha, Phemmy, tcha!'

'Oh!'

'Mere trifles, Phemmy. Trifles! Fiddling while Rome burns. It won't do, Phemmy. *It's not enough!*'

'No, dear, no it's not . . . Ay mean, yes! Oh dear, Ay don't know – '

'You can't cure cancer with cough-drops, Phemmy!'

'Can't you, dear? Ay mean, no, no, of course you can't – well, nobody can, really. Ay know that, but . . . oh, Ay'm sorry, Joan dear, Ay think Ay've rather lost what you're – Ay'm – talking about.'

'Duff,' said Mrs Spurtle.

'Oh. Yes, Ay was afraid that's what you were talking about.'

'It has to be faced. Duff's day is done! I say, that's rather good, all those dees, I must use that in my campaign when – yes?'

Mrs Spurtle spun round – the effect was a little like that of a mattress pirouetting on a centrifuge – and hurled the hatch open in response to a gentle but persistent knocking.

'May I help you?' she thundered, her splendid torso appearing under the gentleman's nose a fraction after her face.

'Toilets,' he said.

'I beg your pardon?'

'Er, t-toilets?'

'If you mean . . .' she paused magnificently before assaulting him with the word '. . . *lavatories*, since I am afraid this establishment does not run to manicure, pedicure, coiffure or costuming facilities, then *it* . . . is there. Through the door marked "Cloaks". First on the left. I doubt if you can miss it.'

'Ah,' said the man. 'Er, th – '

'Peasant!' she seethed, slamming and bolting the hatch.

'Lots of people do call it that, dear,' observed Miss Phemister.

'Lots of "people", Phemister, call a napkin a serviette,

or go to Turkey for their holidays! Lots of people these days don't know what good manners are! So what?'

'Nothing, dear, really,' admitted Miss Phemister.'You were saying, dear, about Mr Duff?'

'Tcha! What is there to say?'

'Well, Ay – '

'I'll tell you what there is: nothing! Nothing at all.'

'Oh, Ay – '

'Unless of course you count the fact that the one improvement effected in this town in the twenty-five years since the man first plonked his backside on a council bench is the patio extension on his own house – *if* you call that an improvement, which I for one do not! Or unless you count the fact that the library van still comes round once a fortnight and hasn't actually lost a wheel in the process – yet – although it cannot have escaped your attention that despite frequent local protests the proportion of so-called Romance upon its shelves is, if anything, higher than ever! Unless you happen to regard the flooding of the McWhirter Playing Fields for five months of the year as a unique opportunity for rice growers and water polo enthusiasts – do you? Or do you think it's a good thing to have a district councillor who calls himself an Independent but who just stands there twiddling his thumbs and sitting on his hands while the politicians cut everything to the bone, and start selling off everything you can think of, from the dustmen to the Maureen O'Rourke Dancers, and half the High Street goes to ruin in fire and flood, I mean just say so, Phemmy, if you do!'

'Oh, well of course there have been cuts and – '

'Cuts, rubbish! It's Duff. Why, do you think I'm *wrong*, Phemister?'

'No, dear, but – '

'*What?*'

Miss Phemister jumped again, but her friend and partner was looking elsewhere. Two doors gave access to the Sanctum Sanctorum of the Bide-a-Wee kitchen: one, its frame chipped and scarred from countless collisions with the serving trolley, opened into the tearoom itself, the other to the corridor leading to the Private Office and the Cloaks. Two heads obtruded through this latter opening, one below the other. One was balding, the other jammy.

'Perhaps,' hissed the widow, 'we should provide a map?'

'There's no flannel,' said the balding head, 'in the, er . . .'

'Toilet,' said the jammy one.

'Really?' said Mrs Spurtle.

'N-no,' said the man. 'I did look.'

'Really?' said Mrs Spurtle.

'Yes. Only of course we did try to get the worst of it off with a serviette, you see, but then my wife had an idea that we might try the, er, for a flannel. Only there wasn't one.'

'No,' said Mrs Spurtle. 'We couldn't find an anchor cable strong enough.'

'Pardon?'

'People – some people, that is – would keep, well, taking them, you see,' said Miss Phemister sadly.

'Have you tried spitting on a handkerchief?' suggested Mrs Spurtle. 'Or haven't you got one?'

'I beg your pardon?'

'Or perhaps you could just stick your child's head down the – '

'Ay'll do it for you!' Miss Phemister intervened wildly. 'If that's all right, Ay mean.'

'Tcha!' said Mrs Spurtle, and turned away in disgust as her weak-willed partner fussed and bothered her way round the infant's glutinous features with her washing-up cloth, then risked life and limb lifting it up to dry its face on the roller towel.

'Mind you don't hang the dear little child, Phemister,' said the widow sourly.

Miss Phemister, panting slightly, handed back to its father the scrubbed and burnished fruit of his loins.

'Thank you very much!' he said. 'So, this is where you do all your delicious baking, is it? All that mixing, and kneading, and – '

'It's a kitchen, if that's what you mean,' said Mrs Spurtle.

'Oh, well!' Miss Phemister twittered. 'We don't do all that, really, not any more. Ay mean these days all we really have to do is – '

'Yes,' cut in Mrs Spurtle. 'This is where we do our work – *when* we're allowed to get on with it. Is there anything else my partner can get for you? A loofah, perhaps? A masseur?'

'Oh no, really, thank you very much all the same,' said the man. 'Well, I won't keep you, then!'

'I should hardly think so,' said Mrs Spurtle. 'Not if what you've spent this morning is anything to go by. Good day to you.'

'Oh,' said the man, and bolted.

The partners faced each other as the door closed weakly behind him, the words 'really Joan!' and 'really Phemister!' framed on their lips.

'Well?' said Mrs Spurtle at last.

'Well, really, Joan! Ay do think you're too . . . hard on people sometimes, really Ay do! Ay mean, it's not his fault if other people . . . take things, is it? And Ay don't suppose they could afford to spend any more, anyway, poor souls, Ay believe it can be very difficult these days for quayte a lot of people who – '

'Pah!' snorted Mrs Spurtle. 'Don't you believe it!

They'll be off right now to the Strathlummock Leisure Centre, you mark my words, or the Blairlummock Highland Ceilidh Experience, or the Inverglair Safari Park at ten pounds a head! *They're* not the ones who are short of ready money, not these days, oh no! Did you hear him say "serviette"? That's the sort of people they are! And besides, that's not what you're really saying, is it? I know you, Phemmy, I can read you like a – I was going to say "book", but you're not such hard work as that. You're needled because I'm going to stand for the council, that's what it is, admit it!'

'Well, Ay – '

'You don't want me to do it, do you? You'd like to Delilah me in my efforts to bring down their dirty rotten temple! You don't want me to make a stand against sloth, and greed, and stagnation, and corruption at Mid Lummock House! Against councillors who starve their communities of funds while they line their pockets thinking up more and more useless committees to sit on! Well, if you think the Tourism, Leisure and Recreation Department's doing such a wonderful job, try looking at our books sometime, that's all *I* can say!'

'But that's just it, Joan dear!' wailed Miss Phemister. 'Ay *do* look! And Ay wonder what's going to happen with you away half the time. Ay mean it's all very well fighting all those things you said on the council, and Ay do admire you for wanting to do it, Joan, really Ay do, but what about the tearooms? Ay can't manage on may own, and Ay don't see how we shall keep going at all!'

'Oh, Phemmy!' Mrs Spurtle's tone was almost affectionate. 'You silly old stick! Haven't you heard of expenses?'

'Well, yes, Ay suppose they'll help with travelling to Duncruddie Mains, and if you need to stay to lunch they'll – '

'No, no, no, Phemmy – I mean loss of earnings

86

expenses! If I have to close the tearooms for council business you don't imagine we shan't be recompensed accordingly, do you?'

'Oh,' said Miss Phemister. 'But then they'll want to see the books, Joan dear, and as you say, Ay mean . . .' The widow's eye was glinting with dangerous humour. 'Won't they?'

'There are books,' said Mrs Spurtle, 'and books.'

'Oh?'

'Yés. Oh come on, Phemmy! I mean there are the books we get old Waddell to do for the income tax, for instance, yes? And then there are the books he could do us for . . . Like insurance and probate, you see?'

'Oh.'

'Precisely. You can't skimp on good government, you know.'

'No,' said Miss Phemister. 'Ay suppose you can't. Shall you . . . shall you be away a lot?'

'Shouldn't be surprised,' Mrs Spurtle replied grimly. 'Twenty-five years' greed and speculation will take quite a bit of undoing.'

They heard the cow-bells clonk, the sound of heavy rain and complaining children.

'Poor souls,' said Miss Phemister.

'Pooh,' said Mrs Spurtle. 'Don't waste your sympathy!'

Miss Phemister sniffed. She had learned over the years that this was the only effective way of registering implacable opposition, however timidly, to her partner's settled opinions.

'And don't sniff me, woman!' growled the widow. 'Come and help me clean up: that'll soon take the shine off your compassion!'

While Miss Phemister brushed and squeegeed under the table, Mrs Spurtle forced herself to stack the sticky plates upon it. An explosive hiss of the venomous variety escaped the widow's lips as she did so; Miss Phemister started and banged the back of her head on a jammy chair.

'What is it, dear?' she bleated.

'Will you just . . . look . . . at *this!*'

The chair rose, like a carapace, on Miss Phemister's shoulders; her ancient head peeped out above the table edge. 'What, dear?' she quavered.

'Mm!' said Mrs Spurtle. A fat and quivering finger pointed to something on the table. 'Mm-mm!' said Mrs Spurtle, covering and uncovering it with a plate to indicate the mode of discovery.

Miss Phemister straightened: her chair fell off, upsetting the water bucket. 'Oh, a fifty pence, dear! How nayce!'

'It is not *nice*,' gritted Mrs Spurtle. 'It's a tip!'

'Oh,' said Miss Phemister. 'Yes, dear, so it is.'

'A tip! What do they – do they think I'm a . . . some little chit saving up for, for nylons? As if they – and after all the – of all the insulting . . . tipping the *proprietor!*'

'Co-proprietor, dear.' Miss Phemister swallowed. 'Don't you want it?'

'That's not the point,' snapped Mrs Spurtle, pocketing the insult. 'Not the point at all!'

'No, dear. Mind, that bit's wet where Ay . . . yes, dear. Oh, look at that!'

Mrs Spurtle looked. In the street outside, a mostly green Morris Traveller rolled silently down the hill. As it drew level with the Bide-a-Wee window it coughed into life and was gone, leaving a thin blue cloud behind.

'It can't be lunchtime already, can it?'

It was not lunchtime, and the two ladies waited in vain for the car to reappear.

Some fifteen minutes earlier, the Semtex Parcel Post

had delivered to the Craft Corner a single large cardboard box, originally intended for the safe transit of Happy Farmer Sunny Yolk Grade C Battery Eggs. It seemed to Mrs Pitt-Holyoake to be a lot easier to carry than it ought to have been.

It was Audrey Pitt-Holyoake's avowed intention to sell only the best, the most exquisite, the most profitable artefacts this season and to this end she had, as has already been recorded, placed her largest order yet with the monopolistic wholesale enterprise in Blairlummock. She had to acknowledge, however, that not all her customers were likely to be as cultivated, as discerning, as well-heeled as she would wish. There would always, for instance, be the draggle of small-to-medium-sized children eager to part with a few coins from their hideous tartan souvenir purses, and with them in mind she had ordered a fair stock of hideous tartan souvenir purses for them to keep their few coins in. She had also ordered furry Loch Ness monsters, Bonnie Craigfieth key fobs, bookmarks and comb-cases (combs not included), I ♥ CRAIGFIETH self-adhesive stickers, a good selection of dangly things (bagpipes, Highland cattle, Fair Maid of Perth costume dolls, fluffy tartan dice) to obscure the rear window of the vacationing motorist, ancient Pict pencil-tops, miniature porcelain lavatories decorated with the old burgh coat of arms and 'Haste Ye Back' inside the bowl, and diverse other examples of (relatively) inexpensive hand-crafted noveltyware to fill up odd corners and make the shop look jolly.

These were what the box contained; these and nothing else. She checked the lid: 'Parcel 1 of 1', it said. Then she checked the invoice, a computer print-out two yards long, clumsily folded and concealed amidst the polystyrene chippings at the bottom. There, sure enough, was her order, printed in full; there, against every single item that was not, strictly speaking, trash was the scrawled legend, 'n/a'.

Mrs Pitt-Holyoake was a person of considerable fortitude, though it was perhaps fortunate that she had no customers for the next five minutes or so. When she had recovered herself sufficiently to trust her legs again she dialled the number of the Highland Craft Centre. '"Not Available",' she muttered. 'I'll give them "Not Available"!'

'*Camera-har,*' said a female voice in business school Gaelic. 'Thank you for calling the Highland Craft Centre, Blairlummock. Unfortunately there is no one available to take your call at the moment but if you would like to leave a message please speak clearly after the tone. *Ha-goo-mar.*' There followed the beginnings of a tinny rendering of the Skye Boat Song. She banged the phone down in disgust.

The third week of March is not usually a good time of year for the Scottish visitor industries, even when Easter is early. It does not, somehow, afford the visitor the sort of experience of which he, or she, might wish to own a souvenir. Mrs Pitt-Holyoake judged her trade that Thursday morning to be slack enough to justify closing the shop in order to upbraid the Highland Craft Centre in person; hence the unwontedly early ignition of her car outside the Bide-a-Wee Tearooms; hence the whiteness of her knuckles on the steering wheel; hence the quantities of puzzled townsfolk left checking their watches in her wake.

Despite the potentially disastrous consequences of her unfilled order, she was not, she decided, unduly alarmed by it. No doubt there had been some mistake; some trainee in the packing department had misread a computer code, or something. She could not believe that the ethnic gorgeousness of late January had now, in March, all passed away, leaving not a wrack behind. Nor could she see how the Centre's suppliers could have disappeared *en masse* in the interim. She nosed the Traveller cautiously round the four hair-pin bends that brought her, eventually, out of the Vale of Lummock and on to the moors to the west of the town. Away in the distance reared the great massifs of the true Highlands, their summits blotched with snow; beyond them lay the west, and the north-west, and the furthest west of all, where she had never been except in fast-vanished dream.

Arable gave way to pasture, pasture to heath, and heath to the holocaust landscape that is the infallible hallmark of recent attempts at self-enrichment on the part of the ludicrously wealthy. It is arguable that the only mitigation for a landscape that has been scored, gouged, trenched and bulldozed into hideous barrenness in the interests of commercial forestry is that it might, one day, produce trees whose lack of aesthetic appeal, a quarter of a century on, will be redeemed by their usefulness. Ruin a hillside now, so the argument runs, and you may eventually have enough pulp for six editions of a daily tabloid newspaper. Lord Margoyle's essay, in this bleak corner of the Lunie Estate, in thus enriching the common weal had not, however, had this desirable effect. Here and there, amid the lunar waste, an occasional withered sprig, mummified in its little plastic sheath, showed where a sapling had failed in its first winter; little corralled groups of fire beaters sprouted at regular intervals and a long, straight, sterile gully had been cut to prevent the spread of inferno from one imaginary sylvan swathe to another. No doubt the tax advantages, while they were available, had proved satisfactory to the proprietor, trees or no trees, and no doubt the rude treatment the moor had received at the hands, or mechanized shovels, of Woganomic Forestry plc had done no actual injury to anybody, the odd species of bog-loving flora and fauna excepted. There was certainly no doubting the feeling of relief at the Kipplerigg Distillery when the plantation failed. Distillers, like trees, need water and the annual growth rate of the Laird's little tax break, measured by the falling level of the Kipple Burn, would surely have put an end to that silent alchemy which, takeovers permitting, so wonderfully transformed its waters into the true Philosophers' Spirit.

Mrs Pitt-Holyoake wondered if Lord Margoyle had thought of that, and, remembering her own little drought at Dante Cottage, realized she had forgotten to report it to Mr Snotter. Perhaps his Lordship knew all along that the trees wouldn't grow. It was impossible to tell, even by keen observation of those whose task it was to do his thinking for him, what – or even if – the Laird of Lunie thought.

Not, she hastily reassured herself as Lord Margoyle's badlands at last gave way to the homely variety of owner-occupancy, that she had herself any cause to complain about her distant landlord. True, there had been that apprehensive period – around the time of poor Godfrey's death – when the lease on Dante Cottage (or Number 23½ Lunie, as it was then unaesthetically called) had run out. Hearing nothing from the estate office, and fretting a little when her letters to Mr Snotter went unanswered, she had begun to think about solicitors; had even gone so far as to make an appointment with young Mr Dunning, of Drubber and Dunning, with a view to clarifying matters. But then, just as dear Godfrey always used to say, 'If you carry a mac it won't rain'; no sooner had she persuaded young Mr Dunning to lower himself to the level of her humble affairs than an answer had come at last from Mr Snotter in the form of a letter inviting the lessee's relict to sign the enclosed Notice of Shorthold Tenancy or, alternatively and within a period of fourteen days, to remove herself from 23½ Lunie with such assistance as the estate might see fit to lend her in the way of lorries and so on. Mr Snotter – she had swept straight past the astonished Belladonna to beard the factor in his inner den – assured her that hers was simply one of a batch of letters sent out to various tied cottage tenants whose continued employment was no longer congruent with the ongoing management of the estate, and that although her own case was of course quite different it had been thought more administratively convenient to deal with everything in one go; that the offer of assistance with removal was merely made in order that anyone wishing to move might not be put off by the cost of doing so, and that the mention of two weeks had been made as a deterrent to the annoying native habit of procrastination, a habit to which he, on behalf of his principal, scarcely felt they were entitled. Mrs Pitt-Holyoake's new Short-hold Tenancy was, of course, annually renewable – that is to say, annually terminable – but this was just the way things were now and he did not think she need worry. 'Unless of course,' he added, 'the Socialists get in. You'd all be out then.' Mrs Pitt-Holyoake, correctly, as it turned out, did not think there was much chance of that. She had stayed in Dante Cottage ever since.

And, moreover, had paid very little in the way of rent: indeed, had paid none at all for the last six years, thanks mostly to the Highland Craft Centre. She frowned as she was thus reminded of the necessity of her journey. She coaxed the car gently round a right-angled bend at the corner of a tattie field – what a splendid picture it would make, the rich brown earth, the first dark green leaves, the infinitely shaded grey of the lichen-splotched stone dyke around it all! Three or four swipes of the roller and it would be captured for eternity – and composed herself for the long haul up to a little pink-washed cottage that sheltered just below the shoulder of Ben Gunn, beyond which the road wound on to Blairlummock.

Having dispensed with the uneconomic bulk of the artisans, the estate's policy towards its remaining tenants was not to hinder in any way such renovations or improvements as they might themselves wish to make to their dwellings. Indeed, when such undertakings could be said – as with the putting in of hot water, or the repairing of a roof – to enhance the value of the property, the estate was perfectly willing to make a corresponding adjustment to the rent. In Mrs Pitt-Holyoake's case they had been most liberal: septic tanks and central heating were one thing, but her Burne-Jonesian taste in design, particularly when applied to the internal walls, was not necessarily everyone's cup of tea. Nonetheless, as profits from the Craft Centre enabled Mrs Pitt-Holyoake to indulge her Pre-Raphaelite leanings yet more lavishly, so had Mr Snotter extended without demur her rent holiday to the complete satisfaction, presumably, of both parties.

'I have an estate to run,' he had explained the last time she broached the subject. 'It suits me well enough if Number 23½ is one less thing to worry about.'

Though she wished he might bring himself to call her home by its given name – he had, after all, raised no objection to it – she was grateful enough for the outcome of this policy of *laissez-faire*. So, she supposed, were the tenants who seemed content enough, for a correspondingly reduced rental, to let their houses crumble about their ears. So long as neither party troubled the other, things went well. Only the occasional troublemaker – that English family, for instance, who had made such a fuss about landlords' obligations to repair – had ruffled in any way the serene calm of Lunie's tenanted acres, and then only briefly. Socialism or no Socialism, the terms of their Shorthold Tenancy had been brought swiftly to bear and

94

they had duly departed, all six of them, three months later. Mrs Pitt-Holyoake had felt rather sorry for them, in a way, but had reassured herself that the council would take care of them. That was what the council was for, after all: that was what everybody paid their Poll Tax for, rich and poor alike; that was the whole point of the thing.

The Traveller's engine began to moan a little, and she changed gear. 'Over halfway now, old girl,' she soothed. 'Then a nice long downhill to cool off in.'

Closing her ears to the car's continued protestations she broke back into her earlier, happier train of thought. Lord Margoyle himself, perhaps, would read of Dante Cottage's renaissance when the article was written. Though largely confined by the infirmities of age and wealth to the more sophisticated comforts of Dottle Hall, Berkshire, the Laird, she believed, still subscribed to *Scottish Country Matters* to keep in touch with the realities of life in John Bull's hyperborean playground. She must be sure to mention him in the rôle of patron to her artistic efforts. He might not understand one word of it, she reasoned, but would be pleased to see his name in print.

There came a sudden violent juddering, then silence.

'Drat it!' said Mrs Pitt-Holyoake.

Two old men – one upright, walnut-faced and bandy-legged, impudently dressed and uncompromisingly loyal to his obscure Cockney origins, the other Scottish, soberly attired, refined of feature and wheelchair-bound – watched at the front room window of Rose Cottage the activities of Half-a-Job, their farming neighbour. Half-a-Job – his real name, which they lived in weekly hope of seeing in the Sheriff Court columns of the *Perthshire Gazette*, was Grant Begg – rivalled the television as a daily provider of provoking entertainment; in the summer, television came a long way second. Early July, they agreed, was the best time to watch, when in the half-ploughed fields the half-hearted struggle between the half-sown crops and the half-poisoned weeds was at its feeble height. Then the spavined cattle, weak from a long winter on short rations of noxiously thin silage, would stumble around their semi-fertilized pastures and the sheep, incompetently sheared by semi-skilled trainees on half wages, would find gaps in the unfinished fencing and new ways in which to terminate their existence in the abandoned ditches of the half-drained wetlands Mr Begg had once had half a mind to grow turnips in. It seemed to be a point of practice, if not of principle, in Mr Begg's system of husbandry that any job not worth doing badly was at any rate worth jacking in after two or three days' fruitless labour. Thus, while the sheep – not the same sheep, of course, though even Oswald had to admit that one member of Half-a-Job's unhappy flock was pretty much like another – staggered on from year to year, half-shorn, half-dipped and, if they were lucky, half-inoculated against rather less than half the ills that mortal mutton is heir to, their owner was from time to time capable, to the exclusion of all other chores, of raising up to a hundred yards or so of fence, complete with gate, to the very highest international standards – and then abandoning it for ever, like some monstrous Daliesque sculpture, for his beasts to hirple round in search of quietus.

Oswald Ochilree, watching Half-a-Job now from his wheelchair at the window, had maintained from the first that Mr Begg was a half-wit; Ganglion, who constitutionally took a dimmer view of human motivation than his friend, was inclined to disagree and had over the years refined a Grand Unifying Theory to explain the wretched man's distressing behaviour. Money, he declared, was at the root of it.

'It's yer subsidies, innit?' he said. 'An' yer grants. Take

yer subsidies: so long as you can get so much per beast wot can stand up without a Zimmer frame, why bovver if arf yer 'erd's got a twenty-five per cent shortfall in the workin' leg department? An' if you can flog the odd one wot turns aht 'arf-way reasonable, why bovver when sum of the uvvers turns their toes up on yer nah an' again? Stands ter reason, if you're a lazy barstud like wot Arferjob is. Contrariwise wiv the grants, ercorse.'

Oswald had looked puzzled.

'Fink abaht it! Far as I can unnerstan' from readin' the papers' – here Oswald thought to remind him that Old Muckspreader in *Private Eye* did not necessarily paint the whole British farming picture, then thought better of it – 'there's these 'and-ahts, right, whereby if you start a job, they dole aht the dosh ter finish it. Well, then! Supposin' if, instead of usin' the cash ter finish it, you puts most of it in yer bum pocket an' uses the little bit over ter start anuvver job, right? Then you gets anuvver grant ter finish that one, and so on. Simple! In fact,' he continued, warming to his theme, 'if we wait long enough, we might find 'e goes full circle, like – finishes the first job 'e ever started, an' works 'is way froo the rest, till by the time we're say, a 'undred an' fifty, 'e'll 'ave got 'imself a reasonably good farm!'

Oswald tutted.

'Nah, nah,' Ganglion remonstrated, 'it makes sense, really. Yew can't blame Arferjob for the system. 'E's in tune wiv the times, inne?'

'He's a gey lousy farmer,' said Oswald.

'Yeah, well, same fing, innit,' said Ganglion.

They watched now in silence for some minutes while Half-a-Job tinkered absently with a one-wheeled trailer and kept half an eye on the lambing.

'I fort 'e said as this field woz all twins,' said Ganglion at length.

'Singles, seemingly,' said Oswald. 'Half-a-twins, anyway. God help the others in that case.'

'Gercher! 'Spect 'e got them muddled up. Twins'll be in the nex' field, drownin' theirselves.'

'Perhaps,' said Oswald.

'Might never 'appen, y'know.'

'What?'

'That plague of locusts, or wotever it is yore broodin' over, might never 'appen. Leg givin' yer gyp, is it?'

'Not really, no. No more than usual.' Oswald sighed. 'Ach, I don't know what it is, really. I'm just glumshy, and that's a fact, and doubtless spending too much time watching friend Begg yonder and wishing I was forty years younger doesn't help any.' He sighed again. 'No' a very profitable line of philosophy, my friend.'

Ganglion grunted.

'Ach, I don't know,' Oswald repeated. 'Take yon, yon . . . sumph out there. I can mind on when I bought this place, years ago, from his father. Oh, man, you should have seen the farm then: no grants or whathaveyou, mind, just work, and hope, and work, and if things went phut, work again. My God, if old man Begg could see it now! There wouldn't be a stone fall out o' a dyke but he'd be there to catch it before it hit the deck. And the kye – that glossy with health you could comb your hair in them! And there's yon bugger now, with his brand-new BMW and a farm like a, like a waste land.'

'Wot're the roots that clutch, wot branches grow outer this stony rubbish?' asked Ganglion rhetorically. 'Good ole Open University always comes up trumps, dunnit!'

'Aye. Well, I wouldn't care to shore any o' *his* fragments against my ruins! I'd fall over.'

'Change an' decay in orl arahnd I see,' Ganglion intoned tunelessly.

'I don't have to look far to see that, either.'

'Oh, ta very much I'm sure!'

'Ach, away with you! You ken fine what I'm at.'

'Oh yeah, yeah, course I do. There's a name fer it, an' all, amongst Crumblyologists.'

'Oh, aye?'

'It's called bein' old, an' feeble, an' pissed off, an' fuckin' useless. Fortunately, there's a sure-fire guaranteed one 'undred per cent fool-proof cure; all you 'ave ter do is go finkin' you might as well be, an' the nex' fing you know is, you are. Works every time, narmean?'

'You're a thrawn old bugger, Ganglion,' said Oswald.

'Glad ter be of service,' said Ganglion, bowing. 'Ouch! Blahdy'ell! Shouldn't a done that. Nah,' he continued, lowering himself gingerly into the nearest chair, 'I do know wot you're feelin'. Bin feelin' it meself lately, wot wiv this soddin' winter goin' on fer ever, an' nuffink but doom an' gloom every time you switch the telly on, an' all the wrong fings 'appenin' ter the wrong people. Talking of which, d'you ever get the feelin' the 'ole bleedin' world's gorn bleedin' rotten an' it's full of greedy unprincipled barstuds gobblin' all the nice people up?'

'Oh, aye,' said Oswald warmly, 'all the time!'

'Yeah. Well that's another symptom.'

'I'm sure it's true, though.'

'Yeah? 'Spect it's bofe, then. There's a cheerful fort, innit.'

There was a peremptory double knock on the back door. 'If that's the Grim Reaper,' said Ganglion, 'tell 'im we're finkin' abaht it.'

Oswald lifted the latch with the notched pole he'd made for himself. 'Mistress Pitt-Holyoake!' he exclaimed. 'Come away in, you're just in time to stop us making away with ourselves.'

'Good gracious! Not with that bare bodkin, I hope?'

'What? Oh! No, this is just a wee tool so's I can get the

door open without banging it into myself every time. Come away in. I'll put the kettle on. Tea or coffee?'

'So long as it's not specially on my account, I'll have tea. Lovely! Good morning, Mr Ganglion.'

'Wotcher, missus! 'Scuse me not gettin' up. Oz an' me woz breakdancin' a minute ago an' I did meself a mischief. Sitcher dahn! That one's filthy an' comfortable, an' that one's cleaner an' gives yer pins an' needles in the bum.'

'I'll go for comfort, I think,' said Mrs Pitt-Holyoake, whose small soft spot for Ganglion had grown softer in her own less corrigible old age. 'I see I shall have to teach you callisthenics!'

'Wossat, then, a new European language?'

She smiled, and agreed that it might just as well be, these days, then went on to explain briefly the practice and principles of her morning routine, though she drew a veil, so to speak, over the more startling details of the practice. Oswald wheeled in three mugs of tea and a sugar bowl on a tray.

'Three, please,' said Mrs Pitt-Holyoake, who did not believe in taking health and beauty too far.

'Mrs P-H woz jus' tellin' me 'ow ter make meself poised an' graceful,' said Ganglion.

'That sounds a thoroughly good scheme.' Oswald handed round the tea. 'Provided you can get the spare parts, of course.'

'Har bleedin' har,' said Ganglion, grinning. 'Cheeky bugger!'

'What a very nice cup of tea,' observed Mrs Pitt-Holyoake, setting her mug carefully on the stained arm of the chair. 'Do you ever think of putting hemp in it, by any chance?'

Oswald coughed; Ganglion momentarily boggled, then composed himself sufficiently to say, 'Wot?'

'Your hemp,' said Mrs Pitt-Holyoake. 'I saw it growing

in your old taxi outside. A bit spindly, if you'll pardon my saying so. Time to harden it off, or it'll go all weak and leggy later on.'

'Oh, aye,' Oswald mumbled. 'That hemp.'

'Reckernized it, did yer?'

'Oh, yes. My father used to grow it, you know. Of course in Oxfordshire it was very hardy.'

'Oh, yeah,' Ganglion agreed weakly. 'It would be.'

'My word, yes. Splendid hedging, every year without fail, and so much nicer as a windbreak than that horrible *cupressocyparis* people grow nowadays. And Mother always found an infusion of the tops of the female plants most beneficial, in Darjeeling tea, when her need arose.'

'When 'er . . .' Ganglion began.

'Every four weeks or so,' Mrs Pitt-Holyoake explained crisply. 'My father always had a little joke about it being the key to a really successful marriage.'

'Ah,' said Ganglion. 'Blimey.'

Oswald, who was not averse to seeing his friend a little bested from time to time, and who had always had something of a weakness for indomitable ladies, chuckled quietly. 'I'm afraid we're denied such good reasons as your mother had,' he said.

'Oh well, I expect we all have our good reasons really, don't we, Mr Ochilree? Tell me, how do you like to use it?'

'We smoke it,' Ganglion admitted, 'mostly. Sometimes Oz puts some in 'is bakin', don't you, Oz? 'Ash brownies.'

'Try tea,' said Mrs Pitt-Holyoake firmly. 'I'm afraid poor Godfrey – my late husband, as you know, Mr Ganglion – he wouldn't let me grow any after we were married. He said he'd seen it do terrible things – out East, you know – when he was a boy. Personally I could never see quite what that had to do with it, but then poor Godfrey was always such a one for the White Man's

Burden, and all that sort of thing. When you look at what gin did to so many of the British out there you can't help thinking they'd have been better off with hemp, but there we are, and of course Godfrey had his way.' She sipped her tea. 'I expect it was all for the best,' she added wistfully. 'I was reading the other day that it's supposed to cause more lung cancer than tobacco, but then surely that wouldn't apply to tea, would it?'

'I'll give you some cuttings to take home with you,' Oswald offered gallantly. 'I'll pot them up, if you'll, erm, pardon the expression.'

Old age had liberated Mrs Pitt-Holyoake from such nonsenses as 'oh you shouldn't' and 'really I couldn't'. 'I should love some,' she said. 'Thank you very much. And you must both come and try my Darjeeling. Now: I'm sure you're wondering why I'm here.'

'Yeah,' said Ganglion, whose liberation from stuffy niceties had preceded Mrs Pitt-Holyoake's by at least half a century. 'Ter wot do we owe the pleasure?'

She told them everything.

'I have a theory, you know,' she concluded, 'that the more things get computerized in the interests of efficiency, the more things go wrong, and the more we develop advanced means of communication, the more we have to rely on delivering our messages in person. My father always said, "Never do business, Audrey, till you can see the whites of their eyes," and I'm sure he did at least as much in one day as any of these smart young things do now, in a week! I also think a horse would give far less trouble than a car, if it comes to that.'

'Better fer the roses, an' all. No probs! We'll 'ide yer keys under the mat an' give ole Duff a ring to get 'im ter come an' tow you away. An' then Oz'n me'll take yer to Blairlummock, won't we, Oz?'

'Fine that,' said Oswald. 'We've never been yet, anyway.'

'Oh really, you mustn't – ' began Mrs Pitt-Holyoake, really meaning it.

'Gercher,' said Ganglion. ''Igh spot of the week fer us normally'd be goin' ter Craigfeef fer the papers'n the odd bits an' bobser shoppin' an' that, we might just as well do that in Blairlum. Might jizz us up a bit. We were just sayin', weren't we, Oz, abaht feelin' a bit stodgy, an'at.'

'In that case,' said Mrs Pitt-Holyoake, 'thank you very much indeed and I'm buying us tea afterwards. I wonder, could I just make one quick phone call?'

'Feel free, ducks!'

For all her avowed mistrust of technology, Mrs Pitt-Holyoake had no difficulty with Rose Cottage's cordless digital. She punched in the number of the Lunie Estate office, frowned heavily for a while, then said: 'Mr Snotter, this is Audrey Pitt-Holyoake, Dante Cottage. My water's off. Again. Thanking you in anticipation.'

She replaced the receiver. 'Another dratted machine! Really, I almost think it's as if people were scared of other people!'

'P'raps 'e knew you was goin' to phone up,' suggested Ganglion.

'You think so? I really don't see why Mr Snotter should be afraid of me. So long as I can have my bath tomorrow morning, that is. Otherwise I really will be one of the Great Unwashed, won't I?'

The reappearance, some three and a half hours later, of Mrs Pitt-Holyoake's car, forlornly hitched up behind Mr Duff's rescue truck, did not pass unremarked in the High Street of Craigfieth.

It was remarked by Hamish Ganglion as he made his way to the Scottish Amiable and Providential Bank to keep an appointment with Mr McMurtry, and by Grace as she slammed the phone down on a highly unsatisfactory conversation with Semtex Transport. It formed the topic of lively debate in the rest-room of the fire station, where Leading Fireman Lockerbie and his ashen-faced crew were recovering from their third call-out that week, this time to a chimney fire at the Duncruddie Mains Crematorium. The Rev. MacAndrew, hard at work on an article for *Life and Work* in the upstairs study his wife called the Heights of Abraham, noticed it and sent up a brief prayer for its owner, whose messy demise was the subject of much ghoulish speculation in the playground of the primary school, until Miss Pleat intervened to put a stop to it. Then she carried the dread tidings back to the staff-room, where it was generally agreed that anyone driving a vehicle more than three years old deserved everything that happened to them, unless it was a Volvo. Hamilton Fingal caught sight of it as he shimmered round the tables of the Fly Bite Restaurant dispensing napery cleverly folded to resemble the Edinburgh Opera House, and thought the High Street quite the wrong sort of place for a vehicle repair workshop, particularly one so threatening to the delicate ambience of Mid Lummock's almost-premier gourmet paradise. At the other end of the street – and of the town's culinary spectrum – Mrs Spurtle, glaring with one eye through the judas-hole in the shutter, observed it briefly before returning her gorgon gaze to the Bide-a-Wee's solitary tea-time client. Savagely, she fiddled, as she glared, with the client's business card. 'EUGENE MKEKWE,' it said, 'EUROPEAN CATERING COMMISSION – ETHNICITY STANDARDS COMMISSARIAT – UNHERALDED INSPECTIONS BUREAU.' Then she harrumphed immoderately, and turned away.

'As if inspecting the kitchen and the store wasn't bad

enough,' she growled, 'without sitting in the window afterwards, frightening people off.'

'Yes, dear,' said Miss Phemister.

'Not that I've any objection, of course,' said Mrs Spurtle, 'to his sort generally.'

'No, dear,' said Miss Phemister. 'Ay should think not!'

'But as I said to him myself, if it's yams and watermelons you're after, I said, you'd do better to try the so-called Scottish so-called Produce Centre!'

'You said that, did you, dear?'

'I did, Phemmy. Oh yes. In no uncertain terms. I make no exceptions for race or creed, as well you know.'

'No, dear. Ay mean, yes, Ay know you don't. Only for . . . the other difference. Ay should say.'

'Sex, Phemmy – mind what you're doing with that knife, woman, you'll have the handle off. By the way, talking of sex, I've just seen Duff the Elder towing the geegaw woman's car up the street. No doubt she has been raped and abducted somewhere, by Duff himself I shouldn't wonder.'

'Oh,' gasped Miss Phemister. 'Mai guidness!'

And then the handle did come off.

Chapter Four

Audrey Pitt-Holyoake's abduction safely accomplished, Ganglion and Oswald left her at the award-winning glass doors of the Highland Craft Centre and set about amusing themselves, as best they could, in Eastern Region's Premier Heritage Leisurespot.

Blairlummock Visitor Village is one of the brightest jewels in the gorgeous crown of Scotland's Visitor Industries Development Board, ranking alongside such paragons of pride and profit as Aviemore's Roger Rabbit Experience, the Loch Ness Monster Centre, Expo Glencoe Massacre, and the Clan Gathering Theme Park 'n' Burgerama, Culloden. It is a regular recipient of the Queen's Award for Invisible Exports and, for all the real competition it ever gets, might just as well nail the Patrick Sellar Memorial Trophy (awarded annually by a representative panel of leading social anthropologists, marketing consultants and travel agents to the Most Unspoiled Village in Scotland) to the shelf behind the foyer of its purpose-built Ceilidh Centre alongside the many gold and platinum discs acquired, in his youth, by the community's entrepreneurial Laird.

It was not always so.

Time was when Blairlummock, far from being unspoiled, was simply, and sadly, neglected. For several centuries it belonged, in the loosest sense of the word, to the Clan Chizzell, and indeed still appears as such on the clan maps of Scotland on sale in its Timespan Heritage Complex, above whose doorway the clan motto (Ne'er

Be Ta'en A Lend O') and crest (a serpent, and a hog regardant) are carved in all-weather styrene polymer. Forced by the changeable exigencies of nineteenth-century economics first to prefer sheep to men, and then to prefer grouse to shepherds, the chieftains of Clan Chizzell cannot be said to have contributed much to the romantic weave of Caledonia's chequered history – or at any rate not since the thirteenth chief, Johann Sebastian Chizzell, allowed himself, during the ill-fated Jacobite retreat from Derby, to be side-tracked just south of Nantwich by the wife of an Anabaptist preacher. The eighteenth chief, Oscar Brangwyn Chizzell, did, it is true, briefly go some way towards retrieving his family's name and fortune. Buoyed up on a wave of patriotic fervour during the reign of Edward VII, of Saxe-Coburg-Gotha, his Anglo-German Trust Company prospered, for a while, so mightily that cabinet ministers and courtiers, princelings and politicians at times outnumbered peasants among the banks and braes o'bonny Blairlummock by more than three to one. Then came George V, of the House of Windsor, and by Christmas 1914 the Chizzell empire, crushed beneath a wave of equally fervent patriotic sensibility, was in ruins. Oscar Brangwyn did not long survive his internment as an economic alien. Depressed by the ingratitude of his countrymen, he threw himself off Chizzell's Loup – this accident blackspot has now, thank goodness, been fenced off – and died, three weeks later, of pneumonia. He left a son, Bertie Keppel Chizzell, a title, and a mountain of debt. Finding no one willing to buy the title, young Bertie was obliged to sell the estate instead before going off, as he put it, to govern New South Wales. Six months later (according to the official account) he was killed by a herd of stampeding kangaroo.

The Chizzell fiefdom, meanwhile, not having participated in the rise of the Anglo-German Trust Company, was little affected by its fall; it merely contrived, in a leisurely sort of way, to revert to the state in which the last Ice Age had left it. This process was not conspicuously arrested by the acquisition of the estate by Montague Dewdrop, the first Earl Chestie. This gentleman, having made his fortune in wholesale fishmongering and having bought his title – fairly and squarely, paying not a farthing less than the going government rate for it – found himself urgently in want of a property to go with it. Blairlummock, being on the market at the time, seemed to him as serviceable as any other.

His arrival in Chizzell Castle – which he renamed Castle Chestie – had little effect on the tenantry, who were reassured by the continuance in office of the Laird's factor that nothing much was likely to change, for them. 'Keep yeerself aloof, my Lord,' the factor advised the newly ennobled Dewdrop. 'And mak' sure to be seen spendin' yeer ain money on yeer ain policies, an' ye'll soon win their respect. Ye may safely leave the rest to me.'

The name of this worldly-wise man was Archibald Snotter.

Montague, Earl Chestie, took his factor's advice and set about remodelling Castle Chestie rather as the mad King Ludwig might have done, had he been working from a photograph of Wormwood Scrubs. Blairlummockonians – among whom the erection in 1809 of a gothic ruin on Ben Buboe by Trismegistus 'Monk' Chizzell, the fifteenth of that ilk, had barely ceased to be a talking point – watched it grow with ironic awe, named it the Dewdrop Inn, and hoped the Laird's zeal for improvement would be confined to his own midden.

Having at last succeeded in establishing himself as a fully fledged ornament of the nobility – the final, clinching accolade being the abstraction, by the dowager Queen Mary, of a positively priceless but possibly rather ugly

Louis Quinze commode from her weekend apartments in the castle – and having noisily expired in the last throes of a thoroughly upper-class social disease, the first Earl Chestie was succeeded by his only offspring, Oswald Bracken Dewdrop, Lord Blairlummock. This specimen was then in his mid-thirties and showing every sign of having been forged in an ermine-fringed crucible. His mother's defection, before his second birthday, to Monte Carlo on the grounds that she could not stand Castle Chestie one minute longer ('The whole bloody place stinks of your father's cod,' she told the uncomprehending infant) was probably the making of the young Earl. Mercifully freed from the debilitating influence of women, Oswald Bracken grew up fostered alike by Snotter and by the English public school. He was thus fitted, when his time came, for the task of being Oswald, Earl Chestie, Laird of Blairlummock, and devoted the rest of his life – which was not a particularly useful one in any other way – to this most puissant vocation with the aid of Snotter the younger (Snotter òg), the third generation of Snotter to tread the potent path of sycophancy. This continuing alliance of principal and agent gave rise to a seditious little nationalistic jingle roughly translatable from the Gaelic as:

A Snotter and a Dewdrop hang together:
A sore affliction indeed is a Chestie complaint!

The second Earl died in 1971, unmarried and untried as to the production of issue, but nonetheless quite worn out with the unbearable lightness of being a landowning peer.

Thus far, then, the history of Blairlummock had been an unremarkable one and the township had fared no better and no worse than thousands of others in the

Scottish feudal hegemony. Then the estate passed to the late Earl's niece, the Honourable Miss Urticaria McPherson-Strutt.

This lady had lived a respectably Bohemian existence for much of a life which was, until shortly before this date, divided between a large bedsitting-room in Chelsea and a small gatehouse in the charming Hampshire stockbroker village of Nether Dibble. A late recruit to the Swinging Sixties, Miss McPherson-Strutt soon showed evidence of a determination to make up for lost time.

At a night-club opening, among the glittering socialites and statesmen-in-waiting, she made the acquaintance of the then plain Wat Tyler (the OBE was to follow some years later in the Prime Minister's resignation Honours List), lead guitarist with Hempen Bicycle, the celebrated exponents of Acid Folk. Romance, of a sort, blossomed; marriage, in the jacuzzi of Hempen Bicycle's Norfolk recording studios, ensued. Astonishingly, the couple were still together three years later at the expiry of the second Earl's mortal lease, and Blairlummock found itself on the map at last as Snotter òg strove to protect the couple's inherited privacy from the impious gaze of the Legions of the Unwashed.

It was also thanks to Snotter that Miss McPherson-Strutt's untimely demise following a fall (or flight?) from the top of Chizzell's Folly never received the thoroughgoing media probing it undoubtedly warranted. The factor's reward, after a fortnight's superlative stonewalling, was not, perhaps, what he had expected: Wat Tyler fired him. His continuance in the post, it was explained, was no longer congruent with the ongoing policy of his principal – a phrase which Snotter himself, in his new creation as factor to Lord Margoyle, was later to employ with great effect.

Hempen Bicycle went their separate ways, some to

explore their own musicality, some to open boutiques, others to the grave. Wat Tyler disappeared completely, for a while, from the public annals.

And then Blairlummock's Great Unspoiling began . . .

'Wot a soddin' awful place.'

'Aye, right enough,' Oswald agreed. 'A bit like a Red Indian Reservation, eh? Only without the Red Indians, of course. It's no' the season for them yet.'

'I spose they do 'ave a shop in this dump?'

Facing away from the Highland Craft Centre (Free Parking! Free Admission! Free Celtic Novelty with Every Purchase Over £20! Coaches Welcome!) which resembled, and, in fact, was, an inelegantly thatched Advance Factory Unit, the nearest likely building – which is to say that it could have been a shopping mall, or a school, or council offices, or a small open prison for low-risk murderers nearing the end of their sentence – turned out, in plastic Celtic script a foot high, to be the Coimhearsnachd Ceilidh Centre. CEUD MÌLE FÀILTE were offered in slightly smaller neon letters underneath; further down another sign proclaimed it CLOSED and a poster gave advance warning of the Mince'n'Tatties Easter Spectacular. Closed also were the Lucky Bawbee Amusement Arcade, the Braemar Gathering School of Highland Dancing, the Killiecrankie Pizzeria and the Wee Whang Indoor Putting Green, all of which lay beyond the locked door of the Hundred Thousand Welcomes. Opposite the Ceilidh Centre was the Blairlummock Village Green and Free Picnic Area, and in its perfect centre was a large electronic noticeboard, an At-A-Glance Guide to the Holiday Community. Ganglion wheeled his friend across the artificial sward to inspect it.

They stood awhile in silent awe.

111

'"So twice five miles of fertile ground,"' muttered Oswald, '"With walls and towers was girdled round."'

'Yeah,' said Ganglion. 'I bet they got sinuous rills, an' all.'

'Aye,' said Oswald. 'There, look: Sinuous Rills Beauty Spot, press button thirty-seven.'

Ganglion did so. The selected amenity began to flash on the map – it turned out to lie about halfway between the Chizzell's Loup Waterfall Viewpoint and the Flow'ry Meads O' Buboe Nature Trail – as did the prescribed route to it.

'Thank you for your enquiry,' said the map, putting the stress on the first syllable. 'The Sinuous Rills were constructed, after intensive aerial research of the Nile Delta and the user-designed beauty spot you have selected is the ideal location to observe their unique natural beauty. Photographic and video accessories may be purchased here. Please wear the helmets provided for your safety and comfort. Thank you. Have a nice day.'

'Anyfink else you wanner be put off of?' asked Ganglion.

'Try button eighteen,' suggested Oswald. 'The Traditional Highland Village Stores. I'm almost out o' traditional Highland matches.'

'Right-ho,' said Ganglion cheerily. 'Don't say you 'aven't bin warned, though.'

'Thank you for your enquiry,' said the map as before. 'Blairlummock's Traditional Highland Village Stores is conveniently situated not two minutes' walk from your present location. Built as an annexe of the Timespan Heritage Experience, the Village Stores is an authentic replication of a typical bygone retail outlet and you may truly imagine yourself transported back in time to the days when shopping, or 'going the messages' to use the traditional Scotch phrase, was an important daily social interface experience and an essential part of the relaxed and friendly Highland lifestyle that Blairlummock Visitor Village has recreated for your enjoyment. Please note that video security equipment is deployed in this facility. Thank you. Have a nice day.'

''Snuff ter make yer give up smokin', innit.'

'Not quite,' said Oswald grimly. 'Let's go and get it over with, shall we?'

'So: wot would you say,' asked Ganglion as they made their way past the grim prison walls of the Wee Totties Crèche and Rumpus Room, 'from your vast experience, was the distinguishin' features of a traditional village stores?'

'The queue,' said Oswald firmly. 'Outside in the rain mostly, on account of the lack of space. And the high prices, on account of the terrible cost of transport, and half the things on your list being out of stock, either because there's no demand for them locally or because they've sold out, and most of the things they *have* got being on a high shelf, or underneath the other counter, or out the back. And they're usually owned by the local councillor, so's folk can have all their grumbles in one go, like.'

'Fair enough for starters! Well: snot rainin', an' there's no queue, so that's two black marks straight off, innit? In we go.' A sticker on the door advised that they were now entering a Smile Zone. They entered it, triggering a traditional Highland burglar alarm and attracting the attentions of three video cameras, which swivelled round and flashed red lights at them.

The shop was a shambles of cardboard boxes, packing material and haphazardly arranged tins, packets and jars, all with labels dating from the Pre-Cambrian era of retail packaging. A large advertisement on the wall sang the healthful virtues of a brand of cigarette Oswald had tried for the first – and last – time behind the gable end of his father's byre. Three-quarters of the way up a stepladder and looking over her shoulder, poised in the act of reaching something down off a high shelf, was a monumental female assistant. A single hair, illuminated by the yellow rays of a light bulb suspended a foot or so away, sprouted from her chin. She seemed quite unruffled and not at all disposed to notice the clangorous din all round them despite Ganglion's frantic gesticulations to her to switch it off.

At last it stopped.

'We're no' open,' said a voice.

Ganglion blinked at the assistant. 'Wot?'

'We're closed,' said the voice again. A teenage girl – fifteen, perhaps, going on fifty, dark-haired and prognathous – stood in the rear doorway. She chewed a quid of gum and was listlessly doing up a blouse button.

'Wot?'

She shambled wearily across the floor, pausing to park her gum on the assistant's ankle and break Ganglion's spell.

'We're – closed,' she said, repeating the words very slowly and leaning heavily on the counter. Oswald, at blouse level, could not decide whether it was one button too few or one too many.

'Oh,' he said. 'Erm, when do you open, then?'

'Easter,' she said.

'Ah,' said Oswald. 'I see. Erm, I don't suppose you could sell me a box of matches, though, could you, seeing we're here anyway?'

'Na,' said the girl.

'Oh,' said Oswald.

'No demand?' asked Ganglion. 'Or is there a war on?'

'Don't sell them,' said the girl, sagging a little on her elbows.

Definitely one too few, Oswald decided. 'Ah,' he said. 'Or a paper?'

'Uh?'

'A paper. *Perthshire Gazette*.'

'Na.'

'Oh. Erm, is there anywhere else?'

'There is the Leisuremarket.'

'Where's that?'

She sighed. 'In the Leisuremarket Centre. It's shut.'

'Till Easter?'

'For lunch. You could try the Timespan.'

'The wot?' asked Ganglion.

'Timespan.' With an apparent effort of will she straightened herself and jerked her head, causing the button to undo itself. 'Next door. The jannie might gie' ye a loan o' his, if y' desperate.'

'Oh, aye,' muttered Oswald. 'Should you no, erm, be in school, lassie?'

She grinned vacuously. 'Work experience,' she said. 'Helpin' ma Da. Only he's at a council meeting.'

''Ow very traditional,' Ganglion observed.

'Eh?'

'Nuffink.' He wheeled Oswald round, upsetting a precarious stack of baked beans and cream crackers. They fell with a curious clonking sound on the stone floor. Ganglion picked up a packet and struck it on the counter, wood on wood. 'Daylight!' he exclaimed.

'Eh?' said the girl.

'Nuffink again. Ta-ra, love.' He opened the door cautiously, but there was no answering peal this time, just a ping from the authentically replicated shop bell.

A hoarse male voice called from the Traditional Highland Stores' inner sanctum. 'Tamsin! Hae ye goat rid o' them yet? Ah'm ready again.'

'Aye, I'm comin',' drawled Tamsin, shambling off.

'That'll be the day,' complained the voice.

They breathed deeply and gratefully outside. 'Blimey! D'you get a loader that dummy?'

'Which one?' asked Oswald mournfully.

'Yeah, good question. Poor cow. Aye-aye, look at that! Reckon you could get a light off of that, Oz?' He pointed to a niche in the Timespan Complex wall. It contained an aluminium structure, artfully contrived to resemble the Torch of Learning, or the Olympic Spirit, or something. A plaque underneath identified it as THE ETERNAL FLAME OF GAELDOM, Officially Kindled by Sir Hector Shoddie, Chairman of the Scottish Visitor Industries Development Board.

'Put yer brakes on, Oz, an' I'll 'ave a butchers.' Ganglion clambered on the wheelchair and peered inside.

'It's gorn out,' he said.

The Timespan Heritage Centre was open, thanks to a clause in its annual grant from the Boasky Trust requiring year-round community access, though on a reduced scale. Many of its more precious exhibits, such as the blue bonnet the thirteenth Chizzell would have worn at Culloden had he ever got there, or the tee-shirt worn by the present Laird at Woodstock and never washed since, had been removed for insurance purposes and would not reappear until the summer. The Wee But'n'Ben Studio, wherein visitors could make videos of themselves performing such traditional crofting activities as spinning, weaving and claymore sharpening, was open by appointment only. The Highland Clearance Participation Show, in which family parties could, for an extra fee, have themselves evicted by holograms of leading TV personalities dressed as bailiffs, was suspended pending negotiations with an agency representing two weather forecasters and the man in the instant coffee commercials.

Also in abeyance for the winter was the ubiquitous

116

graduate of the Thames Ditton Receptionists' College, with her fixed smile, tartan dress and authentic extension of '*kewed mealy falcher*' to the eager punter. In her place was a cross-browed seventeen-year-old Gaelic speaker who said 'yeah'.

'Yeah?' he said.

'We've decided to live dangerously,' said Ganglion. 'See Blairlummock an' die. Open, are yer?'

'It's three pounds fifty,' said the youth. 'Each.'

Ganglion grinned and briefly exhibited his late uncle's Metropolitan Police Authority Hackney Carriage Licence, an invaluable prop on occasions such as this.

'We're from the Board,' he explained, putting it away. 'Official inspection. Testin' yer provision fer the incontinent an' the disabled.' He nodded at Oswald. 'I made 'im go afore 'e come out.'

'Oh, aye,' said the youth. 'On ye go, then. It's all crap anyway. If the illuminated history of Clan Chizzell doesn't work,' he added, 'kick it.'

'Makes it come on, that, does it?'

'Maybe.'

''E deserves to go far,' Ganglion opined as they passed on.

'He's no future in this place, surely,' said Oswald.

'Thass wot I meant.'

'It's funny,' said Ganglion a few moments later, 'but I could swear I've seen that lad before.'

'What, in Craigfieth you mean?'

'Nah, that's wot's funny about it. Years ago – years an' years ago. Which ercorse is impossible, innit. Nah then, woss this? "This way to the Barbara Hypitt-Gorge Exhibition." Mean anyfink to you, Oz?'

'Is she no' that writer woman? Yon books that're four inches thick with gold writing on them?'

'Oh, yeah, vaguely. Wot's she doin' in 'ere, then?'

'Perhaps they're an extinct clan. Exterminated by the McCartlands in the notorious Battle of the Heights O' Pap.'

'By a troop of Archers,' Ganglion wheezed. 'I like it, I like it! Gawd, we get better as we get older, we do. 'Ow's yer stummick?'

'About equal to it, Ganglion, I reckon.'

'Right, then. 'Ere we go!'

The Barbara Hypitt-Gorge Exhibition turned out to be a large, generously furnished drawing-room, carpeted and upholstered in the authoress's preferred shades of shocking pink and revolting puce. An exquisitely fussy bookcase accommodated first editions of all Miss Hypitt-Gorge's copious literary output, though some unseen security device, as Ganglion soon discovered, prevented their removal from the shelves. Dotted around among the variously gilded, scrolled, padded and ruched accoutrements of the salon were little mementoes of her life and times. Several of her agent's letters – all handwritten and beginning with the word 'Darling!' – were carelessly scattered under a locked glass cover on her escritoire, along with the odd enviable royalty statement in nononsense computer type. A sapphire-studded fountain pen turned out to be the very instrument with which was written its owner's latest seminal blockbuster, *The Countess and the Crofter*. 'Miss Hypitt-Gorge,' its label informed them, 'obtains all her pens from Asprey's, and never uses the same one twice.' A sample page of the manuscript, in which the word 'palpitating' appeared three times, lay nearby. Several of the occasional tables (so called, according to Ganglion, because if you put your feet up on them they wouldn't be tables any more) bore framed stills from the television mini-series of the book, starring Lord Olivier as Angus McFud the deaf-mute Kirk elder and Joan Collins as the district nurse, and filmed entirely on location in Blairlummock Visitor Village itself.

The room was dominated by a revoltingly pneumatic sofa, on which reclined a slightly Brobdingnagian figure, obviously from the same studios as the Highland Stores assistant. It wore a ballgown that almost matched the curtains in colour, style and amplitude, a tiara and several very large rings which, though presumably paste, Oswald discovered to be glued, or riveted, to the fingers. One hand pointed languorously to a gilded bellpush on a little table: 'Press this bell,' read a notice, 'to hear Miss Hypitt-Gorge herself speak about her lifelong affinity for the Highlands.'

'If you do that, Ganglion,' said Oswald, seeing his friend's hand already beginning to stray, 'I shall take myself straight off back to the Eventide and never speak to you again.'

'Aw, go on, Oz, bit o' fun, eh?'

'No, Ganglion. No and again no. My gorge has risen. I can stand no more. Gall and wormwood!' He began to wheel himself laboriously away across the thick pile.

'Fair do's, then,' said Ganglion, catching up. 'I know wot you mean, I'd a culture of me own, once. Orf we go, then, see if we can find this jannie bloke.'

Seated on a small Queen Anne chair near the door was a dummy they had failed to notice on their way in. It was dressed in shiny black trousers and a rusty jacket that didn't quite match; a collarless shirt was open at the neck, and the legs ended in a pair of enormous cracked boots that seemed incapable of being filled by the artificial feet within. A cloth cap, pulled down at the front, completed the simulacrum of a man in his mid-seventies, grizzled, unshaven and slightly cadaverous about the gills.

'Item, one genew-ine traditional fully awfentick 'igh-land peasant,' Ganglion announced. 'Completely shagged

119

out arter a night of steamy passion wiv the Cahntess, I s'pose.' He made to check if the model's cap was removable and, if so, whether it would fit him.

'My name is Roderick MacGregor,' said the dummy, 'and if ye touch my cap, I'll gralloch ye!'

Ganglion's mouth fell open, closed slowly, and fell open again. Then, very softly, he began to hum the opening bars of an innocently obscene ditty popular in the benighted loneliness of a Scapa Flow garrison during the long winter of 1940.

'Aye, Ganglion, so it's yourself,' the dummy interrupted, raising its cap. 'You owe me two and thruppence.'

'I never! I won it back, double or quits!'

'That you did not! That, Lance Corporal Ganglion, was the four and six you owed me previously, as well you know. I hope, sir,' he added, addressing Oswald, 'that you have not allowed yourself to be drawn into lending any money to this awful man? He never pays, you know.'

Oswald smiled. 'We share all our debts, I'm afraid. Oswald Ochilree, Mr MacGregor, and I'm very glad to meet you at last after hearing so much about you from the awful man here. I believe we've met your grandson in the lobby?'

MacGregor's eyes twinkled deep inside their sockets. 'Son,' he said shortly, getting to his feet. 'It was a wet night, and my bike had a puncture, and the light was on. That's the way it goes, eh?'

'Oh, aye,' said Oswald. 'Right enough.'

'I've carried precautions since then, mind.'

'Oh?'

'Repair kit,' said MacGregor, patting a tin in his pocket. 'A man has to be prepared, I'm thinking. So, Ganglion, and how's yourself? Are you still having a problem with . . . with your problem?'

'Off an' on,' said Ganglion. 'Mostly on, these days, mustn't grumble though. An' yew?'

'More or less in working order, all the parts I need anyway, most of the time. About as well as can be expected. God's will be done.'

'Aye,' said Oswald, staring at the carpet and not knowing quite how to respond to this divine turn in the conversation. 'Aye.'

Ganglion chuckled. 'Specially when 'E shoves an 'ole in yer inner tube, eh?'

'Well.' MacGregor sucked his cheeks in. 'As I say, it was raining. I intend to enquire no deeper than that.'

'Nah, that's the minister's job, innit.'

'Quite so, quite so. And what may it be that brings you both here, Mr Ochilree?'

'We were, erm, looking for a *Perthshire Gazette*,' said Oswald. Then, thinking this might sound a little idiotic, he added; 'We were told the janitor might have one.'

'And so I have,' replied MacGregor, stalking stiffly across to the sofa. 'Back at the house, Catriona's house I should say. If you'll – just – wait one wee – minute.' MacGregor stooped to lift the hem of Miss Hypitt-Gorge's ballgown and thrust one arm up underneath. 'Where are ye, now, eh?' he grunted. The authoress's glassy smile, they afterwards agreed, became quite appallingly suggestive at this point.

'Ah, I have ye! I call this,' said MacGregor, withdrawing from Miss Hypitt-Gorge's unspeakable regions a nearly empty half bottle, 'the Hielanman's Revenge. There, now. We'll away to the house. Unless,' he regarded them balefully, 'you're wanting to buy something at the Heritage Shop?'

''Ow about it, Oz? Want ter buy any 'eritage today?'

'No, thank you,' said Oswald. 'Nor sell it, either.'

'Mmnn-aye,' said MacGregor. 'Away, then.'

Ganglion bent over his friend as they left the awful room. 'You've rung the bell, Oz,' he whispered. 'That noise 'e makes frew 'is nose is 'is way of sayin' 'e finks yore a good bloke.'

They took a detour to the car park but Mrs Pitt-Holyoake was not there so they left a note with Mac-Gregor's address and followed him round the back of the Highland Craft Centre and through a gate (marked PRI-VATE) in a high stone wall. This gave on to a half-metalled track running through a dense belt of gloomily regimented conifers known locally, so MacGregor said, as the Maginot Line. They emerged after a few minutes into sunlight that was thin and watery but nonetheless warming and welcome after the deadness of the *cordon sanitaire*.

'There we are, now,' said MacGregor. 'The Newtown of Blairlummock. The Native Quarters, gentlemen.'

They stood – in Oswald's case, sat – on the lip of a short, shallowly glaciated valley, a truncated spur of the glen that began a few miles to the north and which ran away to their right, broadening and blurring its edges until it lost itself some thirty miles or so away in the rich alluvial farmland around Craigfieth. On the far side and at an angle of forty-five degrees to the track they were on, a metalled road curled up and over the lip of the depression to join the main road at a junction where, Ganglion remembered, the mainstream of visiting humanity was politely but firmly persuaded to bear left. Somewhere in the apex of this triangle of geographical apartheid, decently obscured by a succession of walls and earthworks and modestly veiled in sylvan petticoats, was the Dewdrop Inn itself, known anciently as Chizzell Castle and now reborn, thanks to the proselytising fervour of teams of evangelical interior designers, as the Blairlummock Towers Conference Centre.

The Native Quarters thus occupied a sort of no-man's-land between the deciduous opulence of the Laird's policies and the sour bogland, generously endowed with rushes, flag iris and, in due season, midges, of the valley bottom, and were – as indeed their only begetter had intended them to be – entirely unsuspected and unvisited either by the heritage-seekers in the Visitor Village or the confrères in the castle.

Which, for the sake of the visiting tourists and businessmen, the image of the region and the economic regeneration of Scotland as a whole, was probably just as well.

The Newtown of Blairlummock, seen now from this little coign of vantage, was in every conceivable respect – from the layout of its eight claustrophobic little streets to the grey stains just below the windowsills in its skimpy harling, from the single broken swing in its concreted playpark to the sagging wire mesh fencing dividing one small square of botanic hopelessness from another – the very image and exemplar of Scotland's peculiar genius (until comparatively recent times) for the Drab Vernacular style of municipal architecture. It looked as if it had been extracted, all of a piece, from the diseased heartland of a post-war urban housing development and dumped in this secluded little strath to huddle into itself and make the best of things. In reality, of course, no such thing had happened: it was merely that the Newtown of Blairlummock had been built to the same plans, by the same builders, and with the same materials and (despite generous assistance from the Community Development funds of Eastern Region, Westminster and Brussels) with the same canny eye to the financial limits of philanthropy. The site had been donated on behalf of the Blairlummock Estate by the present Laird; his retention of feu superiority over it ensured that the inhabitants remained in a state of blissful, biddable innocence uncorrupted by the snares and stews of home ownership.

Ganglion and Oswald blinked and stared while MacGregor, unblinking, regarded them.

'Gawdstrewf,' said Ganglion softly.

'Mmnn-aye,' said MacGregor.

'Is it,' said Oswald. 'I mean, does it . . .'

'There is a primary school, a Spar shop and Post Office, a district nurse, a community hall, and a pub,' said MacGregor. 'The doctor comes Wednesdays.'

Ganglion tried to sound chirpy. 'Everyfink laid on, eh?'

'Aye,' said MacGregor. 'No escape. Except on the Sabbath.'

'Oh?' said Oswald.

'They lay on a bus to the kirk in Ballydull,' MacGregor explained. 'The one in the Village is for visitors.'

'Gawd,' said Ganglion.

'Aye, I'm Free Church myself, as you probably know.'

'Oh, yeah,' said Ganglion. 'I remember. Orlwiz the awkward bugger, you. Wotcher do then, stop 'ere?'

'Not at all. I have the bike.'

'Ah. Oh! Oh-oh!'

'Aye. We'll away and get that paper, then.'

Ganglion bumped Oswald along the track as MacGregor, stiff-legged, led them past clumps of whin to a gate in the township's perimeter fence; a strip of tired-looking grass, a concrete kerb, and they were in Hendrix Street, principal thoroughfare of the Newtown of Blairlummock. A right turn up Joplin Road and a left into Brian Jones Avenue led them to a halt outside the gate of Number 7, differentiated from the other houses in the row by a replica carriage lamp by the front door.

'It's rightly my niece's house,' said MacGregor as if in explanation of the carriage lamp. 'I bide on with her, since my sister died, you know.'

'Ah,' said Ganglion. 'Right.'

'Aye. Away in then.'

They proceeded up the path to the front door, Ganglion concentrating on keeping Oswald's wheels within its narrow confines. The garden ground on each side was some four inches down, and looked wet. 'Take your time, now,' MacGregor advised as he opened the door and left Ganglion to negotiate the two steps up to it.

'Yeah, ta,' said Ganglion. 'So kind.'

'I'm after being prone to hernia, you know,' MacGregor called.

'Wot about wot *I'm* prone to, then?' muttered Ganglion. 'Orlwiz woz an unaccommodatin' ole bleeder, 'e woz, orlwiz somewhere else when 'e woz wanted. Remind me ter tell yer abaht the time when . . . creepin' 'ell!'

Number 7, Brian Jones Avenue was a symphony of purple with cadenzas of green: purple, in all its ramifications of mauve, puce, lilac, violet and fruits of the forest on the floor, walls and doors; green, in uneasy varieties of emerald and algae, in the lampshades, the cushions, the kitchen units and the pouffe. The hall carpet was patterned with bold hexagons, the lounge carpet floral.

'Come away in,' said MacGregor. '*Thig a stigh.*' The lounge suite was old gold. 'We get a Pakistani,' Mac-Gregor said, indicating the suite, the carpet, the room, the house, 'in a lorry. A fine Gaelic speaker, too. Nazir's High-Class Reject Interiors. Catriona saves up. You'll take a dram?' He opened a canteen that played the theme tune from *Neighbours* and with impressive dexterity extracted a bottle and three glasses before shutting it again halfway through the fifth bar. 'You'll not be taking water,' he announced.

'Why, wot does the tap do then?'

'Pollutes the whisky,' said MacGregor. '*Slàinte.*'

'*Slàinte.*'

125

'*Slarnjievore*, ole cock. May yer inner tube never perish.'

MacGregor seated himself on an uncompromisingly upright chair. They drank.

'My, my,' murmured Oswald. 'It's as well I'm disabled already.'

Ganglion blinkered away his tears. 'Wottever – kaa-aah! – yew – aaah! – do, Oz, don't you dare . . . light your pipe.'

'The Heritage Centre,' said MacGregor, taking a second long sip and pausing noisily to scarify his gums with it, 'was after wanting a genuine smugglers' pot still, and it's myself that looks after it for them. On a regular basis, you understand. Remind me to replenish my halfie before we go back. Miss Hypitt-Gorge's reserves are getting a wee bit low, you know.'

Oswald raised his glass. 'What are you calling this, Mr MacGregor?'

''Ighland Clearance?' suggested Ganglion. 'Crofters' Comeuppance?'

'*Uisge gun orra*.'

'Bless you,' said Ganglion.

'Foolish heathen man,' said MacGregor, without overt malice. '*Uisge gun orra* is the drink with no name. Like the MacGregors ourselves when we had a price on our heads, if you know anything about that.'

'Oh, yeah. 'Bout 1944 wasn't it? When all them fags went missin' from the NAAFI stores.'

MacGregor sucked his cheeks and snorted gently.

'Well, well,' said Ganglion, settling himself into the rancid upholstery. 'Fancy yew turnin' up 'ere, eh?'

'Aye, fancy,' stonewalled MacGregor. 'Not to mention yourself, Ganglion. You've not changed.'

'Oh, ta very much I don't fink! Can't see as I can say the same fer you, though. You've really gorn to pieces, ole cock. You used to remind me of a stick insect, now yer looks like a coupler used pipe cleaners. Arfritis, is it, or an overdose of Sunday cyclin'? Seems a queer sorter place though, this, fer you to end up in.'

'Aye, likely it would do,' said MacGregor blandly.

'Do you belong to these parts, Mr MacGregor?' asked Oswald.

'Just lately, aye.' He took another thoughtful pull at his dram. 'Right enough,' he added.

Ganglion put his glass down with a sickening crack on the absent Catriona's smoked-glass coffee table. 'Okay, MacGregor,' he said threateningly. 'Seein' as 'ow we can't stay long on accounter Mrs P-H, an' seein' as 'ow we ain't seen each other since we got pissed out of our skulls on the Thurso to Inverness demob special, an' seein' as 'ow at our age we could easily end up croakin' before this conversation gets finished, 'ow about forgettin' yer 'ighland 'eritage fer once, an 'ow yer great-great-great grand-farver slit seven Campbell froats wiv one swipe of 'is skean doo, an' 'ow it's beneath your dignity to give a bloke the time of day until you've known 'im for ten years, an' answerin' the bleedin' question! Wot're you doin' in this dump? I mean, wot's the set-up, eh?'

MacGregor considered the question. 'Nine,' he said. 'It was nine throats he slit. And it was the battle-axe, the *tuagh-chatha*, that he used, having left his *sgian dubh* in the guts of the tenth.'

'Yeah, well, fine, wotever, same difference. 'Ow do you come to be ekin' out the autumn of yer days livin' in a reject furnishin' ware'ouse an' potterin' about in a museum full of stuffed lady novelists?'

MacGregor slowly swirled the remains of his anonymous dram and stared moodily at the oiliness on the sides of the glass. 'I was a postman in the village,' he said. 'When it was a village, you know. After the war. My sister married a crofter there, a man MacDougall. Lost at Dunkirk, MacDougall was.'

'Killed in the retreat?'

'Aye . . . maybe. Mislaid, anyway. So there I was. My sister, Flora, and Catriona, and me working the croft when I wasn't at the mails, you know? And then Flora died, and the new Laird came in, and Catriona and myself went out, and we stayed here.'

'Wot – you mean, evicted? Didn't Mr Gladstone put a stop to that? I fort they couldn't do that, not to boner fidey crofters, annat?'

'Not at all, not at all. Catriona's in the house just now, making ready for the tourists, you know.'

'Eh?'

'It's part of the Highland Hospitality Hamlet, like a sort o' B and B with extras. It's been unspoiled, like, you know. Catriona goes in to do the meals in the season. She's the hospitality part.'

'Ass 'er job, then, is it?'

'It's her house, Ganglion, sort o'. Partly. Under the Village Management Co-op. Twenty per cent of the incomings, and this place thrown in. Irrespective of the croft, that is. That's all a part of the Lazy Beds Scheme now, of course. She's to be on the MYO this year.'

'The . . .'

'Milk Your Own. It's one of the extras, like, you know. Very popular with the tourists, Catriona reckons she should do well out of it, same rates. The visitors take what they want, you see, for their own use, an' she sells the rest to the Co-op for the souvenir crowdie in the Leisuremarket. I used to help out with the peats myself, till my knees turned on me.'

'Cutting them, you mean?'

'No, no: supervising, just. It's the visitors do the cutting, they take as many as they want away with them

128

at the end o' their visit – there's a dryer laid on – and the rest goes to the Black Houses up the glen. The old village. Where my sister's man's folk were turned out from, last century.'

'I see,' said Oswald, a little dazed. 'That's been restored as well, has it?'

MacGregor's voice was deadened. 'Oh, no. Not restored. Not that, at all.'

'Ar,' said Ganglion. 'Unspoiled, you mean.'

'Aye,' said MacGregor. 'That would be the word for it. Unspoiled. With the grants, and so on.' He put the last of his dram out of its misery. 'It's these management trainees that's in it just now, a dozen or so at a time. The Black Houses is more expensive than the Hospitalities,' he added, 'but these manager folk get a discount for bulk, I believe. It's supposed to make them better at it, managing, you know. Hardier.'

'All the rage, apparently,' Oswald commented absently.

'Must be, aye.'

There followed a longish silence.

'Were ye at the Highland Stores place?' asked Mac-Gregor at last. 'Did you see the dummy goods?'

Oswald nodded.

'Folk buy them, you know. Imagine that, eh?'

'I can, now,' said Ganglion. 'We saw the dummy assistant, an' all. An' I don't mean the one stuck up the ladder, neither.'

'Aye. Tamsin. Folk call her the Blairlummock Bike. Her mother was just the same. More so, even.'

'More like a tandem,' suggested Oswald.

'Mmnn-aye,' said MacGregor. He passed Oswald the bottle.

The wind stirred outside, blattering heavy drops of rain across the window.

'Wot 'appens in the winter?' asked Ganglion.

'More management trainees. Stalking – not with real guns, mind; it's all electronical, the stags have wee, you know, transponders on them. An' there's usually the fillums and the television people around the place, needing extras for programmes about Highland culture, and the like. Take a decent dram, now, that's just a damp glass you have. And the Crafts.'

'The Crafts,' said Ganglion levelly.

'Aye. It's mostly winter production, you know. Take Catriona, now: she's a stuffer.'

'A stuffer.'

'Aye. She's up there most days with her wee foam gun, stuffing clansmen. Wee mannikin things, you know, a very big seller seemingly, in the south. Mail order. They pay a commission. You'll have seen the produce, likely.'

'Yeah,' said Ganglion, looking up from his glass and readjusting his focus. 'As a matter of fack . . .' He swallowed carefully. ''Swot brings-ss-uss-'ere, inner firs' place. Oh gawd, yew tell 'im, Oz, my tongue's gorn too big.'

Oswald explained, briefly, the purpose of Mrs Pitt-Holyoake's mission.

'Oh, aye,' said MacGregor. 'I could have saved Mistress Holyoake the trouble, Catriona was telling me about it the other night. It's in the paper, too.' He moved carefully across the room and extracted a *Perthshire Gazette* from a pile underneath a stuffed donkey with VIVA TORRE-MOLINOS! stitched on its saddlecloth. 'She likes to keep them there,' he explained. 'Where is it, now? It's nearly all advertisements this week and no news at all, I don't know why. Aye, here it is: page seven, Good News Exclusive. *Seo.*'

Ganglion waved it blearily aside. Oswald took it.

'"Who says the Vale of Lummock isn't booming?"' he read.

'Pass.'

'Haud yer wheesht, Ganglion. "Not your Good News *Gazette!* This week's exclusive update on Enterprise Scotland is that the American-based multi-million-dollar HI! International Corporation is set to make a massive investment, right here in Central Perthshire! Yes, folks," – God's sake, what's happened to the *Gazette* since last week? – "Yes, folks, it's time to say . . . to say a big how-de-doody to those good old born-again boys from Detroit, Illinois. First they brought us the very latest in cut-price audio'n'visual gear from Eastern Sight'n'Sound, now they're . . ." poised, I think it must be, it says "poisoned" here, "poised to give the local business scene another good kick up the nineties with their latest scheme to turn a disused army base into a Christian Fellowship Study Centre and Marketing Mall.

'"In an – "'

'A wot?'

'A Christian Fellowship Study Centre and Marketing Mall.'

'Like the moneylenders in the temple,' muttered MacGregor. 'Read on.'

'Aye. Erm, oh yes. "In an exclusive interview with your new Go-For-It *Gazette* – "'

'Facknell! Sorry, Oz.'

'"HI! International's Scottish Senior Executive Vice-President Motown P. Legover said – "'

'Mo – '

'"*Said*, 'My message to the Whingeing Willies and Moaning Moiras is – in Jesus' name, shut up and come alive! We have chosen our site from dozens throughout the UK and we reckon in all humility that our business Gospel is the best news to hit your region this century.

We're going to turn Mid Lummock into the UK capital of sunrise economics.'

'"The site was owned for over sixty years by the Army but has not been used since the Falklands conflict in 1982. It lies just outside Craigfieth which, says the forty-eight-year-old fast-talking former Olympic swimming medallist, will become a boom town by the turn of the century thanks to the trickle-down effect of his business venture. And to show the HI! commitment to the local business community he has already negotiated an exclusive franchizing deal with the Highland Craft Centre in Blairlummock, already internationally famous for its award-winning Visitor Village. 'These native crafts will now enjoy world-wide marketing exclusively through the HI! network of business affiliates,' added Mr Legover. 'We've been there, and we liked what we saw.'

'"Wat Tyler, OBE, local landowner and boss of the Blairlummock Trust, said he was delighted with the deal. 'We have a deep and heartfelt commitment to the unique culture of our Highland Homeland,' he said. 'It's great news for all of us.'

'"Work on the old army base is not expected to start until the end of April, but whizzkids Legover and Tyler are confident that the Centre will be open for business by August. 'We have had detailed planning meetings with Councillor Duff, chairman of the Planning Committee,' said Mr Legover. 'We have satisfied all council inquiries and are ready to go ahead. We're going flat out for this one.' In addition to providing a Craft Superstore for the region, the Centre will also house shops selling a variety of goods from fresh food and baking to state-of-the-art electronics, an Evangelical Missionary Training Centre, a Business College with its own diploma, a restaurant complex, a multiplex cinema, a private hospital and a range of up-to-the-minute financial services – and that's just for starters! 'Our long-term aim,' Mr Legover continued, 'is to make Mid Lummock the Evangelical Business Capital of Northern Europe.'"'

'Is there much more of this, Oz?'

'Only one wee bit, thank goodness. "A spokesperson for the Crown Property Disposal Agency confirmed that the deal with HI! International should be clinched, 'within the next few days. We are in regular contact with the Corporation's legal representatives,' she said, 'and hope to complete negotiations very soon.' Broody's, the top people's solicitors who are acting for Mr Legover, were also optimistic. In a written statement to the *Gazette* they said: 'We can confirm that, subject to all requirements being met, the property formerly known as the Bog – . . . as the . . .'"'

'Oz? Whassermatter?'

'Eh? Oh, nothing, sorry. '". . . known as the Boggybreck Barracks will shortly be assigned to our client." It is understood that a sum in the region of one and a half million pounds is being paid for the site."'

Oswald fell silent.

'Poor ole Mrs P-H,' said Ganglion. 'She doesn't stand a snowball's, does she.'

The rain was now slanting down steadily, pulsing against the window ahead of an icy north-east wind. A car drew up outside the house, the noise of its handbrake being wrenched on clearly audible in the stillness within. MacGregor rose slowly and went to the window.

'It's your woman friend, gentlemen,' he intoned gloomily. 'And from the look of her I'd say she's found out.'

A swift appraisal of her companions convinced Mrs Pitt-Holyoake that she had better drive, and she declined MacGregor's invitation to sample the drink with no name. MacGregor might have been inclined to take offence at this had he not felt in almost supernatural awe of the lady's audacity in travelling the forbidden road to the unacceptably ethnic part of Blairlummock. They dropped him off at the Timespan, where he had a pressing appointment with Miss Barbara Hypitt-Gorge.

They passed a notice on the way out: YOU ARE NOW CROSSING THE HIGHLAND LINE, it said. NA BITHIBH FADA GUN TILLEADH!

'Wot's all that lot mean, I wonder?'

'It's the Gaelic equivalent of Haste Ye Back,' said Mrs Pitt-Holyoake grimly. 'More or less. Sickening, don't you think?'

She treated them to a sepulchral high tea at the Ben Almond Hotel and allowed Ganglion to buy her a double malt whisky to go with her salad. The waitress sensed their mood and hovered for some time, hoping to be let in on it. When she had gone, Oswald said, 'There's another bit about Craigfieth in the *Gazette*.'

'Oh yeah? Wozzat then, they goin' ter turn the McWhirter Playin' Fields inter the Mid Lummock 'Ilton?'

'No, it's not rightly about Craigfieth itself really. Just a wee paragraph: an announcement is expected shortly from MaxProf Associates, financial managing agents for Lord Margoyle, to confirm rumours that the Lunie Estate is to be developed as a residential centre for commercial game shooting. A full report will appear in next week's *Gazette*, it says.'

'Huh!' said Ganglion. 'Your poor ole landlord down to 'is last ten million is 'e, Mrs P-H?'

'Hmph!' said Mrs Pitt-Holyoake. 'I wouldn't know about that. I can't imagine how they think they're going to manage it, though. I can't see Lord M letting the hoi-polloi into the castle, however much they paid.'

* * *

Mrs Pitt-Holyoake thanked Oswald and Ganglion again, repeated the invitation to partake of herbal Darjeeling, and left them with strict instructions to go straight to Grace and Hamish's and drink lots of black coffee. She called in at the Craft Corner, tidied up the detritus of her unpacking earlier in the day, and resigned herself to going full-tilt throughout the summer at her draining-board landscapes. She had better, she thought, see if she had any Taiwan catalogues left.

She collected her car from Duff's and listened patiently to the mechanic's mournful estimation of its life expectancy; he'd been saying the same things for the last ten years at least. She drove cautiously back to Dante Cottage, her senses straining for intimations of mechanical mortality, but heard and smelt nothing new. She parked in the usual way, not caring to trust Duff's to have done anything reliable to the starter motor. She picked her way carefully up the garden path through a gathering dusk that was not, to her distress, quite gloomy enough to conceal the corpses of a seagull, a buzzard and two skylarks pathetically disposed on either side.

She found the water still off, and a letter from Mr Snotter informing her that she had three clear months to find alternative accommodation before quitting Number 23½ Lunie on June 30th next.

Neville was putting the finishing touches to his Rocket to Redemption scheme after his six o'clock work-out that evening when his live-in fiancée interrupted him.

'Business,' she said. 'At the door.' Then she went back to her Home Accountancy Course.

'Hi,' said the girl. 'How are you?'

'Very busy,' said Neville. 'What do you want?'

'My other half back,' she answered. 'Please.'

'Can't manage without it or something?'

'That's none of your business really, is it?' She smiled disconcertingly. 'A deal's a deal, as I'm sure you appreciate.'

'I don't carry money,' said Neville, indicating the classic cut of his trousers.

'And I don't accept plastic. A cheque'll do. I trust you.' She followed him. 'And Gladstone says you can have this back.' She tossed a printed certificate on the table. 'He didn't need it. Thank you kindly,' she said, tugging her dreadlocks.

'Cash it and forget it,' said Neville. 'Okay?'

'Does it self-destruct if I don't?' She turned away before he could answer. 'Oh, and by the way: Mkekwe is one hell of a fucking stupid name for a West Indian, okay? Remember next time. I shan't charge you for the tip. Stay cool!' She giggled, and left.

Neville stored this information and returned to his computer. When the time came to rap and resolve with Clyde Bilt, he would be prepared.

His future official life partner interrupted him again ten minutes later. 'Phone call,' she said. 'Operation Aspirin. It's on for tonight.'

'Better be a few minutes late for work tomorrow then,' said Neville, not looking up. 'Is it a book night?'

'No. Tomorrow.'

'Oh. Just as well really, I have to get this finished. See you in the morning, then.'

Chapter Five

'We didn't want to bother you with it,' said Grace, interrupting Hamish's attempted explanation.

The meal was over, the children coaxed and lovingly bludgeoned into bed, the washing-up left for later. Hamish's inability to dissemble, the product of a particularly tenacious Ganglion gene, had (rather unfairly) provoked his father's ire.

'Why not?'

'Well we – '

'I'll tell you why bleedin' well not! You – '

'Dad – '

'Shurrup, 'Amish! You fort, didn't you, as 'ow a senile ole ruin, e.g. me, couldn't possibly – '

'Dad, ye're no' talk to Grace like – '

'Shur*r*up! If it's any consolation, it's not your Grace I *am* talkin' to, it's you, only it's easier doin' it through Grace, all right? You didn't tell me cos you fink I'm past it, that's it innit? Past understandin'. Past copin' wiv the information. Past bein' capable of anyfink except gerrin' all confused an' wettin' meself, an' makin' you explain the 'ole fing over again. Yah! Don't fink as I've forgotten 'oo it was put me in the bleedin' Eventide an' all, cos I 'aven't!'

'That was different, Dad! Jings, it was *your* idea anyway, an' – '

'Shurrup, 'Amish. Grace 'ere knows wot I mean, don'tcher Grace? Own up.'

'Dad, what Grace means is we – '

'Shurrup, 'Amish. Well, go on! That's the reason, innit!'

'No,' said Grace.

'Yah! Gercher, go on, admit it, you didn't tell *me* for the same reason you ant told Ashley Oz an' Wally, or the bleedin' cat, for that matter!'

'Dad, we haven't *got* a cat!'

'Shut up, Hamish,' said Grace. 'What I meant when I said we didn't want to bother you with it was, we didn't want to bother you with it. And then when you asked why not, I started to explain only you interrupted me and – '

'Yeah! Cos, like I say, I bleedin' well know why not, it's because – '

'Shut up, Dad,' said Hamish.

'Wot?'

'Shut up, Ganglion,' said Oswald.

'Oh. Right then, since there's a consensus, I *will* shurrup. Right, I've shurrup. Go ahead. Go on. I'll keep me mahf shut. I won't say a word. Not a dickiebird. I'll just – '

'Dad!'

'Right! Stum.'

'And what I was going to say,' Grace resumed, 'was, not that we thought you were too old or too daft or anything like that, because we don't, do we, Hamish, and if you were, getting that way I mean, we'd be the first to notice or Mr Ochilree'd tell us, wouldn't you, Mr Ochilree, but because we think you've done enough for us already, what with one thing and another, too much even. Every time we've been in difficulties or even when we haven't, when we've wanted something we couldn't have right away, like this house and the shop, I'm ashamed now – we both are, aren't we, Hamish – looking back, the way we behaved over that. I think, we think, it would have been better for us to wait, we were like a couple of bairns wanting sweeties before lunch. I mean, you didn't have folk coming to your rescue when you were our age, did you? And it's time we . . . stood up for ourselves, I mean – stopped running for help all the time, stopped using you as a . . .' she glanced Freudianly at Oswald and hastily amended what she had been going to say '. . .as a cushion.' It wasn't such a striking metaphor but it would have to do.

'I see. An' 'at's wot you fort, is it, 'Amish?'

'Aye, well, erm – '

'We've talked about it, haven't we, Hamish?'

'Oh, aye,' said Hamish feelingly. 'We did, Dad. Honest.'

'I see.' Ganglion sighed. 'Well. In the first place. Item one: when I was about your eldest's age, Grace me old plum duff, I nearly died of tonsillitis, right? So, I 'adter 'ave the bleeders out, see – on the kitchen table, wiv a lumper dry ice ter take me mind off of it, har har, an' a fing wot looked like a pair o' fire tongs ter drag 'em out wiv, right? Bleedin' barbaric, *an'* it cost me poor ole mum two an' ninepence, but that woz just the way fings were, see?'

'Yes, but – '

'Paid in advance, an' no money back if dead. Nah, if you're sayin' you fink wot was good enough for my generation's good enough fer yours, or young Wally's, or your grandchildren's when you 'ave 'em, if you're sayin' fings shouldn't get better, an' easier, an' kinder, an' more just an' equitable, an' less of a bleedin' 'opeless struggle all the time, or that people shouldn't be'ave as though they orter, then thass fine by me, luv, you can go right on finkin' that, an' votin' Tory, an' lyin' awake at night listenin' to all the groans an' wails of all the good people 'oo fought an' struggled an' wore themselves out tryin' ter make the world a bit better place for those wot woz comin' after 'em – *if* that's wot you wanner fink, is it?'

'No, but – '

'Right, then. Item two: I 'ear wot you say, about lookin' back on yerself, the way you woz, an' feeling squirmy about the way you looked at fings then, an' the fings you did an' said, wantin' everyfink now, this minute, an' finkin' you 'ad a right to it, just cos it was there, an' you 'adn't got it. It's called bein' young an' immature. An' the way you fink now an' the way you look back, that's called growin' up. 'Appens to all of us, eventually, even 'appened to me. You wait till you get to my age, girl, yew'll squirm yerself inter knots remembering wot you done when you was fifty! You foller me?'

'Oh, yes, and that's wh – '

'You mentioned sweets: d'you let your kids 'ave sweets every time they asks for 'em?'

'No! Of course not. We – '

'Why not?'

'Well . . . I mean it's obvious, they're bad for the bairns' teeth, and it would make them greedy, and, well, it would be wrong. But – '

'Right, that's agreed then. So: you never let 'em 'ave sweets, right?'

'No, I – '

'Wot? No? But they're bad for 'em! You juss said! Bad fer their teef, bad fer their guts, bad fer their moral fibre! Why not, then?'

'I . . . we . . . well now and again doesn't hurt them, does it? As a treat, for instance. So long as they don't whine on all the time for them it's all right, and I trust Ashley Oswald not to eat his before his packed lunch at school. And we make sure they brush their teeth.'

'Right, fine. Nah, then: sposin' sweets cost a 'undred pound a packet, wot then?'

'Well then they wouldn't have any, we couldn't afford them, but – '

'Right! So – you decide, then, don'tcher? Eh? Wot's right fer them an' wot's right fer you. Like I did over that money fer the shop an' that, okay?'

'Well . . .' Grace sighed. 'Yes, all right then.'

'Good. Which brings us to item free: don't you ever, Grace an' 'Amish Ganglion, go dictatin' ter me wot I can an' cannot stand ter know about, or do somefink about, or fink about, right?'

'But we – '

'Cos if you do, like decidin' not ter tell me about somefink because you know better'n I do wot's right fer me to do if I know about it, then you're treatin' me like a dribblin' infant wot can't be trusted, see? Which is where we came in, innit.'

'Yes,' said Grace miserably. 'I suppose so.'

'Hang about!' said Hamish. 'Now *you're* doing it!'

'Wot?'

'Now you're just saying to us exactly what you've just been telling us off for, for saying to you! Except, by the way, we didn't.'

Ganglion sighed. 'Afraid you've lost me, son. Must be me senile dementia.'

'Look: you're saying we mustn't tell you what you should do, right?'

'Bang on.'

'And now you're telling us that we shouldn't do what we want to do, cos you don't like it! Or not do, come to that. Why *shouldn't* we stand on our own two feet?'

'No reason at all, son! No reason at all. 'Cept it'd be four, unless Grace 'ere was standin' on yours as well, which would be pretty painful, no offence, luv. That's the point, though: if you tell me you're in shtuck wiv your business an' I say, oh dearie me wot a shame, we can't

141

'ave that, 'ere's a million quid – some 'ope – yore perfeckly entitled ter say get knotted, or words to that effect, we'd rarver sink on our own two knees, four knees or wotever, fanks very much all the same. Course you could say that! Wouldn't bovver me. Well, it would, but not in that way. See? It's not – bein' allowed – ter know . . . Oh, sod it, I'm worn out wiv this, you tell 'em, Oz.'

Oswald stared silently at the reproduction of Rodin's *Kiss*, an anniversary present from Hamish to Grace, on the mantelpiece. 'Being disregarded,' he said at length, 'is a bugger, right enough.'

'There y'are!' Ganglion was triumphant. 'In a nutshell, good old Oz. Bein' disregarded – which is ter say, bein' ignored, an' left out of account as bein' not quite up to the mark veez-ah-vee wot's goin' on. Or, which comes to the same fing really, bein' 'andled wiv bloomin' kid gloves an' gettin' special treatment on account of dicky tickers an' white 'airs an' 'at. In uvver words, we're every bit as free an' equal an' grown-up as wot you are, gorrit?'

'Yeah, Dad, okay. We've got it. Haven't we, Grace?'

'Yes, Mr Ga-, Dad, I mean. Sorry.'

'Ass okay! So long as you remember we're piteous ole crumblies wot need constant 'umourin' an' panderin' to, we won't 'ave any more silly squabbles. Cos one day I'll be dead an' you'll be sorry, as me dad used ter say, an' then one day 'e was an' I wasn't, 'orrible old bugger. Nah then, let's get this straight, shall we? You're tellin' us, a bit late in the day but never mind eh, that 'Amish is about to go on a one-way journey up Queer Street fanks to a buncher cut-price cowboys from Dunbrofe, an' Grace ditto on accounter some transport firm wot doesn't see why she should be entitled ter reg'lar deliveries of sellable fruit'n'veg. Right?'

'Right, Dad.'

'An' that you don't fink it's mere coincidence that arf

the 'Igh Street looks like it's bin used fer a remake of *London Can Take it*?'

'What's that?'

'A film about the Blitz,' Oswald explained.

'Oh, yeah. Yeah, right.'

'Right. An' your suspicions are confirmed when you open up this week's Two Minutes' Silence an' reads about this buncher Jehovah's Capitalists an' their plans fer Boggybreck Barracks, right?'

'Right.'

'Well, just ter show you 'ow right you were to be worried about me comin' ter your rescue, I'll tell you wot I can do about it, shall I?'

'What, Dad?'

'Absolutely sod all. Nuffink. Norra sausage.'

'Oh.'

'That makes yer feel easier, does it?'

Hamish grimaced.

'Apart from lyin' awake tonight worryin' about you both, ercorse.'

Grace winced.

'As is my right, seein' as 'ow I loves you both, an' your sprogs, more'n I'd care to say wivvaht a big drink in me. Any advance on that, Oz, speakin' as a godlessfather?'

'Erm, well – ' Oswald began. The telephone rang and he fell gratefully silent while Hamish answered it.

'It's for you, Dad.' Hamish put one hand over the mouthpiece. 'Mrs Pitt-Holyoake.'

'The Dope Fiend of Dante Cottage? Speck she's checkin' to see if I've sobered up yet. Ta, son. 'Ello, missus! As God is my witness, I walked in a straight line ter speak to you, 'ow's that!'

'Oh?' Mrs Pitt-Holyoake's voice sounded remote and abstracted, as if she had been interrupted by someone else. 'Oh yes, I see. Mr Ganglion?'

'Yeah, smee. Wot can I do fer you?'

'Mr Ganglion, you're the only person I can think of.'

'Ah. Look, Mrs P-H, before you go any further there's somefink you ought to know.'

'Oh?'

'Yeah. It'd never work.'

'What?'

'It's the curse o' the Ganglions, see. 'Ereditary. Look at 'Amish. We could never 'ave kiddies, Mrs P-H. Don't torcher yerself, my dear, you'll find a better man.'

'Oh, yes, I see. I'm going to be evicted, Mr Ganglion.'

'Eh? Wossat?'

'Thrown out. Do you remember Mr Ochilree reading about the plans for the estate in the paper this afternoon? There was a letter waiting for me when I came home. Three months' notice. From the wording of the letter I presume they want all our houses.'

'Oh my gawd. Look, er, I dunno as I can, I mean you'd be welcome but Rose Cottage is kinder cramped as it is, wot wiv – '

'I feel so dreadfully lonely, Mr Ganglion. Tomorrow morning I shall consult a solicitor, I suppose, and I'll have to go round all the other tenants to form a . . . well, a group or committee of some sort I expect. But at the moment I . . . well, I should like someone to be gloomy with, I suppose. Would you mind awfully, and Mr Ochilree as well? Oh – Oh dear, there I go, I'm forgetting you're not at home, are you? Oh no, I couldn't possibly impose on your son and his wife, I'm so sorry, I – '

'Ow's yer water?'

'I beg your – oh, yes, yes, I see. Still off, I'm afraid.'

'Come an' 'ave a good long tub,' said Ganglion. 'Grace won't mind a bit, will yer, Grace? An' then we'll see about the glooms afterwards, all right?'

'Oh, but surely I, I mean aren't you – '

'Ass an order! Okay? If yer not 'ere in arf an hour,' Ganglion put on the Ugly Troll voice he used to frighten Wally with at bedtime, 'I'm . . . comin' . . . ter GET YOU!'

Mrs Pitt-Holyoake's laughter lacked something of Wally's uninhibited delight but was nonetheless genuine and grateful. 'In that case, very well then, I will. And thank you.'

'What won't I mind?' asked Grace.

Ganglion explained.

Grace assured him that she didn't. 'Would she be wanting to spend the night, though?'

'Dunno.' Ganglion shrugged. 'Why, you got the spare room let to long-distance City commuters, then?'

'No, Mungo Beauly. He's out, but he might come back tonight.'

'Mungo Beauly?'

'Yes, you remember, he used to call himself "Slim",' Grace giggled. 'He's staying with us just now.'

'Wot, you mean that fat spotty kid 'Amish used ter knock around wiv?'

'Yeah, that's him,' said Hamish. 'Only he's a lot thinner, and he's lost the spots and wears a suit. He was editor of the *Gazette*.'

'Woz?'

'Was. New ownership. As from this week.'

'He told me just what the new *Gazette* would be like,' Grace confided. 'I thought he was pulling my leg till I saw it.'

'He's away to Edinburgh today – he's been helping out in the shop the last couple of days – trying to find out more about these Clinch McKittrick people who're buying up the houses. He said he'd be back some time this evening or mebbe the morn's morn.'

'Ah. Well, we'll see about that when 'e gets 'ere, then,

145

shan't we. 'E can always kip at Mrs P-H's, come to that, don't spose 'e'll mind not washing. Let's see 'ow poor ole Mrs P-H is first, anyway. Gawd.' Ganglion shook his head. 'Wot a fing, eh? Wot a fing. Where's she s'posed ter go, at 'er age?'

Hamish nodded gloomily. 'That's what Mr McMurtry said.'

'McMurtry? Bank Manager?'

'Yeah. I went to see him this afternoon about a – for some advice. An' that's when he said it.'

'Wot, about not 'avin' anywhere to go? Blimey, wot's 'e done? Lent a fiver to a deservin' cause?'

'They're closing the bank,' said Hamish. 'Well, merging it, same thing. It's going in with Melmotte's; they're both shedding their surplus staff capacity, and that includes him.'

'Poor 'im. Strewf! Comes to somefink when yer feels sorry fer a bank manager, dunnit!'

'Aye,' Oswald muttered. 'Always supposing I was.'

'Mr Ochilree!' Grace was shocked. 'That's not very nice.'

'No,' Oswald agreed. 'I suppose poetic justice doesn't require a commentary, right enough.'

'An' yew orlwis fort 'e was such a nice ole codger!' Ganglion cackled.

'Has he, I mean . . . did he . . . do something bad to you?'

'Not me, no.' Oswald looked uncomfortable. 'A neighbour. Ach, never mind it now.'

'Was it – very bad?'

Oswald sighed through his nose. 'Depending on your point of view, aye, it was bad enough. The upshot being that for the sake of one season's poor calving, a farmer saw all his land and his house, stock, everything, advertised for sale in the *Gazette* one week, enquiries and all

146

offers to the Scottish Amiable and Providential. Would you no' say that was bad?'

'Oh, that's terrible! What happened?'

'To the farm? The estate bought it; it was cheap enough at the time, even for them. That's how they come to own Mrs Pitt-Holyoake's house, come to think of it; it had been the cowman's place. It cleared the debt, just about.'

'Oh, so he was all right then, in the end? Your neighbour, I mean.' Grace waited anxiously for the happy ending.

Oswald offered catharsis instead. 'Depending on your religious outlook, aye, maybe. He went out after rabbits, slipped or tripped on something, and blew his head off. So the Sheriff Court decided, anyway. The insurance no' being much, but better than nothing. If you see what I'm driving at.'

'Oh,' said Grace.

'Aye, well, I dare say two wrongs never did make a right. Difficult sometimes to squeeze a tear, though, right enough. At least he'll have his pension.'

'Yeah, well, erm, no, I don't think so,' Hamish mumbled. 'He said something about how they'd been after him to take early retirement only he didn't want to. So there's a redundancy payment, but nothing else. He said he'd got another seven years before his pension, the old age pension I mean.'

'How the other half lives, eh?' said Oswald. 'Did you get your . . . advice then, after that?'

'No' really,' Hamish admitted, 'as such. He said it was out of his hands. He did give me a leaflet, though.' He drew a glossy crumpled thing out of his jacket pocket. 'Here it is.'

'Scot-Melmotte One-Stop Moneyshop,' they read. 'A New Concept in No-Fuss Financial Counselling.'

Oswald unfolded it. 'Nice pictures,' he commented

after a while. 'I don't see you in them, though, to be truthful.'

Grace snorted. 'They all look like Neville! Including the women.'

'Yeah,' Hamish agreed. 'That's what I said.'

'You said that? To Mr McMurtry? What did he say?'

'He said he thought they all looked like his investment manager.'

'And? Then what?'

'We didn't really say anything after that,' Hamish admitted. 'There didn't seem to be anything much left to say. Oh, except we'll be getting a free filofax when the account's transferred. As a loyalty bonus, or something.'

'Well we can forget that!' Grace said firmly. 'If that Mr Parkinson at Melmotte's is going to be the new manager we shall just go somewhere else! I don't like his eyes,' she explained. 'And his hair smells.'

'Oh, no, it's not him. He told me that, Mr McMurtry I mean. Parkinson's got himself a job with those MaxProf people, the firm that was in the paper today. Birds of a feather, McMurtry said. I got quite embarrassed by the end of it, really. He wasn't himself at all.'

'Wish I'd a bin there ter see that,' said his father.

'Why, Dad? You've nothing to do with him, have you? I thought you always used the Post Office.'

'Let it pass, son, let it pass. Secrets of the dyin' sepoy. Oo's got the job, then?'

'Kirk,' said Hamish.

'Oo's 'e, when 'e's at 'ome?'

'The investment manager,' said Hamish. 'He's the same age as me, McMurtry said. I think he was being nice when he said it.'

'Beam me up, Scotty,' muttered Ganglion.

'Yeah. Set phasers to stun.'

'I'll have to get this room ready,' said Grace, launching

herself to her feet and getting brisk with the cushions. Hamish blenched instinctively, checking himself for flaws. 'Why, pet?'

'Mrs Pitt-Holyoake's coming, silly. You know what she's like.'

'No,' said Hamish. 'Neither do you, do you?'

'Well you can imagine, can't you? Excuse me, Mr Ochilree. I should have thought it was obvious, think of all the things she's got, antiques and things.' She magicked a tissue from somewhere about her person and began scrubbing at the lid of the hi-fi. 'And she'll be here soon, it's nearly half past eight!'

'Eh? Oh Chr – help ma bob!' Hamish jerked upright and blundered off to the door.

'Hamish? Where are you off to?'

'The meeting! It started half an hour ago!'

'Oh, *Hamish!*' Grace's hand flew to her mouth. 'I forgot! Wait – have you got your file? And a pen? And that clipboard I got you from Haq's?'

'Yeah, yeah.' Hamish fidgeted in the doorway. 'It's all in the kitchen under the bread bin.'

'Oh Hamish, you can't go like that!'

'Eh? Like what?'

'You've not got your proper shoes on, or your suit, or anything!'

'Blahdyell!' Ganglion exploded. ''E's not bin an' gone an' joined the Stags, 'as 'e?'

'Naw, Dad. It's the Gala Committee, I'm on it.'

'He's the secretary!' Grace barked proudly. 'Hamish, you've got to go and change!'

'Too late,' said Hamish. 'I'll have to explain. Cheers.'

'Don't wake the – '

The door slammed and he clattered off down the stairs.

'It's the first meeting,' Grace explained. 'They asked

him at the weekend, when Mr Borden had his accident.'
She started bullying the pot plants on the windowsill.

'Wot, ole Butcher Borden? Wot did 'e do, leave a
finger in the pork soss?'

'No,' said Grace, threatening the magazine rack. 'He
crashed his van on that dangerous bend by the golf course.
Something happened to his brakes and he went off the
road.'

'Poor ole sod. Was 'e badly damaged?'

Grace drew breath for the announcement. 'He broke
three ribs,' she said, 'and his right arm, and, oh, what was
it, something else. Something beginning with f.'

'Forehock?' suggested Ganglion. 'Flank?'

'Femur.'

'Ouch! Wossat, then?'

'Thigh bone,' said Oswald quietly. 'Like I bust that
time, only with me it was both.'

'Oh,' said Ganglion. 'Jeez. Poor ole sod.'

'So,' Grace continued, falling to her knees to intimidate
a rug, 'naturally there was a vacancy after that, and they
asked Hamish to come to the rescue. Mr Glencairn senior
proposed him himself.'

'Ah,' said Ganglion, failing to deconstruct this
statement.

'That's a very great honour, I should think,' said
Oswald, doing better.

'Yes,' said Grace simply. She harassed the loose covers.
'I can't think how he's going to manage without his suit,
though, these things are so important, aren't they? It's all
my fault really, he relies on me to look after that side of
things and I've been – well . . .'

'Garn!' said Ganglion, allowing kindness to overcome
fatherly cynicism. ''Snot the clothes, it's the man wot
matters! I don't suppose they chose 'Amish for 'is suit, do
you?'

'N-no,' Grace admitted. 'But it's the sort of thing they expect, isn't it? Sayeed Haq always wears one, and he isn't even a committee member. Not a proper one, anyway.'

Again, Oswald was alert to the hidden agenda. 'Is that so?' he asked, feigning genuine interest.

'No!' said Grace, meaning yes. 'Hamish says he's offered to negotiate some sort of sponsorship this year, from his business contacts. It's all very hush-hush at the moment, and of course it'll be Hamish who writes the letters. You know they lost the council grant.' She broke off to tyrannize the curtains. 'Because of the rationalizations.'

'Oh, yeah, them. Like we lost our 'ome 'elp, wot we told ter get knotted four years ago, cos of the reforms in the social services.'

'You shouldn't have done that!' Grace gave the curtains a respite while she dealt with her father-in-law. 'You should always take what you're entitled to.' She made it sound like a nasty medicine and followed it with a bitter pill. 'It's your right!'

'She told me off for swearin',' Ganglion pouted, 'an' Oz off for smokin', and bofe of us off for not keepin' the place tidy enough fer 'er ter come in an' clean it.'

'And,' added Oswald, 'she kept telling me how nice the garden would look if I got it concreted.'

'So we told 'er ter get knotted.'

Grace was awed. 'What happened?'

'They sent a social worker,' said Oswald.

'Oh, Mr Ochilree!'

'Aye. But we dealt with her too. Didn't we, Ganglion?'

'Gawd yes, not arf!' Their eyes glittered, remembering. 'Dancin' on the table, wasn't she, Oz? After 'er second 'elpin' of hash gateau!' The two old men wheezed uproariously.

'You didn't tell us any of this.'

'Dint wanner bovver you wiv it,' said Ganglion blandly. The doorbell rang.

Ganglion answered it, Grace having unfinished business with a fire engine, a sticky teaspoon, three Lego bricks and an undressed bendy Postman Pat discovered under the frilly petticoats of the best armchair. As she hastily transferred this collection to the reproduction brass-style coal-box by the log-effect gas fire (where she found a number of other things, including a very ancient bib with most of a nourishing deglutinized and additive-free meal still adhering to it) and Oswald tidied himself out of harm's way, they heard snatches of an ascending conversation in which the words 'too silly of me' and 'too bad of me' strove to make headway against a disclaiming stream of Ganglionese.

''Ere we are!' he whispered hoarsely, remembering the children were asleep and then forgetting again as he let the door crash open. 'I made 'er leave 'er stick an' 'er spotty 'andkerchief downstairs.'

'Do come in, Mrs Pitt-Holyoake.' Grace laughed nervously, trying to look appropriately solemn at the same time.

'Oh, Mrs Ganglion, I'm such a silly old woman,' said Mrs Pitt-Holyoake. 'Hello, Mr Ochilree too, this really is too bad of me.'

Oswald offered a wordless rebuttal as Grace conducted her to the best armchair, and caught Ganglion's eye. Their late companion already appeared altered somehow, demoralized; as if some internal spiritual spring mechanism had become suddenly fatigued, or overwound. Her frame seemed to have shrunk, minutely but perceptibly, so that the skin, like the clothes, hung a little more loosely about it and the crown of shocked white hair seemed in danger of slipping off to one side. Her eyes were pouched and moist, and both hands trembled slightly as she lowered herself awkwardly into the chair.

'I really don't know what I could have been thinking about,' she continued, rubbing anxiously at a muddy ladder in her stocking. Her legs, below the hem of her splashed skirt, looked all skin. 'At first I thought I would ring you up, Mr Ganglion, and ask you to come over and then I realized of course that would be a selfish thing to do, all that way, and then I thought I would go to you instead, and I went to the telephone to ask if that would be all right, and of course dialled this house – which meant looking it up in the book first of course – because I really knew all along you would still be here! Only, I forgot it was this house, Mrs Ganglion, if you see what I mean . . . I'm not sure that I really know what I mean myself . . . I do hope I'm not disturbing you? I really don't know why I should be so stupid, I . . .'

'Nah, 'sall right, innit, Grace?' Grace nodded yes, energetically. 'Don't you fret yerself nah, eh, Mrs P-H! You're 'ere now, that's wot matters. You'll be as right as rain after a good 'ot barf an' a nice fat whisky, won't she, Oz?'

'Aye!' said Oswald, thinly cheerful. 'Never fails!'

'Oh!' said Grace. 'I'd better just, erm, find you a towel, Mrs Pitt-Holyoake.' She had suddenly remembered the fleet of boats the boys had left behind earlier, not to mention the scattering of cotton buds and the adhesive grey tidemark. 'I'll just, um, make sure it's, erm,' she added.

'Oh now really,' exclaimed her guest, flashing all her horselike front teeth at once, 'you mustn't, I mean it's not as if I really need one, I shall be quite happy just to –'

'Nonsense!' said Ganglion. 'You indulge yerself, luv. I don't spose young Wally'd mind if she played wiv 'is dinosaurs, would 'e, Grace?'

'Oh! Er, ha-ha!' said Grace, who had forgotten about the dinosaurs. 'It's really no, er . . . I'll just.' She went.

'I don't want to be a fuss to people,' said Mrs Pitt-Holyoake miserably. 'You shouldn't encourage me.' Feeling very foolish, she thrust her hands down the sides of the cushion out of a childhood habit of hiding them whenever she did something she thought she might wish she hadn't. One hand reappeared holding a toy car, just as Grace re-entered looking more flustered than ever.

'I meant to offer you coffee, or tea of course if you'd prefer, Mrs – oh! Oh I'm sorry, Mrs Pitt-Holyoake, it's the two-year-old, he will keep hiding things, I'll just – '

But her guest had relaxed a little and was happily discovering that the doors opened and the steering wheel really worked.

'There's a wee catch underneath, too,' Oswald confided, 'for opening the bonnet. He always gets me to do it when I'm here.'

'What, you mean this thing h – ooh! I say! What a splendid looking engine! It certainly looks more real than my poor old crock's!'

'I'll . . . just be, then,' Grace said lamely, and left them to it.

'The things they think of nowadays,' mused Mrs Pitt-Holyoake, closing the bonnet and making it spring open again. 'It's a shame they can't make it easier for little fingers to manage, though.'

'He can manage the child-proof medicine bottles handily enough,' said Oswald.

'Really? Oh well I shall have to get him to do mine for me in that case! Do you know, Dr Ghouleagh gave me some new arthritis pills last week and I have to jam the wretched bottle in the door and push hard with both hands, like *that*, which of course doesn't do my arthritis any good at all!'

They laughed, and she parked the car exactly flush with a line of inlay on the table at her elbow. There was a muffled banging from above.

'This is really very naughty of me,' she said, 'and of you, too, making your daughter-in-law go to all this trouble just for the sake of a bath for me. I did manage my usual tub this morning, before the water went off. And she really shouldn't be doing all this tidying-up, because that's what she will be doing, I'm sure. Good gracious! If she could see the state of my bathroom – of course . . . when I say "my bathroom" I don't . . .' Her voice caught. 'Oh dear, I'm . . .' She fumbled uselessly in her sleeve, then put a hand up to her face as if about to stifle a sneeze. 'I'm so sorry, I . . .'

Ganglion lurched across, heedlessly cracking his shin on the corner of Grace's coffee table. ''Ave an oily rag,' he said, producing one. 'Sorl right, it orlwis looks like that when it's washed.' He laid an arm, not too heavily, across her shaking shoulders. 'Fings do it to you like that sometimes, I know.'

Oswald, quietly at the sideboard, found where the Ganglions kept their spirits and poured an unladylike dram of Kipplerigg's finest. He set it without comment on Mrs Pitt-Holyoake's table, next to the car.

The door opened; Ganglion looked up.

'I'll make some tea,' whispered Grace, and closed it again.

''Ave a good blow,' Ganglion advised. 'Then you can carry on without worryin' about the side-effects. We're yer mates, remember.' The advice had the desired effect; Mrs Pitt-Holyoake wept afresh and freely, while Ganglion massaged her neck.

'I don't . . . what Godfrey would think if he could see me now,' she said at last.

'I expect he'd think of giving you a cleaner hanky,' murmured Oswald.

The widow guffawed briefly through her tears. 'Oh dear!' she spluttered, searching for a dry corner of Ganglion's oily rag. 'I don't know about that, Mr . . .' She found it. 'I always – had to starch them for him, you know, and I don't think he ever used one for . . . for this sort of thing. He used to go to the bathroom. I teased him about it once, you know . . . oh dear! He said he – he thought bodily emissions were better dealt with in private!'

She collapsed backwards, one hand coming up to take Ganglion's and squeeze it, and gave way to torrential giggles. Grace, blushing deeply, entered the room and set the tea tray down, passed her a box of tissues and blushed deeper still when this triggered another wave of tearful mirth.

''Sall right, luv,' Ganglion muttered, patting Grace on the arm. 'You'll understand when you gets to our age.'

'Nah then, Oz,' he said when Grace had passed the tea round and Mrs Pitt-Holyoake, now looking a great deal healthier, had recomposed herself. 'You're the cool brains of our relationship. What should the lady do?'

'Go to a solicitor,' said Oswald firmly. 'Right away.'

'Yes, I suppose you're right, and I know it's what Godfrey would say. Only . . . well, are you sure it'll do any good?'

Oswald smiled fleetingly. 'Well, put it this way, my dear: lots of folk do the football pools every week but it doesn't stop them going to work to earn a living while they wait for the jackpot.'

'Oh . . . yes I see . . . I think I see what you mean, Mr Ochilree. You don't make it sound very hopeful. And besides,' she added, 'I suppose really the estate are only doing what they're entitled to do, by law, upsetting as it might be for me. It is their house, after all. Still,' she sighed, 'it'll probably be as well to have it confirmed.'

'Ah, well,' Oswald coughed. 'They'll maybe find that being within the law isn't necessarily the same thing as being home and dry, still less being in the right. However, we shall just have to wait and see about that. What I meant was, you should have a lawyer looking at it for you, but you maybe shouldn't just leave it at that.'

'What else should I do, do you think?'

'Over to you, Ganglion.'

Ganglion drew his breath and adjusted an imaginary tie. 'Kick up shit,' he said.

Grace coughed.

'Granted,' said Ganglion.

'That sounds *very* tempting, Mr Ganglion! What do you have in mind?'

'First off, I 'ave in mind fer you ter stop callin' me Mister Ganglion. Nah that I've rubbed yer neck it sounds a bit kinky, narmean? So drop the mister.'

'And I'm Oswald,' said Oswald. 'Even though I was stuck at knee level.'

'An' 'at's Grace,' Ganglion added. Grace blushed.

'Jolly good,' said Mrs Pitt-Holyoake. 'Audrey.'

'Get the papers on to it, Ordrey. The good old free press, har har. No, seriously, I mean it. Same wiv you'n 'Amish, Grace, an' your bitser bovver, in fact even more in your case. Nobody's done nuffink wrong to you – 'ceptin' tryin' ter put you out of business – so it's pretty well the only thing you *can* do. An' ercorse – I'm speakin' as a perfessional 'ere, you unnerstan', nuffink personal – it's just the sorter sob stuff they go for, innit? Corner shop squeezed out by cut-price sharks; local business frettened by takeovers; pore white-'aired ole lady turfed out into the snow by millionaire landlord; see wot I mean?

It's like Craigfeef Academicals versus Real Madrid in the European Cup. They'll lap it up.'

'Ye-es,' said Grace doubtfully. 'But what good will it do?'

'Get a reaction,' Ganglion replied promptly. 'By which I meantersay, "no comment" is a reaction of sorts, innit? Embarrass the barstuds. Make 'em squirm a bit. You never know. Plus, ercourse,' he added, 'it's always good fer a laugh.' He cackled.

Grace pursed her lips. 'That's not – I mean, I don't think that's right, really.'

Mrs Pitt-Holyoake came to her aid. 'I know just what you mean, dear, and I agree, it's not really the right attitude. But you see, sometimes it's better to have a good laugh than . . . well, than dwell on less happy things.' She sighed. 'Well, I must say I never thought I'd be looking forward to my interview in quite *this* way!'

'What interview's that, Mrs Pi – erm, Audrey I mean?'

'Oh, of course you won't know, will you! That was my other letter today: I've been expecting a Ms Partleigh-Noble from *Scottish Country Matters* and a photographer to do a little piece on my – on Dante Cottage, and now they've written to say they'll be coming next week, on Thursday afternoon. I had asked if they could make it an early closing day, so isn't that nice of them!'

'Oh, aye,' Oswald commented. 'And a bit of luck, too, it being a sort of – well, landlords' magazine, like.'

'Yes, isn't it? I shall feel quite like a spy in the enemy camp!' She took another swig. 'I do feel awful,' she giggled, 'being the only one drinking your whisky, Grace.'

'Yeah, so do I,' Ganglion agreed.

'Oh!' Grace jumped up. 'Of course, I . . . actually, it's not ours, it's Mungo's but I'm sure he won't mind.'

'Mungo!' exclaimed Ganglion. 'Ercourse! The very bloke!'

'Oh, I don't think so now, though,' said Grace. 'He's not the editor any more and from what he said I don't think the *Gazette* will be much use.'

'Stuff the *Gazette*! They'd 'ardly need ter bovver printin' the bleedin' fing if people was ter stop dyin'. Nar, I mean when it comes ter the nashnalls, the ole tabloids, 'e'll 'ave the contacks, won't 'e? Stanster reason.'

'Who is Mungo?' Mrs Pitt-Holyoake enunciated carefully.

'Wot is he, tralala!'

'Wheesht man, Ganglion! It's uncanny, Audrey, is it no', what the sight of a dram will do for some folk?' Oswald explained who Mungo was.

'I say!' said Mrs Pitt-Holyoake when he had finished. 'What a stroke of luck! Oh, Grace my dear, you shouldn't have,' she added, meaning the second whisky. 'Bottoms up, though, just the same.'

'Actually he's hoping to help us, I mean that's why he's here . . . partly,' said Grace. 'About those people who bought next door, where the flood was, and the house that went on fire up the street. He's looking up in the Register of, what was it? Cecils, or something?'

'Sasines, I expect.'

'Yes, that's right. It's a big list of who owns what in Edinburgh, the list I mean, not the people. It's a building,' she concluded helplessly.

'And what people would these be, my dear?'

'Well that's what he's trying to find out. He said they wouldn't, the real owners I mean, wouldn't necessarily be the ones whose name was on the window things.'

'The agents? No, they wouldn't I suppose. Not that I can remember seeing anything in the windows myself, though I can't say I ever looked particularly. Who were they, a local firm? Drubber and Dunning?'

'No.' Grace took a sip of her small one. 'Clinch McKittrick.'

'Oh, them!' said Mrs Pitt-Holyoake, becoming gnomic in her cups.

'Beg pardon?' said Grace. 'Do you know about them then . . . Audrey?'

'Oh, well! Not all about them, no, just that they're agents, property agents you know, and they seem to specialize in development – horrible word! – buying up derelict properties, old warehouses and that sort of thing, on behalf of . . . well, of builders I suppose, or those other people, you know, the ones who make money knocking things down and letting other people put things up. Funnily enough, it was my sister-in-law who told me about them – Godfrey's younger sister, that is, the one who married a coffee planter and had a rather peculiar time with the Mau Mau, poor thing, that Godfrey said he could never quite get to the bottom of. Anyway, when the authorities finally gave in and declared her husband to be officially dead she bought a little house in Bath – it always used to remind me of a doll's house I had when I was a gel, you know, all fanlight and plaster and whatnot but very little in the way of actual house – anyway, where was I? Oh, yes, them. Well, she said it was a very funny thing, because she'd been thinking for some time that she ought to, you know, sell up, and go into one of these places like a cross between a seaside hotel and a kindergarten with a bit of nursing home thrown in; she's always been a great one for her comforts, of course, especially since Kenya, only she never really quite had the nerve to . . . well, she had a visit from a very presentable young man – her words, you understand, not mine – and he arranged the whole thing for her, just like that! And he turned out to be these people, Clinch McKittrick. She seemed to think because they had a Scottish sort of name

I'd know all about them but then of course the English are so very ignorant of that sort of thing, don't you find? And they were going to – well, do something pretty beastly as it turned out, but Phyllida said she honestly had no idea at the time, to the Crescent where the house was. Was, I'm afraid, being very much the operative word as it turned out. So there we are, that's them!'

'Oh,' said Grace.

'Although she did say that quite a lot of the houses in the Crescent were in pretty poor shape by that time, standing empty, you know, and being vandalized and so on; it was one of the reasons she thought it better to go, you see.'

'Oh,' said Grace.

'Yes, she said even the Council people – and you know what they can be like, always slapping conservation orders on things and then doing nothing about them afterwards – even they thought the area was beyond redemption. In fact, I'm not sure they weren't actually involved in some way with the whole scheme, in the end, with one of these grants, you know.'

'Oh,' said Grace.

'Er,' said Ganglion. 'I fink your water orter be ready now, Ordrey luv.'

'Mm? Oh goodness gracious yes! Well now, if you're sure, Grace . . . well, this is lovely! I shall take my whisky . . .' She tittered, tripping to the door. 'I say, it's just as well it's not gin, isn't it!' She tripped out.

Oswald cleared his throat, jolting Grace from her reveries. 'She seems . . . happier, anyway,' she said.

'Wisteria,' said Ganglion. 'That an' whisky. She'll come down off of it.'

'Oh,' said Grace.

'Yeah. She'll need catching when she does.'

'Yes.'

'Cheer up, luv! It might never 'appen.'

'Yes,' said Grace. 'No.'

'*Nil carborundum!*'

'That's what Mungo said.'

'Well, there y'are, then. Reckon it'll be any use, wot 'e's doin' up in Auld Reekie?'

'I don't know. I think he thinks he'll find it's very difficult to find out just who the real owners are, but I missed the bit when he was explaining why, I was that busy trying to sort out these deliveries.'

'Oh, yeah, them. Any joy?'

'Not really, no. I rang these International Retail Supplies people and spoke to someone who said my input was greatly appreciated and would be fully considered in the next ongoing network review, so I said, what's going to happen just now? And she said, nothing.'

'Did she tell you to have a nice day?' asked Oswald.

'She might have done, I don't know. I put the phone down.' She took another messy swallow of her small one. 'Oh . . . sugar!' she said.

'There must be other suppliers, surely?'

'I tried all five in *Yellow Pages*. One was a recorded message telling me to phone International Retail Supplies, one spoke Chinese at me, at least I think it was, and two'd been cut off.'

'Oh. Erm, and the fifth?'

'Oh.' Grace looked embarrassed. 'Well I don't think he'd really be – suitable.'

'Eh? Wot, 'ow d'yer mean, suitable?'

'Well . . . he didn't sound very nice.' She brushed something off her lap, several times.

'Yeah, but . . . I mean, beggars can't be choosers, luv! Wot way not nice? I mean did 'e drop 'is aitches or woz 'e just after yer body?'

'No! I mean – oh, I don't know . . . well: what he

actually said was, he could get me anything I wanted, no – no problems.'

'Anything? Blimey, wot's wrong wiv that, then?'

'It was the way he said it! Like, I said, could he receive an order for wholesale fruit and vegetables, and he laughed, and then he said . . .' Her voice dropped. 'He said, "Honey, you can give me an order for anything, any time, any place." Then . . . well, so then I said could I, you know, read him my list of requirements and he said yes, so I did and then he just laughed again and said that I – I was a crazy lady but that he liked doing deals with crazy ladies and he'd get back to me. I'd . . . I'd given him the shop name, you see, when he answered the phone.'

'Yeah, well, it does sound a bit peculiar, still . . . wot's the name of this outfit, then?'

'The – the Magic Banana,' Grace said. 'Yes I know,' she added. 'Do you think the telephone people might have put them in the wrong section by mistake?'

'Oh, probly, yeah!' Ganglion guffawed. 'Mine jew, buggered if I know what the right one'd be!'

'I did wonder,' Grace stammered, 'if . . . if it might be, well, you know . . . drugs.'

'Wot, in *Yellow Pages*?'

'Well you never know, it could be a, you know, a front.'

'Why drugs, though?' Oswald asked.

'Well, you know . . . bananas. You know what they say, don't you?'

'About bananas?' asked Ganglion. 'No. Wot *do* they say about bananas?'

'Well, I don't know really' – Grace sounded rattled – 'but I do know it's not very nice.'

'Well I'd give it a go, if I woz you,' Ganglion advised.

'Even if it does turn arf Craigfeef into Olympic affletes, I reckon it's worf a try.'

'Oh well,' Grace shrugged. 'I don't suppose he will ring back anyway. He didn't sound a well organized sort of person.'

'Yeah, well, wait an' see. So in the meantime you're stuck wiv Semtex, are you?'

'Yes, and they're not due again till Monday week! I don't know what I'm going to do. Hamish thinks we ought to go to MegaMessages, buy all theirs, add on fifty per cent and sell it in the shop.'

'Ass not a bad idea! Specially fer 'Amish! No, really an' truly, 'snot. Why not? 'Slegal, innit?'

'Well . . . maybe,' Grace agreed reluctantly. 'And that's what Hamish said too, only . . . well, I mean, imagine us *doing* it, though! I'd be so embarrassed.'

'We wouldn't, would we, Oz?'

'Not at all,' Oswald agreed bravely. 'One of the perks of old age, doing daft pranks like that. I doubt we'd need to borrow a van of some sort, though.'

'Tell yer wot,' Ganglion offered, his eyes shining. 'Oz an' me'll do it, in the Doo Shevoo, just fer a practice run, like, first off. Then we can see wot 'appens, 'ow's that? Can't guarantee 'ow much we'll squeeze in, mine jew, but we'll see, all right?

'We-ell . . .'

'Right, that's settled then! Termorrer, Oz?'

'Aye, well . . . afternoon, anyway. I've, erm, twa-three things to see to the morn's morn.'

'Oh yeah, Friday's the mornin' you wash yer 'air, innit. Right, then: stand by ter receive a waggon-loader goodies around tea-time then, okay?'

'Well if you're . . . I'm all right for cabbages, mind.'

'No fart bombs, right, gotcher.'

'And turnips, I've got plenty of them.'

'Good, bleedin' great 'eavy fings'd probly bust the springs anyway. Anyfink else you don't want?'

'No, I think that's it, if you're really sure – '

'Positive! Shame 'Amish can't do the same, innit? No point in 'im sellin' the stuff dearer'n wot folks're gettin' shoved froo their letter-boxes, though.'

'No. And have you seen the prices?'

'Yeah, saw'm in the paper smornin'. Must've bin a bleedin' big lorry orl that lot fell off the back of. Wot 'appens when it all breaks dahn, though, ass wot I'd like ter know! Can't see them cowboys takin' it back an' fixin' it, can you?'

Grace sighed. 'I don't know. I know Hamish can't, though. He can't even send things away now.'

'Sumfink'll turn up,' said Ganglion vaguely. 'It usually does fer us Ganglions. Talkin' of which, I fink sumfink just 'as – 'ass your front door, innit?'

They heard footsteps on the stair, the cupboard on the landing opened and closed and then a rather aggressively hangdog Hamish appeared.

'You're early!' said Grace.

'Yeah,' said Hamish. 'Grace, did you know there was someone in our bath?'

'Audrey,' said Grace. 'Mrs Pitt-Holyoake.'

'Oh yeah, right, forgot. Any of Mungo's whisky left?'

'A – a bit, yes.'

'Good. Dad, Oswald?'

Oswald signalled no.

'No fanks, son,' said Ganglion. 'I'm swerving all over the road as it is.'

'Right.' He poured himself a large pub measure, looked at it, then tipped the bottle again and turned it into a real drink. 'I need this,' he explained, catching Grace's eye.

'Did your meeting . . . go all right, Hamish?' Grace asked.

Hamish considered the question. 'Depends,' he said.

'Depends? What do you mean, "depends"?'

Hamish swallowed. 'On your point of view,' he said.

'*Hamish!*'

'What?'

'What's the matter, Hamish? What happened?'

Hamish repeated the question to his glass and seemed to decide it would answer better on a refill. His eyes met Grace's again. 'I've resigned,' he said.

'Oh, Hamish! You haven't!'

Hamish sniffed. 'No,' he said. 'You're quite right, I haven't.' He took another tilt at his glass. 'I got kicked off.'

'*What?*' Grace blanched; Oswald scrutinized a rust spot on his wheelchair. Ganglion put on his Ganglions-will-be-Ganglions look.

'What . . . for?' whispered Grace.

'Claiming first-class postage on second-class letters?' suggested Hamish. 'Sorry, just wanted to see how you'd react, pet. No, they're going to be sponsored, you see.'

'Sponsored,' Grace repeated. She had once, at a railway station, fallen into conversation with a man who introduced himself as the Duke of Buccleuch, and had treated him in much the same way. 'That's nice,' she added.

'No it isn't,' said Hamish.

'No, all right then,' Grace agreed.

'I said I wouldn't write letters to them, you see.'

'No, I see,' said Grace. Then she cracked. 'Why not, Hamish?'

'See for yourself.' He tossed her a glossy booklet.

'"The HI! International Community Trust",' she read. 'I know we're not very religious, Hamish, but – '

'Open it,' said Hamish. 'Now, read that bit, there where it says "affiliate co-donors".'

' "The United World Redemption Church of Christ the Communicator," ' Grace read. ' "Transatlantic Satellite Systems, Inc, Good News Industries plc, Tollgate Road Factors plc, Melmotte's Bank, the Mid Lummock Water Company, MaxProf Associates, Scottish Penal Institutes Ltd – " '

'Down near the end,' Hamish interrupted. 'Three names, where I've marked them.'

' "Eastern Sight'n'Sound, Euro-Kay Electronics, and . . . and Semtex Transport." '

'Yeah,' said Hamish. 'Right.'

'Yes, I see,' said Grace. 'But surely, I mean – when you'd explained, didn't they . . .?'

'Didn't they what? Throw their hands up in horror and say, oh well of course if it's that sort of money we don't want to touch it? No, not so's you'd notice. Well, one or two of them did, sort of. One, anyway. Old Glencairn.'

'What did he say?'

'Oh, you know, the usual, what he always says. That the Gala's always been a community effort ever since he helped to start it, and help from the local council was one thing but he would always like to believe that it was first and foremost a community thingie, you know, endeavour. That sort of thing.'

'Good for him,' said Oswald.

'Yeah, right, spose so.'

'Then what happened?'

'Then? Oh, then Sayeed Haq read a letter from his old man, House of Commons notepaper, the lot, saying how especially pleased he was that his own home town should be among the first in Scotland to take full advantage of the government's liberalization of regional fiscal policy and the economic regeneration of things generally, and that he'd be delighted to open the Gala himself as he believed it would be the beginning of great things to come. All that sort of stuff. So I said I couldn't see how putting local shops out of business was good for anybody except the people who were doing it, and they voted me out. I mean, right off. Off the committee. Five to one. Half the usual folk weren't at the meeting.'

'The one being old man Glencairn?' asked Oswald.

'That's right. And the five being Sayeed Haq, Mr Kirk, Mrs Fingal from the restaurant, Clyde Bilt and Glencairn junior.'

'Kenny voted against his own father?'

'Yeah. Said they'd agreed to differ.'

'And that was it?'

Hamish shrugged. 'More or less. Oh, old Solly Chisholm's off too. He resigned cos they wouldn't let him do the printing this year. I left them discussing how they were going to get the WRI and the BBs and the Stags and folk like that to modify their input to mesh in with the main thrust of the programme.'

'??' said Grace.

'The main programme's being organized by the Bilts,' Hamish explained. 'On behalf of these HI! people. It's one of the conditions. Bilt said it was vital that the presentation shouldn't look too "homey".'

'Oh,' said Grace. 'I see.'

'Yeah. Oh, and Mr Borden sent in his resignation – off the committee, I mean. They're moving! Selling up. As soon as he's well enough.'

They digested the news in silence.

'They got themselves a new secretary, I suppose?' said Grace.

'Oh yeah, no bother,' Hamish replied, killing his whisky. 'They co-opted Neville.'

'Wot's all this about bein' busy termorrer mornin'?' Ganglion demanded. They had left Grace putting Audrey to bed and leaving a note to explain to Mungo why he was sleeping on the sofa, and he had driven soberly back to Rose Cottage. 'We're not plannin' anyfink wild after breakfast, are we?'

The question brought renewed banging noises from Oswald's bedroom.

'Oz? You all right?'

The bedroom door was half pushed to. Ganglion knocked, waited, then poked his head around it. 'Gawdstrewf! Wotcher doin'?'

Oswald was hunched forward, rootling through wodges of paper in an open chest. Discarded documents littered the floor all round his chair. 'Ah,' he said, straightening. 'I was looking for this.' He unfolded a fragile document, heavily creased and one-eighth stained, and passed it to his friend.

Ganglion screwed his eyes up and read it. 'I fink,' he said slowly, 'you'd better be seein' a solicitor yerself, me old mate.'

Chapter Six

The long-established legal practice of Drubber and Dunning, solicitors and notaries public, still occupies the premises in Hope Street, Duncruddie Mains, acquired by its founders in 1923 after they had helped to ease the previous occupants, the Mid Lummock Husbandmen's Welfare Association, into mutually beneficial liquidation. The founders – Walter Cairns Drubber and Patrick Minto Dunning – were leading lads o'pairts in a generation remarkable for its talent, its manliness and its fair promise; a generation sorely depleted, alas, by Flanders, Passchendaele and Ypres. Young Walter and young Patrick, however (and much to their mortification no doubt) were denied their chance of foreign glory and found themselves tholed instead to desks at the War Office, where their steadfast courage under a bombardment of pleas, petitions and protestations enabled the great work of conscription to go ahead on a sure legal basis. At the very moment the last soldier (a twenty-one-year-old poet and mathematician described at his Appeal Tribunal as a scholar of not inconsiderable abilities) fell to a sniper's bullet at 10.58 A.M. on November 11th, 1918, they were able to unbend their war-weary backs at last and declare, without fear of contradiction, that they had served their King and Country faithfully and well. They were then awarded Service Medals and Honourable Discharges and fared homewards, having made several useful contacts in the great machinery of state, and happily unaffected by the merest trace of that dangerous *ennui* that afflicted so many of their contemporaries in the years following. They fixed their brass plate to the wall of the British Linen Bank in their home town, employed a disabled ex-comrade to do their clerking for them, and carried on their practice from two rooms on the first floor above the manager's office. Within a twelve-month they had prospered to the extent of being among the leading subscribers to the town's War Memorial at whose base they dutifully laid their annual wreath to the memory of those of their old schoolmates destined never to grow old.

Four wreaths later, they who were left for the years to condemn experienced a sudden access of capital and transferred to Hope Street.

A few more years of steady profit enabled each partner to take a wife and, in due and seemly course, to produce a single male heir and to enrol him on the books of Doctor Thin's Academy in Edinburgh, whither both striplings, having served their educational apprenticeship amongst the commonality of Duncruddie Mains, were duly despatched at the age of eleven.

After university (Edinburgh: Law) and training (in the ineffably splendid establishment of Messrs Broody's, WS) young Sinclair Kitchener Drubber and young Alistair Haig Dunning returned to their native sod, there to take up the legal reins from their ageing progenitors (whom they now called Papa) and to impress and dazzle the lieges with their learning and their polish (or rather, pawlish). Being as they were bred, rather than drawn, to the seal and the signet they had of course no aptitude whatever for the law, and no particular desire to commingle with those of their generation (last met at the age of eleven) who sought to pester them with their grubby little suits and piffling transactions. They yearned for the rarefied atmosphere of Broody's, for the riotous nights in Rose Street and the long and palely languorous mornings after, and they deeply resented having to spend the rest

171

of their days in the clouded, scummy backwaters of Mid Lummock. They dree'd their weird, however (to borrow a phrase of Sir Walter Scott's) and did not falter. They had inherited guile. They had acquired pawlish. Above all, they had an intimate knowledge, gained in their years of tender infancy before shades of Dr Thin's enclosed them, of all the blackest secrets of their community (not to mention their papas) and this – coupled with the ability, only recently denied the honest practitioner at law, to work for both parties in a transaction, thus doubling both their innate stock of duplicity and their fee – saw them through.

Nonetheless they were determined that their own sons – when, in due and inevitable course, they had them – should never have to suffer, as they had suffered, the indignities of direct contact with their litigious or transgressing fellow-citizens. The third generation was destined not to practise in Mid Lummock, nor even in the hallow'd suites of Broody's, but instead was sent out with the most puissant blessing of both families to pass advocate and practise at the Scottish Bar, where it would never, never, *never* have to meet any common people – save, on exceptional occasions and as learned counsel, at the other end of a perfectly enormous rosewood table with a sleek-suited minion of Broody's to act as go-between and net court judge.

The fourth generation, it may confidently be predicted, will go one remove further and take up medicine, where the rewards are higher, the effort less and the clients more compliant still, provided one chooses one's field carefully. In the meantime it is brought to Mid Lummock for its half-term holidays, abjured to remark what a bonny place it is, and quickly taken away again.

Thus the long-established legal practice of Drubber and Dunning, solicitors and notaries public – which in three generations has pretty much reverted to what it was in the days of Mr Walter and Mr Patrick, where the present partners, Mr Tozie and Mr Cosh, each carries on his broad back a moiety of Mid Lummock's mundane hopes, fears, loathings and peccadilloes, where the advice and assistance of Broody's ('our Edinburgh agents') is always to hand should matters threaten to become too complex or too likely to throw their incompetence into sharp relief, and where, this March morning, Mrs Audrey Pitt-Holyoake, shopkeeper, and Mr Oswald Ochilree, retired farmer, waited uncomfortably to be condescended to while the firm's receptionist, immaculately starched and gelled, polished the leaves of a peculiarly monstrous *Monstera deliciosa*. Soft noises off, as of the reverent sifting of ashes and the laying-on of paper hands, offered muffled testimony to the minutely ponderous workings of the great machinery of justice, remorselessly and blindly grinding out the unceasing harvest of human frailty in the rooms beyond.

The two elderly clients suffered, meanwhile, in silence. Though they had met on the street outside – it being the settled opinion of Mr Tozie and Mr Cosh that car parks belonged strictly to the realm of trade – and had exchanged words of surprise, of pleasure and (in Oswald's case) of brief explanation, they had been afflicted on entering the precincts of Drubber and Dunning with a disabling species of numbed reticence, of the sort that afflicts the denizens of doctors' waiting-rooms who apprehended both the vulgarity and the embarrassment inherent in a discussion of symptoms. Oswald moodily observed the receptionist through the holes in the *Monstera*; Mrs Pitt-Holyoake, incredulous, read the problem page of the *Investor's Chronicle*. At length a buzzer buzzed discreetly in some concealed region of the receptionist's workstation; she finished off the leaf she was

173

working on, shimmered across her expensively piled portion of floor, and bent privily to attend to it.

'Mr Ochilree?' She posed the question as if there might, at some unspecified future date, be real cause to challenge the reliability of the reply.

Oswald looked at Mrs Pitt-Holyoake, scanned the reception area for concealed namesakes, and cleared his throat. 'Yes?'

'Mr Keechie will see you now.' She delivered the information with the air of one grudgingly bestowing unmerited largesse.

'Mr . . . Keechie? Erm, it was Mr Cosh's secretary I spoke to when I – '

'Mr Keechie is available,' said the receptionist.

'Oh,' said Oswald. 'Ah. Where do I, er . . .?'

'Up those two steps,' the receptionist replied, as if to distinguish them from the non-existent three steps, or thirty-nine steps, or Alpine range. 'Along that corridor' – there was only one – 'and it's the door at the end, with Mr Keechie's name on it.'

'Up those two steps?'

'Ye-es.' Persons in need of a lawyer, her tone suggested, should take care to bring both legs with them. 'The partners' consultation rooms are on the first floor.'

'Oh, aye, no, I meant . . .' He indicated his physical inferiority to the mainstream of society. 'You see.'

'Yes,' said the receptionist. Mrs Pitt-Holyoake gave up trying to sympathize with Underperforming, Chalfont St Giles, and rose to assist.

'If you could maybe . . .' Oswald suggested.

'Oh,' said the receptionist. 'Well, if there really isn't any other . . .'

'You can't get vertical take-off models on the NHS, you know,' Mrs Pitt-Holyoake cut in tartly. Oswald blushed with admiration.

'In that case I suppose I'll have to,' said the receptionist. Oswald could not quite decide whether the utter neutrality of expression with which this statement was delivered was cause for forgiveness or for enhanced offence. She grasped one handle of the chair in much the same way as a person of average sensibility would, with a pair of tongs, remove a dead rat from a dustbin.

After the two women had hauled him backwards up the two steps (Mrs Pitt-Holyoake having nonetheless to reach across and assist with her left hand the effete efforts of the other's right) Mrs Pitt-Holyoake bent to retrieve a red curve of fingernail from the deep beige weave of the carpet.

'Is this yours?' she enquired politely.

'It *was*,' said the other, flouncing back to her workstation. The cheeseplant cringed as she passed. Oswald tooled himself off down the corridor leaving his friend to return to her seat and be glared at for fully three minutes until the telephone warbled and the receptionist condescended to answer it.

'*Drubber* and *Dunning*,' she cooed. 'Can I *help* you?'

Oswald considered head-butting his way through the imperfectly varnished plywood door of Kevin Keechie, LLB, Dip LP, but decided instead to go for the crabwise knock conventionally employed by what one of his therapists had once referred to, unsmilingly, as the ambulatorarily challenged.

'Come!' said a disagreeably nasal voice within. Oswald raised an eyebrow; he had thought that only people in TV dramas said that.

Oswald, beholding a solicitor's office for only the second time in his life, was momentarily nonplussed. His previous experience – gained while negotiating the purchase of Rose Cottage with old Mr Foustie, of Foustie and Fuffle – had taught him that lawyers habitually dwelt in large, poorly heated, once-glorious drawing-rooms where the deceased ashes of an antique fire gathered venerable dust in a coldly marbled fireplace behind a warped japanned screen, where the ceiling wanted only a plaster acorn or two of its former magnificence and the skirting board still climbed eighteen imperious inches up the flocked wall, where the window had clearly – or rather, opaquely – not been ravished open since the last partner but two had leaned out of it to wave a flag for Victoria's diamond jubilee, and where the client's strip of carpet was worn to its timeless skeleton by the countless pacings of pursuers and defenders, deponers and deponees, testators and heritors, accusers, accused and litigants of every airt and part, all long a-mouldering; said threadbare portion being located in front of a desk doomed to outlast the Apocalypse and piled high with the urgent litter of dreary legal ages, behind and above which peered and spiered the great adviser himself, a character begat by Mr Dickens or the Rev. Mr Sterne, a legendary creature of crags and bags, of nicotine and sealing-wax of finely tapered safebreaker's fingers and pale, watery eyes rimmed with aeons of world-wearying human burthen.

Mr Keechie, on the other hand, looked like Hollywood's idea of the liftboy at the Ritz, inhabited a generously proportioned broom cupboard and spent his working hours behind – or before, or on, as the mood took him – a multi-tiered space-saving module festooned with electronic officery of every conceivable description and inconceivable purpose, cluttered only by a drift, not of paper, but of five-inch floppy disks, each carefully and efficiently muddled in among the others. An abstract print, designed to promote cerebral tranquillity in the beholder, hung upside-down above Mr Keechie's licence to solicit on the otherwise lavatorially bare walls. A small storage heater kept the chill apartment uncomfortably stuffy. There were no windows; instead, a dirty ventilation brick sucked the air out from around Oswald's ankles while a small electric fan stirred the carbon dioxide round his head. He backed the door shut with his chair, shook the clammy flabby thing held out to him by way of greeting, and waited for the lawyer to cease his fascinated scrutiny of the screen at his other elbow.

'Fine,' said Mr Keechie to the screen. Then, to Oswald, 'I understand you have some matter for me.'

'Erm, oh, aye,' said Oswald, struggling to throw off the unpleasant surgical connotations of Mr Keechie's opening gambit. 'As I was explaining to Mr Cosh's sec – '

'Take me through it again,' said Mr Keechie. 'Mr Cosh has remitted your matter to me,' he explained. 'Something to do with a lease, I understand.'

'Well, aye, no, not exactly,' said Oswald.

'Fine,' said Mr Keechie, artlessly glancing at his watch. 'What is it exactly, then?'

'Well.' Oswald cleared his throat. 'It all starts with my father, you see, with my father's farm, I should say.'

'Ah! A boundary job!' Mr Keechie looked wistful; he was thinking, perhaps of his outstanding finals paper on Use and Custom *in re* the March Dykes Act of 1661.

'No,' said Oswald.

'Oh? It usually is.'

'Aye, well . . . erm, it's not.'

'Oh. Go on, then, if you will.'

Oswald drew breath. 'He had this bit farm, you see – my father this is we're talking about still, you understand – that he bought just at the end of the Great War, and – '

'1945?' said Mr Keechie, making a note.

'No, 1918,' said Oswald. Mr Keechie put a neat line through his note. 'You mean the First World War then, do you?'

'Aye,' said Oswald, puzzled. 'The Great War, like I said.'

'I . . . see,' said Mr Keechie, making another note. 'Wilfrid Sassoon and all that, eh?'

'Erm . . . aye. Well, as I said, he bought it, the farm that is, not . . . anyway: he made what go of it he could, it not being weel-luckit, like, and – '

'Not being what?'

'Very suitable for agricultural purposes,' Oswald translated. 'Owre many bogs an' rocks, and suchlike. So he – '

'Oh, ho!' said Mr Keechie.

'Beg pardon?' said Oswald.

'Tell me, Mr Ochiltree, is this – '

'Ochilree.'

'Eh? Oh. Very well then, as you please. Tell me, you aren't about to land me in a cause of *aemulationem vicini*, are you? Emulous behaviour, and all that?'

'Erm . . . I don't . . . I don't think so, no.'

'Oh.' Mr Keechie had done a rather dazzling little *viva-voce* on it. 'Proceed.'

'Aye, er . . . where was I?'

'Bogs and rocks.' He consulted his notes. 'And suchlike.'

'Oh, aye. Well, like I say, erm, there he was, you see, then in 1923 he was spiered at by a gentleman from the War Department – that is,' he amended hastily, sensing the interruption, 'he had a visit, erm, asking him would he consider letting the government have the land for military training, exercises and such. You, er' – Oswald essayed a little grin – 'you know the saying, the army always fights the next war as if it was the last one!'

'No?' said Mr Keechie.

'Oh. Well, erm, it's just a saying, like. Thinking o' the Falklands, for instance.'

'Oh. Really?'

'Aye, well, never mind.' Oswald coughed. 'Anyway, my father said, if they wanted practice fighting in stour and gutter, that was their business – so long as the price was good, naturally enough.'

'Naturally enough,' agreed Mr Keechie. 'I do hope,' he added, showing the first signs of professional animation, 'your father went to a solicitor?'

'Oh, aye! He came here! Well, not here actually, but to Drubber and Dunning, right enough.'

'I see. And a sale was agreed, was it?'

'Oh no, no. No' a sale. A lease, just. He insisted on that – my father, that is. I wasn't around at the time. He told me afterwards he said he wasn't minded to part with anything for ever, not even a wee bit boggy farm, no' to the government, no' at any price!'

'I see,' said Mr Keechie, making another note. 'Something of an anarchist, was he, your father?'

'He was a Lance Bombardier and a Kirk elder!' Oswald protested.

'Takes all sorts,' observed Mr Keechie. 'So, then: we have a lease, do we? What was the ish?'

'Pardon?'

'The ish – lengthy, expiry date?'

'Ah,' said Oswald. 'That's just it, you see.'

'What is?'

'The point,' said Oswald. 'Why I'm here. You see, what he did was – this was on the advice of Mr Drubber himself, by the way, to keep the thing straightforward and above board seemingly – what he did was, he took a fixed sum down in return for letting the army boys do their bit shooting and suchlike for as long as . . . well, for as long as they wanted the use o' the land to do it on. It made the whole thing simpler.'

'Did it?'

'Well . . . so Mr Drubber said, seemingly.'

'I see,' said Mr Keechie, who didn't. 'So what . . . I mean, what did it look like, then, this lease?'

'Like this,' said Oswald.

Wrinkling his nose, Mr Keechie took the offered document and opened it out.

'Is this all of it?' he asked.

'Oh, yes. Just the three pages – the initialled ones – and a map, and a dod of sealing wax and signatures on page four.'

'Extraordinary,' muttered Mr Keechie. His lips moved soundlessly as he scanned the rusty copperplate. 'Mmm – mmm, huh, huh, yeah. Trouble is, of course,' he added, laying the document aside and brushing the tips of his fingers on his lapels, 'with this sort of gimcrack lease – meaning no disrespect to the departed, I hasten to add – is proving the lessee, in this case the army, have actually finished with it. Ve-ry, very tricky! Who's to say they don't want it any more, hmm?'

'It was in the paper,' Oswald faltered, suddenly mindful of his father's admonition not to believe a word he read in it.

'What was? Which paper?'

'The *Perthshire Gazette*,' said Oswald, answering the second question first. 'Sale of Boggybreck Barracks.'

'Boggybr – '

It would be untrue to say that Mr Keechie's knuckles whitened: they were too deeply embroiled in subcutaneous tissue to accomplish the feat. It would be breaking the bounds of credulity to report that his jaw dropped, since there wasn't really enough of it to be noticed if it had. Nor did his eyes – being of a peculiar matt texture unsuited to scintillation – glitter. It was, however, impossible not to entertain the fancy that the sockets, had their owner been a cartoon character, would have rung up twin pulsating pound signs as the intelligence behind them processed Oswald's information.

'You . . . are,' began Mr Keechie, in a voice tinged with something passably close to emotion, 'the heritable proprietor of . . . of,' he waved Oswald's document feebly, heedless of the dust, 'of the subjects concerned?'

'Oh, aye,' said Oswald smugly.

'You're . . . sure?' Mr Keechie's mental faculties hummed with *res perit domino et judicata*, not to mention *merae facultatis*.

'I'm my father's son! His only son. His only anything, after that fashion.'

Mr Keechie made a mental note to hug himself. Then he gulped, foreseeing another difficulty: 'And the . . . the property,' he croaked, one hand plucking at his collar, 'is intact?'

'Well, erm, I can't rightly . . . Will I tell you the story of it?'

'Do,' gasped the lawyer.

'Well. You see.' Oswald coughed, easing himself into the narrative. 'With the money he got from the let of Boggybreck, my father bought Newbiggings – with an agricultural mortgage, naturally – and married my mother, and had me. He, erm, he was aye a methodical man, in that sense, and when he passed on he willed the whole to me, my mother having predeceased. And then I . . . well, I made over the farm like, to my own son . . . for the usual reasons, like, with the tax and such, only' – Mr Keechie's face was threatening to dissolve – 'I kept Boggybreck separate-like, to myself. I don't rightly know why, exactly. I expect maybe you would call it sentimentality.'

'Oh, yes,' said Mr Keechie, happy for the time being to admit to anything, however outrageous. 'Yes, of course.'

'Aye, well . . .' Oswald shrugged. 'So there it is, I suppose.'

Mr Keechie was suddenly very still. 'You have the deeds, I take it?'

'As good as,' said Oswald.

'As . . .' Tiny beads of solicitous perspiration began to appear in the narrow and debatable region between the lawyer's downy eyebrows and his prematurely receding hairline.

'They're lodged with you. As . . . I don't know, security, maybe? Ah!' Oswald's right index finger, viewed from across the solicitor's office module, appeared as a bony blur. 'I mind it on now! It was something to do with Drubber and Dunning taking over my mortgage on New-biggings after the original people, what were they now, the Husbandmen's Something-or-other, anyway, after they went bust.'

'Aaah!' Mr Keechie permitted himself the sort of expiration normally associated with red mists and compliant virginity. He swiftly recomposed himself. 'Mr Ochilree,' he began, with all the portentiousness at his command, 'let us suppose that you are the owner of Boggybreck.'

'I am!'

'Then let it be so supposed. We shall be dealing, Mr Ochilree, with some truly formidable adversaries.' His fingers twitched, as if already turning the laudatory pages of the *Scottish Law Journal*. 'The Ministry of Defence. The Scottish Office. The Property Disposals Agency. To name but a few.'

'Er, yes,' Oswald concurred.

'As to the question of fee.'

'Ah,' said Oswald. 'Aye. Could I maybe . . . pay as I go, like . . . for as long as I *can* go?'

Mr Keechie smiled alarmingly. 'Mr Ochilree, not everything that comes from America is unwelcome, you know.'

'No?'

'No, Mr Ochilree! I'm talking commission basis here, you understand.'

'Ah! Er . . .?'

'A percentage. Of your . . . this . . . heritable asset. You see. Shall we say . . . one, ahem! . . . and a half . . . per cent?'

'Payable if we win, you mean?'

'When, Mr Ochilree, when!' He offered the flabby clammy thing again. 'A pleasure,' he said 'to have you as my client, Mr Ochilree!' And indeed he really did look as though he meant it, as he did also when he added, 'Now I'm really very sorry but I'm afraid you'll have to excuse me because I have another client I'm supposed to see.'

'Aye, yes,' said Oswald, turning himself through one hundred and eighty degrees in the few narrow feet between the agent and his door. 'Poor Mrs Pitt-Holyoake.'

Keechie frowned. 'Did you say "poor"?' he muttered; then, brightly, 'I'll be in touch, Mr Ochilree!'

'Aye. Oh, erm, I'll have my papers back. If you don't mind.'

With a fair imitation of good grace Mr Keechie made a photocopy, returned the original, and opened the door for him.

'Can you give me a wee shove, to get me started?' asked Oswald. Keechie gave him special client status, and did so.

'What's he like?' whispered Mrs Pitt-Holyoake as she bumped him down the steps.

'No' bad, considering,' Oswald admitted, earning himself a scowl from behind the *Monstera*. 'So long as you keep reminding yourself that he's a grown-up just like yourself.' The scowl matured into a glower. 'We'll wait for you in the car, see how you get on.'

It was raining heavily outside, and Hope Street bore abundant witness to the challenge of competitive tendering. Chimp-like, Ganglion pranced over to help a dispirited-looking woman with a pushchair across the worst of the pavement lakes and assist Oswald and his chair into the weeping interior of the 2CV.

''Ow are yer, then, me ole mate?' he asked, clanging the door to. 'Pounds lighter, eh?'

'Not at all. I kept my hand in my pocket.' Oswald explained the nature of his arrangement with Messrs Drubber and Dunning.

'Blimey! Well, that all sounds very 'opeful then, dunnit! I mean, if 'e'd a thought you was a dodgy case, 'e wooder've stung you fer 'is fifty guineas on the spot, woonty?'

'Ah, well, maybe,' said Oswald. 'Maybe not.'

'Ur.' Ganglion nodded. 'So, wosse doin' now, then?'

'Oh, checking up, I should think – I should hope. He wouldn't be much of a lawyer if he took everything on trust, would he?'

'Like wot you don't, eh?'

'No' with lawyers, no.'

'Ur. Oz?'

'Aye?'

'Can I arst you a personal question?'

'It never stopped you before, Ganglion.'

'Yer, no. But.'

'My goodness! Go on, then.'

'Oz, woss your motive? I mean, is it the principle of the fing, or, I dunno, buggerin' up these international god-bashers an' doin' a few folk a good turn? Or wantin' ter die rich? Or wot?'

184

'Mmmn,' said Oswald. He frowned and thought, and frowned again. Then his face cleared. 'I don't know!'

'Ar.'

'I mean, a bit o' everything, I suppose, and . . . oh, I don't . . .' he sighed. 'Drawing the line somewhere?' he suggested. Then, half to himself: 'Why should the deil hae all the best tunes?'

'Ar. Ass fine, then.'

'Is it?'

'Oh, yeah. Fine.' Ganglion cleared his throat and scrutinized the odometer. 'Yer a good bloke, Oz,' he said.

Oswald blushed at the gear stick. 'Ach, havers!' he admonished it.

'You don't believe all that stuff about Craigfeef's economic miracle then, do yer?'

'What, like it said in the paper you mean? No, of course not! Nothing miraculous about a few rich folk getting richer, as far as I can see.'

'Nah.'

'Mind,' Oswald frowned. 'That's not to say there's no' a few folk who do. Believe it, I mean. Look what happened to Hamish last night for instance.'

'Oh, yeah. Still.' Ganglion shrugged. 'There's orlwis plenty o' suckers, though, ent there? Or worse.'

'Mm . . . aye.' Oswald sounded doubtful. 'Mind you, I'm not just so sure it's up to us to – ' He jumped as a set of unseen knuckles rapped on his steamed-up window. He opened it, failing as usual to avoid a little flash-flood of rainwater that cascaded into the crook of his elbow.

A stooped Audrey Pitt-Holyoake dripped on the pavement. 'Gawd – 'ere,' exclaimed Ganglion. ''op in!' She cascaded on to the back seat.

'That was quick,' Oswald observed.

'Yes,' said Mrs Pitt-Holyoake. 'All very simple and

straightforward!' She arranged her skirt so it clung below the knee.

'Your . . . case, you mean?'

'My eviction,' said Mrs Pitt-Holyoake.

'Oh, my dear,' said Oswald hopelessly.

'Din't wanner know then, did 'e? I see. Bleedin' –'

'Oh, no!' Mrs Pitt-Holyoake seemed to be having a little difficulty with her breathing. 'On the . . . on the contrary!' She giggled uncontrollably as the two men looked on, anxious and bemused. 'Oh dear, I'm so sorry! But really I – you – can't help seeing the funny side of . . .' She wiped her eyes with the back of one gloved hand, snorted, took a deep breath, and began again. 'You see, far from "not wanting to know", he – it turned out – knew all about it already! That is to say that he, Drubber and Dunning, I mean . . . they are acting for – as local agents for . . . for the solicitors acting for . . . for *them!*

'Do you know,' she added, recovering herself again, 'I felt just like that silly couple in those films, you know, the ones who always go straight to Dracula's castle to shelter from the thunderstorm. Although I must say . . .' she pulled off a glove to find her handkerchief '. . . of the two of us I think he was the more taken aback. His face! Oh dear! You were quite right, Oswald. Like a little boy caught with his hand in the biscuit tin! You see, he couldn't help it. I'd been telling him my story and he'd been making little notes and nodding and humming, you know, all very correct and proper, and then he asked me if I'd had any formal note from the solicitors and I said yes, I had – I picked it up at the Post Office this morning, you see, which was just as well as it was a Recorded Delivery thing and I wouldn't have been at home, of course, to sign for it otherwise – and so I gave it to him and he took it and . . . well, as I say, his *face!* The poor boy just couldn't hide it, could he? Not at all like Mr

Horning, Daddy's old solicitor; Daddy used to say you could murder Mr Horning and he'd simply watch you over the top of his glasses and work out your plea in mitigation while you did it. Whereas poor Mr . . .'

'Keechie.'

'Such an unfortunate name. Whereas all he could do was sit there going redder and redder until I actually thought he was going to cry!'

'I expect he's no' used to seeing the end product of his dealings yet,' said Oswald. 'Being so young.'

'Oh? Oh yes, I see what you mean. And I know it's awful, really, for me, I mean. I suppose I should be the one to cry. Still!' She sniffed. 'I just don't seem able to at the moment. Now then, I wonder since it's so wet, could you give me a lift to my car?'

'Yeah, sure,' said Ganglion. 'Where is the ole girl?'

'Straight down this road to the end, then left. I had to find a hill, do you see. Oh dear,' she sighed as Ganglion smeared a patch on the windscreen and turned on the ignition, 'I suppose I really ought to open the shop and see if I've got any customers though I must say I don't feel like it. Perhaps I shall just go home and see if anything's happened to my water. Not that I really want to do that either, for some reason.'

'You could always come wiv us to MegaMessages, if you like. We could do wiv two cars.'

'Oh? What's this, a hold-up?'

'Not as such, Ordrey luv, no. It's a little scheme, like, to 'elp Grace wiv 'er delivery problems.' He outlined the problems and explained the scheme, which their companion declared sounded a perfectly splendid one especially if you didn't like all these big shops anyway, which she herself never had.

'I say,' she added. 'You wouldn't mind awfully if you had lunch with me at Dante Cottage first, would you? It wouldn't seem quite so bleak, somehow, if I had someone with me – friends, I mean.' Silently she scolded herself for the unintentional offensiveness of the request she had begun to make.

Oswald said that sounded like a splendid scheme, too.

'We can always get water from the burn,' she added. 'If we have to.'

Audrey Pitt-Holyoake's affair with the Pre-Raphaelites did not, fortunately, extend to her basic domestic arrangements. The freezer, which slumbered under a tapestry in the scullery, produced three High-Energy Low-Calorie Gourmet-Style Meals For One; 'Prepared for Today's Lifestyle', the packets said, 'With YOU In Mind!'. There was a picture of a young woman wearing a man's business suit and taking photographs of something from the back of a Range Rover. The hostess's microwave (concealed in a linenfold Pre-Raphaelite kitchen unit) soon had them thawed out, molecularly agitated, and fit for rapid consumption, whatever they were. They accompanied the feast with one each of three kinds of sherry Audrey 'found' in her sitting-room sideboard.

Afterwards, Ganglion washed up in a cacophony of orgasmic-plumbing which produced, after one or two false ejaculations, a miserly trickle of scaldingly hot brownish water. 'Perhaps they've been cleaning the system,' Audrey suggested. 'It's always filthy for days afterwards, when they do that.' A percolator seethed dyspeptically on a gas ring ('I know electric ones are quicker,' Audrey explained, 'but they look so brutal, don't they, and besides this one was only fifteen pence at a WRI jumble.'). She had offered herbal Darjeeling but they decided against it, on account of the driving they had to do later on.

Ganglion's generous nature having extended to liberality with Audrey's detergent, he was up to his fascinatingly scrawny elbows in suds when his portable telephone began to chirrup. 'Get that coodjer, ducks?' he called over his shoulder. Mrs Pitt-Holyoake, hovering nearby with a tea-towel, dived into his jacket (unfortunately its owner had left it on the back of his chair) and produced the instrument, along with a cascade of old shopping lists, tissues and sweetie wrappers.

'Pull that,' Ganglion instructed, 'an' press that.'

'Hello?' she said. 'Yes, he is. One moment.' She held it against his ear. 'It's for you,' she said, a little unnecessarily. He had little whorls of grizzly hair on the back of his neck, she noticed, and smelt agreeably of tarry string.

'Yer? Oh, wotcher, 'Amish! Wot? Oh, Ordrey. Yeah, Mrs Pitt-'Olyoake, wot's . . . wot? Never you mind, filthy bugger! Yeah . . .'oo? Oh, 'im, yeah. . . . Yeah? Fine, more the merrier. Big car, is it? Right, we'll – wot?. . .Blahdy'ell! Wotever next, eh . . . Yeah, right, tell me later, right. Cheers, son.'

'That was 'Amish,' he told them. 'In case you didn't know. Mungo's back wiv some info on these property sharks, dunno wot, an' 'e sez 'e'll come wiv us this arft, in 'is car, to do Grace's shoppin'.'

'Oh, very good!' said Oswald. 'We should just about strip the place between three vehicles.'

'Right. Oh, an' there's bin a break-in or somefink at Meiklejohn's, the 'ole place is swarmin' wiv designer filth an' MacEachran's guzzlin' 'is way rahnd the 'ahses makin' enquiries. Enough stuff gorn ter light up the 'oler Perfshire – accordin' to ole blabbermahf Monzie, that is, so it's probly no more than an Olympic sprinter's-worth. Anyway, they've got an Alsatian out sniffin' up everybody's trouser legs, an' there's five of them, 'Amish says, givin' poor ole Meiklejohn a right grillin'. 'Amish reckons they reckon 'e dunnit.'

'That's nonsense!' snorted Mrs Pitt-Holyoake.

'Yeah, so it's probly true. Anyway, Mungo's rarin' to give MegaMessages wot for, so we'd better sup up an' off, ant we? Yew gorra downstairs karzi, Ordrey luv?'

Mrs Pitt-Holyoake blinked. 'Yes, under the stairs.'

'Fank gawd fer that, means Oz an' me'll be arf an hour between us, 'steader free-quarters, wot wiv my bag an' 'is fix. Gotcher stuff ready, Oz? Woodjer believe it, forty years o' stickin' needles in cows' bums, an' 'e can't bear ter jag 'isself!'

'Ach wheesht man, Ganglion,' Oswald winced. 'Audrey doesn't want to hear that.'

'Ter lose one leg, Mistah Hochilree,' Ganglion parodied, wheeling his friend to the door, 'is a misforchoon; ter lose two would be . . .'

They went off arguing good-naturedly about whether cattle feel pain.

Mrs Pitt-Holyoake sighed happily as she dried the plates and forks: one little cloud, that had been on her horizon since the morning before, had just delightfully vanished. Herbal Darjeeling was one thing, but she had been rather worried about the used hypodermic needles in the bathroom at Rose Cottage. Then she frowned. What sort of a world was this, she asked herself reproachfully, if someone like her could instantly assume the worst of a pot-smoking diabetic? Then she gasped as a twist of the cloth brought an answering stab from her arthritic right wrist.

Poor Oswald. As if simply being old wasn't beastly enough on its own.

Scrymgeour, flat on his belly in the fodder radish, waited until both vehicles were out of sight before proceeding to

190

paint the intestinal remains of a stag with a liberal dose of alphachloralose. Then he backed carefully off. A swarm of flies buzzed greedily, but not for long, around the gruesome mess.

Neville was spending part of his lunch hour rapping at Jerusalem House. A slim file, professionally marked 'Rocket to Redemption', lay open on the stripped pine table in front of Mr Clyde Bilt. Chylblayne Bilt, dressed as usual like a Thanksgiving Day Barbie Doll, sat with wifely deference at his side.

'It's basically a chain letter system,' Neville explained. 'Only with money, and the added bonus of eternal life rather than the threat of bad luck. And it's interactive,' he added.

Bilt ran his professionally blue eyes over the document, occasionally flipping back a page or two to check a reference. 'Neat graphics,' he commented. 'Your own program?'

Neville agreed modestly that it was.

'When you say "eternal life",' said the evangelist, closing the file, 'you mean you're equating the born-again experience with the big dollars?'

'I thought the two could go together, yes.'

'Ah like it,' said Bilt. 'Chylblayne honey, do you like it?'

'Ah think we, uh, ought to give Neville the opportunity to explain it to us in his own way,' said Mrs Bilt, catching her husband's eye. 'Ah'd like to hear it.'

'Okay with you, Neville?'

'Oh, fine, check. Well, the concept is to pyramidize the work of the UWR triple C, basically. You take, say, five reliable people – we call them Redeemers – and each one forms round himself, or herself, a group of six others, and at this stage I'd say let these groups, these five groups of seven, have a sub-text, which in our case is, well, Bible study, or prayer, or . . .'

'Fellowship,' said Bilt.

'Right! Great label. Okay. Now the Redeemer in each group must choose two of the others to be Penitents, right, leaving the other four as Sinners. I'd suggest some simple test of Faith to expedite this process. Now, each member of the group puts in – well, let's say ten pounds, to keep it simple in our example – that makes seventy pounds in all, which is divided up as thirty pounds for the Redeemer and twenty each for the Penitents, leaving the Sinners all ten pounds down, for the moment.'

'You'll like this bit, honey,' said Bilt. 'Go on, mah frayund.'

'Okay. Well, now is the time for the two Redeemers to declare themselves – you know, their Faith, er – to come out – '

Bilt frowned. 'Ah don't think we'll use that, uh, expression, Neville, you know? We prefer to say "Born Again".'

'Oh, right. Anyway, this is where the Redeemer comes in again: he – or she – tests the Penitents, they, er – '

'Let Jesus into their hearts,' Bilt prompted.

'Walk with the Lord,' said Chylblayne.

'Oh, nice, right. And then become Redeemers themselves, you see? Each one going off to start a new group – another Rocket – with two of the original four sinners as Penitents, each having to find two others, two new Sinners, to bring his group up to strength.'

'So you get two new groups, you see, honey? Each group of Sincere Seekers goes on to bring two new groups to Jesus.'

'Praise the Lord!' said Chylblayne absent-mindedly. 'But hey, Neville, these new Penitents. Ah mean aside from findin' Jesus, they're just gonna break even, aren't they?'

'Oh, right, yes, but then they stand to collect when they become Redeemers. Of course, they can always up the premium first, if they're really motivated. I mean, er, if they've truly let Jesus in, that'll motivate others, won't it? Their Faith.'

'Oh, right,' said Chylblayne. 'What happens to Redeemers afterwards?'

'Up to them,' said Neville. 'As First Division Believers you'd expect them to be up to finding six new Sinners to launch a new Rocket. Think of the dividend.'

'Three hunnerd per cent on each deal?' hazarded the evangelist's wife.

'Two,' Neville corrected. 'Being a full-time Redeemer for the UWR triple C, you wouldn't grudge a third of your gross for the Lord, would you?'

'Well, now Ah –'

'Tax-deductible?'

'Assuredly not!'

'Neat, eh, honey?'

'Ah'll amen that, sugar,' said Chylblayne.

'Earn-as-you-save, you see,' said Neville. 'And frankly, I think we're looking at a Redeemers' market on this one, given the sure-fire cash incentive.'

'Let us thank the Lord Jesus Christ,' Bilt intoned, 'in our hearts.'

'I'll go for that,' said Neville.

They prayed, thanking God that they, as baptismal market-makers, were not as other men – or, in Chylblayne's case, persons.

'Ah gottan inspiration back there, brethren!' Bilt's face was flushed. 'Right there in mah heart a message sorta flashed through, like it was mainlining from the Glorious Kingdom!'

'Praise be to God!' breathed Chylblayne.

'Great!' said Neville.

'Like this whole concept, Nev, it's for the kids, yeah? Like the Supreme Redeemer said, suffer the little children to, uh, like – '

'Do God's business, you mean?'

'Oh, mah Sweet Lord!' Bilt's ecstasy extended on each hand to Chylblayne's wrist and Neville's thigh. 'Neville, we are humbled by your Holy apprehension! You know what I am going to say?'

Neville smirked. 'Let it be declared before the Lord,' he foxed.

Chylblayne gasped.

'Amen!' said Bilt. 'Fawn and Hall, mah frayund, Fawn and Hall!'

Neville blinked, cleared his throat, played for time. 'Amen!' he said.

'A-mayun! Our beloved little ones, mah frayund, will bring the Good News to their little playfellows at their very own primary school! Mah inspiration tells me fifty, uh, pence would be acceptable in His sight.'

'Well, er – '

'Clyde,' said Chylblayne, leaning in to Neville and inhaling to superb effect, 'has a high strike-rate, prayer-wise.'

'Oh,' said Neville. 'Great!'

'Ah know!' said Bilt. He raised his hands, shot his cuffs and pressed his fingers to his temples. 'Ah know, mah frayund, what you are thinking. Gimme twenny-four hours and God's Will . . . will be done. Ah assure you. Aaaaaaah!' The evangelist's eyes fluttered shut.

His wife hunched her exquisitely sculpted shoulders and leaned in closer still. 'He's walking with the Lord,' she whispered, panting slightly. A sharp tongue flicked across her all-American teeth. She drew little circles with her finger on the back of Neville's hand. 'He is letting . . . Jesus . . . in!'

'Ah – ' Neville began.

'Sssh!' She stood up, bringing Neville with her, led him along the passage and backed him against the front door. She took his hand in both of hers and looked at it.

'Clyde says you're divine,' she informed it. Neville concocted a suitable smile. 'I'm not divine,' she continued, 'being a woman.' She drew his hand up to face level. 'But Ah am fervent!' Her hugely perfect saucer eyes met his little piggy ones. The afternoon mail shot out between Neville's legs and fell suggestively to the floor. They ignored it.

Neville made a little noise in his throat. '. . . fervent?' he said.

'Yeah, fervent. In heah!' She pressed his hand to her heart, or near enough. The action brought their faces closer. 'Ah'm told,' she breathed, 'Ah have the gift of tongues. Mmmnlmnflmnll,' she added, demonstrating it.

Neville nearly fell over when she stopped. She skipped away and flounced demurely back along the passage. 'Clyde takes our dear ones to the studios Fridays,' she said. 'Straight after school's out. To record *Family Togetherness Hour* for the HI! station.'

'Oh?' said Neville. 'Ah. Does that . . . take long?'

'Depends,' said Mrs Bilt, tossing her hair and looking at him sideways. 'Sometimes they stay over, you know? Sometimes they don't.'

'Oh,' said Neville.

'Clyde always rings at eight,' she added. 'To let me know.'

'Ah,' said Neville. 'Right.'

She frowned. 'We live in the sight of the Lord, Neville.'

'Oh? Oh, yes. Oh.'

'So that kinda saves *others* looking, y'know?'

'Oh!' said Neville. 'Check!'

Chapter Seven

Aeneas Meiklejohn, BSc, Dip Pharm, independent retail chemist and sundriesman, was having a terrible morning. He had overslept, waking foozily and feeling every day of his age. Young Miss Huxtry, his assistant, had been late – again – arriving at the shop door, her rain-defying thermoplastic coiffure synthetically immaculate, as always, just as he, his bowtie askew, his shirt buttoned on the wrong holes, his laces undone and his goatee uncombed, was stumbling blearily through the rear entrance to the private apartments above.

'Oh good,' she had said, swaggering through to the staff powder-room, 'I'm not late after all, then.'

Peering round the right breast of the cardboard Kodacolor Girl, he had seen the pavement outside devoid of impatient custom. Ah, where were the queues of yesteryear! Straightening painfully he had felt suddenly dizzy and had knocked the gorgeous creature over; stooping to pick her up he had got his foot caught in one half of his trailing tri-coloured braces and had fallen forward, sprawling and struggling, his hands clutching her unyielding shoulders, his feet flailing to free themselves from entanglement. He had hauled himself, grunting and panting, to his knees and caught the reflection of Miss Huxtry, her face a mask of continent derision, in the security mirror above the door. It seemed to him to bespeak rather less of human warmth than did the inane rictus of the Kodacolor Girl.

'I shall be, ahem,' he'd said, fiddling with the loops in his shirt front, 'if anyone wants me,' and bolted.

He'd had time to wash, shave, brush, comb, powder, polish, button and lace, and was nearly through his nutritious morning bowl of sugary old rope before Miss Huxtry had occasion to require his services in the dispensary. He squinnied at the prescription, tilting it one way with his head cocked the other; making Dr Ghouleagh's writing run uphill this way seemed to slow it down a bit and make it slightly less indecipherable. Did the physician do it deliberately, he wondered, to plague his failing faculties? Not that Ghouleagh himself was getting any younger, of course. He shuddered. The thought of a revivified Ghouleagh did not bear contemplation. More tablets for Miss Pleat, it was; and what would she be needing *those* for at her age, and she a schoolteacher? He fussed himself into his pharmacist's bridals and checked his beard in the kitchen mirror for dietary fibre. Oh, that old Ghouleagh was an awful man, right enough. They should have taken him off the register when they had the chance; hadn't it been tax evasion that tripped up Al Capone, in the end?

Miss Pleat stood like a granite obelisk, grey and obdurate beside a carousel of depilatory accessories and ozone-friendly intimate anti-perspirants. What on earth, he asked himself, receiving no reply to his 'good morning' and thinking again of Ghouleagh's prescription, was going on inside that bodily carapace known to the world as Miss Pleat, the schoolmistress? He shuddered again. Thank goodness he'd bred no hostages for her to practise on. Had not the unspeakable Miss Huxtry been a star pupil, a Primary Dux, a Pleat Girl through and through? Perhaps old Ghouleagh had a point, after all.

He unlocked the dispensary door – finding the correct Yale key first time for once – switched on the light, sat down at his bench, assembled bottle, scales and funnel and selected the little key for the DD cupboard, so called

(as per regulations) in case, presumably, the pharmacist should ever suffer a brainstorm and forget which
one it was. He half rose, bracing his shrunk shanks
against the edge of the bench, and made to unlock it . . .
. . . And remained thus, like a costumed ape, his flesh
coldly drenched with sweat, his brain feverish, his lips
trembling, for fully ninety seconds.

'Guard the door, Simison,' said Sergeant MacEachran
after he'd persuaded Miss Pleat of her need to seek
chemical solace elsewhere.

'But it's raining,' said Constable Simison.

'I know,' said Sergeant MacEachran. 'It's been a terrible spring altogether, hasn't it?' He closed the door on his
associate, changed the sign to SORRY – CLOSED and
pulled down the blind. Then he walked through the shop,
taking great care not to touch anything except the floor,
and upstairs to the first-floor kitchen, where he found Mr
Meiklejohn and Miss Huxtry sitting at the table, one
looking shockingly dazed and vacuous, the other quite
normally so.

The former looked up as the sergeant came in, and
tried without much success to collect himself. 'A – a cup
of tea, Sergeant?' he said.

'Oh, aye, that would be very nice,' said the Sergeant.
Mr Meiklejohn began to get up; Sergeant MacEachran
laid a hand on his thin shoulder; Mr Meiklejohn started,
and made a little squeaking noise. 'Will I make it for us?'
said MacEachran. 'While we wait for the others to arrive.'

'Others?' piped Mr Meiklejohn.

'Oh aye, I'm afraid so.' The sergeant filled the kettle,
ran hot water in the teapot – an old line of Mrs Pitt-
Holyoake's, charmingly contrived in the form of a
thatched idyll – and swirled it slowly round, hugging the

pot to his ample trunk and gently swaying with it, his feet planted firmly apart, his serge buttocks spilling over the draining board. 'Drugs Squad. From Dunbroath, you see.'

'Oh,' said Mr Meiklejohn.

'Aye,' said Sergeant MacEachran. 'Ah, there we are, now! One each and one for the pot, is it? There now, we'll just let it draw. Now then, Mr Meiklejohn.' He produced a very small black notebook from a very large pocket, removed its pencil – despite himself, Mr Meiklejohn was fascinated to see if the sergeant would lick it, like the policeman always did in Act One, Scene Three of Craigfieth Arts Club productions, but he didn't – and located a page free of parking offences, bicycles without lights and vexatious urinations.

'Now, then. You locked up last night, when?'

'Well, erm, not last night, Sergeant.'

'Oh?'

'Early closing. I shut the shop at one, er, tidied up a bit, you know, and left it at, well, by half past, anyway.'

'Half past one?'

'Y-yes.' The sergeant wrote that down. 'And the locking, Mr Meiklejohn, what does that involve?'

'I beg your pardon?'

'Which doors – what locks – that sort of thing.'

'Oh, yes I see. Well, the shop door, of course – that's a Yale lock and a, a whatd'yecallit, a mortice, and two bolts, and the dispensary door, another Yale, and this one here' – he indicated a door leading to a raised patio and the back garden – 'that I use to come and go, that's a Yale too.'

'And the back door? Downstairs, I mean, to the storeroom?'

'Oh, a big lock, you know – key like this.' Mr Meiklejohn held up two fingers six inches apart. 'From the

199

inside, which is always locked because of draughts. I never use it, to go out I mean.'

'Aye, I see. And did you?'

'Did I what?'

'Go out, Mr Meiklejohn. Milk and sugar? No? Miss Huxtry?' He sighed heavily. 'I have to manage with these.' He produced a little tube of sweeteners. 'They're horrible,' he added, dropping two in his cup. 'But that's the way it goes, eh?' He patted the dark blue expanse between his rib cage and his pelvis. 'Got to watch the waist. There we are, now. Did you go out, Mr Meiklejohn?'

'Oh no,' said the pharmacist. 'No, I was in all afternoon and evening. I – ' He broke off; there were reasons why he couldn't add, 'I have witnesses'. He changed it to, 'I can assure you of that,' instead. 'And I went to bed straight after – I mean, very early, about nine o'clock. Straight after my evening meal.'

'I always get indigestion if I do that,' Sergeant MacEachran complained. 'What would you suggest, Mr Meiklejohn?'

'Pardon?'

'For the heartburn.'

'Oh I see, well, er, there are of course a number of proprietary brands available, Sergeant, all more or less variations on the same basic antacid formula. I always use bicarbonate of soda myself, followed by a glass of milk – when I get it, of course. Which I don't . . . er, very much that is. And certainly not last night.'

'Ah,' said the sergeant. 'I expect it's more a question of diet, really. Myself, I can't resist the cheese on toast, I'm afraid.'

'Ah,' said Mr Meiklejohn. 'Oh. Er . . .'

'What's your secret then, eh?'

Mr Meiklejohn jumped. 'Eh? Wh-wha . . . er, secret?'

MacEachran's face was a picture of tuberous guilelessness. 'For the sweet repose,' he said. 'I mean, for instance, what were you after having yourself, last night?'

'Oh! I er, yes I . . . er.' The pharmacist rolled a frantic eyeball round the kitchen until it lit on a bowl and spoon by the sink. 'Muesli!' he said.

MacEachran nodded slowly, meaningly. 'Ah,' he said.

Mr Meiklejohn gulped and squawked.

'It's what my wife's always telling me I should have,' the sergeant continued. 'Last thing, if I'm peckish. Well, well. My, my.' He shook his head wonderingly. 'Muesli! Tt-tt. Fancy that, eh?'

The wretched Meiklejohn broke out in a grey guilty sweat, his bowels frozen and uneasy. He was also considerably annoyed, in the first place because this investigation, by a deliberately dull-witted sergeant intent on discussing his digestive disorders, of the theft of a whole cabinet full of expensively lethal substances, smacked too much of the Craigfieth Arts Club to be tolerable; secondly because, even as he felt another damning trickle slide down his spine, he knew himself to be telling the truth, or at any rate all the truth that really mattered. He *had* gone to bed at nine o'clock; the reference to an evening meal had simply been a conversational device to . . . well, to fix, to account for it, in case anyone should think it peculiarly early. He'd been feeling tired, that was all – he had things on his mind, that was probably it – too tired, in fact, to eat anything at all. He just hadn't been feeling hungry, and that was that. And now here he was, caught up in a ludicrous discussion with a policeman about eating muesli at night when what he should be doing was . . .

'Eh? I, er, beg pardon, Sergeant?'

'I was after saying, Mr Meiklejohn, you heard nothing in the night, then? No suspicious noise of any kind?'

'No, no, nothing at all, Sergeant, nothing at all.' Which

was true. 'And I'm a very light sleeper,' he said, which was true, too. 'Always,' he added, which wasn't.

'Except this morning,' Miss Huxtry cut in acidly.

'Eh?' Mr Meiklejohn felt a fresh Niagara break out between his shoulder blades.

'Except this morning, Mr Meiklejohn. You overslept. Your clothing was disarranged.' She primped her lips in the manner recommended by Miss Pleat for such examples of gross moral turpitude. 'And you hadn't combed your beard,' she added spitefully. She favoured Sergeant MacEachran with a gaze of marbled frankness. 'It was all sticking out sideways,' she said.

'Ah, well, yes, I, erm,' mumbled Mr Meiklejohn. 'Hardly ever.'

Sergeant MacEachran was sympathetic. 'It's these dark mornings,' he said. 'Hardly worth getting up for, as you might say. It's always the way, the first few weeks after the clocks change.'

'Ah, er, I –'

'Now as to the actual theft.' The sergeant changed inquisitorial gear abruptly, launching himself clear of the sink and advancing ponderously on Mr Meiklejohn. 'What exactly was, er . . .?'

'The cabinet,' said Mr Meiklejohn.

'Aye, fine that. But what was taken exactly?'

'The cabinet,' said Mr Meiklejohn.

'The . . . whole –'

'The cabinet,' said Mr Meiklejohn. 'It was padlocked, of course,' he added.

'The cabinet,' said Sergeant MacEachran levelly, 'was padlocked.'

'Yes.'

'A *dhuine*!' exclaimed the sergeant. 'My goodness,' he translated.

'Ah,' said Mr Meiklejohn. 'Yes.'

MacEachran scribbled copiously, though not furiously.

'About three foot six,' said Mr Meiklejohn, anticipating the next question, 'by two foot, roughly. Grey, metal. With DD on. One D on each door, that is. In red.'

'D . . . D,' the sergeant muttered, writing it down in black.

'Yes. For "Dangerous Drugs", you see.' The pharmacist coughed. 'Regulations. I, er . . .' MacEachran looked up. 'I keep it, ahem! on, that is, above, my bench. On a very strong and, er, secure . . . shelf.'

'Shelf,' said Sergeant MacEachran.

'Yes,' said Mr Meiklejohn.

'I see,' said Sergeant MacEachran.

'Not thinking, you see, that . . .'

'No. Of course not.'

Miss Huxtry sniffed. Sergeant MacEachran wrote it down.

'I really don't understand it at all,' said Mr Meiklejohn miserably.

'You mean with the doors being locked. And no windows in the dispensary. And yourself not hearing anything.' Mr Meiklejohn nodded. 'You have a burglar alarum, I see.'

The pharmacist leaped gratefully to his feet and drew MacEachran's attention, conjuror-like, to a cupboard on the wall. 'Two,' he said. 'One on this door, one for the shop, both being controlled by a switch' – he opened the cupboard, removed three packets of cereal and stood aside – 'here.'

'Very good,' said Sergeant MacEachran. 'And you'll have switched that off yourself this morning, will you?'

Mr Meiklejohn looked at the policeman, then at the switch, and felt his sweat suddenly evaporate. 'I always do,' he heard himself say.

'And your keys were . . .'

'Oh, yes! As always.' Mr Meiklejohn felt his feet touch bottom again and managed his first smile of the day.

Sergeant MacEachran took careful note of the little wooden plaque on the back of the cupboard door. 'KEYS', it said helpfully, above a plastic hook; below, 'A   NT FROM   FIETH'. Mr Meiklejohn matched his keys to the worn semicircle where the missing letters weren't. The sergeant nodded.

'It would have gone off if he hadn't,' said Miss Huxtry. 'When I came in.' Her employer smiled again. 'Will I be paid for the time the shop's kept closed?'

The smile vanished. 'That, erm, dep – '

'Ah!' boomed the sergeant. 'This sounds like my colleagues from Dunbroath. I'll just fill them in on what you've told me, Mr Meiklejohn, though I don't suppose it'll save you having to go through it all again, I'm afraid. If you'll just' – Miss Huxtry had made to leave – 'wait here for them.'

The assistant rolled her eyes to the ceiling, pouted, and glared accusingly at Mr Meiklejohn. Mr Meiklejohn, however, was staring at the cereal cupboard, so she stopped glaring and sniffed instead. Finding even this had no effect, she decided to hand in her notice. Neville was right, she told herself. It was time to move on.

Besides, there was nothing to keep her here now.

Downstairs, MacEachran made a quick survey of the five young Drugs Squad detectives and addressed himself to the most pubescent-looking.

'Sergeant MacEachran, sir,' he murmured.

'DI Snow,' said Detective Inspector Snow, disdaining to risk his hand in the sergeant's paw and nodding instead to his colleagues. 'DS Crack. DCs Horse, Speedie and Grass. Show.'

'Eh?' said Sergeant MacEachran. 'Oh aye, sir. *Seo*.' He handed Snow his notebook.

'Yes – yes – yes – yes,' said Snow, once for each page. 'Check.' He gave it back.

'A, hrm, a real "locked room mystery", eh, sir?' ventured MacEachran. Crack and Horse stuck their jaws out at him.

'You think so, do you, Sergeant?'

'No, sir,' said MacEachran. 'Of course not.'

'Good,' said Snow.

'Will I, erm – '

'Yes,' said Snow.

'Sir,' said MacEachran.

The five plain-clothes men went upstairs to give Mr Meiklejohn a bad time. MacEachran sighed to himself and ushered Simison into the car. Craigfieth's community constable was looking, as MacEachran put it, 'pooksie'.

'I'm older than they are,' explained Constable Simison.

MacEachran spread his legs and adjusted the crotch of his trousers. 'Aye,' he sighed comfortably. 'So am I.'

Simison looked pooksier still. 'What d'ye reckon, then?' he asked.

'We-ell,' said MacEachran, taking a packet of jelly babies from the glove-box. 'I should say there's no law that I know of against eating muesli two meals running.' He found a black one. 'He had some on his beard,' he added.

'Oh,' said Simison. 'Right. What?'

MacEachran explained.

'I see,' said Simison.

'What you might call a three jelly-baby problem, my dear Simison,' said the sergeant, popping in a fourth. 'Or wouldn't you?'

'Should we no' tell' – the constable jerked his head shopwards – 'yon Thunderbirds clones in there?'

MacEachran shook his head. 'We're not detectives,' he reasoned. 'Besides, it's a free country, isn't it?'

Simison declined to answer.

'Aye,' agreed MacEachran. 'Still, ours not to reason why, eh? Ours but to do the house-to-house enquiries.'

Simison ground his teeth and pouted gloomily.

'Ach, away, man!' MacEachran comforted. 'What other job do you know of that lets you spend all day having elevenses *and* getting paid for it? Let's see now.' He considered the task ahead. 'I'm thinking we'd better start at the manse.'

'Aw, c'mon, Sarge! That's half a mile away, they won't have – '

'Jessie MacAndrew's baking,' said his superior firmly, 'always makes a very good foundation, in my experience.'

It turned out a long and trying day, that Friday, for some.

For Darren Pocks, manager of MegaMessages, the disappearance of his entire stock of fresh fruit and vegetables (turnips and cabbages excepted) threatened at one stage to spell the end of a promising career in massmarket retailing. Yet what else, he asked himself helplessly as he watched the motley convoy depart, could he have done, except agree with the piratical-looking one in the terrible tartan hat that one person's credit card was as good as another's, and that there was no notice on display limiting purchases in the Green'n'Goodly section to so many kilos, or even tonnes, per person? How was he to know that a delivery normally sufficient to satisfy both the Late Night Crush and the Saturday Scrum – and still leave enough over for the Monday Morning Dribble – should on this occasion be completely exhausted by half past four on Friday afternoon? How could he, in this day and age (he asked himself) say 'no' to a one-legged old man in a wheelchair? Regional management would tear him to pieces for that!

Instead of which, he told himself as he surveyed the

pillaged emptiness of Green'n'Goodly, they're going to tear you to pieces for *this* . . .

But for Darren Pocks – who was, after all, a good enough citizen, in his way, having never knowingly disobeyed a rule, exceeded a limit, or broken a heart – help was at hand. For MegaMessages is but one island in that great archipelago of commerce known as ShoppingLand, Scotland's Premier Consumer Village, and news travels fast in villages. By half past five a two-mile queue of cars had built up in the motorway approaches to the ShoppingLand exit, their occupants determined not to suffer as a consequence of the latest rumoured shortage. Half an hour later there was not a leaf in any of the archipelago's many super-, hyper- or gargantuamarkets, save in MegaMessages alone, where the young Mr Pocks was offering a free cabbage or turnip with every purchase over twenty pounds and looking forward to receiving, once again, the ShoppingLand Manager of the Month Award.

Kevin Keechie, LLB, DipLP, on the other hand, was plunged in a despair made no more bearable by the knowledge that it was largely of his own making. Having disposed of that wretched woman, Holysmoke or whatever her name was (a sleek-suited brother lawyer at Broody's had warned him he might expect the odd irritating twitter from that quarter) he had cancelled all appointments (quite easy, this, as he hadn't got any) and plundered the archives of Drubber and Dunning in search of material for the career-enhancing case of Ochilree vs. A Lot Of Embarrassingly Important British Institutions.

The archives occupied a cellar – originally intended*

---

* See (for instance) *Neuks and Byeways of Auld Lummock*, Duncruddie, 1898.

for the concealment of Covenanters unaccountably unwilling to make the acquaintance of the Bonny Earl of Montrose – which ran the full width and depth of the Hope Street premises. Soon, it was planned, a Workfare Scheme would see the whole lot (with the exception of such deeds and titles as required to be preserved in their original holograph or probative form) put on computer tape; in the meantime the archives mouldered on in a variety of more-or-less unsuitable containers underneath the fashionably deformed feet of the firm's receptionist. Hither young Keechie besought himself, heedless of the dry-cleaning bill – which would count as professional expenses anyway – for his cob-webbed and mould-polluted suit.

After two or three timeless hours (at least three-quarters of one of them spent in an awed perusal of a farm boundary dispute that had been going on, by use and custom, since 1721) he found what he was looking for: a box file whose yellowed label (after it had flaked off and he had picked it up) bore the legend 'In Re Ochilree & Heritors: Boggybreck, Newbigging, &c'. The file fell to pieces as he opened it; inside, a bundle of stained papers and two ounces of rust were all that remained of its internal organization. He spread the lot out on the floor and searched through it, discarding first two substantial tranches of correspondence relating to the transfer of a mortgage on Newbiggings Farm from the Mid Lummock Husbandmen's Welfare Association to the original Messrs Drubber and Dunning, and to the farm's subsequent transfer from Mr Oswald Ochilree, its unburdened proprietor, to Mr Angus Ochilree, his sole heir. Then there were the actual deeds of Newbiggings, together with a certificate of final discharge of mortgage dated August 3lst, 1953; finally (and with reluctance) Mr Keechie laid aside a rather interesting-looking bundle of papers relating to a dispute between Mr Oswald Ochilree and three sucessive Ministers of Agriculture concerning the disappointing performance and questionable sexual proclivities of the Piper O' Dundee, an under-achieving Ministry bull. Some of the language used seemed, to Mr Keechie's modern mind, quite gratuitously candid.

This left a dingy brown envelope with a pencilled inscription just legible as the word 'B'breck'. Mr Keechie opened it. Inside was a single foolscap sheet with the words 'Conveyed to HMG/War Dept 8.8.23' and the initials 'WCD'.

It was then that Kevin Keechie made his big mistake. Every experienced lawyer in the possession of information which, if proved, might annihilate his client's case, knows that it is up to the opposition to do the proving; otherwise the law itself would surely be brought into disrepute and individual lawyers reduced to penury. Mr Keechie, however, was not an experienced lawyer. Instead of quietly replacing what he had found in the dusty obscurity in which he'd found it, he took the damning foolscap sheet, together with his photocopy of the late Mr Ochilree's lease, to the office of Mr Tozie, and showed it to him.

It seemed to Mr Keechie that his superior's gaze remained fixed on the documents long after he'd read them.

'Why,' asked Mr Tozie after an unconscionably long pause, 'do you bring me these?'

'To, er, to, to . . . ask your advice, Mr Tozie. There, um, seems to be a bit of a sort of dichotomy here, to me. Um,' said Mr Keechie. He could have sworn the partner's face relaxed when these words were out.

'Very good, Mr Keechie. I'll deal with this now. I'm sure you have a lot of things to be getting on with.'

'Well, actually – ' began Mr Keechie; then he registered

Mr Tozie's expression. 'Er, yes, actually,' he said. 'Thank you, Mr Tozie.' He shuffled doorways across Mr Tozie's broadloom prairie.

'Mr Keechie.'

'Y-yes, Mr Tozie?'

'You have done well, Mr Keechie. It shall not pass unremarked.'

'Thank you, Mr Tozie!'

I'll bet it bloody won't, he thought bitterly as he returned to his broom cupboard; even a fat cat like you couldn't fail to remark on one and a half per cent of a bloody gold mine. 'Fool!' he wailed to his four claustrophobic walls. An eternity of legal aid certificates seemed to stretch out before him. He could have wept, had such a thing been permissible.

Detectives Snow, Crack, Horse, Speedie and Grass left Aeneas Meiklejohn a broken man, doubting his ability to carry on (single-handed, thanks to Miss Huxtry's resignation 'for moral reasons') a retail pharmacy business, even if they had allowed him to re-open it, which they hadn't.

'Further investigations,' they said.

'For how long?' he'd asked.

'For as long as it takes, chummy,' Snow had replied, his expression allowing the words 'to catch you out' to remain unspoken.

They had searched every room for clues, dusted every surface for fingerprints, looked (it seemed to him) into his very soul for the damning evidence that would lead to his conviction and sentence for the theft and reset of drugs specified on a list supplied by him and of certain other items found, to his intense embarrassment, to be missing from the shop after he'd spent a gruelling two hours compiling an inventory for checking against his records.

Fury-like their questions returned to haunt him as he

sat that evening at his dusty kitchen table: had he locked this, secured that, switched on, switched off, checked, rechecked and checked again? Yes, of course he had!. . . hadn't he? Aeneas Meiklejohn did not, in truth, rightly know; but then he didn't rightly know anything, any more. Outnumbered five to one (six, counting Miss Huxtry) he began to suspect himself. It seemed, after all, to be the likeliest explanation, and who was he (or, more to the point, who would he be when the case of Regina vs. Meiklejohn came on) to fly in the face of all the evidence, or evidential lack of it?

He groaned, sending little devils of fingerprint powder swirling across the table and on to the floor.

Yet he hadn't given in: no, not though it might have strengthened the case for the defence. 'A matter of business confidence,' they'd said, 'crucial to the outcome.' Mr Meiklejohn had understood only too clearly what that meant. It meant that a most acceptable offer – cash – for his ailing business and its notional goodwill would vanish like midsummer snow should he so much as breathe a hint of it abroad. And so he had kept silent, had willed himself not to tell how he had conducted two potential buyers' agents round the premises at seven o'clock, and seen everything secure; how he had checked again after one of the two had let himself out at eight; how he had rechecked (despite an almost overwhelming weariness) an hour later, when the other took his leave.

He had kept mum; had – what was the phrase again? Oh yes – had protected his interests. Yes, that was what they'd said.

Besides, it wouldn't do just now, if his fellow-townsfolk knew he was about to deal with Clinch McKittrick. He'd have more local standing as a convict. And he'd still have the capital when he came out . . . wouldn't he? Or did the seizure of drugs-related assets extend to the proceeds of sale of a high street chemist's, these days?

He groaned again, throwing Sergeant MacEachran's left handprint into stark relief on the table top.

The owner of the handprint completed his house-to-house enquiries in Grace's kitchen just as the raiding party returned, gleeful and heavily laden, from its sortie to MegaMessages.

'Evenin' all,' said Ganglion, saluting. 'Fancy givin' us an 'and unloadin' a few tons of fruit'n'veg, officer?'

Sergeant MacEachran hastily crammed in a last morsel of shortbread and gulped his tea. Constable Simison put away his notebook.

'I'm afraid not,' he replied fuzzily. 'Catriona'll be getting my tea. Thank you very much for all your help,' he added, scooping up his cap and turning to Grace and Hamish.

'I'm sorry we couldn't really tell you anything,' said Grace. 'We always sleep very heavily, don't we, Hamish?'

'Ach, well, that can't be helped.' The sergeant bent over Wally's highchair and tickled his cheek with a blunt forefinger which he quickly withdrew before the infant incisors could meet it.

'Unk,' said Wally, making do with second best.

'Not to worry, madam,' said Constable Simison. 'Very often the absence of unusual activity can be a useful indication in itself.'

'The things they teach them nowadays, eh?' grumbled his superior officer.

Ashley Oswald ran to the top of the stairs. 'I'll see them out, Mam,' he called. Grace made a what-do-you-do-with-them gesture.

The sergeant smiled solemnly. 'That's quite all right,

my dear,' he said. 'He asked to see our IDs when he let us in.'

Grace blushed. Hamish said, 'I blame the television, myself.'

'Makes a change from blamin' me,' muttered Ashley Oswald's grandfather.

'Not at all,' said the sergeant. 'Goodness knows it's a sensible enough precaution, these days.' The two policemen negotiated their way tactfully round Wally's chair and left.

But Ashley Oswald did not show them to the front door; instead he motioned them to silence, and led them down the passage to the back of the shop. There he perched on a sack of potatoes and cleared his throat.

'I wish to make a statement,' he said.

The constable began to expostulate; the sergeant stopped him with a subtle tap from the heel of a size eleven boot. 'Do you want your mam and dad here before you make it, son?' he asked gently.

Ashley Oswald shook his head vigorously. 'No!' he whispered. 'It's a, sort of a, secret statement.'

'Oh.' Sergeant MacEachran nodded slowly. 'One of those. I see. On ye go, then.'

'There was a – an unusual activity in the middle of the night,' said the boy.

'Oh?' said Constable Simison. 'And what would you be up to at that time of day then, eh?'

Ashley Oswald looked puzzled. 'It wasn't day,' he objected. 'It was the middle of the night. I needed the bathroom but my watch had stopped but I know it was after midnight because I had to use my torch.'

'Aw, fer – '

'Ah, yes,' cut in the sergeant. 'The street lights were out, then?'

The boy nodded.

'Very good! You're a fine detective. And you noticed something, did you?'

'Yes,' said Ashley Oswald. 'A Ford Siesta GT Turbo Hacienda Special with stripes and low profile tyres, registration K519 MUL.'

'Goodness!' said the sergeant. 'Make a note of that, Constable. And what about the driver, son. What like was he?'

'I don't ken,' said Ashley Oswald. 'It was too dark to see anything.'

'Aww!' Constable Simison stuffed the notebook back in his pocket and glared at the witness. 'So in that case you couldn't have seen the *car* then, could you?'

'No,' said Ashley Oswald.

'So,' said Simison heavily, 'in that case, sonny, you've been wasting our time, haven't you? And wasting police time, young man, is a very – serious – offence.' He emphasized the last three words with a prodding finger; at the age of fifteen the constable had nursed ambitions to become a teacher before being dissuaded by a comparison of the salary structures. Policing's loss had been education's gain.

'Thank you, Constable,' said MacEachran. He stared at Simison's finger until it wilted. 'Is that true, son? You *didn't* see anything?'

Ashley Oswald shook his head. 'No, it was too dark. I heard it.'

'You – heard – a . . .'

'A Ford Siesta GT Turbo Hacienda Special,' the boy repeated, 'with low –'

'I got all that, thank you,' said Simison nastily. His feet were hurting and he was missing *Neighbours*.

'Aye, but,' began the sergeant. 'I mean, how d'ye *know* that's what you heard? Had you seen it before?'

'Oh yes, loads of times,' Ashley Oswald assured him.

'Well, at least three. Me an' Tammy Spr – ' He blushed. 'I mean, I can tell just by listening, honestly. An' I spot car numbers, so I looked it up after.' A car door slammed in the street outside.

'Wheesht, now,' said MacEachran. 'Tell us what this one is, then.' They waited for the noise of the engine; when it came the boy grinned broadly.

'That's easy! It's the minister's Metro. It sounds like a canful of midges with a bad cough.'

MacEachran peered round the store-room door and through the shop window. 'My, my,' he said. 'And you say you've seen this, this Ford Fandango or whatever, about the town before? And did you notice the driver then?'

Ashley Oswald stared at his feet. 'Not really,' he mumbled.

'Ah well, not to worry. You've given us some very useful information, sir. Hasn't he, Constable?'

'Eh?' said Simison. 'Oh, yeah, I s'pose. I mean aye, sure.'

'Aye,' said MacEachran, ruffling the boy's hair and turning to leave.

'And there was two of them,' said Ashley Oswald. Simison stiffened. 'Two car doors went bang,' the boy explained.

'Well?' asked Simison in the car. 'Are we going to pass that on to the Drugs Squad, then?'

'No,' said MacEachran.

'Ah,' Simison sneered knowingly. 'Useless then, as I thought.'

'No,' said MacEachran. 'If I'm late for my tea,' he added, 'I shall tell Catriona to blame you.' The constable scowled and turned the key.

Inside the Scottish Produce Centre store-room Ashley Oswald listened, then frowned, then thought. Then his

215

face cleared. It *was* the police car, all right. That funny scratchy noise would be the starter motor about to pack up.

Neville and Miss Huxtry switched off *Neighbours* and checked out their Manual of Stable Relationships. Five point four eight minutes later they recorded their response quotients (in pencil) in the space provided and studied the results.

Neville whistled softly. 'Is that an unbalanced plateau reading,' he asked, 'or what?'

'Mmyes,' his paramour agreed. 'There! Look, I knew you were doing that part wrong. It should have been second and third fingers, look, not first and second.'

'Hmmm,' Neville agreed dispassionately. 'Different frictive coefficient, then.'

'Mmyes.' Miss Huxtry regarded her left nipple. 'It's quite sore actually.'

'Which would raise the libido threshold, then, from your point of view.'

'From my point of view, yes.'

'Mmm.'

'Mmm.'

'Did you have the balls of your feet together throughout?'

'Does it say that, "throughout"?'

'Yup.' Neville pointed to the relevant diagram. 'Here.'

'Oh, yes. Sorry, I thought that was a clenching aid for the climacteric.'

'Oh, right, no, that was that other one, remember, number twenty-eight.'

'Mmyes. I remember now. Never mind. We have got the rest of our lives, after all.' She slid out of the bed and put on her dressing-gown. 'I'm going to shower, okay? Mind the sheets, Neville.'

'Oh,' said Neville. 'Wanna take it off, then, or what?'

'Does it say afterplay for this one? I didn't think it did.'

'Oh, er, wait a minute – no, no it doesn't. Not compulsory, anyway.'

'There you are, then,' Miss Huxtry pointed out. 'Time *is* money, Neville.'

'One down,' said Neville, holding it up for examination, 'one hundred and forty-three to go. Roughly a year's worth, if we stick to the book.'

Miss Huxtry drew the shower curtain. 'I don't know what you mean by "if", Neville,' she called over the noise of the water.

'Yeah, but, contingencies,' Neville objected. 'Like, what about your interview with Kirk next week?'

'Oh, I've got some for that sort of thing! I took that big box just for us. We agreed to keep things like that separate, remember?'

'Oh, right, check. Career moves one thing, relationships another. Might as well use different brands, save confusion. Mind if I join you?'

'Better not,' said Miss Huxtry. 'It might have unwanted results. Remember what the book says about deferred spontaneity being one of the Five Keys. Besides, I've finished.' She emerged wrapped in a large white towel. 'You can have one now, if you like.'

'No, it's all right,' said Neville. 'Did you tell Meiklejohn you were taking them as your staff bonus?'

'Why should I? I should have thought it was up to him to ask.'

'Oh, right, I just . . . Hey!' Neville signalled amusement. 'I wonder if the police are out looking for a drug thief with a hundred and forty-four wiggly-wogglies?'

Miss Huxtry frowned. 'That would be silly,' she said. 'By the way, Neville, I want to go on using them after we're married. It's safer than the pill, health-wise, we'll both still be needing them, career-wise, and anyway I think it's more natural, all right?'

'Oh, right, check. Makes sense to me.'

'Yes. And Neville – don't look, please, I'm going to dress – Neville, I need to be sure it was all right, what I did at Meiklejohn's. You know?'

'"All right" – what, you mean morally? Yeah, of course; you did what the man paid you for, didn't you? Preparing the ground?'

'I didn't mean that. I meant being associated with what happened last night – Operation Aspirin.'

'No chance. And anyway, all the stuff's been disposed of safely so the whole thing'll fizzle out after a few days. Except for Meiklejohn of course.' He laughed. 'Bet he's still wondering what it was in his coffee made him so sleepy. Anyway, he'll be out of our way pretty soon. It's no different from what I'm doing with the videos, after all. Can I turn round now?'

'Yes, if you want. Has anything happened yet, with the videos?'

'Not yet. But it will very soon. And when it does it won't be my signature on the invoices, okay? Any more than it was you putting sleeping pills in Meiklejohn's coffee last night or hiding in his staff toilet waiting till he'd gone to bed. So stop worrying. We're just enablers, that's all.' She allowed him a chaste kiss.

'For the time being,' he added.

'That's all right, then,' said Miss Huxtry. 'You out tonight?'

'Oh . . . yes. Yes, actually. Possible career move, in fact, meant to tell you.'

'Oh, right, brill, tell me afterwards . . . you won't take ours, though, will you, Neville? I do want them to last.'

'Oh, no, right. Actually I don't think I'll be needing any.'

'What do you mean, Neville?'

'Oh, right, no, it's okay. I mean, I think they'll be provided.'

'Oh, Neville!' Miss Huxtry regarded her fiancé with undisguised admiration. 'Go for it, darling!'

'I will,' said Neville. 'Don't worry. I won't blow it.'

Sergeant MacEachran's return call from the Driver and Vehicle Licensing Centre interrupted his second helping of rhubarb crumble and left him thoughtful.

'And what,' he asked his wife, 'do you suppose Mr Andreas Laagerlaut would be up to in the back lane of Craigfieth High Street in the wee small hours of this morning?'

'That would depend who he was,' Catriona replied sensibly.

'Indeed,' said the sergeant, who knew his wife's methods. 'An Honorary Consul of the Republic of Bophuthatswana,' he read from his notebook. 'Among other things, no doubt.'

'Maybe he was trying to organize a rugby tour.'

'Aye, possibly. He'd need good tyres for that, would he not? Perhaps we'd better check them, just in case.'

Catriona started to clear the table. 'I hope you're not going to start a diplomatic incident, Donald,' she said. 'I don't want you getting promoted just when I've got the house nice.'

'Ach, well,' her husband replied, rescuing his pudding before it disappeared into the compost bucket. 'I dare say I shall be the soul of diplomacy, Catriona *ma gaoilean*. Am I not always?' He relinquished the empty bowl. 'Grace Ganglion's expecting again, a wee girl, did you know?'

'Away, Donald!'

'She is so! Pink baby wool in her shopping basket, *and* she hid it when Hamish came in. Mind you met her at the surgery the other day: old Ghouleagh's probably told her it's twin boys. Is there any cheese in the fridge, Catriona?'

'Well, it's pretty much as we thought,' said Mungo, flicking open his Co-op Big Value Reporter's Notebook and being generous with his choice of personal pronoun. 'Or to put it another way: forget Clinch McKittrick.'

'Huh!' said Hamish. 'Fat chance. Wait till they flood *your* airing cupboard.'

'Ah, well, that's different,' reasoned Mungo, who'd never had one. 'What I mean is,' he continued, before his friend could berate him with more outraged domesticity, 'they don't figure as the big boys in this operation at all; like Audrey here was telling you last night, they're just the winklers.'

No one seemed inclined to oblige him with the obvious flattering question, so he carried on anyway. 'Winkling out, you see. Getting rid, one way or another, of any inconvenient owners or tenants who might get in the way of the developers, greasing a few palms here, kicking a few shins there, that sort of thing. And then disappearing, of course.'

'They haven't greased our palms,' Hamish complained.

'That's because you're not palm-greasing material, pal. You have to be a councillor or a planning official for that sort of thing. Or get yourself a nice job at the Scottish Office – you'd qualify for a whole body massage then, I shouldn't wonder. Meanwhile, as far as they're concerned, the family firm of H and G Ganglion is simply two pairs of shins just asking to be hacked to pieces.'

'Yes but then why don't they just offer to buy us out?'

Grace asked. 'Like they did Mrs Quaich, or the Cummingses?'

'Or the MacTavishes,' Mungo replied, 'or the Gordons, or the Grahams, or the Calderwoods, or the Blacks, heirs of the late Miss Thomasina Pitcairn?' He grinned at his audience of gaping mouths. 'Told you I'd been busy, didn't I? And although I can't prove it was Clinch McKittrick behind all of them I've got a pretty good idea – but I'll explain that in a minute. To answer your question, Grace: are you over seventy years of age? No? Or about to be made redundant in your job? No, of course you aren't! Or dead? Right, that's why. You're young, fit and thriving, with no particular desire to sell up and move. Yet.'

Hamish spoke. 'You're not . . .' He shrugged helplessly, unable to cope with his careering train of thought. 'Are you?'

'Listen: let's take a situation that's happened so many times in real life people don't take it seriously any more when they see it in plays on the telly, right? Let's pretend you're sitting tenants in some crumbly old tenement your wicked landlord wants to flog to an oil sheikh who's looking for a nice cheap site for an office block, okay? Only he can't force you to leave, because the law won't let him, and you don't want to leave because you're comfy where you are and all your friends and family live just down the road, blahblahblah and all that. So, remembering this is a play on the telly, what does your wicked landlord do? Answer: first he's terribly sorry but "his workmen" are just that wee bit too busy just at the moment to see to your leaky roof, damp bedroom, blocked drain, whatever. Then, maybe, said workmen do come round, only woops-a-daisy and fancy that, they go and stick a chisel through your rising main while they're testing the wall for dampness, or they smash the drains to

221

bits trying to unblock them, or they find the only way they can get at the roof is by removing the staircase. Accidents will happen, after all. Meanwhile your landlord gets chatting to this man in a pub – zoom in on landlord's meaningful look, cue sinister music on synthesizer – about these snivelling little scumbags who're standing between him and his rightful share of Britain's economic upswing; if only, he says, getting another round in and shooting meaningful glances all over the place, if only something would happen that might persuade them to see sense, only of course it's not legal, more's the pity, cos if it was, as God is his witness, it'd be worth a few grand of his money to make sure it did happen, not that he'd want to know anything about it, personally, even then . . . fade out pub scene and cue vandalized windows and petrol bombs through your letter-box, cue closing shot of you moving out and taking up residence in a cardboard-box, cue the BBC switchboard jammed with complaints about left-wing bias, end of play.

'Only,' he broke the ensuing silence, 'this isn't a play and you're not tenants, you're owner-occupiers and proprietors of nice little businesses that are humming along quite nicely, thank you very much, or at any rate nicely enough to take care of the mortgage and the housekeeping and your non-chronic illness medical insurance, and so on. Or were, until . . . dot, dot, dot.

'Put it this way,' he added. 'If you were to get an offer for your businesses in a few weeks' time, would you expect it to be more, or less, than you'd have expected a few weeks ago?'

'Less,' said Mrs Pitt-Holyoake, 'in my case, I don't mind admitting. But can you prove any connection?'

'In a word, no,' said Mungo. 'But don't you think it's a bit odd that of all the properties I looked up on the

Register of Sasines in beautiful downtown Edinburgh, not a single one, *not one*, seems to be owned by real people?'

'"Real people"?' said Grace. 'What do you mean, Mungo? Who does own them?'

Mungo flipped through his notebook. 'Eurocal Developments, Blacktrouser Properties, Albacorp, Intercontinental Estate Managers Incorporated, New Horizon Realty Factors and Sayeed Haq (Holdings).'

'Sayeed *Haq*?'

'Yeah, bit of a bonus there. Just for fun I looked up the old homestead, you know, my parents' council house in Logie Baird Avenue, and bingo, there he was, your friendly neighbourhood entrepreneur. According to the electoral register he's got eight voters living in it, too. All with different surnames. Makes you think, eh?'

'Yeah, but, I mean hang on a wee . . .' Hamish shook his head. 'I mean, okay, there's all these houses but then . . . I mean, I know my end, right, there's Euro-Kay and Eastern Sight'n'Sound, and it turns out they're part of this HI! thing. Fair enough but that doesn't mean to say they're behind all these other people on your list, does it? And then there's the Produce Centre, Semtex and International . . . thingy. I mean . . . oh, I don't know, I know I suggested it as a joke, like, but . . . surely . . .?'

'Well no, all right, maybe not,' Mungo conceded. 'And we'd have to go to Companies House or something to find out and even then we probably wouldn't if they've covered their tracks. And I know what you're saying, why should they all be in it together, what have they all got in common apart from giving you a hard time of it one way and another? A cut-price electronics firm, a transport company, a lot of property speculators, a bank, an American Evangelical Church, and so on. It doesn't make sense.'

'Right!' Hamish was relieved. 'It doesn't, does it?'

'Until you realize the one thing they *do* all have in common, that is.'

'Oh?' said Grace.

'Like, oh, let me see, Jacob's Cream Crackers and Camel cigarettes, Castlemaine XXXX and the *Observer*.'

'Wh-what's that, Mungo?' Grace asked.

'Money,' said Mungo.

Audrey Pitt-Holyoake returned home to find another four avian corpses disposed about the herbaceous borders. She swept them into a shovel and gave them a decent if hasty burial in a large hole, once intended by poor Godfrey as a fishpond and now pressed into service as a miniature plague pit, in the far corner of the garden. Then she coaxed a murky bath's-worth out of the hot tank, and went to bed.

A leprous moon rose over the blanched Lunie acres. An owl hooted, once, twice. . . the third hoot was rudely forced and abruptly terminated. There was a silent scream of feathers, and a soft plump in the canary grass. Then silence.

Chylblayne Bilt has the chain off while Neville's finger is still on the bell. Her black cotton housecoat, severely belted, proclaims the nakedness beneath. 'Ah've been waiting,' she says, chaining and bolting the door. She turns and takes his hands.

'We'll fuck upstairs,' she says. 'It's all ready.' She leads the way, her feet springing on the treads, her buttocks straining left and up, right and up, left . . .

'Does that excite you, that word, fuck?' she asks without stopping, left and up, right . . . 'That word in mah mouth? Fuck? Let's fuck. Fuck me. That send you?'

'No,' Neville fibs.

They arrive. It is the marriage bed. There is a TV, a

video, a telephone. A *Playboy* centrefold, framed on the wall above the pillows, shows Chylblayne in her blonde period.

'Find a video for us will you, Neville?' She is out of the housecoat now, plumping the pillows, kneeling, anus winking at him. 'Clyde at Madison, last fall. That one really sends me.' Awkwardly, Neville finds it. The slot in the machine gobbles it greedily.

The phone rings; Chylblayne answers it, on her back now. Splayed. She motions him to undress.

'Hi! Honey, it's you!' Neville tears a button off; she waves her hand impatiently, squirming. 'Oh! Say, that's just . . . yes, honey, he's right here, you wanna rap with him? Oh, okay. Yeah. Yeah.' The hand again; Neville has forgotten to take his shoes off before his trousers. 'Yeah, honey . . . yeah! Ah don' know yet.' Then the shorts. 'Yes, honey, he is circumcised. Uh-huh! You bet. God be with you too, honey. HI! and goodbye.' She hangs up.

Neville gulps. 'He . . .' (wilting) '. . . *knows*?'

'They had to stop over,' she explains, smiling at both ends. 'Fawn's brace keeps flarin' on the cameras.'

'You . . . *told* . . .'

He is being grinned at now. 'Clyde, Neville dear, knows how to treat a lady. Okay, listen, before your goddam' penis disappears for ever: Clyde had a career castration, okay, just after we were married; he was with the Tennessee Brethren then, they're highly fundamental, screwin'-wise. Okay, so he needs the up so he can take the out, y'know? He makes out okay on testosterone and he gives pretty good head, but: no babies! So,' she shrugs, sending Neville into fresh agonies, 'we get to choose donors. Correction: Clyde gets to choose. It's a father's duty, wouldn't you say? Now put that tape on, y'hear, and get your ass over here. Ah gotta few little treats organized for later on tonight, if you happen to be needing that kinda thing. Meanwhile, quit watchin' me playin' wit' mahself an' get fuckin'. Ah gotta conception to organize.'

Clyde, Chylblayne and Neville attain their object together. It is a very short tape and Chylblayne does have a head start.

The treats are many and various. Some involve the video player. Others take place in the bathroom. Appliances are the work of the devil, she tells him. God gave us bodies to use. She shows him what she means. It is from the bathroom, showered and powdered, that she returns much later to wake Neville up.

'You're a daddy,' she says. 'Good night.'

He dresses on the landing and finds his own way out. A stray cat has crawled in to die under the Bilts' privet hedge. He does not notice it. Dawn breaks. He stumbles home.

Chapter Eight

Joan Spurtle was not, perhaps, so much a woman of action as a living monument to the irresistible force of obduracy once it has got an idea in its head. A lesser person might have frittered away hours, days, weeks even, in a fruitless search through the groves of Eurobureaucracy for those responsible for unleashing Eugene Mkekwe, unheralded inspector and persecutor of Scottish widows, as a ravening pike in the douce waters of genteel catering; she, Joan Spurtle, founder-chairperson of the Brighter Gardens and Neater Wynds Action Group, went straight for the jugular. She wrote to the *Perthshire Gazette*, enclosing a photocopy of the letters she had received, the day after the visit, from the Bureau des Petits-Fournisseurs, PO Box 23221, Strasbourg. Her letter was brief without skimping on the issues, imparted the right tone of outrage without appearing defensive, and was forceful without (thanks to a lot of self-control) being unprintably rude. Though its main purpose was, of course, to mobilize popular antipathy to male bureaucrats in general and Mr Mkekwe in particular, it aimed also to serve the secondary functions of alerting public consciousness to the excellence of the Bide-a-Wee Tearooms (trade being far too slack lately) and the shiftless duplicity of local government as practised by the Mid Lummock District Council. It would do no harm, after all, to let off the odd opening shot in her campaign to unglue Duff from his seat on the Tourism, Leisure and Recreation Committee. That threats to honest trade in the burgh of Craigfieth could be made, seemingly with impunity, by the distant mandarins of Belgium or Luxembourg or whichever piffling little statelet Strasbourg was in, was, she pointed out, a damning comment on the ineptitude of certain so-called stewards of the public interest in the smoke-free rooms of Mid Lummock House. That tens of thousands (if one counted back to 1961 it must be at least that many) of satisfied customers of the Bide-a-Wee Tearooms (she managed to mention the name three times, four counting the address) should be denied their right to enjoy her Traditional Scottish Scone Selection on the spurious grounds that the flour came from Canada, the cream from Jersey, the sugar from the Caribbean and the honey from More Than One Country was, she suggested, an example of precisely the sort of creeping socialism that the *Gazette*, as a self-proclaimed champion of Scottish enterprise, should be eager to root out and throttle. Finally she challenged any reader inclined to doubt the excellence of her establishment's culinary delights to come and sample them in person.

She read the letter over and, feeling that it lacked a certain something to fulfil the whole of its purpose, was inspired to add: 'PS: Any customer producing a copy of this week's *Gazette* will receive a 10% discount on the bill.' She smiled, sealed the letter, and stamped it.

She'd get Phemmy to shove the prices up on Monday. It was Easter next week, anyway.

Neville slept late, a small and frightened infant in the unholy realm of his newly matured consciousness. He dreamed. He dreamed of falling. He dreamed of carrying things – sofas, elephants, the Craigfieth Mercat Cross – up spiral staircases. He dreamed of being in school assembly with no trousers on. He dreamed he was copulating with his mother's vacuum cleaner but it turned into a computer-enhanced image of Miss Huxtry, who said he shouldn't be doing that, it wasn't scheduled until page five hundred and thirty-eight. He dreamed he was feeling pleased because he'd grown all his pubic hair back until he heard his own voice telling him it was only a dream and everything would be awful when he woke up. He woke up. It was. His fiancée was bending over him.

'I'm sorry,' he mumbled. 'I skipped a few chapters.'

'What?' said Miss Huxtry.

'Waaa-urgh,' said Neville.

'You've got a visitor.'

Neville's hand slid involuntarily, protectively, to his genitals. 'Wh-who?' he quivered, fearing the worse.

Miss Huxtry eyed the disturbance under the sheet. 'Mr Bilt,' she said.

Neville relaxed.

'I hope for our sake, Neville, that all this is going to come off.' Miss Huxtry went back to her office room to record, on a commission basis, some more cassettes in the personae of Wicked Wanda, Nadine The Nite Nurse, Sexy Sado Sadie and Lesbia Longlash, the Lustiest Lip-Licker in Leith.

Neville groped his way into last night's clothes – his boxer shorts seemed unaccountably to have shrunk – and stumbled a little bow-leggedly downstairs and into the lounge. Clyde Bilt stood with his back to the door, his hands hidden, his face bowed as if in prayer. The sulphurous afternoon light was failing, on the whole, to struggle through the curtains.

Neville shuffled shiftily in the doorway. His skin crawled. He tried to swallow a couple of times, but found he couldn't. Clyde Bilt looked very large in a sculpted, American sort of way, especially from behind. Neville fancied he'd read a thing or two, somewhere, about nymphomaniac wives. He wished he hadn't. Apparently they couldn't always be relied on to tell the truth about

229

. . . and what was the man praying *for*, anyway? Neville opened his mouth. A dry crackly noise came out. The evangelist swung round.

His eyes shut, Neville was still trying to work out whether he should be glad his glasses were not on or sorry he had left them off when he felt himself taken in a crushing embrace that smelled of sandalwood and worsted. He opened his eyes. Bilt's lip trembled; his eyes were moist. His jaw rippled beneath the razored face like a rabbit trying to kick its way out of a suede handbag. He stood back an inch, fixed his eyes on the youth, then rolled them heavenwards.

'This is my beloved son,' he breathed, 'in whom mah dear wife Chylblayne is well pleased.'

'Urp,' said Neville.

'Amen,' said Bilt.

'It,' said Neville. 'Um, all right, then?'

Bilt smiled. 'Gard's Will,' he said, 'has been enabled.'

'Ah,' said Neville. 'Great!'

'Great is the word for it, mah son. Great is mah estimation also. Gard's Will is always – great!'

'Yeah,' said Neville. 'Right. Amen.'

'Amen and praise the Lord. Speak His name, Neville. Utter it now!'

'Er, uh – God's, you mean?'

'Our son's, mah frayund. The Holy Fruit of Chylblayne's womb. Name it.'

'Oh. Ar. Er . . .'

'Nothing Jewish though, y'hear? Or Hispanic. This kid's got prospects.'

'Oh, right, fine. Er – Branson, then.'

'Rantzen? Say, isn't that a – '

'*Branson*. Buh. Bee.'

'Branson. Branson Bilt. Branson B. Bilt, I like that. I like that with the B, don't you?'

'Oh right, check. Like, er, Franklin D. Roose – . I mean, er . . .' Was 'velt' Jewish?

'Harry H. Truman?' said Bilt. 'Ulysses S. Grant, Dwight D. Eisenhower?' He was beaming.

Neville beamed back. 'John F. Kennedy,' he suggested. 'Richard, M. Nix – oh, um – '

'A misunderstood man, Neville, a very misunderstood man.'

Neville nodded gravely. 'Oh, right,' he said. 'He did what he had to do,' he added, wishing he could remember what it was. Bilt nodded too, so that was all right. They nodded together in manly commune.

'You're, er,' Neville began. 'I mean Chyl – , your wife, even though it was only last – she's, um, sure, is she? That it's, he's, a . . .?'

'Gard speaks to her, Neville. To *her*. To mah wyuhf. God spoke to her in the bathroom.'

'Oh,' said Neville. 'Oh! You mean when she – yes, yes I see. Amazing!'

'Divine eugenics, Neville. You cannot argue with divine eugenics.'

'No,' said Neville. 'No, I should think not.'

'Gard called me,' said Bilt, pressing Neville's right hand in both of his, 'to be celibate, as you probably know.'

'Yes I, er – '

'To be, like Joseph son of Heli, the husband of my children's mother.'

'Ah.'

'Ah know not temptations of the flesh, Neville, in that regard.'

'N-no? No, I see.'

'Eve's curse tainteth not mah member, Neville.'

'No, well, it wouldn't really would – '

Bilt's grip tightened. 'Now in your case, Neville,' he said.

'Ulp,' said Neville.

'Gard had . . . other plans.'

'Oh, yes! Right. Fine!'

'Tell me what those plans were, Neville.'

'Me?' said Neville.

Bilt smiled, squeezing. 'Don't be afraid,' he murmured, chillingly. Neville swallowed. 'Tell me, Neville.'

'To, er, to-to, have, er, with your . . . to make, um . . . you know.'

'Think, mah frayund, think. To . . . give . . . mah wyuhf . . . to give . . . go on, Neville.'

'A good time? No! No, er, to give . . . er . . . your wife – a baby?'

'Go on.'

'To – to give your wife a b-baby, to make her . . . pregnant, to, to, impregnate your wife . . .' Neville's mind raced. How many other ways were there of putting it, man to – to – 'To sow my seed in her, um . . . in her, to –'

'Yes! *Yes!*' Bilt's eyes glittered. Neville felt two of his fingers crack. 'And has not the Lord Gard looked on that seed, Neville; and blessed one, just one, to do His Holy Will in the sanctified womb of mah wyuhf and Gard's handmaiden Chylblayne Bilt *née* Poindexter?'

'Oh, right!' Neville grinned and nodded very rapidly. 'I see! Great!'

'Blessed be her name!'

'Bl – , right.' Bilt's eyes had closed, his tongue was working in the corners of his mouth. Somewhere, from afar, Neville seemed to hear two thousand voices about to join in, and wished he couldn't. It was doing things to things he didn't want things being done to. Also his circulation was now cut off at the wrist.

'Blessed be the Lord, blessed be the name of Bilt in the legions of the Lord, blessed be the child of this Thy

servant, Lord, blessed be he in Thy name, and' – Bilt
loosed one hand and let it drop below, between, closing
it – 'blessed be the power of this Thine instrument of
gloreagh!'

'Huuuu-ii!' said Neville.

Bilt was breathing heavily, rapidly, in time with his
hand. Neville closed his eyes, too, and groaned. Bilt fell
to his knees, scrabbling. Neville understood why the
curtains were drawn.

'Reveal unto the Lord!'

'Ow!' said Neville as the zip snagged. Then he removed
his mind and thought of the Nikkei Futures Index.

When it was over Bilt produced a very clean handkerchief and dabbed his chin with it. Neville toppled backwards into a chair, feeling cold and empty.

'Be very glad mah name ain't Cronos, frayund,' Bilt
remarked amicably, putting the handkerchief away. 'He
ate 'em hatched!'

Neville watched his bruised penis creep back into
shape, leaving a little slug-trail on the dralon. The evangelist's wife, he noticed, had missed three golden pubic
hairs on his left testicle. He heard himself say, 'Are you
mad?' He shivered.

Bilt chuckled sanely. 'Well now,' he said. He produced
a card from his breast pocket and gave it to Neville,
snapping the corner with an immaculately clean fingernail.
Neville read:

HI! – HOSANNAH INTERNATIONAL – HI!
Neville G. Wringhim
Scottish Executive Vice-President (Special Projects)
'DOING GOD'S BUSINESS ON EARTH'

'Are you?' Bilt asked. 'That's the question.'

'What – '

'Lemme tell you,' said Bilt. 'Blairlummock Conference

Centre, Friday, from nine A.M. All Day Feast of Motivation. Be there. You'll meet the other enablers; ask them.'

'What – '

'Fawn,' said Bilt, 'and Hall. See what it did for them.'

'What – '

'Take time off work.' Bilt chuckled again. 'Like the rest of your life, okay?'

'Okay,' said Neville. 'What – '

'The G,' said Bilt, leaving, 'is for Gloreagh!'

'Ah,' said Neville. His penis checked its retreat. He dressed, put the little card safely in his pocket, and went to find his intended.

'. . . in my nice warm hands and press all of its throbbing length against my steamy hot quivering – '

'I did it,' said Neville.

Miss Huxtry stabbed the pause button and looked up from her book. 'I'll have to start that all over again now, Neville. Did what?'

'Made it come off.' He showed her the card. 'Starting Friday, in Blairlummock. All Day Feast of Motivation. In the Conference Centre.'

Miss Huxtry sighed happily. 'I've always had faith in you, Neville,' she said.

Neville blushed. 'Thanks.'

'Talking of doing it, Neville.'

Neville gulped. 'Y-yes?'

'What do you think might be best with Mr Kirk? That's next Friday too, you know.'

'Oh . . .' Neville felt slightly nauseous. 'I'd just, er, leave it up to him, really.'

'Mmm.' She seemed doubtful. 'You don't think that would make me look a bit, you know, passive?'

'I'd say that depends,' said Neville. 'Really.'

'Mmm. You're probably right. Oh, Neville, before you go – what's this word mean?'

234

Neville bent warily over the book. 'What, "consummation", you mean? Dunno, really. Just another name for rumpy-pumpy, I think.'

'Oh,' said Miss Huxtry. 'I'll leave that bit out then. There's quite enough of that here as it is.' She rewound the tape. 'I'm wearing my peep-hole bra,' she said, 'and my naughty pink suspender belt, just the way you horny men like it, with my matching fur-lined crotchless panties. Could you help me with these rubber stockings? My hands are a bit wet because while I was waiting for you to call I've been . . .'

Neville closed the door, very softly, showered and went back to bed, his future assured. Not that it hadn't been fun, while it lasted, fooling about in the shallow end with the likes of Sayeed Haq, though he'd never intended to spend more than six months at the outside on that kind of small-town stuff. He'd see Haq tomorrow, tell him to find another rent collector. All over now, prentice work. Of course (he pulled the duvet up over his ear) they'd have to find somewhere else to live, probably. Haq would want the house back – so what? Hi! would provide . . . or Melmotte's . . . whoever. The shape of things to come. No more enabling for him . . . hard work . . . dedication . . . he could have sworn . . . never mind . . . those tapes she had . . . must've been Ganglion himself who'd served her . . . funny no one else complained though . . . never mind. He slept, dreamlessly, the sleep of the morally vacant.

Hamish Ganglion, unassisted, sold a three-pin plug, a Jimmy Shand cassette and a record cleaning cloth. He did quite a brisk trade – enough, he calculated, to pay the whole of Ashley Oswald's School Book Fund for next term – in weekend video rentals from the absent Neville's newly arrived stock, all of it devoted, as far as he could judge from the titles, to nature documentaries of one sort or another. It was funny the things people wanted to watch on video these days, he thought, though right enough there didn't seem to be nearly so many programmes like that on TV, it was all pop shows and quizzes unless you paid extra for things like documentaries, and news, and films, and so on. Hamish shrugged. The wee nyaff had to be good at something, he supposed, though it was a pity it wasn't Sounds Good machines they'd all be playing their tapes on. On and off through the day he saw an Eastern Sight'n'Sound delivery van and was sure it would be visiting the homes of all the people who had brought their hired recorders back on Thursday and Friday. He'd have to put an ad in the *Gazette*, try and flog them, though the price he'd have to sell them for to compete with Eastern Sight'n'Sound's new ones wouldn't exactly show very much in the way of profit. Opening his post – half of it circulars from business finance houses, the other half bills – he wondered if he and Grace shouldn't just give in, sell up, go somewhere else. One of them could get a job, or retrain, or something. He tried to dismiss the thought but it kept on returning, especially during the one-and-three-quarter-hour gap between selling the plug to the minister's wife and the cleaning cloth to the minister (who returned the plug because it was faulty and had to have his money back because it was the last one in the shop and the new lot still hadn't come in) and it brought with it little attendant questions, little imps that whispered in his ear. What's this town to you? they asked. Or you to it? Look what happened the other night. What's your future here? What happens when the next mortgage payment comes due? What's the point? He could not shake them off. Encouraged, they brought some friends round to join in the fun. They wanted to know about Grace, what she'd be thinking about having a

236

failure for a husband, a man who left home every day and came back richer to the tune of half an hour's worth of a real man's wages . . . And what about Mungo then, eh? Mungo could look after himself, they pointed out, Mungo was clever, and witty, Mungo'd always land on his feet, Mungo would, hadn't he always? A born provider, Mungo. He knew a thing or two. No one kicked Mungo around and what was Hamish, then, in comparison? Hadn't Mungo got the papers to help Oswald? Mungo could do things Hamish couldn't. And what was Hamish doing, apart from going quietly bankrupt . . . what were they up to, Grace and Mungo, did he know that? And who could blame her, eh, who could blame her, married to him? Mungo made her laugh. Does she still want you, Hamish boy? You know – that way? So what's it been like lately then, eh, you and her, eh? Eh?

The door opened to admit Fawn and Hall Bilt, the latter with a carrier bag proclaiming JESUS TAKES THE LOAD.

'Momma says to take these back,' the child announced, fixing Hamish with a wide blue stare of appalling frankness. 'Momma's tired today.'

Hamish unloaded *Wildlife of Westphalia* Vols I-IV, ticked them off in Ashley Oswald's old school jotter, and put them on the shelf. 'Did she enjoy them?' he asked.

Hall shrugged. 'Ah guess so. Ah heard her tell Poppa they were adequate for their purpose.'

'Momma's going to have a baby boy,' said Fawn, as if by way of sequitur.

'We know where babies come from,' said Hall.

'Um . . . right,' said Hamish.

'Poppa told us.'

'Oh, good. Erm . . .'

'You wanna hear it too?'

'Well er, actually I – '

237

'Okay. Momma takes her temperature – '

' – in her vaginal opening – '

' – and Poppa says a special prayer to Jesus – '

' – and an angel comes – '

' – and puts a seed – '

' – in Momma's uterus – '

' – and then she has a good rest – '

' – and Poppa says a very special thank you – '

' – which we don't need to know about – '

' – because we're not emotionally mature – '

' – yet.'

'See?'

'Erm . . . yeah. Right.'

'Is that how your wife got her babies, mister?'

'Erm, well . . . no' quite, no, I mean – '

'Aw, shoot, Hall, ain't no use asking him. He ain't God's People.'

'Oh, yeah. Say, does that mean he's gonna fry in Hell for ever?'

Fawn shrugged. 'Guess so. Ain't no business of ours, anyway. We're okay.'

Hall looked at Hamish again. 'Guess he looks kinda crummy already. We'll check it out with Muzz Pleat next semester.'

Hamish blinked. 'Miss *Pleat*?'

'Yeah.' They wandered over to the video shelves. 'She's at our house right now. Poppa's bringing her to Jesus in his study.'

'Jings,' said Hamish.

'You got anything suitable for us, mister? Momma said we could have it if you did.'

'Erm . . . well there's cartoons, like, on the bottom shelf there. Disney, Tom and Jerry, er, there should be a few Thundercats too unless my son's – '

238

'Cartoon images are a blasphemous abomination and a mockery of God's creation,' said Hall and Fawn.

'Oh,' said Hamish.

'Don't you have anything that won't corrupt our spiritual welfare?'

'Oh, aye,' said Hamish, doubting it. 'Erm . . . oh! This'll be all right, I'm sure. *Life on Earth*. It was on telly a few years ago. It's all about nature and volcanoes, and, erm, you know, dinosaurs and that, how everything . . .' He faltered.

'You mean *evolutionism*?'

'Well, er.' Hamish recoiled a little. 'Yes, I suppose – '

'Evolutionism is a false prophecy – '

' – begotten by Satan himself – '

' – an' a perversion of God's Holy Word – '

' – to confuse the unnerstanding of suggestible minds – '

' – an' lead them into doubt an' heresy – '

' – an' Muzz Pleat's gonna program it right out – '

' – next semester – '

' – so Poppa says – '

' – 'cause he's on the Board of Management – '

' – an' he can *make* 'em do it!'

'Oh,' said Hamish. 'Here, then.' He took a box off the top shelf. 'What about this?'

They shrugged. 'Okay, looks clean.'

He took their money. They put *The Last Temptation of Christ* in their carrier, and left.

Made a right arse of that one, didn't you, Hamish boy? said the imps.

To hell with it, thought Hamish. He took *Wildlife of Westphalia* Vol I for the kids to watch, locked the shop, and went home early. Staying open during the lunch hour had not been a success, and he was hungry.

There were a lot of customers in the Produce Centre,

many of them strangers. Thinking Mungo might need help – and quite taken with the idea of actually selling something, for profit – Hamish apologized his way through the customers. It was not Mungo, however. It was Babette, obsessively attired in state-of-the-art retail interface chic and apparently coping quite well with the pre-packaged, pre-priced plunder of the day before. Mungo, he remembered, had volunteered to redo all the price labels. 'Hi,' he said. 'Where's Mungo?'

'Dunno,' said Babette. 'Scuse me, you're in the way.'

There was no one in the house. He checked the back lane, and found Mungo's car gone. He searched the house again but there was no note. He caught himself looking in Grace's wardrobe and felt ashamed. Then he felt ashamed and angry; then just angry. Then just miserable. He made himself a peanut butter sandwich and didn't want to eat it. Instead he phoned Rose Cottage. There was no one in there, either. He sat at the kitchen table and abandoned himself to bills and daemons.

[Warning: Perusal of the following digression may risk criminal proceedings under the National Interest (Obsession With Secrecy) (Scotland) Act of 1989. Unfortunately it is reasonably crucial to the plot. The publishers apologize for any inconvenience this may cause.]

Boggybreck Barracks – or, to give it its proper and classified title, Her Majesty's Security Services' District Sub-Regional Establishment Number 23 (Central Eastern Zone) – had been for nearly sixty years tangible proof of Milton's comforting dictum concerning the usefulness of those who only stand and wait. Acquired (one way or another) as a bulwark against the tidal wave of pacifism that swept the realm after the great hurricane of 1914–18, it was in fact used only once as a barracks *per se*, and that only for one week in 1926 when a battalion of the King's

Own Royal Perthshire Periodicals (the 'Auld Despicables') stood by to save Mid Lummock from the rapine of bolshevism then threatening to sweep away the very principles of chauvinism for which so many had recently made the supreme sacrifice. When the ravening hordes turned out to be merely trade union leaders in wolves' clothing and the General Strike was over, the Auld Despicables went back to their allotments and the barracks – a large, floorless wooden structure originally intended by Oswald's father as a coarse-weather shelter for his grazing stock – collapsed, leaving the Ochilrees' abandoned but and ben (brilliantly whitewashed in honour of the Despicables' officer élite, who had used it as a casino) as the only visible indication of Boggybreck's vital rôle in the national defence.

Two years later the military authorities, in grudging obligation to the spirit of the Geneva Protocols, dug a large, secret hole wherein was tenderly laid to rest a considerable quantity of high explosive gas bombs. Having shovelled the bog back and made a swift strategic withdrawal, they left the place more or less to the elements for another twelve years, though not without taking the very sensible precaution (by way of showing His Majesty's continuing lively interest in it) of erecting a very ugly barbed wire perimeter fence and putting up a notice absolving themselves from blame in the event of trespassers being shot. The land thus became, for a while, something of an accidental wildlife park, being used as a refuge from the sporting gun by the more intelligent and athletic game on the neighbouring Lunie Estate, and consequently the subject of much bitter correspondence (most of it one-way) between the House of Margoyle and the Joint Chiefs of Staff, who demonstrated by a refined form of dumb insolence that it is possible, in very rare cases, successfully to defy the Scottish Landed Interest.

The deer grazed safely on until the winter of 1939, when Lord Margoyle's Uncle Siegfried, lately Scottish affairs adviser to the British Union of Fascists, had the dubious satisfaction of watching from the window of Hut 18b of the recently constructed Boggybreck Internment Camp as they were rounded up and shot by a group of marksmen from the Local Defence Volunteers, led by one Corporal Borden, a Reserved Occupation worker in the firm of Borden's Family Butchers, Craigfieth, an establishment whose success against the odds of wartime rationing might be said to date from this incident.

Boggybreck had a quiet war, as wars go, ridding itself of its last remaining internee when, in 1942, the Margoyle solicitors were successful in persuading the War Office that the mental health of Uncle Siegfried had deteriorated to a point which even his closest family now recognized as one of harmless insanity. He spent his remaining seventeen years, at his own request, in the top floor apartments of a garret in Lunie Castle, where he laid elaborate plans for the annexation of the Faroes by a team of hand-picked storm-trooping gamekeepers. An obituary notice in *The Times* recorded the passing of 'one whose talents were, alas, destined to be drowned by the clash of arms in Europe'. Few who knew him would disagree. The Mosleys sent a wreath by diplomatic bag.

Boggybreck's sole claim to a footnote in the national annals was the construction, late in the war, of several large buildings designed to appear to Axis spy planes as irrefutable proof of a Second Front in Norway. While it remains unclear even to military historians of the period quite what German High Command was supposed to make of such frantic preparations, forty miles inland, for a seaborne invasion of Scandinavia, it seems likely enough that the immediate object of the project, that of Baffling Adolf, was indeed achieved. A document salvaged from the smoking ruins of the Reichstag records an Intelligence report to the effect that a Norwegian-based *Aufklärungs-flugzeug* had spotted an unspecified outbreak of *Rüstungs-industrie* close to the spot believed to have been chosen as a landing strip by Rudolf Hess three years earlier. 'Local agents' (alas unspecified but possibly observing from a garret at Lunie Castle) were instructed to communicate further details.

This subterfuge, however successful at the time, presented something of a problem to post-war military planners. The army, as is well known, hates waste, and while many if not most of its wartime emergency structures could be expected to revert to dust and rubble if not overly attended to within five to ten years, Boggybreck – built not by British craftsmen but by Italian prisoners of war fresh from joining up the South Isles of Orkney – showed every sign of holding firm for decades to come. What, then, was to be done with it? Was there anything, indeed, that could usefully be done with a structure of undoubted military provenance but undisputed military worthlessness? Memos flew; the file thickened; its cover page, having accumulated in the first few months such gems of civil service thinking as 'Use it as a target', 'Offer it to the Yanks' and 'Intern Aneurin Bevan there' finally became the playing board for a very popular Whitehall game in which each contestant writes 'You touched it last', initials it, and passes it on to the next. At last, in the autumn of 1946, the file was accidentally mislaid by a Deputy Second Assistant Secretary going home on the Bakerloo line and found by a quite exceptionally dim-witted schoolboy, who wrote 'Keep things in it' on the front and handed it in at a police station – a public-spirited act which earned him a clip round the ear, a warning not to poke his nose into other people's affairs, and a life-long hatred of men in uniform.

The effect was immediate: within a month, Boggybreck had acquired windows, ventilation, humidity-controlled central heating and one hundred and seventy-five thousand austerity-style demob suits all ready and waiting for returning heroes from the war in the East. In 1947 the remaining one hundred and forty-seven thousand, six hundred and thirty-eight unclaimed charcoal-grey two-piece civvies were despatched, as a good-will gesture, to the newly independent Indian civil service.

The Indian government sent them back again for the Festival of Britain.

Boggybreck's key function in NATO planning was firmly established, along with the small staff of civil servants, typists, security personnel and military liaison officers – about forty in all – necessary to oversee the efficient, professional storage of such strategic items as trench puttees, desert capes, Sam Browne belts, ostrich plumes, ceremonial spats (Lt-Col And Above) and 'Khyber Pass' long-life guaranteed one hundred per cent frostproof mackintosh condoms, North-West Frontier garrisons for the use of (L and XL only).

In 1977 extensive secret operations were carried out, as part of a nationwide nuclear war contingency programme, in, around, and underneath Oswald's father's but and ben. The cottage itself was renovated and refurbished, then locked and abandoned. An inner security fence was erected and radiation hazard signs posted (shooting of trespassers no longer being thought quite the thing). Staff at the storage depot were asked not to look out of their windows during these operations.

The *Perthshire Gazette*'s claim that Boggybreck was last in use during the Falklands conflict was, like so many press reports, true only insofar as it went, and was therefore misleading. It is correct to say that the facility was operational during the liberation of Port Stanley;

indeed a consignment of trench puttees, too late to be of any use, was despatched by RAF Hercules that very day in response to an urgent plea by Mr Max Hastings. It is a matter of record that a policy of Progressive Military Disinvolvement (to use the Whitehall phrase) was implemented shortly afterwards, following an account-ants' report on the operational efficiency of the Ministry of Defence Procurement. However, since Boggybreck's principal use at this time was as an emergency tampon store for the Women's Royal Army Corps it is doubtful whether, as the *Gazette* implied, it played any very active part in the drama of the South Atlantic. Pre-emptive negotiations with a high-level team from Hosannah Inter-national then began, during which the main buildings themselves, despite vociferous protests from architectural conservationists, were razed to the ground, without prej-udice, by way of making the site more attractive for development. Minutes of these meetings, particularly as they applied to Oswald's father's Top Secret Cottage, are unfortunately not due to be considered for declassification until 2039, though rumours of a lease-back 'Holocaust Clause' should probably not be discounted, given the prevailing political and economic climate.

Thus Boggybreck became once more an anonymous wil-derness, the bleak domain of hoodie crows – most of which, this raw Saturday afternoon, turned out to be dead. Ganglion toed one in the air and pretended to shoot it with a finger; Oswald, watching from the front seat of a Datsubishi 4WD Yomper nearby, tch'd in disapproval. They had gained entry, courtesy of the fearlessness of their two companions from *Scotland Now!*, by the simple expedient of lifting a padlocked security gate off its hinges and driving in.

'You're daft,' said Oswald.

'No dafter than Lord M an' 'is pals when they goes out shootin' tame pheasants. In fack,' Ganglion added, preparing to launch another corpse, 'I'm not sure a dead crow doesn't make a more sportin' target. Flies 'igher, for one fing. Ptchew! Ptchew! There y'are, see? I missed.'

'That's not what I meant,' said Oswald. 'I was thinking of how they came to be dead in the first place. I hope yon pair know what they're doing.'

The two newshounds had flung an anorak over the barbed wire that topped the cottage gate and were scrambling over, using a DANGER – RADIATION notice for support.

'S'long as they don't croak till they've got us safely home again. Oi, thass a good one, innit! Croak – 'oodie crows – geddit?'

'Very droll,' said Oswald. 'You're forgetting gamma rays are catching, aren't you?'

'Gercher! I spect it's just a try-on, scare people off. Like my uncle used to take an envelope marked 'VD Clinic Report' to the pub so's people wouldn't nick 'is beer when 'e went for a slash. Same fing.'

'I don't suppose,' Oswald remarked, 'that everyone at the Ministry of Defence is like your uncle, Ganglion.'

'They better not be! Suffered terrible wiv 'is bladder, my uncle did. Eye-eye! They're comin' back.'

The reporter – an attractively podgy, provocatively scruffy young woman wearing jeans and a sweatshirt proclaiming POWER OF THE PRESS – vaulted the gate with astonishing ease and waited for her companion, a lugubrious, grey-skinned photographer of indeterminate middle age who rejoiced in the name of Campbeltown Fotheringhame. The reporter's name was Smith. She strode up to them. 'Weird place you've got here,' she said. 'Two-way windows. Or do I mean one-way? Reflective on the outside, anyway. Wonder what they don't want us to see, eh?'

'There speaks the true investigative journalist,' said Fotheringhame, panting slightly from the effort of walking. 'What about it, Smith? Want me to lean on one of the panes and reveal all?'

'Shit, no! It's the *un*answered questions that sell papers. You got everything you want, Fothers?'

'Mmnyeah, just about. If I could just get our friend here to pose in front of his dad's home clutching the lease an' looking sympathetic that'll be me finished.'

'God's sake!' exclaimed Oswald. 'You must have taken thousands already.'

The photographer shrugged, knocking his cameras together. 'Who's countin' when you're no' payin'?' he reasoned. 'Manage it with the chair, will you?'

'Not without an engine,' said Oswald. 'What about the radiation?'

'Forget it,' said Smith. 'Standard procedure on the part of Them when They don't want Us getting too close. Oldest trick in the book. Besides, the wind'll be blowing away from us. Come on, I'll carry you. Never mind my boobs, they don't damage easily.'

'Cworr,' said Ganglion as Smith picked Oswald up and strolled away with him. 'Ever fort of bein' an au pair, luv?'

'Too busy being a babysitter lately,' Smith called back. 'Will you manage the chair by yourself, Fothers?'

Campbeltown Fotheringhame looked at it. 'I might, if I pull it behind me,' he said doubtfully.

They had a little trouble with the photo: Oswald's facial muscles, normally disinclined to give him any trouble with the unconscious registration of emotion, flatly refused to co-operate in the simulation of a sympathetic attitude for the camera. They offered instead wistfulness, vague yearning, psychotic despair, vacuous dissatisfaction and, finally, ennui. Fotheringhame settled for the ennui and used up most of a roll on it, including the radiation notice for gratuitous good measure. Then, with unwonted athleticism, he crouched and leaped round the building, framing it from various angles with both hands.

'You flipped, Fothers?' asked Smith.

'I'm just . . . tryin' to see . . . if we could . . . sorta . . . get a moody . . . kinda . . . reflection aff o' they windies,' he replied. 'Shame we canna line up a bulldozer or something, bounce it off. Distorted, like. Wi' aw them big black clouds.'

'Aw, c'moff it, Fothers,' Smith snorted. 'This is *Scotland Now!* you're working for, not the bloody *Independent*. Print the mug and spell the caption wrong, that's this comic's motto.'

'Yeah, awright, awright,' growled the photographer. 'Nothing wrong wi' a bit o' artistic integrity once in a while, is there? Hey!' He grinned cariously. 'Fancy doin' a feature on all these deid birdies, hen?'

'Fuck off,' said Smith.

Fotheringhame cackled. 'Our wee Smithy here,' he explained, 'did her journalistic apprenticeship on the *Daily Mail*, ye see. Remember "Save Our Seals"? They sent her tae interview them.'

'Never work with children or animals,' Smith shuddered. 'Especially dead smelly ones. Besides, I was brought up to believe that the only good hoodie is a dead hoodie, so there.'

On the way home – they stopped to put the gate back on its hinges to make the nation safe – Smith copied the letter Oswald had received from Drubber and Dunning that morning, a short epistle regretting their inability to advise him further and enclosing their account for seventy-eight pounds, forty-six pence including VAT.

'Going to pay it?' he asked.

'Am I more newsworthy if I don't?' he replied cannily.

'Oh, sure. Rebel Grandad In Won't Pay Shocker. One-Legged OAP Tell Lawyers To Hop It.'

'In that case,' said Oswald, 'I'll pay.'

'Wot did you mean by "babysitting" back there, Smiff?' asked Ganglion. 'Not referrin' to your friend 'ere, was yer?'

'Charming,' said Fotheringhame.

'My last assignment. Six whole days in the exclusive company of Darleen McGlinchy.'

'Who?'

'Darleen McGlinchy. Wife of Ogilvie "Spud" McGlinchy, the Bearsden Ripper.'

'Oh, 'im. Jeezers. Why?'

'Why? To keep her away from all the other reptiles, of course. Next week in *Scotland Now!* – Stand By Your Man, Says Delectable Darleen, twenty-eight, Blonde Bombshell Wife of Terror Rapist. Exclusive: My Years Of Lust With Hell Hubby. Slayer's Sex Slave Secrets.'

'I don't believe it,' said Ganglion.

'You're dead right! It was more a case of once a week with the light off, if you ask me. Still, that's human interest journalism.'

'That's bloody awful!'

'Too right! A whole week, nearly, stuck in the Holiday Inn, Paisley – her choice, need I add – guarding her interests while she knocked back the Tequila Sunrises and shovelled in the scampi and chips and told me it wasn't his fault, really. Ugh! Talk about where there's muck there's money.'

''ow much?'

'Ninety-five thousand – she fancied a bungalow on Loch Lomond – and a modelling contract.'

'Hmph,' said Oswald. 'What am I getting?'

'Your piccy in the paper, old son,' said Fotheringhame. But it was not to be.

The pictures were developed and the story written the next day according to the paper's strict literary guidelines: no polysyllables, no sentence to exceed ten words, no abstract concepts. The whole was submitted to a sub-editor who reduced it by half, transcribed Oswald's name wrongly, headlined the piece '"It's War" Says One-Leg Oz, 72' and passed it on to the editor, who read it, frowned, and lifted his red telephone to speak to the proprietor.

The proprietor interrupted his acquisition of a Swedish pulp mill and a small academic publisher in Wellington, NZ, to take the call. He frowned, too, then advised his editor to fax the story down to the office of Rear Admiral ███████ at the National Committee of ██████ and ███████ Rear Admiral ███████ was not there, of course, it being Sunday, nor was he at home in ██████████, but a call to the ███████ Club established that he might be found celebrating the start of the █████ fishing season with his friend Lord ████ on the River ████████████. A despatch rider was sent out who, having blazed down the M██ for █████ hours at ██ mph, being escorted for part of the way by officers of the ████████shire Constabulary, caught up with Rear Admiral ███████ shortly after ████: █████ m.

' ███████████████; well, ███████ me! ██████████, ██████ ██████████, bloody ████████, █████████████,' he said, giving the characteristic sideways ██████ with his ████ so well known in ██████████, ████████, and at the BBC. 'I'll tell ██████ the answer's ██, and put out the usual ████████████,' he barked. Then, pausing only to land a six-pound █████, he muttered the instruction to his ███████████████.

The editor of *Scotland Now!* took the call in his car as he drove home from evening service at the Lord MacKay Street FP church in Milngavie. He pulled up to call his paper.

'It's a pull on that cripple story, as we thought,' he said.

'Run the roller-skating goldfish instead, and issue the usual reminder.'

Smith was duly given the usual reminder and sent off to cover the Michael Jackson Come-back Concert at the British Legion Club, Dunoon with instructions to forget all about One-Leg Oz, 72. 'Who's he?' she said.

Thus, dear citizen, is it demonstrated that the price of freedom is eternal vigilance; and that the guardians of our ancient liberties are ever viglant, yea, even on the Sabbath Day are they vigilant!

It was after closing time when Grace and Mungo came home, flushed and frivolous, to find Hamish miserably sweeping up in the shop.

'Oh, there you are, then,' he said.

'We got badges, Dad,' said Ashley Oswald. 'Look.' 'ROLL ANOTHER ONE', his badge said. 'JUST LIKE THE OTHER ONE', said Wally's.

'Oh,' said Hamish. 'Fine.'

'You'll never guess where we've been Hamish!' Grace giggled.

'No,' said Hamish, ostentatiously putting the broom away. 'Since you didn't leave a note. Where were you? Haight Ashbury? I wouldn't like to think what sort of a mess Babette's made of the till, by the way.'

'Oh, that's all right, it's a new one, Mungo got it. We – '

'*New?* Mungo?'

'It's okay, pal,' said Mungo. 'It's not really new. Friend of a friend of a friend, sort of thing, with a little bonus I got off *Scotland Now!* Think of it as rent.'

'It's fantastic, Hamish! It adds up and works out the change and stores all the information for cashing-up and everything all by itself. That's why I was able to get Babette back.'

'Guaranteed one hundred per cent idiot-proof,' Mungo grinned.

'Oh well, better get me one then, hadn't you? Pal.' Hamish savagely rearranged a display of oranges. Two fell out. 'Or am I the exception that proves the rule?'

'Hamish!'

'Oh, sorry, sorry. Here. I'll pay for them.' He dug a fistful of change out of his pocket, dropped quite a lot of it, and banged thirty pence down on the counter. 'One day's net profit from Sounds Good. Go on, put it in Mungo's till. One of us better earn a living.'

'Silly Daddy,' said Wally.

'We'll pick it up, Dad,' said Ashley Oswald, grabbing his brother and diving for cover. Grace looked upset. Mungo looked apologetic.

'Yeah, listen, sorry about the note, pal, that was my fault really. I kind of whisked Grace off her feet.' Hamish cast him a baleful look. 'I'll rephrase that.'

'We've been to the Magic Banana, Hamish,' Grace said tightly. 'We thought it would be a surprise.'

'Consider me surprised, then. What's the Magic Banana when it's at home? A vegetarian restaurant or something?'

'Dad . . .'

'Keep it,' said Hamish wildly.

'Hamish! It's that place I tried ringing before, you know, about supplies for the shop. Don't you remember? The man said he'd ring back and we didn't think he would but he did, this morning, and Mungo answered it and realized it was an old friend of his, a Mr Zimbalist, and – '

'Who?'

'Zimbalist,' said Mungo. 'Ephraim Zimbalist junior, but not *the* Ephraim Zimbalist junior. At least I don't

252

think so. He's a . . . well, how would you describe him, Grace?'

Grace giggled again. 'You'd like him, Hamish. He listens to that music you know . . . what's that group you used to play me the records and I didn't like them?'

'Grateful Dead,' said Hamish.

'That's it! I told him you liked them too, and he said anything you hadn't got, he could probably get it. He's . . . a bit odd, actually, but in quite a normal sort of way, if you see what I mean. Quite old, though.'

'He's the last of the Beautiful People,' Mungo explained. 'Well, probably the last in Dunbroath, anyway. He was there when they levitated the Pentagon.'

'Really?' said Hamish

'Oh yes, Hamish, he told us all about it, they all joined hands seemingly and, well, you know, concentrated, and chanted tarantulas and things, and sort of willed it to lift off the ground!'

'And did it?'

'Well, he said he wasn't sure, really, but lots of people thought it had at the time and he showed us the press cuttings and everything. It was really interesting, like watching history come to life.'

'*Village Voice*,' said Mungo. 'Nice little paper. Good layout. Great small ads.'

'I see,' said Hamish. 'And he's a fruit and vegetable supplier is he, this hippy type?'

'Well . . . not really actually as such, no, but he knows lots of people and sells lots of things and after I rang the other day he sort of, you know, asked around a bit and, well, there we are really.'

'Are we?'

'Oh yes, it's all right, Hamish, really. He showed us. There's everything we could need here, well more really,

253

just . . .' She shrugged. 'Lots of things. Whatever we want.'

'Like, mushrooms, man!'

'Yes, he's got lots of those, a bit on the small side but quite nice fried, he said, and oh, Hamish, some of the things – like huge marrows, really enormous, and everything sort of *bigger*, really, and healthier-looking too. Goodness knows where he gets them from.'

'Findhorn, at a guess,' said Mungo. 'They do things to them there. Talk to them, you know. Pray a lot. Like Prince Charles, really, only more obsessive. One of them wrote a book about it. I've got a copy if you'd like to borrow it. As a writer I'd say he was very good at market gardening, but it'd give you the picture.'

'Right. I see. Well, fine that then. And he delivers, does he?'

'Ah,' said Mungo.

'Well,' said Grace.

'You see,' said Mungo.

'What?'

'He's a . . . a non-driver, Hamish. On religious grounds.'

'Except for his rickshaw of course,' Mungo added.

'Oh, fine! Great! So every time you get a customer wanting a cauliflower all you have to do is lift the phone and hey presto! Arnold Schwarzenegger comes pedalling his balls off over to Craigfieth! Should make a great scoop for the *Grocer*, eh Mungo?'

'That's what we thought you'd say,' said Grace. 'So we . . . that is I mean I . . . I'll tell you what, pet, why don't I make us some tea? And, good gracious, it's Wally's bedtime already – nearly,' she added as Wally's face began to gather itself in protest. 'Let's go and get comfy anyway.'

'So you what?' said Hamish, preparing to panic.

'Well, yes, all right, Hamish, but that's not the point you see, the – '

'What isn't?'

'What you think it is – I mean the point is, Hamish, Ephraim – Mr Zimbalist – 's got all sorts of things, I mean you really wouldn't believe, would he, Mungo? I mean things you never see these days, in the shops I mean, not the normal ones anyway and you know what the shops are like round here, I mean where would you go, Hamish, if you wanted just an ordinary coal scuttle, a metal one? Or plain old-fashioned flowerpots, not plastic ones, or – oh, Hamish! he had hundreds of these – plain ordinary plates and jugs and bowls, nice ones I mean, but not expensive designer ones or crafty ones, just nice china plates where if you break one you can get another, or wooden toys or bicycles that aren't stunt ones – you know what we said to Ashley Oswald when he wanted one of those – or nice clothes where you don't pay a fortune for the label but they don't look like catalogue ones, and pots and pans, cheap but good quality, you could see that, or small carpets or, and, oh just everything like that?' Her eyes were shining.

'Dunno,' said Hamish. 'Did you say bikes?'

'Yeah, Dad,' said Ashley Oswald. 'Only fifty pounds. I had a go on one of them, it was great *and* I went four whole pedals without stabilizers, really, honest! I could save up, Dad. I've got two pounds forty-eight you gave me already.'

'And what I thought was, Hamish, why shouldn't I – or we, why shouldn't *we* – well, go in for some of them? Round here. I mean there are lots of people who haven't got cars, aren't there, and you know how hopeless the bus is nowadays and it costs a fortune, I mean for instance old Mrs Flews was only saying to me the other day she'd been wanting a poker since the year before last only she didn't see why she should have to buy a whole set of fire things to get one, well we could sell her that!'

'A poker,' said Hamish.

'Yes! For instance. And all we'd need, really, is a . . . a . . . Well, some sort of truck, perhaps.'

'Does he do electronics?'

'Well maybe not electronics as such, Hamish, but. . .'

'What?'

'Well all right, no he doesn't, he says they're, well . . .'

'Not wholesome, man,' said Mungo, making a peace sign. 'Unbrotherly. Dark side of the Force.'

'Oh,' said Hamish.

'Yes but the point is, *if* we had a – a truck of some sort – say the biggest you can get without an HIV test or whatever it is you have to pass before you can drive one of these things that's too big for an ordinary licence – if we had one of those we could . . . could use it. For transporting the things in. As well as the fruit and vegetables, I mean. Hamish?'

'Oh, yeah, fine!' Hamish laughed bitterly. 'Triffic, wonderful. I mean apart from the fact that we've nowhere to put anything like that. I mean had you thought where to put it?'

'Well there's the back-room, the store. If we got regular supplies in we wouldn't need it so much, would we? We could knock a door through. And,' she continued before Hamish could object to knocking a door through, 'if that didn't work there's – well, we could talk about that when the time came, couldn't we. I mean I know trucks are quite expensive, good second-hand ones I mean, but – '

'Quite expensive! I should say expensive, that is if you don't just want a bucket of rust with a wheel on each corner. Have you any idea how much a decent vehicle'd cost?'

256

'Well yes, Hamish, roughly, and I know a thousand pounds is a lot of money, in some ways, but – '

'A *thousand*?'

'Well, twelve hundred and something actually but it would be money well – '

'And where're you proposin' to get a halfway decent truck for that much?'

'At the Magic B – . . . at Mr Zimbalist's,' said Grace. She swallowed quickly. 'Only we'd have to give him a decision by next weekend or he'll send the deposit back because he's got a – '

'Deposit? How much?'

'Only a hundred pounds, Hamish, and he says we can get it checked over, by the AA for instance, any time between now and then.'

'But we aren't in the AA!'

'No I know, but Mungo – '

'What?'

'I've got a pal,' explained Mungo. 'Does AA approved work. He'd give it a going-over for a couple of notes. My treat. As well as getting you a couple of hundred for the car.'

Hamish gaped. 'Car?'

'For spares,' said Mungo. 'They're quite difficult to get hold of since they stopped making them.'

'I mean it's not as if we used the car much, as a car, Hamish, is it? Even when it's going properly. And if it was broken up Mr Zimbalist'd get the number plate.'

'Wha – . . . why?'

'Because it's got 666 in it. That's why – well, partly why – the truck's so cheap. To us, I mean. He's got a friend who's a wizard.'

There was silence for a while.

'Don't do that with the melon, Wally dear,' said Grace absently. 'Give it to Uncle Mungo, that's right.'

'That still leaves us short of a thousand,' Hamish said at last. 'I can't see old McMurtry giving me a thousand pennies, let alone pounds. Or Kirk, for that matter.'

'N-no,' Grace began. 'But.'

'But what?'

'But, well . . . I mean, it wouldn't have to be . . . I mean *I* could . . . couldn't I? On my own – I mean, for this shop.' She looked at the floor. Mungo played peep-bo with Wally's melon. Ashley Oswald had slipped through to the house.

'Oh, yeah,' said Hamish quietly. 'Fine. Right. Go ahead then. I'll – make the kids' tea, shall I?' He blundered round the counter. 'Better make it a thousand and forty-seven pounds fifty-two,' he added thickly. 'The lad can have his bike then, can't he?'

Grace and Mungo caught each other's eyes, then Grace looked away. 'Come on, Wol,' said Mungo. 'Let's go and give your dad a hand, shall we?' He picked the infant up and touched Grace, very briefly, on the arm as she bent to empty the till.

Chapter Nine

The next three days were relatively uneventful. In the United States of America, Federal Tax Commissioners ordered a covert investigation of the affairs of Duncan Trombo, the billionaire property developer, and his many business associates in Wall Street, the White House and Detroit, Illinois. In Britain, the Department of Enterprise decided not to refer to the Monopolies and Mergers Commission the proposed takeover of Universal Regionals plc (proprietors of the *Perthshire Gazette* and some seven hundred and twenty-eight other titles worldwide) by Hosannah International (UK) plc (Say HI! To Global Diversification) on the grounds that since Felix Krüll, the merchant banking arm of Melmotte's, were acting for both parties there was no occasion to fear that shareholders' interests might be compromised. Her Majesty's Customs and Excise reported a sharp drop in the total of UK cocaine seizures and sparked a lively debate as to whether or not this was a good thing.

Mid Lummock district councillors met to approve the awarding of commercial contracts for a wide range of local services. Afterwards they announced an eight and a half per cent reduction in the Community Charge and went off to set about getting themselves re-elected three weeks later.

Craigfieth witnessed a few more little unravellings of its threadbare social fabric. At a thinly attended meeting of the WRI on Monday night it was resolved (pro: five; con: three; abstentions: eight) to dissociate the organization from all preparations for the Gala, since (as one speaker pointed out) the Gala didn't seem to have any use for the WRI's services anyway. Mrs Jessie MacAndrew (treasurer) reported proceeds of fifty-eight pounds and seventy-three pence from the Daffodil Tea. There followed an interesting talk, with slides, on the rôle of women in Azerbaijan, and a Basket Whist.

Craigfieth Community Council met on Tuesday night in the Community Centre at 8 P.M., sat around until 8.23 P.M. and, with the late arrival of Ms Maureen O'Rourke, became quorate and had a meeting. There being only one item on the agenda, Ms O'Rourke was asked to give her thoughts with regard to community involvement in the Gala. Ms O'Rourke stated that as she was, so to speak, an interested party in the case – being a co-director of the Body Development Dance Workshop Artistes and hence under contract to the Gala Committee to provide terpsichorean relief – she hoped they would understand that hers must be a position of the strictest neutrality in the matter. It was speedily resolved (a) That this Community Council would not involve itself in matters which, strictly speaking, were outwith its remit and (b) That this Community Council write a strongly worded letter of protest to Warm-U-Up (Dunbroath) Ltd re the total lack of heating facilities in the Community Centre since the previous October, which was obliging clients of the Craigfieth Playgroup to keep their anoraks and mittens on. The meeting closed at 8.46 P.M.

Wednesday night saw an extremely disaffected gathering of Stags in the rear function suite of the Ben Almond Hotel. Even as the Brother Stags passed through the Arcane Portal, depositing Spoor and donning Pelt after the Ancient Custom, it was clear that trouble lay ahead. Bruce Waddell (Spoormaster Seneschal) looked grim; Kenny Glencairn junior (Velvet Templar) looked nervous. The Most Puissant Ceremony of the Musk Oath was got through with, some felt, unseemly haste. Tension mounted as all those present – Royals, Rutters and Rogues alike – waited for the rather messy Initiation Rites of young Jimmy Duff (grandson of Councillor Duff, grandnephew of Duff the Elder, of Duff's Garage, and the ninth fireman to take the Antler) to end. When at last Mr Glencairn senior rose to his aged feet to give the traditional Herdmaster's Bellow no one present was in any doubt that what followed would not be mere ritual.

Nor was it. Briefly (for him) Mr Glencairn outlined the history of the schism which, fifteen years before, had threatened to split the Stags into two herds, viz the Coherers, who held that the ancient and terrible Bond of Secrecy forbade any sort of Staggish involvement in the affairs of the uninitiated, and the Diffusers, who (being mostly shopkeepers) maintained that certain Outsider's Affairs (e.g. the Shopping Gala) were most unlikely, in this day and age, to jeopardize the Order and could, indeed, be of tangible benefit to some of its favourite charities – such as the Indigent Hinds' Welfare Association and the Fawns' Annual Outing to St Andrews. At that time he, Mr Glencairn senior, had attempted to heal the breach by planting a foot (or ought he to say two hooves?) in each camp (here he paused to let the beauty of this metaphor linger upon the incense-laden air of the rear function suite) and becoming Honorary Life President of the Gala Committee while simultaneously taking up the Mantle (here he paused to adjust it) of Herdmaster and Stag Royal Supreme of the Craigfieth Lodge.

He ventured to think that this arrangement had worked very well.

Recent events – here he broke off entirely and fixed his son, Kenny Glencairn junior, with a watery glare of myopic reproach; Kenny shuffled his feet and sweated under his mask – recent events had forced a change in his

261

long-standing business arrangements, and the imminent removal of himself and his hind, Mrs Glencairn senior, to a bungalow on the Silver Threads Retirement Estate in Bonquhars. (Here you could have cut the air, as someone put it in the cocktail bar afterwards, with a knife.) This would, he pointed out, leave the Gala Committee bereft of an Honorary Life President of any active utility (the Silver Threads Retirement Estate being, by implication, one of those bournes from which no traveller returns) and the Craigfieth Stags looking for a new Herdmaster. In order to avoid certain unfortunate things happening (fissiparousness might have been the word he was after) he felt it might be better if these two posts were to be filled – if at all – by two different people. He thanked his fellow-Stags and closed his Bellow with the traditional couplet of demotic Doric.

The three resignations – one each from the WRI, the Community Council and the Stags – were duly delivered to Sounds Good (formerly the Bonaventure Wireless Shop) where Hamish informed the bearers that he didn't know where Neville was, only where he wasn't, i.e. Sounds Good, his resignation from the post of Temporary Trainee Assistant Retail Manager having been delivered by proxy on Monday morning. They took their resignations to Sayeed Haq instead, who received them with an inscrutable smile and a little speech to the effect that these things were very often for the best.

Kenny Glencairn junior announced his translation to the status of sole franchizee for Gospel Wholefoods in Dunbroath on Thursday morning. The closing-down notice and the ubiquitous little sticker appeared in the window of Glencairns (Estab 1887) shortly after lunchtime.

Miss Phemister, hearing the news, ventured to observe to her friend and mentor that this must surely be good for

262

the business of the Bide-a-Wee Tearooms. Mrs Spurtle fixed Miss Phemister with a curdling look and asked her if she had ever wondered why all the shoe shops in Duncruddie Mains were in the same street and practically next door to each other. Miss Phemister had to admit she hadn't. Mrs Spurtle, massively vindicated, left it at that.

All was not gloom, however, in the empty Tearooms that Thursday afternoon. Mrs Spurtle re-read her letter in the *Perthshire Gazette* (printed in full and with only three mistakes), smiled in a delphic sort of way, instructed Miss Phemister to order more supplies of Mother McGoody's Instant Castle of Mey Scone Mix (No Egg Needed) and sat back to await developments.

Audrey Pitt-Holyoake, half-exhausted from late nights with the paint-roller, received a visit at Dante Cottage from Miss Xanthia Partleigh-Noble of *Scottish Country Matters* and a photographer, none other than Campbeltown Fotheringhame, moonlighting from *Scotland Now!* on the pretext of having a touch of flu.

Miss Partleigh-Noble gushed her way from apartment to apartment. Campbeltown Fotheringhame pointed his camera where he was told to, and said nothing. He knew his place and the money – cash, no National Insurance – was good. Four more outings of this sort, he calculated, and his wife could have her hip done.

The significance and provenance of every part of Dante Cottage's fabric, furnishings and decoration safely recorded for browsing posterity on film and in Roedean-taught Pitman's, Audrey left them in the drawing-room while she popped out to make some Darjeeling (herbal? No, better not) prior to the 'background part' of the interview, during which she hoped to enlist the support of Miss Partleigh-Noble's magazine in her campaign to avoid homelessness.

'There we are,' she said, returning with the tray. 'Now then – that's goat and that's cow, there's cube, granulated or demerara if you want sugar, and those are Bath Olivers.'

Miss Partleigh-Noble took goat and no sugar; Mr Fotheringhame asked for two, please, and just as it came. Audrey thought he might have been happier with a mug, but did not say so. Instead she said, 'I expect you must go to all sorts of interesting places, Mr Fotheringhame, being a press photographer?'

The lensman thought immediately of an epic bender he'd had in Orkney, covering the visit of HM Queen Elizabeth the Queen Mother to St Magnus Cathedral in Kirkwall. Good old Queen Mum! Always did her bit for the media and left you to spend the remaining five hours and forty-two minutes of your assignment to get local colour in the pubs. Then he considered his surroundings. 'I went to Turriff once,' he said.

'Oh . . . really?' said Audrey. 'I don't think I've ever been there.' Should she have remembered, she wondered, if she had? 'And it was . . . interesting, was it?'

'Oh yes,' said Fotheringhame. 'Very interesting.'

Audrey wondered if the ball was now in her court. 'A – er,' she began.

'They showed me an emporium,' he said. '"You must go to Archie's Emporium," they said. "It's very interesting."'

Audrey glanced across at Miss Partleigh-Noble, but she had retreated behind her chair and was writing something in her notebook.

'And . . . was it?' she asked helplessly.

'Oh, aye,' said Fotheringhame. 'Sure. Ve-ry interesting. About the most interesting place I've been, I'd say.'

'Ah,' said Audrey.

'That . . . man . . . Archie,' Fotheringhame continued

heavily, clutching a tiny cup in his great fist, 'do you know what he had? In his emporium? He had *seven* Perkins Diesel Generators! It was unbelievable.' He shook his head. 'Seven. All in one place, you understand? Before, I'd just thought, ach, what's an emporium, y'know?'

Audrey nodded rapidly.

'But this place. Well, *I've* never seen anything like it. Before or since.'

'Good gracious,' Audrey murmured.

'And then . . .'

'Yes?'

'Then they says to me: "Go and see Hughie's bike." Just like that. Go . . . and see . . . Hughie's bike.'

Audrey gave up. Miss Partleigh-Noble turned a page.

Fotheringhame sighed. 'Sometimes,' he said dolefully, 'I wish I had.'

'Now then,' said Miss Partleigh-Noble, constipating the o and making the e balance on a razor's edge. 'I understand that your' – her eyelids fluttered a fetching little excuse-me – 'your *lend*lord, haha! is Lord Margoyle?'

'Yes,' said Audrey sweetly. 'Worse luck,' she added, not so sweetly.

Fotheringhame stirred out of his reverie.

'Oh!' said Miss Partleigh-Noble. 'Haha!' she added, playing for time. 'Could you, I mean . . .'

Audrey smiled. 'He's evicting me,' she said, breaking a Bath Oliver in two. 'Throwing me out. Giving me the boot. Not for not paying rent, I should add. Nor for anything specified in the various Acts of Parliament discussed at great length by the late Messrs Gloag and Henderson.' She patted a big book in a brown paper cover on her occasional table. 'Just thrown out.' She smiled again. 'More tea?' She was rather enjoying herself. Miss Partleigh-Noble weakly proffered her cup and saucer. Campbeltown Fotheringhame came to life and took a biscuit.

'But why,' said Miss Partleigh-Noble, 'would he do that?'

'You're the journalist,' Audrey replied, pouring without the hint of a tremble. 'Ask him.'

Miss Partleigh-Noble visibly shuddered. Her cup and saucer rattled in sympathy. She put them down hastily and made various decorous gestures indicative of her innocence of the charge. 'More features, really,' she explained.

'Ersa feature,' said Fotheringhame through his biscuit. 'Little old lady. Eviction. Nice, these.'

'Do have another,' said Audrey, getting up. She crossed to her escritoire and returned with a sheaf of letters.

'Notice of Intention to Repossess,' she said, handing it over. 'Notice to Quit. Copy of my letter about constant interruption of water supply, unanswered. Letter to Broody's asking for an explanation of their silence. I haven't had the silence back for that one yet.' She sat down again, obliging Miss Partleigh-Noble to read them. She looked round her pretty, cosy little room. 'Rather a shame, wouldn't you say?'

Fotheringhame nodded vigorously.

'Oh yes,' agreed Miss Partleigh-Noble. 'Yet it *is* such a shame because I was at school with his daughter, you see.' She looked quite distraught.

'I'm not sure I see the sequitur,' Audrey replied equably, 'but I take the point.'

'Oh dear!'

'What?'

'Well I see here it says you're to . . . remove, at the end of June.'

'That's right. That's what they want.'

'Oh, well . . . That's it then. My article wasn't due to come out until September, you see.'

The silence seemed very long. 'Really?' said Audrey at last.

'Yes. So you see . . .' Miss Partleigh-Noble gestured at her notes. 'All a terrible waste, really.'

Fotheringhame froze in mid chew.

Audrey stood up. 'I expect,' she said levelly, 'you'd like to leave now, wouldn't you.' It was not a question.

'I think I'd better, rather,' said Miss Partleigh-Noble gratefully.

Fotheringhame heaved himself upright, spilling crumbs on the gracefully faded carpet. His colleague walked quickly to the front door as if determined not to draw breath until she was safely through it. Fotheringhame let Audrey go first, then shambled after her. Miss Partleigh-Noble was now almost running up the garden path. Then she screamed in a most unladylike and almost pitiable way, and nearly fell over. Audrey feigned indifference, Fotheringhame shambled on.

'More deid birdies,' he commented.

'Horrible!' said Miss Partleigh-Noble.

'Yes,' said Audrey. 'I pick up at least half a dozen a day, and bury them at the back there.'

Fotheringhame trod across Audrey's little lawn to the hedge, bruising the grass with his size twelves. He bent down and, with a stupendous effort stood upright again and plodded back, a tiny shivering thing cupped in his hands.

'A wee larkie,' he said. 'Deein.' He peered at it. 'Alphachloralose,' he grunted. 'Kills by hypothermia.'

'You mean it's – it's poison? I thought it was just this awful weather – cold, and wet, and . . . are you sure, Mr Fotheringhame?'

'Oh, aye. Death by natural cold's quick enough;

267

alphachloralose takes a bitty longer, an' you get the sudderin', you see. Like that.' He turned his back and did something quick and merciful.

'It gets intae the food chain, y'see,' he continued, his hands empty now. 'You get the poisoned bait put down, say: hoodies get it, and buzzards, things like that. That's the idea, see? Then they die, an' get eaten, and things that eat them die, an' so on. Includin' flies, of course. Then yon wee insectiverous creatures . . . phht!'

'Horrible,' said Audrey.

'These farmers!' said Miss Partleigh-Noble vacuously.

'No farmer that I know of, round here, would do a thing like that,' said Audrey.

'Oh?' said Miss Partleigh-Noble, not understanding but not interested anyway. 'Well, we'd really better . . .' It started to rain.

'Aye,' said Fotheringhame. He looked at Audrey. 'I'll send ye the photies,' he said.

'Thank you. Thank you very much. That's very kind of you.'

The little red Renault whined off down the lane. Audrey went back in and closed the door. She wanted to lock it, too, but her wrist was hurting and her hand shook too much to manage the key.

Ganglion clicked his phone off, then clicked his tongue.

'Trouble?' asked Oswald.

'Grace,' said Ganglion. ''Avin' a bit of a time of it. School 'olidays. 'Amish. An'at.'

'Oh, aye.'

'I said we'd take Ashley Oz off of 'er 'ands fer a day, termorrer. Gawd! Finker somefing ter do, Oz.'

'An outing, somewhere?' Oswald suggested vaguely.

'Yeah, spose so.' Ganglion sighed.

'Did you ask?'

'Wot? Oh, that, yeah. Same. Nuffink in.'

'That's it, then,' said Oswald. 'It's been four days, there's no point in looking any more.'

'No. Spose not. Wonder why, though?'

'Might as well go on wondering,' Oswald grunted, wheeling himself through to the kitchen to make another pot of tea. 'Seeing as how every time we ring the paper and ask for Miss Smith they ask who's ringing and then say she's not available.'

'Yeah. Oh well. Speck there's some perfickly good an' utterly cruddy newspaper-type reason for it.'

'Like censorship, maybe.'

Ganglion coughed. 'You, er . . . you don't fink you might be bein' just a touch paranoid, Oz, sayin' that, do you?'

Oswald clapped the lid on the pot. 'A few years ago, perhaps.' He thought of making it *à la* Pitt-Holyoake, remembered marijuana was a mood enhancer, and decided not to. 'Say ten years ago. Not now.' He wheeled the tray through. 'I've been thinking,' he said.

'Ar! Fort you woz very quiet lately. Finkin' wot?'

'About this.' Oswald fetched his father's lease, now well thumbed, from the sideboard, and turned to the last page. 'See that,' he said. 'What do you notice about what's on it?'

Ganglion looked. 'Same as before, Oz,' he said, a little helplessly. 'A plan of Boggybreck, a few lines of legal waffle about this agreement bein' signed an' sealed an' wotnot, your dad's signature, some geezer at the War Office's signature an' a whole lot of other signatures in Witness Whereof. An' a dollop o' wax.'

'Right.' Oswald smiled grimly. 'Now, what do you notice about what's *not* on it?'

Ganglion shrugged. 'Well . . . I dunno. The secret recipes fer Worcester Sauce an' Guinness Extra Stout?

Pictures of nude women wrestling in fresh fish? Wot you on about?'

'What's *not* there, my friend, is anything to indicate whether this document is a lease, or a contract of sale, or an agreement to – to let the Maureen O'Rourke Dancers practise on the land on alternate Shrove Tuesdays – or anything. *And,*' he added before Ganglion could reply, 'you'll notice, will you, the way all the pages are fixed together.'

'Stitched,' said Ganglion. 'Ar.'

'Now then.' Oswald settled grimly into his exegesis. 'Let's just pause there, and remember what else was going on at the time my da put his name on this thing, shall we? Item: Drubber and Dunning persuade him to take an attractive lump sum in lieu of rent in perpetuity, just enough, surprise surprise, to put down as a deposit on Newbiggings; item: he takes out a mortgage with the Mid Lummock Husbandmen's, who shortly afterwards go phut; item: Drubber and Dunning come to the rescue of the Husbandmen's, and buy – oh, aye, I got young Mungo to check it for me in Edinburgh – *buy* a posh set of offices in Hope Street, cash down. Now then, assuming my da put his signature on *two* leases, this one and a copy, what do you suppose happened to the copy, eh?'

'Unstitched, last page of lease taken out, put into dummy deed of sale,' said Ganglion, 'an' stitched up. Bob's yer bleedin' uncle. But wait a minute, Oz – there's his initials, look, on every page; 'e wouldn't 'ave gorn an' done that on every page of a, wossname, deed of sale or wotever it's called, now would 'e?'

'Aye, no but look at his initials, Ganglion! See? And remember, practically everyone wrote copperplate in those days, if they'd been taught to write at all. I mind they were still teaching it when I was a bairn. It would be 'no difficult matter to forge two letters of the alphabet, would it? And then – out with the needle and thread.'

Ganglion looked at the lease again. 'The witnesses bein' either employees of the lawyers or a load of dimmocks hauled in off the pavement. Yeah. I see.'

'So who would you say,' Oswald asked, 'were the very last people on earth I should have gone to for advice?'

'Yeah. Right. Oh gawd.'

'And what simple fact can you tell me about anything to do with the activities of the Ministry of Defence?'

Ganglion thought. 'Everyfink they do costs five times as much as the original estimate, an' even then it doesn't work.'

'Apart from that. Apart from that, everything they do is a state secret. In the public interest. Including being the proud owners of a forged set of title deeds to Boggybreck. Can you see the powers that be owning up to being receivers of stolen property and missing out on one and a half million pounds? Hardly, eh? So what are they going to do when they find a newspaper starting to sniff round the story? QED, my friend. Kew-ee-dee.' He drank his tea and poured them both a refill, leaving his friend to digest the theory in silence.

'You cannot 'ope to bribe or twist,' Ganglion recited softly, not taking his eyes off his lap,

> Fank Gawd, the British journalist;
> But seein' wot the man will do
> Unbribed, there's no occasion to.'

'Or woman, Ganglion,' Oswald corrected. 'Or woman. These are the nineteen nineties, after all.'

'So wot're we goin' to do about it?'

Oswald shrugged. 'I don't – '

The phone rang. ''Allo? Yeah, ass me . . . oh, 'allo

there, me old mate, 'ow are – Wot? . . . yeah . . . yeah
. . . yeah, well I – Oh, yeah, but . . . oh. Yeah, well, all
right then. Yeah. Yeah. Right . . . yeah. Right . . .
Termorrer, right . . . Right. No, no bovver. Right.

'Facknell! Well, there we are, Oz! Like my old Sunday
School teacher used ter say when she woz turnin' us
upside down ter shake the pennies out, there's always
someone worse off than wot you are.'

'Oh?'

'You better believe it. That woz our friend MacGregor,
phonin' from beautiful downtown Blairlummock. Seems
'e's bin caught in a compromisin' position wiv a bottle of
hooch an' a stuffed lady novelist, an' given the sack; and,
get this, as a result 'is niece is chuckin' 'im out. Termorrer.
Can we go an' get 'im, can 'e come an' stay wiv us till 'e
gets 'imself sorted. Says 'e's got 'is own camp bed. So, all
we need to do is find 'im somewhere ter put it, eh?'

'You'd better put the roof-rack on, then,' said Oswald.

'Oh, I dunno, Oz, be a bit draughty for 'im, kippin' up
there. An' wot about when it rains?'

'Idiot! Ach, we'll manage somehow I suppose. That
can't be all he's got, though, can it?'

'Pretty well, accordin' to 'im. That, an' a few clothes
an' 'is pension book, an' 'is Bible no doubt. 'E sez ter
forget the bike, 'e'd be just as 'appy ter listen to the
service on Radio Scotland instead.'

Oswald sighed. 'Now there's something to look forward
to! Oh, well, if that's really all he's got, the poor old
bugger, you could take Ashley Oswald with you – I expect
there'll be more things open now it's Easter. I could stay
here, tidy up a bit.'

'Right-o,' said Ganglion. 'Oi, Oz – never a dull
moment, eh? 'Ere, you don't fancy a smoke on it by any
chance, do yer?'

* * *

Campbeltown Fotheringhame arrived home later than he had intended. The whole sordid business of money – especially, it seemed, *his* money – had been too utterly distasteful for Xanthia Partleigh-Noble and he had been obliged to accompany her to the offices of *Scottish Country Matters* – an outstanding example of neo-Nazi business architecture in the very heart of the Greater Glasgow Enterprise Zone – in order to get it. 'Never trust the bosses' might not sound very much in the way of a store of wisdom acquired over twenty-nine years of service, man and boy, to the moguls of the Newspaper Publishers' Association but it was, he reminded himself daily, pretty well the only thing worth knowing.

Even here he had some difficulty. The Greater Glasgow Enterprise Zone was, apparently, a cashless society and the legions of clothed robots on the staff of *Scottish Country Matters* seemed determined, to a zombie, not to soil their hands with the stuff if at all possible. No, he explained (looking inside his greasy coat to check) he did not have any micro-link credit facilities; no, he did not go in for electronic banking, power cuts being what they were these days and no, he would not take a cheque. He wanted his wages crisp and blue – even soggy and grey would do – and all nicely done up with a wee rubber band, and there he would stay until he got them. He sat down heavily on something that probably wasn't a chair to prove it, feeling like Priapus might have felt in a Vestals' dormitory, had he happened to be suffering from leprosy and syphilis as well.

At last a sufficient quantity of folding specie was procured somehow and handed over to him – they had run out of sterilized tongs, apparently – in a sealed white envelope. Fotheringhame opened it, counted the money (lingeringly) and gave them the envelope back. He called in at the Building Society and deposited the money in his wife's account, the Inland Revenue having about as much respect for decent privacy these days as the Department of Social Security. Then he went home.

His wife had had a reasonable day: average-to-moderate pain, average-to-poor mobility. The bulb had gone in the sitting-room ceiling light, and that was a nuisance because she couldn't manage the chair to fix it, but otherwise she was happy enough, she said, and very glad to see him. She got the drinks, he cooked the tea. When they had unwound a little she showed him the letter she'd had from *Scotland Now!*'s employee health insurers.

'Yeah, well,' he said when he'd read it. 'As I told you, hen. Don't worry, we're nearly there.'

'But it's so unfair, Cambie! I'm not a chronic case!'

'You are unless you can afford the operation,' he pointed out. 'Catch-twenty-two, see? No, stay put. I'll wash up.'

Later he changed the bulb and settled her by the fire with her coffee. 'I'll just be,' he told her. 'Got a wee phoney call to make.' The telephone was in the kitchen; moving it from the icy hall had been one of their few concessions to modern living.

He dialled (they weren't that modern) an Edinburgh number. 'Helloo!' he cooed in his Sunday-best Bearsden. 'Would that be Clay Loan, official freelance representative of Her Majesty's quality press? Fotheringhame frae the gutter speakin'.'

'Campbeltown!' said a voice. 'Hi! How's filth?'

'Filth,' said Fotheringhame feelingly, 'is not what it used tae be. Clay, I've got a wee taster for you. A truly tasty morsel: about three inches by one and a hauf, excludin' feathery appendages, typical of the family Alaudidae, an' deid, five hours ago, of alphachloralose.'

'Sweet Jesus. Are you sure?'

'Short of eatin' it masel' tae find oot, yes I'm sure. If

you fancy payin' for a P-M it's in the freezer right now. In clingfilm, mind.'

'Mmm. Right, go ahead and have it done. Yes, dear boy, Clay will pay. Now let's see – skylark, you say? Where found?'

'On the Lunie Estate, Lord Margoyle prop, Central Perthshire.'

'My, you *do* get around, old thing! Would this by any chance be Lunie as in MaxProf Associates as in shortly-to-be Scotland's leading shooters' paradise?'

'The very same.'

'Oh, thank you, God! Thank you, thank you, *thank* you, God!'

'No' at all,' replied Fotheringhame drily. 'Feel free tae pray tae me ony time, ye miserable sinner ye.'

'Yes, quite, thank you too, of course, dear boy. Now then, tell me: any chance of getting something a bit more . . . you know . . . like a golden eagle perhaps?'

Fotheringhame thought. 'Doubtful. It's past lambing now, they'll be headed back to wilder places. I can, however, offer you buzzards, hoodie craws, any quantity of flies an' bluebottles, an' probably the odd deid cat if ye looked hard enough.'

'Mmm. Cats might be an idea, I suppose. Or dogs, even better. The rest . . . well, not quite cuddly enough, really. Especially the bluebottles. Even A, B and C1 readers like their conservation issues to be cuddly, you see. Now if it was *seals* . . .'

'I have a suggestion,' said Fotheringhame. 'Get yer breeks dirty an' hae a look yersel'!'

'Point taken, my dear, point taken. I dare say I could don the old green wellies and the Barbour jacket with prickly hat *à la mode*.'

'Yeah. You do that. An' when ye find somethin' – remember who tell't ye, eh?'

'Oh, I will, I will. You can do the snaps, old thing, I promise.'

'Yeah, yeah. So you should. Actually I was thinkin' of a percentage like, y'know? As your unimpeachable source, so tae say.'

'Oh, ho! The old Fotheringhame holiday fund running low is it?'

'What's a holiday? I was thinkin' more o' the Mrs Fotheringhame hip operation fund, *ectualleigh*.'

'Oh. Ouch. Sorry. Yes of course. Fear not. When this lot hits the fan I'll make sure a substantial dollop flies in your direction, okay?'

'Good. Hey an' listen – make it big, y'understand? Like, big. TV, Sunday supps, the polis even. Make it stink, Clay, you hearin' me?'

'Dear me! Do I scent the whiff of an ulterior motive, old fruitcake? I mean, I know you're heavily into the wee birdies and all, but . . .'

'I'm rootin' fae another endangered species, if ye want tae know. An endangered species o' human birdie, what has nae news value these days on account o' bein' too commonly extinct. You just do as I say, okay?'

'Message received, old man. Over and out.'

'And hey! Before ye go. Make it this side o' June 30th, you hear me? Well this side. Or I'll tell all tae the *Sunday Sport*.'

'You cad, sir!'

'Aren't I just. Do it, pal. Do it.' He put the telephone down and stared at it for some time with great intensity. Then he joined his wife.

'Who were you ringing, dear? If it's not a secret, I mean.'

'A hack,' said Fotheringhame, 'wi' a ploom in his mouth, correction, plummm in his mowth. Fortunately,' he continued, lowering his weary buttocks into the second best armchair, 'unlike most he's got a fair allowance o' the real stuff between his ears. I hope,' he added.

Neville had a curious telephone call shortly after six o'clock, a curiously twangy voice that asked for him by name.

'Yes?' he said.

'A frind tills me,' said the voice, 'thit you used the services of a Mr . . . Eugene Mkekwe, the other day?'

'Up to a point,' said Neville, being witty.

'What?'

Neville gulped. 'I mean yes. Yes I did. Wh – '

'Good. Use him again, will you? Tomorrow evening six-thirty at the bick of the Ministry of the Interior. Got thit?'

'The f-furniture place, you mean? Yes, yes I've got that. Wh – '

'And frind – if you want to stay frindly – a word of caution.'

'Y-yes?'

'Don't be there.'

He met his fiancée in the bathroom; fortunately she was only cleaning her teeth.

'Going out?' she asked.

'Yes, a – business, actually.' He felt himself blush.

'Oh. Good. Look, about my interview. There's an extra part to it. Tonight.'

'Oh? Oh, right, check. Well, good luck then.'

'Yes. It probably won't take as long as yours did, Neville, but – don't wait up, okay?'

'No, of course not. Um, see you in the morning then?'

'Possibly. You have to leave early, remember. Anyway, *ciao*.'

'Yeah, *ciao*. Right.'

Neville walked, shoulders hunched against the driving rain, to the house on Fleming Way.

'Oh! Lawks-a-mussy, massuh!' wailed the girl. 'I jus' doan hab de rent moneah dis week! Please, massuh, doan take ma li'l piccaninny away fro' meah!'

'You're being silly,' said Neville.

'I know,' she said. 'People with a sense of humour usually find it amusing. What can I do for you, Mister Man? And if that isn't a safe question, fuck me if I know what is.' She giggled. 'You wouldn't, would you? I mean, you just *couldn't!*'

'Couldn't what?'

'Fuck me.'

Neville flinched.

The girl laughed again. 'I'm sorry,' she said. 'Should have put a condom on my tongue before I said it. But I mustn't mock. Speak, O Android of the Briefcase!'

'I need your brother again.'

The girl gasped. 'So that's it! I think I ought to warn you, you know, just because black men have proverbially big dongs doesn't necessarily mean they – ' She caught his dead eye. 'Sor-ee!'

'Can't we get off sex, just for a minute?'

'I find it hard. But I expect you don't. Okay, what do you want him for?'

'Business.'

'What else? Okay – where? When?'

'At the back of the Ministry of the Interior – you know the place?'

'Crap furniture, never open. Yeah, yeah.'

'At half past six. In the evening. Tomorrow.'

'Okay, I'll tell him. Anything else?'

'Er . . . yes. Tell him to call himself what he called himself last time. He'll understand.'

'That stupid Afro name again? God, you really are stupid.'

'Just tell him.'

'Right, right, right. Anything else? You wanna jerk off in the bathroom? I got some lovely pictures of money stashed away – '

Neville slammed the door.

The girl shrugged. 'Was it something I said?' she asked herself.

Mrs Spurtle heaved a long, contented sigh.

'Twenty-eight, Phemmy! Twenty-eight!'

Miss Phemister was head down in the suds. 'Yes, dear,' she said.

'And only eight of them wanting ten per cent off! It's just as I always say, Phemmy, people are idiots.'

'Yes, dear.'

'They'll fall for anything!'

'Yes, dear.'

'Thank God!'

'Yes, dear. Is there any more washing-up?'

'No, that's the lot.'

'Oh! Thank guidness!'

'Never mind, Phemmy! *Courage, mon amie!* Never mind just now – a few more weeks of this, Phemmy, and we can get a dishwasher!'

'Ooh! Mai guidness!'

'Or maybe months, we'll see. Anyway, you must agree it's worth it, don't you? After all, what's a few plates and cups and things when the very life-blood of the Bide-a-Wee is at stake?'

'Oh, quayte. Yes dear, Ay'm sure.'

'Good. Now then: the next thing to do is to see about getting my nomination papers for the election, and get your name down on them.'

'Oh!' Miss Phemister dropped a plate. 'B-b-b-.'

'As proposer, Phemmy, as proposer. Or seconder or something. Good God alive, woman, you don't think I'd let *you* loose in Mid Lummock House, do you?'

'Oh no, dear. Thank you.'

'Hmph! One thing's for sure, I'll have no trouble getting my signatures, the crowds we'll have in here the next few days. Ha! Ha-ha!'

'Wh-what is it, dear?'

'I've just had a thought, Phemmy! Stop twittering and I'll tell you: my thought is, Phemmy, what if they allow you secretarial help?'

'Oh! Ay . . . what, dear?'

'A secretarial allowance, you stupid woman! For secretaries! For councillors!'

'Oh, Ay . . . Ay – oh no, Joan! No, please, Joan, Ay –'

'Oh well.' The widow shrugged. 'Just a thought.' She rubbed her hands. 'Oh ho, Mister Eugene Mkekwe, you are going to regret the day you crossed Joan Spurtle's path!'

'Yes, dear. Ay'm sure you're right. May Ay . . . may we . . . go home now?'

Chapter Ten

Ganglion set off early to relieve his daughter-in-law of Ashley Oswald and take him off to Blairlummock. Oswald stayed behind to spring-clean, at any rate up to a height of about four feet six inches, the communal apartments of Rose Cottage, starting with the bathroom on the principle of getting the worst done first. This accomplished with liberal doses of bleach (and to hell, thought Oswald, with the septic tank just this once) he returned to the sitting-room where his reforming gaze was immediately assailed by Ganglion's collection of art prints, a series of six variations on an eternal theme, whose originals had evidently been drawn long before the adoption of leanness as a prerequisite of feminine allurement and which paid scant regard to the limitations of three-dimensional anatomical possibility. MacGregor – who as a regular churchgoer of the more grimly joyful persuasion would surely draw a clear distinction between practice and principle and have little time for the frivolities of art – would not like them. In fact MacGregor, being MacGregor, would actively disapprove. Which was just too bad for the time being, because they were out of Oswald's reach and therefore, he decided, none of his business. In any case, being a good host had to have its limits and if MacGregor knew of a better hole then he was perfectly entitled to go to it. He'd hardly notice them at all if they put his bed directly underneath.

A vapid shaft of sunlight broke through the gloom and washed feebly over Half-a-Job's sour acres. All the animals had gone, Oswald noticed: probably, he thought, in

281

a last defiant act of collective hara-kiri. The farmer's trailer, now completely wheelless, rotted uncomplainingly where he had abandoned it.

The sun strengthened a little, revealing a million specks of dust in the disturbed air of the sitting room. Bother spring-cleaning, Oswald thought, I'll just pop out to the taxi and get those pot plants ready for hardening-off, like Audrey said. There would be plenty of time to finish off indoors; it was bound to rain again later on.

Babette was serving in the shop; Grace was in the kitchen. 'He's just outside,' she said. 'Playing with Tammy Sproat. Erm, would you mind . . .?'

'Takin' sprog Sproat as well, you mean?'

'Yes, if you could, only he's Ashley Oswald's best friend at the moment and he says he's bored.'

'Blimey! In that case yes, I'll take the little bleeder. Gawd knows there are few fings in this life more danger-ous than a bored Sproat. We'll all squash in some'ow, I dare say.'

'Thanks. Only I've got someone to look after Wally for the day, you see – I was going to put him to playgroup only I don't like him being in the Community Centre when it's raining, I don't think it's good for his chest and we're going to get this truck today.'

'Wot, you'n 'Amish?'

'No. Me and Mungo.'

'Ar. And 'ow *is* 'Amish?'

'Oh,' she sighed. 'Difficult, you know. Not, you know, against it really, but . . .'

'Difficult.'

'Yes.'

'Yeah, I see.'

'You do think it's a good idea, don't you? I mean I've been to the bank and everything and they're quite happy.'

'Oh, sure, luv. I fink you're on a winner, frankly. Swot this dump's bin cryin' out for fer years, few ask me. Play yer cards right wiv this Banana bloke an' you could be set up for life, bofe of you. Only it's difficult for 'Amish, don't yer see?'

'Oh I know, and I do see, only it's so hard to get through to him without being afraid of upsetting . . . especially when there's already something I haven't . . .'

'Wot?'

'Oh, nothing really, it's all right. It won't be for much longer, I hope. Only I'm so worried about him. I'm . . . I'm afraid he might be going to, you know, do something.'

'Cworr! Don't 'old yer breath, luv. No, that's not fair really, 'e's all right is our 'Amish, underneef. Wot sort of somefink?'

'Well, like – sell the shop, for instance. His – your old – shop.'

Ganglion sniffed. 'Mightn't be a bad idea.'

'Do you . . . really think so?'

'Well I meantersay, if a business is dyin' on its feet, like wot 'Amish's seems ter be, not entirely through 'is own fault I freely admit, wot's the point in goin' down wiv it, I arst you? Might as well give it yoofanasia, I'd say. Put yerself out of its misery.'

'Yes. Only you see I . . . I think it's you he's mostly worried about really. He thinks – that is I think he thinks – he's afraid he'd be . . . you know, letting you down, or something.'

'Lettin' me down?'

'Well, yes. You know . . . destroying what you built up, or being a failure where you'd been . . . well, not been.'

'Oh, Gordon bleedin' Bennett! Well fer a start I dunno where 'e got orl this lettin'-the-fambly-estate-go-ter-the-moneylenders rubbish from, cos it wasn't me, honest, 'e must've read too much when 'e woz pubertin'. Look, orl my ole Bonny-Vencher Wireless Shop ever did – orl it ever *'ad* ter do, I should say – was keep me an' 'im clothed an' fed. If it did any more'n that it was an unexpected bonus, far as I was concerned. An' besides, fings was very different then than wot they are now, people dint fink of goin' somewhere else ter shop, fer one fing, not ter mention there wasn't all these discount places an' cata-logues, an' big manufacturers doing deals wiv the big stores fer cut price computers an'at wot the customer, stupid git, as ter throw away after a couple o' years cos there's no spares. Snot 'Amish's fault, all that.'

'No, I know. I mean, I know that, and you know that, but . . .'

'An' you know I know you know I know you . . . yeah. But 'Amish . . .'

'Well . . . I mean maybe he does but he doesn't know he does.'

'Ar. An' so you want me to 'ave a word wiv 'im, is that it?'

'Would you?' Grace's eyes widened.

'I dunno, luv, frankly. One, I dunno that 'e wouldn't just ignore it cos it dint fit in wiv 'is mood an' because it woz comin' from me anyway; two, I'm not sure as 'e really oughter take it from me in the first place. See wot I mean?'

'Oh yes I . . . no, not really.'

'Purrit this way: don't you fink it might be even worse, in the long run, if 'e *didn't* make 'is own mind up? 'Owever painful that might be? 'Owever wrong, come ter that?'

'Yes.' Grace looked unhappy and unconvinced. 'I sup-pose so.'

Ganglion's resolve weakened instantly. You stupid old bugger, he told himself, half your trouble's always been not being able to say no to girls who said please. Got about as much will-power as a sherry trifle, you have. 'Listen,' he said softly, taking Grace's hand. 'Give it a little longer, orl right? An' then – if you ask me again – orl right, I will. Okay?'

'Yes. Thanks . . . Dad.'

'Nah then, nah then! That won't do!' He bit his lip. 'You've got your fortune ter make, remember?'

'Yes.' She smiled, sniffing. 'I'll go and get Mungo.'

'Yeah. Er, Grace luv? You, er, you dont fink 'Amish might be a bit – well, jealous, sort of fing, do yer? Or even – an' I know this is stupid ercorse – even a bit, well, anxious, narmean?'

Grace looked puzzled. 'About . . . about Mungo, you mean?'

'Well . . . yeah. Said it was stupid, mind.'

'About me and Mungo?'

'Um, sort of, yeah.'

'Oh, but that's – I mean, *Mungo?* What on earth would Hamish have to be jealous about?'

'Well, this is it. Right! Thass wot I fort, too. Good.' He opened the kitchen door. 'Oi, you two! I left five minutes ago!'

The wind played tunes in the roof rack as they drove out of Craigfieth. After about five minutes Tammy Sproat said, 'Why are we going the wrong way?'

'Aha!' said Ganglion. 'Oh-ho-ho! Shurrup.'

Ten minutes later they stopped at Boggybreck. 'Okay, my two little Accessories Before The Fact, 'ave a butcher's round, see if anybody's watchin'.'

The two boys, their senses alert from days of car-spotting, soon reported that Boggybreck was deserted except for a few stray sheep and an awful lot of dead birds. 'Right,' said Ganglion.

'Nah then,' he said when they had ignored the notices

285

and reached the improbably restored cottage. 'I'm goin' to ask you somefink: do you, young Ashley Oswald an' you, young Tammy, want ter put yer innocent little feet on the steep an' slippery slope wot leads ter crime, an' immorality, an' a lifetime of lookin' over your shoulder in case the Bill nabs you unawares?'

'No!' said Ashley Oswald, horrified.

'Depends,' said Tammy Sproat.

'Ar. Well, let me purrit this way then: you turn your backs while I pick this 'ere lock, okay? An' no peeping, Tammy Sproat!'

'No, Mr Ganglion!' said Tammy, turning his back and palming a small mirror from his anorak pocket. 'Promise.'

'Right, then.'

'Deserve ter be burgled, some people,' said Ganglion thirty-eight seconds later. 'Nah then, let me paint a little picture for you, right? There's this big blue policeman, right, an' 'e sez ter you, 'allo 'allo 'allo 'e sez, or if it's Sergeant MacEachran the Gaylick equivalent, your grandad, 'e sez, or in your case Tammy your best mate's grandad, is in serious bovver wiv the law, an' like ter be banged up in the Tar Er London wiv a whole loader desperate convicts like insider dealers an' pension fund managers. Nah then, 'e sez, wot exactly woz that old reprobate up to at. . .' he checked his watch ' – ten firty-eight precisely, this mornin'? Woodjew wanner tell 'im, an' condemn me to a life of durance vile eatin' tinned peas every day an' 'avin' ter wipe wiv shiny bog paper?'

Both boys shook their heads firmly, eyes goggling. 'Never tell the Filth onnything, my dad says,' Tammy piped. Ashley Oswald blushed and hoped his grandfather would think it was the cold wind.

'Right. Well now, the simplest way ter say, "I don't know nuffink about it, hofficer," is – ter know nuffink about it. Hignorance is like a tender exotic froot,' he added, opening the door. 'Touch it, an' the bloom is – gorn!' He closed it again, behind him.

'Is he always like that?' Tammy asked.

'Mostly, yes,' Ashley Oswald admitted.

'I wish he was *my* grandad,' said Tammy.

They strolled back to the car, half-heartedly playing Celtic vs. Rangers with a dead crow.

Ten minutes later Ganglion rejoined them, blew on his fingers and started the engine. 'Everyone orl right?' he called over his shoulder.

'Yes thanks, Mr Ganglion,' said Tammy. 'I had ma pee. Thanks fae stoppin'.'

'Ar,' said Ganglion. 'Right.' Gawd, he thought as he drove off, I wasn't as fly as that at his age, was I? Seventeen, perhaps – but *seven?*

The rain duly came on, but not before Oswald had got the plants thinned, repotted and set out in seed boxes under the sitting-room window in the lee of that bitter spring's prevailing north-easterly wind. What they really needed, of course, was a cold frame, or at least a few cloches. Ah well. He just had time to transfer the tomato plants from the sitting-room to the taxi before the wind gathered itself for a really wicked blow and the heavens opened. MacGregor's lot, no doubt, would say this spring was God's punishment for man's wickedness. If that was the case then he, Oswald Ochilree, common man of this parish, wouldn't help feeling it was a bit much of God to be so indiscriminate in His wrath. When it came to targeting the sinful the Almighty was about as accurate as a United States bomber pilot.

Ganglion dropped the boys off in the Visitor Village car park with strict instructions to be there, or thereabouts, two hours later.

'C'mon, Ash,' said Tammy. 'Let's head for the Lucky Bawbee. How much've you got?'

'Two pounds forty-eight,' said his friend. 'And a pound Mam gave me for emergencies. Only I'm supposed to be saving for a bike.'

'Nae problem, Jimmy!' Tammy grinned. 'I've got this system, see?'

Ganglion parked the 2CV, deliberately left the gate open and rang the bell of Number 7. It played the opening bars of the *EastEnders* theme. Someone had vandalized the carriage lamp.

The door was opened by the niece. As well as being possibly the worst (though by no means least expensively) dressed woman he had ever seen, the niece possessed a pair of muddy-coloured, unintelligent eyes, the sort of backside you could keep your encyclopaedias on supported by the sort of legs you see propping up the underground car parks, and a mouth which suggested she had once (in early puberty, say) bitten on a lemon and had been savouring the taste of it ever since. Or so it seemed to Ganglion.

'Ar,' he was about to say.

'Come for him, have you?'

How did you say all that without moving your lips? he wondered. 'Ar,' he said.

'He's in there, I'm going out. Some of us,' she added, ostentatiously closing the garden gate, 'have our work to go to.'

'Enjoy your stuffin',' muttered Ganglion.

'What?'

'Er, I said I got some stuff in, er, my boot.'

'Don't get it on the carpets, then,' she said. 'They're all paid for and I have enough to do as it is.'

Eat your heart out, Sigmund Freud, he thought. He found MacGregor sitting on his hard chair in the middle of the dining-room floor, the little heap of possessions at his side topped by a birdcage with a canary in it. It, too, seemed prepared for the worst.

'Wotcher, cock,' said Ganglion. 'This it then, is it?'

MacGregor raised a pair of very slow eyes. '"Nothing I have here is mine", Ganglion,' he said, '"or is generated by me." Know who said that?'

'No,' said Ganglion.

'General Ojukwu, leader of the Biafran uprising, remember? After it had been put down.'

'Ar.'

'He was in exile,' MacGregor explained. 'They gave him a nice wee house, on the Gold Coast.'

'Ar,' said Ganglion. 'Fancy you knowin' that, eh?'

'I think of those words,' said MacGregor, 'often. Did you see Herself?'

'I did.'

'Did ye speak to her?'

'Up to a point, yeah?'

'What did ye say?'

'"Ar", mostly.'

'You did well.' MacGregor's head sank again.

'Yeah. Well – sorl over now, innit, orl that! You won't never 'ave ter speak to 'er or see 'er, ever again.'

'You promise?'

'I promise.'

'You may not be of the Lord's people, Ganglion,' observed MacGregor. 'But you're a man.'

'Ta,' said Ganglion. 'I'll drink ter that!'

'Mnnaiee! Would that you could, my friend!' MacGregor shook his head disbelievingly. 'Would that you could. She poured it all away, Ganglion. Poured it all away! Down the lav! All ma lovely *uisge gun orra!* Ah! What it is to have a guest at your door and not a drop of hospitality by you! *A dhuine, a dhuine!*' He sniffed. 'That's one of the Riddles of Fionn,' he explained.

'Ar,' said Ganglion. 'Well your mate Fionn can just riddle off, can't 'e, cos I brought this.' His hand went to his inside jacket pocket, in, out, and produced a flask. 'Not ooshkie goon orrer, I'm afraid, just Co-op cheapo. 'Ope it'll do.'

'My good friend,' said MacGregor simply, taking off a good dram. 'Aaah! *Seo!*'

'Ta, ole cock. You've just proved a pet theory of mine.'

'Oh, and what's that?'

'Never you mind,' said Ganglion, his pet theory being that if offering a slug of Clan Campbell to a MacGregor, and getting away with it, didn't prove that all this whisky snobbery was a load of cobblers, his name wasn't Ganglion.

'That's an acceptable dram,' said MacGregor, taking another one. 'For all that it's the piss of Red Colin.'

'Oh,' said Ganglion. 'Bum.'

MacGregor produced a wheezy, grating sort of noise which on closer inspection turned out to be laughter. The canary joined in.

Tammy Sproat's system proved successful – successful enough, at any rate, to have them thrown out of the Lucky Bawbee after fifty minutes' concentrated play.

'That's no' fair,' Tammy commented outside. 'Grown-ups at casinos get bribed tae stay away.'

'I can't wait to be a grown-up,' said Ashley Oswald. 'You can do things then.'

'Aye. Best tae be young, though, really. What'll we dae now?'

'Dunno. It's ages yet.' He dug in his pockets and produced fistfuls of gaming tokens. 'What are we going to do with these? It says inside you've got to spend them, not swop them for money, only they won't let us go back.'

'Dinna fret,' said Tammy. 'My dad knows a man who'll gie ye eighty pence in the pound for them, that'll gie ye . . .' He cast an experienced eye over the gleaming hoard. 'About hauf a bike anyway. Honest.'

'Okay,' said Ashley Oswald, handing it over. 'Do you want to go to the Timespan?'

'What's tha'?'

'A sort of museum I think. Mam says museums are good for you.'

'She's queer, your mam.'

'Isn't!'

'Is so, then, like shopping your dad's licence plate in for a crappy old van. I know a man who'd pay five grand for that. He's a pervert.'

'How did you know?' Ashley Oswald was shocked. 'I'm not supposed to!'

'I hear things,' Tammy leered.

'Oh. Well anyway, it's not a crappy old van, so there. It's business transport and tax-deductible, I heard Uncle Mungo say so. And it's not Dad's licence plate, it's Mam *and* Dad's, cos they're a partnership.'

'Queer family!'

'Shut up.'

'Okay, then.' Tammy reckoned life was already too short to waste on grudges. 'Tell ye what, let's go tae that posh car park, not the Visitor one, the other one, where aw they rich businessmen an' that hae their conferences.'

'What for?'

'Holy shit, don't you know onnythin'? Tae guard them, o' course. While their owners're inside, a pound a go.'

Ashley Oswald frowned. 'Guard them against what?'

Tammy grinned. 'Us, ye dummy! Away, I'll explain it as we go.'

* * *

Neville was having a most gratifying morning, and was not the least bit daunted (for example) by the fact that Clyde Bilt was the only man present – indeed, the only person, since the only females there were waitresses, who didn't count of course – whom he knew, or that most of his companions tended to look the same: close-cropped, bronzed (or bronzered), suited and gleaming: slightly older, fuller-fleshed versions of Neville himself, in fact. Besides, they all wore badges, large rectangular ones pre-printed with the legend, 'HI! I'M..........'. All sported middle initials: 'HI!' Neville advertised himself, 'I'M NEVILLE G. WRINGHIM.' Clyde Bilt (rather unimaginatively, Neville thought) had awarded himself a Z. Neville, understandably enough, was not to know that Bilt had been christened (on more than one occasion) Clyde Zachariah.

The day began with aerobics. A tall girl in a green pudenda-sheath (she didn't count either) and half a tee-shirt was the session leader for this one, inviting them (to strains of an appropriate musical noise) to clap their hands above their heads while bending, legs splayed, at the knees. Neville noticed that when she did this her breasts disappeared, as indeed did most of the sheath. This lasted ten minutes, and was invigorating. There was orange juice, deglutinized rolls and low-fat spread to follow, which the girl did not stay to share.

Then Clyde Bilt himself introduced a middle-aged young man with a guitar, who was going to perform a Motivation Anthem for them all to join in. This musician, Bilt told them, was a very close personal friend of 'one of our leading Christian music stars', adding in a rather double-edged way that this particular leading Christian music star had a lot of very close personal friends. The Motivation Anthem was quite long but only involved three chords and was easy to chant along with.

When you got
Attitude, aggression, aptitude, attack,
Attitude, aggression, aptitude, attack –
Go for it!

When you got
Blessedness, brilliance, boldness, balls,
Blessedness, brilliance, boldness, balls –
Go for it!

– and so on through all the spiritual business virtues and all the letters of the alphabet, omitting some of the trickier ones. Neville thought the last verse – zeal, zenithmindedness, zymurgy, zip – particularly clever, though he didn't know what zymurgy was and was half-sure the man on his left had shouted 'zits' instead of 'zip' which (if true) was rather galling as he, Neville, had taken particular pains all week not to have any.

There was wild applause afterwards, during which Wat Tyler, OBE, himself, looking very sloppy and incongruous, slipped into the room, had an intense little conversation with some of the waitresses, and slipped out again. They resumed their seats, flushed and motivated, each to find in his place a little pamphlet entitled *20 Ways to Hone Your Killer Instincts*. Number one involved beating a rolled-up newspaper on the table saying 'Today's going to be a *great* day!' Neville made a mental note to start buying a newspaper.

Then Clyde Bilt got to his feet again. Neville thought the deference shown by most of his new colleagues – who all seemed to be section heads, principals, directors and vice-presidents of one sort or another – worthy of remark, and congratulated himself on having started at or near the top. He remarked also on the few who seemed to show less than outright adoration: clearly they were the ones to cultivate next. He turned in to his current mentor's remarks.

' – an' especially mah very dear frayunds and colleagues Mo Legover and Nash Hump, who have been so truly enabling in bringing about the miracle of Hosannahville, whose natal day, mah frayunds may Ah remind y'all, is now with Gard's Grace only a few weeks up ahead of us.

'Now, mah frayunds and associates, Ah wish to interdooce to y'all a very special person who Ah jus' know is gonna fit right inner our organization like a li'l ol' weevil in a boll. Already he has done untold service in the cause of light an' progress an' opportoonity as exemplified foh us all by the glorious network that is our very own HI! organization – '

'HI!' said everyone. It was a custom apparently.

'Mah frayunds, let me tell y'all jus' some of the truly wunnerful thengs this young mayun has done, for Ah know that in his modesty he will not object if Ah do, uh, jus' tell y'all some of them right now. He has done, dooty, mah frayunds, way over an' above the common call, in the vital an' necessary work of, uh, site preparation for the wunnerful developments we all at HI! – '

'HI!'

' – have playunned for his own li'l ol' community right there in Craigfieth which, thanks in no small part to him, we playun to have fully functioning as a Hosannahville satellite service an' residential zone way ahead of schedule. Thanks, frayunds, and only thanks, to his own efforts in regard to this, assisted at tahms it is true bah an enlightened local businessman who, though not of the One True Faith, has many of the right beliefs an' attitoods, thanks to him we at HI! – '

'HI!' It was a bit like 'Simon Says' for grown-ups.

' – can rest assured that no fewer than fahv, Ah say *fahv*, prime objectives have already been secured, or are about to be secured, at a cost well within our budget strategy.'

There was polite applause.

'Yet that is bah no means all, frayunds and brothers, not bah *no means* is that all! In addition he has devahsed, exclusively foh our benefit, a with-profits proselysation scheme, suitable foh all ages, that will ensure both a steady flow of recruits at the base end, pyramid-wise, of the national an' innernational network, an' a steady flow of income – all of it, Ah am assured bah mah colleagues in accountancy, one hunnerd per cent free of taxes – to promote Gard's message throughout the European Sector an' who knows the good ol' United States also if the noo White House staff gets certain misadvahsed charity legislation struck off in Brother Donald's first term! Say HI!, mah frayunds, say HI! to Capital Growth!'

'HI!HI!HI! to Capital Growth!' The applause this time was markedly more enthusiastic.

Bilt nodded vigorous agreement with it, took a sip of orange juice, and continued: 'This scheme will furthermore enable us to, uh, redeem the hitherto relatively untapped fahv-to-sixteen age group which as y'all know grows more fahnnancially meaningful every day. Ah say there is a job foh him some day in the Hosannah Business Education Trust! Finally, mah frayunds an' co-staffers, an' in some ways to me personally the most wunnerful an' meaningful of all, he has shown his loyalty, devotion an' dedication – Ah should also say discipline, mah frayunds, the most precious commodity of them all – in certain very special ways known only to two others present here today, and to the Lord Jesus Cryest Himself.'

(And to Chylblayne, thought Neville, forgetting for the moment that women were God's Sacred Vessels and therefore didn't figure in the sum.) The audience, mostly ignorant of what Bilt was talking about, nonetheless gave solemn approbation to it.

'Frayunds, brethren an' colleagues, this young mayun

has a great future with us, an' that future is NOW! Frayunds, Ah give y'all Neville G. Wringhim! Stand up, Nev! Stand up an' be counted!'

Neville stood up, and they counted him, and clasped his hands, and slapped him on the back, and gave him another orange juice. One or two older brethren gave him the Kiss of Peace, too.

'Next session at midday,' someone called over the hubbub. 'Rap at random, guys, till then.'

Bilt swarmed over, his hands stretched out in greeting. 'Nev, mah frayund. Ah wanna innerduce you t'two very special an' wunnerful people.' He led Neville through a crowd of rappers to a slightly quieter corner of the Blairlummock Conference Facility. 'But first, there's some-then' Ah wanned t'say to you. This, uh, frayund you have, this Miss Huxtry, huh? May Ah give you one word of advahce, mah frayund? Think very carefully an', uh, maybe, think about waitin' a li'l while longer, huh? Ah mean, maybe, think about not gettin' tahd down, you get me? Now then . . .' He swung Neville round to face two large men with glasses of orange juice.

'Nev: Mo; Mo: Nev; Nev: Nash; Nash: Nev; Nev; meet Nash an' Mo, your brothers in Gard's Holy Work.' Neville grinned blankly. 'Your fellow-enablers, Neville.'

'Oh!' said Neville. 'Right!'

'Pleased to greet yuh, Nev boy!'

'Put it right there, Nev baby!'

'Hi,' said Neville.

'HI!' said Nash and Mo.

'Excuse me a while,' said Bilt.

'Motown P. Legover,' said the first large man. 'Senior Executive Vice-President (Scotland).'

'H-hello.'

'Nashville D. Hump,' said the second. 'Senior Executive Scottish Vice-President (Development). I hear great things about you, Nev baby. I hear how you mean to get on in the organization.'

'An' I'm sure, Nash, that Nev is going to tell us himself, right now. How, Nev boy?'

'Well,' said Neville, struggling to recall the less forgettable lyrics of the Motivation Anthem. 'Through, er, dedication, diligence, er, drive and, er.' He improvised. 'Sheer hard work.'

'Oh, ri-ight,' said Legover. 'Not to mention godliness, guiltlessness, guts and go?'

Neville nodded.

'Or,' said Hump, 'purity, perseverance, push and power?'

Neville nodded again.

'Or,' said Legover, 'gobbledegook, geckos, gum and gophers?'

'Or cup-cakes, candy bars, candelabra and cant!'

'Or in fact anything else that you may be told to go for from On High!'

'HI!' said Neville, not thinking.

'Bearing in mind,' said Hump, wagging a finger at him, 'that the Word from On High is Holy Writ!'

'It surely is, Nash. For as Clyde Bilt himself has said to us on many occasions, Nev boy, there is no other agency but the agency of Our Lord Jesus Christ!'

'Oh, right,' Neville agreed. 'Which agency is that?'

'HI! Publicity Associates Inc,' said Hump.

'We have the exclusive account,' said Legover.

'Right!' said Neville.

'So,' said Hump, 'you're Special Projects are you?'

Neville checked his badge. 'Yes, that's right.'

'He'll have to meet Cousin Andreas, won't he, Mo?'

'Cousin?'

'As opposed to brother. We kinda like to distance

297

ourselves from some of our more semi-detached opera-
tives. Andreas is a kinda special case. I expect you've
liaised with him already, at a distance, if what I read from
Clyde's remarks is correct. You'll meet him today, he's
around someplace.'

'Oh,' said Neville. 'Right.'

'You make out okay with Chylblayne?' Hump asked,
catching Legover's eye.

Neville coloured slightly. 'Yes, thank you.'

'Score first time, did you?'

'What my colleague means, Nev boy, is – how long?'

'Oh.' Neville thought. 'Till she said, you mean?' They
nodded. 'Eight hours, I think. Maybe nine.'

Hump whistled 'Eight-nine *hours?* Jesus! Wanna guess
how long I had to keep my pecker up? I'll tell you: two –
whole – *nights*. And a day.'

Neville looked suitably impressed.

'On account of the lady had her dates wrong, for
Chrissake! Course, that was Fawn. Hall's daddy here' –
he nudged Legover – 'he came later. The lady had
scientific predictors for that one, that right, Mo?'

'Yeah, right, Nash. Mind you, Nev, what Brother
Hump here doesn't tell you is – I enjoyed my period of
service. Know what I mean?'

'Oh,' said Neville. 'I mean, well, so did I actually,' he
lied.

'I guess I ain't gonna hang around listening to your
insinuations,' said Hump, dumping his orange juice in a
nearby parlour palm. 'See y'around, Nev. Be lucky.' He
shouldered off.

'Good ole Nash,' Legover grinned. 'Such a great guy to
tease, if you know how.'

'What does he . . . actually do? In the business I mean?'

Legover shrugged. 'The usual, I guess. Makes the
moves. Calls a few shots sometimes, when the Word

comes, y'know. Kicks a little ass, that's when he ain't doing something quite other to it.' He grinned again. 'Hey kid, you see me in the paper back there?'

'The *Gazette* you mean? Last week?'

'You got it! Great little piece, I thought. Fact I said so much to . . . certain quarters: hey listen, fellas, I said, this is one li'l ole turkey you ain't gonna have to buy for Thanksgiving. For why? Because why waste your money on a turkey's gonna walk right in that there oven of its own sweet vohlition, is for why! Made no difference.' He shrugged. 'The fellas bought it anyway. Hey! That's a great little outfit you got here in England, that Department of Enterprise. Real sweet.'

'Scotland,' said Neville.

'Uh?'

'I mean, this is Scotland. You meant the UK, I think.'

'Oh, yeah. Whatever. Pissant li'l island, you fall off it before you know you're there. Guess it's kinda hard to get that fine detail sometimes.'

'Oh, right,' said Neville. 'I agree, actually.'

'Good,' said Legover. 'You're learnin' fast, boy.'

'Thanks. Could you tell me, er, Mo . . .'

'Ask,' said Legover, adjusting the crotch of his trousers, 'and it shall be answered. Only keep it brief.'

'Right. What exactly does Clyde Bilt do . . . er, exactly. In . . .'

'Don't say it! I can get a little tired of Red Indian games, y'know? Just call it the Organization. Simple answer, kid: Hosannah International's a GEBO, right? A Global Evangelical Business Organization.'

'Right.'

'Well, Brother Bilt's part of the evangelical side.'

'Yes?'

'An' the rest of us is the business organization.'

'Ah.'

'Doctrine of Mutual Interdependency, see?'

'Right.'

'Fine man. *Fine* man.'

'Bilt?'

'The same. Tell me, did he get you to do your business for him?'

'What? Oh . . . that. Yes.'

'Yeah. Kinda makes you think, huh? Like maybe Jesus Christ ain't everything there is, y'know? Don't worry. It won't happen again. HI! takes care of its own.'

'Ah,' said Neville.

'Aren't you forgetting something?'

'What? Oh, sorry. HI!'

'Right. Just testin'. No, Brother Bilt be a bit lackin' between the legs but he's AOK brainwise. You gotta girlfriend? Screwin' partner?'

'Fiancée.'

'Oh, right, sure, cute. And has Brother Bilt done a little counselling on you in regard to that?'

'Um, yes, actually.'

'An' I bet you're just itchin' to know why?'

'Well act – . . . I mean, yes.'

'Yeah? Right: fact is, Brother Bilt may be a pill-poppin' castrato himself but he sure knows what a man's gotta do in this game, right? I mean, like relaxin' from execkertive stress.' Legover shifted from foot to foot, his hands in his pockets. 'Like, take me: I wouldn't just say the Lady Chylblayne was exactly my cup of tea sexually, y'know?'

'No?'

'Hell, no! I mean, okay she makes the moves an' what-all, but she's kinda on the high and wide side for my likin', y'unnerstan'? Me, I go for greener fruit, like firmer, y'know? Nice – an – tight!' He glanced across at a group of waitresses standing by with fresh supplies of Florida's finest. Two of the girls detached themselves from the rest and moved towards the great pine staircase installed by the fourteenth chieftain of Chizzell after a raid on Glamis Castle.

'Like I say, boy, we enablers get our meat order reg'lar. See y'around, Sperm Bank Junior. Be lucky.' He strode swiftly, and stiffly, off.

The two boys found no customers in the Blairlummock Towers car park, somewhat to Ashley Oswald's relief. He was about to suggest going to the Timespan after all (it was cold, and Mam would be bound to ask) when Tammy gave a cry and grabbed him by the sleeve.

'Empire Starfighter ten degrees,' he hissed.

Ashley Oswald looked beyond his friend's pointing finger and saw a black Ford Siesta GT Turbo Hacienda Special, registration K519 MUL, with stripes. They loped off to investigate.

It was locked, of course, and empty save for a long cardboard box, covered with a sheet, on what little there was of the back seat. They held a whispered conference, then squatted down behind a nearby BMW 4WD GLi Coupé to await developments.

Neville felt something poke him in the small of his back. 'Frind!' said the Honorary Consul of the Republic of Bophuthatswana. Neville turned round, very slowly. 'Andreas Laagerlaut,' said the man. 'Plizzed to mit you.'

'You're –' Neville gasped.

Laagerlaut cautioned silence.

'Cousin Andreas?' Neville whispered.

'Ah, so you've heard about me alriddy then? In thit case you'll know I sometimes hiv . . . other clients, yes?'

'I see, yes,' said Neville. 'And' – he dropped his voice – 'tonight's . . . is other clients?'

'Tonight's tonight. Tomorrow is . . . another day.'

301

'Oh, right,' said Neville. 'Absolutely.'

'Today it might be – a Mr Meiklejohn, shall we say? Or a little plumbing job? Or some illictrical wiring? Tomorrow . . . who knows?'

'Are you . . .' Neville's eyes widened in admiration. 'Are you . . . Clinch McKittrick?'

The man laughed, briefly, then stopped. The effect was not pleasant. 'You mean there are some things even a vice-prizzident of Spishal Projects doesn't know?' he sneered.

'Not yet, no. I only started today.'

'Ah! So you're the proud father, are you?'

'I – I'd rather not answer that.'

'Good. Then I shall tell you, my frind. Clinch McKittrick is – a name.'

'Yes?'

'Thit's it. Just a name. Use it in two or three places maybe – three is the most – throw it away. Just business. Put money in – for a sphishal project, shall we say? – take money out – end of story. End of name. It saves . . . certain pipple a lot of time, and wastes the time of certain other pipple. Which is very expedient, wouldn't you say?'

'Oh, right,' Neville agreed. 'Nice.'

'Like a motor car,' Laagerlaut added, half to himself, 'that you don't want to be seen in too often.' He looked at Neville. 'You like to buy a nice fast car soon, maybe?' Neville nodded. 'Don't buy mine, frind. It his a history. Excuse me, I hiv a phone call to make.'

'Oh, right. See you around, then.'

'I shouldn't think so, my frind.' Cousin Andreas smiled. 'I think I shill shortly be owed a nice long holiday. *Ciao*, as they say.'

His work finished, as far as he could finish it, Oswald lay on his bed, the door closed for warmth, and read one of

302

his father's old breeding books to help him relax. The phone began to ring; Oswald started the exhausting business of getting out of bed, then checked himself. If it was anyone he knew, they'd try Ganglion on his portable. If it wasn't, he didn't wish to speak to them. If it was Ganglion himself he'd ring again. He flopped back on the pillows and carried on reading.

The phone shrilled for quite a long time. Then it was blessedly silent again.

For Neville, the next five minutes lasted a very long time yet seemed scarcely sufficient for their purposes. At first he was aware of a low, pulsing sound above, or below, the male chatter of the conference room, a sound that seemed somehow to issue from the walls themselves. Then Wat Tyler, OBE, made a second appearance and spoke quietly to a grey-haired forty-five-year-old Neville remembered had been introduced to him as Klaus von Auschwitz, Head of Operational Methodology. Von Auschwitz – whose accent turned out to be as transatlantic as everyone else's – looked startled at first, then his expression gave way to outright panic. He muttered something to Laagerlaut, who nodded coolly, replaced the payphone receiver, and left. Then he caught Neville's eye and almost ran across the room to him.

'Stay close,' he said. 'I'm gonna need you.' Then he stood on a chair. 'Brethren!' he shouted. 'Brethren! Okay, listen: we have a suspension of the schedule. We have a visit from The Man.'

The effect was electrifying: everywhere, suits were adjusted, shirts tucked in, ties tightened. There was an outbreak of mutual grooming as the cream of Hosannah International examined each other for fluff, crumbs, stray hairs and flakes of non-executive dandruff. Von Auschwitz came down off the mountain and grabbed Neville's arm. 'Okay now, you go straight to the third floor, suite twenny-eight – got that? And you go right in there and unscrew Motown P. from whatever piece of under-age ass he's gotten himself into, okay? No questions, just say The Man's here.'

'Right.' Neville panted as they turned on the first half-landing.

'I gotta deal with Hump,' his colleague added grimly. 'Fourth floor. I coulda sworn I saw that goddam fag slidin' off with the bell-hop.'

'Right.' They were thundering up to the second floor. 'Who – is – The – Man?'

'Jesus H, the kid doesn't know yet!' Von Auschwitz was sufficiently shocked to stop running. 'Okay. Get it once, get it good, okay? This guy we are talking about is the Supremely Reverend Gil E. Martin, known to his closest associates as the Son of Man, known to the rest of us as The Man for short. All you gotta remember is he's the head of everything, right? Every goddam thing. An' if he finds any single one of us screwin' ass at a Motivation Day, we are *all* gonna get our asses busted! Now go for it!'

Neville pounded up the remaining one and a half flights and down a nightmarishly narrow grey corridor to suite twenty-eight where he quickly found that Motown P. had gotten himself into both his companions. He shoved them off him and they both sat down heavily on the floor looking ludicrously desirable.

'What in the name of fuck – ' Legover began.

'The Man's here,' said Neville.

Never was there such a rapid detumescence. When, less than a minute later, Legover had dressed and gone (Neville made a note to remember the usefulness of snap-on-ties) the two girls – Neville made another note to remember it wasn't true what he'd heard about Philippinos – made to follow. Neville shook his head. They smiled, took their clothes off again, and got into bed. Neville left the room, turned the key in the lock and dropped it in his pocket. They'd been bought and paid for, after all. And a week was beginning to seem a long time. The Son of Man might not stay for very long.

Hump tore past him on the stairs. 'Don't they have no goddam elevators in England?' he wheezed. Neville followed at a more sedate pace.

He thus had a grandstand view of the entire assembly as it dropped to its knees before the advancing figure of a man, dark-haired and balding, considerably under the six-foot norm of HI! senior staffers, and looking every minute of fifty-five. He was dressed in a corduroy jacket, faded denims and an open-necked lumberjack shirt but Neville, even from that distance, could feel the Presence like the slam of stale air in an underground railway tunnel.

He also felt rather out of place, as the only non-kneeling member present. It was too late either to retreat to the half landing or advance the six steps to the conference floor. His knees began to shake. The Man was at the foot of the stairs, coming straight for him.

The two boys had deserted their hiding place to get a better view of the helicopter and the black car was almost on them before they realized their peril. They jumped back just in time to avoid being run over as the car roared past them, tearing up the pea-pebble and doing hundreds of pounds' worth of damage to the vehicles parked on either side. The boys covered their eyes, but not before they'd had the chance to see what was under the sheet as it slipped off the box on the back seat.

Ashley Oswald looked at Tammy. 'What'd he want empty milk bottles for?' he wondered. They wandered off to keep their appointment.

* * *

Halfway to Rose Cottage, Ashley Oswald asked the question that had been nagging him since the weekend.

'Grandad?'

'Hmm?'

'Grandad, you know when a lot of men and ladies go into a room together and take their clothes off and start putting each other's things into their mouths?'

MacGregor choked.

Ganglion cleared his throat. 'Do I know wot about it?'

'Is that where babies come from?'

'In a word, son – no. Okay?'

'Okay, Grandad.' Ashley Oswald smiled with relief. He didn't know much, but he knew enough to know what he wasn't supposed to know about.

'Son?' said Ganglion.

'Yes, Grandad?'

'Djew mind my askin' 'ow you came to ask me that?'

'No, Grandad! I saw it on a video. It was called *Wildlife of Westphalia.* Dad said it would be about animals.'

'Ar. And did you – tell your Dad about . . . all them men an' ladies?'

Ashley Oswald blushed a little. 'No, Grandad. I just put it back to the shop. I didn't want to embarrass him.'

'Ar.'

'Are – are you going to?'

'I fink I'd better, yeah.'

'Oh.'

'Not mentionin' no names, ercourse.'

'Oh!' Ashley Oswald's world was restored; he had, after all, watched all of it. 'Thanks, Grandad!'

MacGregor recovered his breath. Tammy Sproat tried to teach the canary bad words under his breath.

'Looks like Half-a-Job's been at it again, Grandad,' said Ashley Oswald as they breasted the last summit before Rose Cottage. A messy smudge of black smoke

306

drifted up from the dead ground in front of them before being whipped away on the wind.

'Looks like 'e's bin workin' fer once, yeah. Burnin' 'is farm accounts, most likely.'

'I think not, Ganglion!' MacGregor's voice was urgent. 'Put your bloody foot down, man, never mind ma bed! That's a house on fire!'

It was. It was Rose Cottage. Ashley Oswald had never seen men scream and cry before; Tammy had, but then Tammy had seen more of life generally.

Smoke poured out of all the windows at one end and a little gout of flame, the colour of congealed blood, poked through the roof.

'Get back you two!' his grandad screamed as, tears pouring down his face, he and MacGregor ran futilely to the back door, which opened only to unleash a great lion of flame and smoke. They hauled it shut again and blundered, half-blinded, to an end window. Ganglion peered in, cupping his hands round his face. 'Oz!' he screamed. '*Oz!* Oh, sweet Jesus, no!'

The boys watched as the two old men searched for something to break the window with. 'I'm good at this,' Tammy muttered, picking up a stone.

It was a superb shot, straight and deadly. The window seemed first to sag, then to collapse inwards. Ganglion struggled up on MacGregor's bony shoulders and got the catch open; then he wormed through, his bottom and legs disappearing into the blackness inside.

'Grandad! No! No, Grandad!' Ashley Oswald started to cry, and ran forward. He reached the house in time to help MacGregor, who was shaking violently, heft the unwieldy weight of Uncle Oswald and lay it in the grass at a safe distance.

'Go on!' yelled Tammy, waving them back.

The wheelchair came next, then a brass-bound chest

(how did Grandad manage?) and bundles of papers, books, bedding. Then they pulled out Ganglion himself, and the boy had a brief and sickening vision of a door apparently melting away as another lion, more ferocious than the first, rushed to gobble his grandad up. Then they had him out and were staggering away.

Ashley Oswald did not want to look around.

'Sorry about your dirty pictures, old friend,' said a voice.

MacGregor and the two boys made themselves useful for a while. Ashley Oswald, at unthinking risk, made a tour of the blazing building and rescued the marijuana crop. When he got back, Uncle Oswald was sitting up with Grandad's arm round his shoulder. They had all moved further back. MacGregor was picking up pieces of paper and stacking them neatly under a stone. Tammy was drawing heavily on a squashed cigarette he'd been saving for emergencies.

'It'll give you lung cancer that will, laddie,' said MacGregor.

'So do caged birds,' said Tammy. 'The BMA sez so.'

The roof of Rose Cottage sagged, sending flames exulting into the filthy air. They all moved back further still.

'I heard a car,' said Oswald, beginning to tremble a little now. 'So I looked through ma window, and there was this man carrying a box. An' I thought, oh it must be a parcel for us an' I was about to get into ma chair when I heard a smashing – the windows'. He caught his breath. 'An' so I keeked round the door an' saw the – saw the flames, an' I knew fine the only hope for it was to shut it again, an' just hope. I couldna' get ma window open,' he added apologetically. Then he said: 'It was a black car. With stripes down the side.'

'Okay, mate, okay. I'll give PC Plod a ring an' get 'im to come out. An' I spose I'd better phone the fire brigade

308

too, for all the good it'll be. An' 'Amish – oh no, course not, they can't come an' get us, can they? Car's away to Dunbroath.'

'The Filth'll gie us a run,' said Tammy, looking eager to break the family code for once.

'Ar,' said Ganglion. 'Ass right.'

'Oh well,' Oswald smiled wanly. 'I guess it's the Eventide for us this time, ma friend.'

'No chance o' that,' said MacGregor. 'Did you not see the paper yesterday? They've closed it. Something to do with care in the community.' He spat.

'Tha's right,' said Tammy gloomily. 'Mam says I've tae share wi' Lance an' Debbie cos Grandad's comin' tae stay wi' us.'

'Gawd,' said Ganglion. 'Er, listen fellas . . . sposin' I woz ter tell you I knew a place, goin' beggin' right now, wot 'as bedrooms, beddin', furniture, crocks, potsanpans – everyfink, in fack, in that line, plus stocks o' food. Plus, central 'eating, 'lectric an' all that laid on free. Would that cheer us up, djer fink?'

Oswald laughed. 'Who's paying?'

'Nobody,' said Ganglion.

'Oh – ho! So who owns this paradise, then?'

'You do,' said Ganglion. 'Wait an' see.'

Somewhere a lark began to sing.

'Grandad,' whispered Ashley Oswald as they heard the first siren. 'Is this the place we're supposed to forget about?'

'Yeah,' said Ganglion. 'So you'd better just forget about it all over again.'

Neville arrived home late, after a long private conference with Gil E. Martin and an even longer session with Mo Legover's compliant leftovers. He was excited, triumphant, exalted . . . Motivated. The only small problem was how best to break it to his fiancée that their relationship was no longer viable.

He let himself in. Miss Huxtry was not there. Instead there were two policemen, who arrested him.

Chapter Eleven

April ran its course, leaving little of any freshness or great historical significance in world affairs. In the Horn of Africa the various warring statesmen continued, like revellers in a dance of death, to fight each other to the last starving baby for the basic right to exercise ideological supremecy in the region. In the Gulf a series of mass murders (some with accompanying mutilations, others not) among certain leading families in the rival theocratic groupings encouraged hopes in the West that the forces of moderation might be temporarily in the ascendant. Somewhere in Beirut – somewhere, to be more precise, in the mainly Muslim, mostly Shiite, partly undevastated and utterly insane sector – a hostage whose own narrow, selfish interests failed to coincide with those of any important government, chalked up, on April 29th, his three thousand, seven hundred and twenty-eighth day in captivity. On April 30th his captors took away his stick of chalk as a gesture of reprisal against alleged ballot-rigging in the latest Lebanese presidential election.

In the civilized world, a meeting of NATO members agreed unanimously to treat the latest Soviet proposal – a sixty per cent reduction in the remaining conventional forces of the Warsaw Pact in addition to the unilateral nuclear disarmament already proposed, allied to a promise of free elections throughout the Soviet republics, supervised by the UN – with extreme caution, regarding it as probably no more than a bargaining ploy at best and, at worst, a smokescreen to blind world opinion to open disaffection in the Baltic States. The United Kingdom government announced new security measures for Northern Ireland, under which all inquests were in future to be held *in camera* and all autopsies on suspected members of outlawed organizations conducted by an impartial army surgeon. The State President of the Republic of South Africa proclaimed his intention to hold preliminary talks in the near future with the object of setting up a legislative chamber to represent the legitimate interests of persons of mixed English and Afrikaner parentage.

The sale by British Aerospace of its Royal Ordnance division to HI! Peace Shield Products Inc was hailed on both sides of the Atlantic as a major advance in the war against international terrorism.

Floods swept Bangladesh. A hurricane devastated the Caribbean and odd unstrategic bits of Mexico. There was an earthquake in a remote part of northern China. The Dow Jones Index fell ninety points following the arrest by the FBI of property billionaire Duncan Trombo for alleged 'revenue irregularities'. Seventeen backbench Conservative MPs courageously abstained in a vote on the Second Reading of the National Insurance (Non-Compulsorization) Bill. Zimbabwe beat England by an innings and one hundred and eighty-seven runs in the final Test at Harare to take the series three-nil. It was an unexceptional month for major news.

In Craigfieth, however, public excitement ran at near fever-pitch for several days following the discovery, at half past seven one Friday night, of one Gladstone Fredericks (twenty-two) in a wooden packing crate in the High Street premises of the Ministry of the Interior, and its unforeseeable consequences.

Sergeant Donald MacEachran (acting, it was widely supposed, on information received) had been proceeding in a northerly direction in the vicinity of the premises when his attention was drawn to a parked car at the rear. (That his attention had, in fact, been drawn to it by Tammy Sproat whistling at him from behind the garden wall of an unoccupied house nearby was one of the intriguing aspects of the case not to find its way into the official reports.) On investigation the sergeant did indeed discover an area of worn tread on the off-side front tyre of a saloon-type private car, registration number K519 MUL. Suspecting this to be merely the first in a potential catalogue of offences against the various Road Traffic Acts, MacEachran then tried all the doors. They were locked, of course, but his action did at least have the most satisfactory effect of triggering the car's burglar alarm. Thus alerted to the possibility of a serious criminal offence, the officer used his initiative – though not, as yet, his personal radio – and decided to investigate further.

He was struck – as indeed was the High Court judge six months later – by the curious incident of the lights in the windows of the Ministry of the Interior. Twenty-two years in the force had taught the sergeant a trick or two about human nature, and he thought it reasonable to expect that any ordinary, law-abiding citizen, alerted to the possibility that his pride and joy was in the process of being taken and driven away in the street outside, would have reacted, at that dim hour of a filthy April night, by switching his lights on in his efforts to avert the felony. The occupants of the Ministry of the Interior, however, switched theirs *off*. This, the sergeant said, made him think. And this time – having thought – he radioed Simison for assistance. The constable abandoned his compilation of the quarterly crime figures (depressingly low) and leaped into the police car with the intention of rushing the five hundred yards or so to his colleague's aid. Moments later he leaped out again (the starter motor having finally packed up) and instead commandeered a blue Fiat Curia, property of the Mid Lummock Presbytery, whose driver the Rev. Gilleasbuig MacAndrew, had been about to visit a convalescent old lady next door with some of Jessie's baking.

Simison slammed the door shut. 'Drive,' he said.

'Fast?' asked the minister.

'Yes!'

'Oh, good!' said the minister, and did so.

MacEachran meanwhile (in accordance with the provisions of the Scottish Police Acts) knocked very softly with one diffident knuckle on the rear doors of the Ministry of the Interior, waited about half a second for a reply, and walked in.

The black air was suddenly filled with flying bodies, scuffling feet, grunts, obscenities and thuds. Something large and meaty hit MacEachran in the stomach and bounced off. The doors were wrenched open and in the sulphurous haze of a street lamp the sergeant saw five, maybe six silhouetted figures run out into the night. He stumbled forward, hearing more groans, tripped over and fell heavily on something soft. He heard a car engine revving, and the squeal of rubber.

Simison saw the five men scrambling into a battered minibus parked in front of the shop.

'Stop them!' he barked.

The Rev. MacAndrew was a sincere believer in divine providence; he was also glad it wasn't his car. He aimed at their front off-side wing and put his foot down. Simison, still cowering, watched between his fingers as the minister afterwards lumbered out of the car in pursuit of the three men who had emerged, somewhat dizzily, from the back of the minibus and who were now running off along the Dunbroath Road. Not for nothing had the minister been a member of the Divinity Students' XV on the occasion of its famous (and unrepeated) victory over the Medical

School in the season of 1962–63. He afterwards preached a stirring sermon on 1 Samuel 24:19: 'For if a man find his enemy, will he let him go well away?'

The two remaining desperadoes flung themselves in the ditch to avoid being knocked flat by a speeding black Ford. They gave themselves up an hour later, after asking directions to the police station.

MacEachran picked himself up and groped about for a light switch. Finding it, he saw himself to be in a large workshop and surrounded by large quantities of tatty old rubbish in various stages of transformation into desirable interior design components. At his feet lay a young, dark-haired man in his early twenties, apparently senseless. The cause of his senselessness, a large wooden crate labelled, *EXPORT FURNITURE: THIS SIDE UP!* seemed to be emitting faint tapping sounds. He put his mouth to a knot-hole near the top (or bottom). 'Hello?' he said.

'Hnhnhnnk,' said a weak voice inside.

The figure at MacEachran's feet began to stir. 'Uuurgh,' it said.

MacEachran knelt down and produced his identity card. 'I'm a police officer,' he said, trying not to sound unnecessarily severe about it, 'and I'm charging you with complicity to unlawfully detain this gentleman here.' He patted the crate. 'To be going on with.'

'I want to say something,' said the young man.

'You're not obliged to,' MacEachran pointed out.

'No, but I want to.'

MacEachran took out his notebook. Seen from behind, Craigfieth's solicitous sergeant might have been mistaken for a soutaned priest administering extreme unction.

'I'm ready, son,' he said. 'What is it?'

'Stop knocking my teeth out with your truncheon, officer,' said the young man, and passed out again.

The trial judge seemed quite put out when Dr Ghouleagh's evidence showed this allegation to be utterly without foundation.

Simison and MacAndrew, having secured their suspects with handcuffs and Presbyterian tow rope, helped the sergeant prise the lid (or base) off the crate. A timid figure emerged, blinking. They took his gag off and untied his hands.

'I'm not really called Eugene Mkekwe, honest,' he said.

'I'm sure I wouldn't be minding if you were, sir,' said MacEachran, and sent him off with the minister to restore himself with tea and home-bakes at the police house.

Simison emerged from behind a heap of valuable lumber. 'Look what I've found, Sarge,' he crowed. MacEachran looked. The cabinet was empty and had been flung unceremoniously into a corner, but the letters DD were still clearly visible, one on each door.

'I think it's time we called Dunbroath,' said MacEachran.

Had the questioning of Gladstone Fredericks been left to the plodding MacEachran it is quite possible that Neville (and a great many others, in the end) might have been spared at least one more night sleeping the sleep of the upwardly mobile. The sergeant and his wife would, in all probability, have inclined to the view that the poor soul was in every respect an innocent party to the affair and more deserving of a dram and a comfy bed for the night than a vigorous debriefing in the police station's poky interview-room. In the morning the young man might well have allowed himself to forget that Donald MacEachran was a policeman and told him everything, anyway. We shall never know.

Instead, at eight thirty, Fredericks found himself under interrogation by two plain-clothes officers from the Eastern Regional Fairly Serious Crime Squad and forced to remember that policemen were policemen, and that young male West Indians only had themselves to blame for not being born otherwise.

He held out for fully forty minutes. Then it occurred to him (no doubt quite mistakenly) that he was in imminent danger of finding himself arrested and charged with having chloroformed himself, gagged himself, and nailed himself up in a packing crate, contrary to the We Never Asked To Have Your Sort Here In The First Place Acts (1948 *passim*). So he gave in and told them all about Neville, and his sister in Craigfieth, and the Bide-a-Wee Tearooms, and many other things besides.

Thus it was, ten minutes later, that Neville discovered that being young, white and prosperous was not necessarily a safeguard against all life's little upsets. Not even a nodding acquaintance, via his transcontinental business associates, with the Risen Christ, seemed adequate proof against the infernal legions of the secular constabulary.

The Bophuthatswanan High Commission that night reported one of its cars stolen. Andreas Laagerlaut disappeared without trace, although his image appeared, eighteen months later, on a confiscated BBC News videotape of unrest in one of the newly constituted English townships in the Transvaal.

At about the same time that Knightsbridge police were logging the stolen diplomatic vehicle, D.I. Snow and his associates were conducting a search of the Ministry of the Interior, High Street, Craigfieth, with the assistance of Edwina, a three-year-old alsatian bitch trained to sniff out illegal substances through up to six layers of polythene, waxed mackintosh or spermicidally lubricated latex.

The dog betrayed no affinity for Mr Meiklejohn's cabinet, which was hardly surprising considering that its contents, though alarming, had not been illegal as such.

During the next half hour it showed intense interest in three areas of the premises: these were thoroughly probed and found to conceal a rubber ball, a packet of salami sandwiches, and a cat. All three were removed for tests. Edwina then advanced on a Welsh dresser, hackles up and jowls slavering horribly. She planted her nose in the crack between the doors and remained there, snorting, tail up and bearded anus dilating and contracting with professional enthusiasm.

'It's locked, sir,' said D.C. Horse.

'Smash it open then,' said Snow. 'Here, use this.' He tossed across a regulation issue Drugs Squad hatchet. Horse blanched. His fiancée, WPC Rexine Clampit of Traffic Division, had been saving up for a stripped pine dresser for fifteen months; acquiring it had become almost a precondition of their oft-postponed nuptials. To ravage open this one, with a hatchet, seemed to Horse like a violation of his beloved's own long-preserved virginity. Nonetheless he had his career to consider. Crack and Speedie held the dog back as he lifted his arm and swung . . .

The Mid Lummock cocaine haul was hailed by the media the next day as a crushing blow for Scotland's drug barons. In fact, as embittered Customs and Excise officers did not tire of pointing out to each other for weeks afterwards, it was nothing of the sort; for them it represented, rather, the complete waste and ruination of eight months' patient surveillance in two continents, was precisely the sort of emperor-sized balls-up they might have expected from the Eastern Regional Weenyplods, and was a major setback in the unremitting all-out war between the two law enforcement agencies. They reserved their most pungent ire for Sergeant Donald MacEachran, which was perhaps a little unfair, however, understandable.

At ten o'clock the next morning the real Mr Eugene Mkekwe, described in a press release as 'an Edinburgh-based representative of the African National Congress', denied all knowledge of the previous night's events; he had, he said, been in Argyll at the time, attending as its guest speaker a local conference of the Scottish National Party where he had found among the crofters and tenant farmers in his audience, ready sympathy for the plight of his people. He added that he had no doubt that, but for a piece of unaccountably mistaken identity, he would now be winging his way by diplomatic bag to the top floor of an interrogation centre in Johannesburg.

Gladstone Fredericks was held for questioning under the Prevention of Terrorism Act until Monday afternoon. Then he returned to Dunbroath to find he had lost a week's dole for failing to sign on.

Never before – not even in his time of triumph only twenty-four hours earlier – had so many people shown an interest in Neville G. Wringhim. He hardly knew whether to curse his ignorance or bless it. By Monday morning he hardly knew what day it was. At ten thirty he was taken before the Duncruddie Mains Sheriff Court and committed for trial on charges of conspiracy to kidnap, conspiracy to steal, conspiracy to traffic in drugs, and making multiple applications for shares in BritCure plc, formerly the Primary Health Division of the NHS. The last charge was added as a result of information supplied by an anonymous 'former associate' of the accused. The sheriff, last of a dwindling band of believers in the presumption of innocence, granted the defence application for bail but set it, in view of the seriousness of one of the charges, at twenty-five thousand pounds. Within an hour it had been paid into the court by a person desiring his identity to remain secret; the prosecution, naturally enough, had no objection to secrecy of any sort and Neville was released from custody shortly after one o'clock. At five to two a tractor driver transporting a load of superphosphates to the Clashmahavers Garden Centre stopped to let him ride on the trailer.

He had plenty of time to think during the journey and his thoughts, for the most part, focussed on Miss Huxtry, his bride-to-be. He remembered, too, his thoughts of the previous Friday night and realized of course that he had been . . . no, obviously not 'wrong' since that was an entirely unviable concept, but misinformed – yes, that was it – *misinformed* as to the precise degree of supportiveness and compatibility coexistent between himself and his prospective long-term partner in safe sexual practice. Clyde Bilt had been premature in his anticipation of Neville's free-standing capabilities in regard to that one, certainly. Gil E. Martin was just a jealous old man. He realized, too, how lucky he had been, in a way: if this little blip in his ongoing life-plan had occurred just one day later he would have acted on Friday night's resolve and hived the girl off. He sweated slightly, in spite of the bitter cold. Now was the time, if ever there was one, to draw some income from his capital investment; as Neville had planned Miss Huxtry's rise, so she should now prevent his fall, until all these misunderstandings had been cleared up – especially as all his banking accounts would stay frozen in the meantime.

The thought froze him as he imagined what life would be like without her . . . whereas if she'd landed that job with Melmotte's . . . He'd left home that morning – how long ago it seemed! – too early to find out. Presumably he would still pick up his retainer from Sayeed Haq; perhaps he could also get on with planning special projects – as soon as he knew what those were, of course – for HI! Clyde had obviously been too busy to come and see him in custody; he'd call round there tonight. In the meantime, there was Miss Huxtry. He began to feel more his old self again. Quite apart from everything else, they'd missed – two, was it? No, three – three sessions with the Manual, what with one thing and another. Over a week! And it evidently wasn't true what they said about prison tea: he for one felt ready, willing and able. He tried to conjure up a vision of his beloved, failed, and settled for the relevant anatomical bits instead. Suite twenty-eight at Blairlummock didn't count, of course, not being anything to do with true love or meaningful relationships.

The driver set him down at the Dalglumph crossroads. He walked the two remaining miles in the drizzle, not minding it a bit, splashing through the puddles but avoiding the squashed birds.

He arrived home to find Miss Huxtry packing the third of her set of three matching business-class suitcases, a relationship anniversary present from Neville.

'What are you doing?' he asked.

'Packing,' she said. 'Why, what does it look like? Do you mind, you're dripping on them.'

'Oh, right,' said Neville. 'Sorry. Er – going somewhere?'

'That's right,' she said, snapping her briefcase shut. 'Unlike some I could mention. Now then, Neville, I've put the phone, Hydro and gas bills on the table with my cheque for half the amount, I think that's fair, don't you? And of course I'm taking my PC portable that I lent you – it's all right I've saved all your stuff on disk, for what it's worth now – and I've sent the sheets and bedding ahead but your single's made up. Okay? Oh, and these of course.' She indicated a large box of condoms in the suitcase, then zipped it up. 'I expect they issue heavy duty ones in prison anyway. Right.'

'Ahead?' said Neville dully. 'Ahead where? Why . . .?'

'The fact you need to ask, Neville,' she replied briskly, slipping into her designer pack-a-mac, 'is itself the answer. I mean, ya, sure you performed well in the early stages, but then – huh! You worked the moves all right, did the stuff, fine, okay, then what happens? The first big break you get – you blow it! Right – out of – sight. You just – blew it. Oh, and talking of that – I'm taking the Manual, right? Kirk was on the same page in his last relationship only the cow took it with her when they split. Okay? I mean it's not as if you'll be wanting it really.'

'Kirk?' Neville dogged her into the lounge. 'Melmotte's Kirk?'

'Mmm, ya.' She was peering round the net curtains. 'James T. Got the job of course, thanks for asking – estate agency side, going to be a big sector. Plus an offer I could not refuse after what you got yourself into – whatever stupid little mess it is you *have* got yourself into. My own Renault, aerobics room, IBM compatible, the lot. Plus he's a lot less sexually arrogant than you are, Neville, and that's really got to be a drag lately. He's very proficient and doesn't waste valuable time over it. He's caring, Neville. Our schedules fit.' She dropped the curtain. 'Women – real women, that is – plan their own sexual fulfilment these days, Neville, as, when and if they want it. They exercise control. There's my taxi. *Ciao*.' She left him dripping on the hall carpet.

Two hours later Neville's phone rang. It was Clyde Bilt.

'Oh,' said Neville gratefully. 'HI!'

'Yeah,' said Bilt, not returning the ball. 'Listen, Nev, just wanned you to know that Chylblayne and I are one hunnerd per cent with you at this moment in time, okay?'

'Oh! Tha – '

'Although naturally it would be entirely anti-expeditious for either one of us, company-wise, to meet right now. Ah'm jus' sure you appreciate that don't you, Nev?'

'Not meet? B – '

'Yeah, sure you do. Y'see, Nev, theng is with this ball game you gotta, y'know, step back occasionally, like, distance yourself from people from time t'time irrespective of whatever your true feelings might be, y'know?'

'Yes b – '

'Good, good, sure y'do! An' Gard, Nev, Gard knows what those true feelings are! So listen, till this theng gets rightways-up, we'll just be right in there prayin' foh you, okay?'

'Aw, c'mon!' Neville whined angrily. 'I mean what about all the – '

'Neville.' Bilt's voice hardened. 'You do surely appreciate Chylblayne's position in all of this? I mean, like, supposin', right, y'all don't git outa this, where's that leave her? I mean, you got any conception of the lengths our sorta people gotta go through t'hush up a termination, given our situation creedwise? Blood will out, Neville, we have th' Word of Gard on that. Listen, like Ah say: we're prayin', Nev. Suggest you git y'self some prayin' too. S'long.'

Ganglion paid an unannounced visit to his son's shop, intending to hang around outside for a while until the coast was clear for them to talk in private. In the event he did not have to wait.

'Wotcher, son,' he chirruped as the door clunked shut. 'Eye-eye! Cracked yer bell, 'ave yer?'

'Sign of the times,' said Hamish, stuffing three threats of civil action for debt and one disconnection notice under the counter. 'How's your – ' He scanned the walls for ears. 'Your new – you know?'

'Smashin'! Ta fer askin'. Gizzernuvver few days ter settle in, you'll 'ave ter come an' see us fer dinner. Roast beef of ole Argentina an' free veg do yer? Wiv treacle

323

sponge an' custard ter foller? Or would you prefer your chewin' gum spearmint flavoured?'

'Chewing – ! You mean all that stuff . . . like astronauts? Yuck!'

'Yeah, 'sright, tons an' tons of it. In addition ter good ole-fashioned tins an' packets an'at. Oz reckons they must've bin plannin' fer two years minimum, the stuff they got laid in. Kinder makes yer fink as they knows somefink the guvverment leaflets don't let on about, dunnit? Bet you never knew you could microwave a Christmas pud, didjer?'

'Well, yeah, actually I did. That one we had last year was, didn't Grace say?'

'Wot? Yuck ter you then, in that case! Still, that's enough about me. 'Amish, er, these, you know, naycher videos wot you got laid in, there's somefink about 'em I fink you oughter – '

'Yeah, I know.'

'Oh. Ar. You . . . know wot's really on 'em then?'

'Some of them, yeah. I expect the rest are the same, though. One of Neville's bright ideas.'

'Ar. Er, 'Amish . . . since when? I mean, when did you . . .'

'Yesterday morning. Old man Sproat was in straight after they kicked him out of the Eventide. Said he'd heard *The Secret Life of the Danish Beaver* was the best one and could he have it for a week. Knowing him I pretended not to have it, gave him *The Cherry Orchards of Bangkok* instead, which probably wasn't much different. I'm sending the rest back as soon as I can find out who to send them to. Don't suppose old Sproat'll bring his back anyway. Why, Dad – you weren't wantin' one yerself, were you?'

'Nah, course not, I got me – correction, I did 'ave – me art prints. Oh well. Dare say I can always go an' see ole

324

Wanker Sproat if I'm desperate. No, fing, was I was worried in case you got any aggro off of 'em, you know, like bein' tarred an' fevvered by the Neighbour'ood Watch or somefink.'

'Yeah, that's probably what Neville had in mind too. No, I didn't have one single complaint – not about those, anyway. Which you might think was kind of odd, considering some of the folk who've been borrowing them lately. Or then again, maybe not.'

'Nah, prob'ly not. Oh well, thass orl right then, if you've not 'ad any bovver wiv 'em.'

'Not with them, no.'

'Oh?'

'Yeah. Funny, isn't it? I mean, if Neville *was* trying to get me in trouble he actually needn't have bothered. Turns out I did it for him. Here.'

He rummaged among his creditors' hate mail and produced a formidably expensive-looking white envelope.

'Wossat then? You'll 'ave to tell me, I left me seein'-froo glasses in the car. These are the ones I use fer not fallin' over.'

'I'm being sued for blasphemy, Dad.'

'You *wot*?'

'Blasphemy. You know, saying bad things about God, and that. Well, Jesus I should say, in my case. Mrs Bilt is suing me for slandering the Living Jesus, according to this. I suppose it's a way of getting round not being able to libel the dead. Mind you, I can't help wondering who'll get the damages.'

'Gawd almighty! Wot did you say?'

'I didn't say anything, Dad – well, unless you count saying 'Oh Jesus!' the other night when I dropped a milk bottle on my foot. No, I uttered it, seemingly. To be precise, I uttered a video of *The Last Temptation Of Christ*. Actually I uttered it to those horrible kids of hers, which strictly speaking I shouldn't have, cos of the certificate, only seeing she'd just sent them back to the shop with four volumes of *The Wildlife of Westphalia* I don't see that she's anyone to talk. Still, there we are: solicitor's letter. Broody's Edinburgh. There'll be one from the Court of Session to follow, so it says.'

'An' all cos of this, wossname, this film?'

'Yup.'

'Yeah, well, I can see as 'ow 'Im booting out the moneylenders in the temple might've gorn against the grain a bit wiv that lot, but even so – '

'Oh no, it wasn't that bit seemingly. There's this bit where Jesus wonders what it would've been like if He hadn't been, you know, if He'd been an ordinary person, like, sinful, an' married an' so on, and he imagines having sex with . . . I dunno, some biblical wife or other, I haven't actually seen it. Anyway, it's this bit's got her going.'

'Bugger me.'

'Yeah. All go, Dad, eh?'

'Not arf. I must say you seem remarkably cheerful about it, considerin'.'

'Yeah. Well. Spose it's good publicity, as Mungo would say. Besides, it's no' really my problem, or won't be soon enough.'

'Oh aye?'

Hamish put on a pugnacious look. 'Aye.'

'Since when?'

'Friday mornin'.'

''Oo too?'

'I don't see it matters wh – '

'Ar. I see. Clinch McKittrick then, eh?'

Shame, perhaps, made Hamish more aggressive. '*So?*'

Ganglion shrugged. 'So, nuffink. Got the money, 'ave you?'

'No' yet – but I got their signed offer an' everything, and signed by me an' copied, and sent to a solicitor. So they can't back out of it. Be funny if these Clinch McKittrick people really are mixed up with the Hosannah lot, won't it? Mrs Bilt could end up suing herself.'

'Yeah, 'ilarious. Told Grace yet, 'ave yer?'

'No' yet – but I'm goin' tae. When I'm ready, okay?'

'Yeah, fine. Fine. 'Ow much?'

Hamish told him. 'It's awright, Dad, really, it's under control. I ken what I'm doin'. Really.'

'Oh, I believe you, son, I believe you. Honest. Watch my lips: I believe – you. Okay? See yer.'

Ashley Oswald came home from school the following Thursday clutching a copy of the *Perthshire Gazette*, rather battered from being gleefully mauled all day by Tammy Sproat, who had given it to him at four o'clock saying it was all right, he could always nick another from Haq's on the way home.

'Mam! *Mam?*'

Grace was in the store-room trying to organize the Magic Banana's latest mixed consignment of potatoes, cauliflowers, grapefruit, non-stick kitchen utensils and children's shoes in four width fittings.

'What is it?' she called fuzzily from behind a rack of imitation fur jackets.

'Mam! Look!' He spread the paper out on a boxed twenty-four-inch Teletext TV she wasn't going to tell Hamish about just yet. 'That's *him*, isn't it?'

'Who, pet?' She glanced across at the page. Her son's finger was pointing at the third from the left in a double-page spread of photographs.

'That man, Mam. You know, the one who . . .' He remembered he wasn't supposed to know about his mother's visitor the day the flood happened and tried to think of another way of telling her the good news. 'I mean, I think it might be the one, er, cos – '

'Mungo! Mungo, come and look at this!'

Mungo straightened and took his glasses off. 'Yup, that's our friend all right. Remanded in custody, too, along with all the others except Neville. Good.'

'It doesn't say anything here about Clinch McKittrick, though. It says he's a trainee stockbroker.' Grace frowned. 'He doesn't look like a stockbroker to me.'

'No?' Mungo smiled. 'I'd say he looks as though he was born one, actually. Not that I suppose it's true anyway – he'll just be an hourly-paid cretin like all the rest of the goons. The big fish'll have got away by now, like they always do. Still, that's not our worry, is it!'

'No,' said Grace. 'I'm glad they've got him – locked up I mean. I know prisons are horrible and everything, but – ' She shuddered. 'Those eyes!'

'Yeah. Ought to be a special offence, oughtn't it? Conspiracy to look like a shifty, ruthless bastard. Mind you, they'd have to build an awful lot of prisons.'

Grace's business – sooner or later she would have to find a new name for it – began to mushroom magically. Word spread that all sorts of things hitherto unavailable in rural Mid Lummock – or only available in packs of twelve, or by mail order, or as part of an otherwise unwanted set, or available, at a price, but turning out to be not at all as one remembered them to be – could now be obtained, at the cost of a little scrummaging, in the High Street of Craigfieth. Sometimes customers disappeared for an hour or more in the wholesale turmoil that filled the shop and the store-room, once Grace had had Hamish take the old counter out to make room. It was certainly unhygienic, and probably insecure (several dozen storm-proof clothes pegs, unavailable in the burgh for twenty years, disappeared without payment) and possibly even a little dangerous in places, but it was fun, and exciting, and different, and people – even Babette, who found herself performing miracles of arithmetic – liked it, and waited for Grace's little sapling to grow, somehow, into a giant commercial oak.

She sold quite a lot of magic mushrooms, too, having consulted her old pocket English-French dictionary, used her imagination a bit, and christened them Champignettes. Wally demanded them at every meal. Finding herself too busy to visit the hairdresser in Duncruddie Mains she just let it grow and decided to like it that way. She also wore more comfortable clothes; looser, longer ones with room to move about in. People remarked how well she looked, despite all the hard work, and in truth she did feel well – a little tired, perhaps, in the evenings and sometimes a bit odd first thing in the morning as well, but that was to be expected.

And something would have to be done, or rather said, about that, too. She waited for the time for saying it to be right.

In the meantime the only small cloud on her horizon – apart from Hamish, of course – was the small, nagging matter of what it was exactly that Ashley Oswald had been getting up to at school after requesting, and getting, 'Fifty pence for Jesus' on the second morning of the new term. Alarmed further by what happened a week after that, she had a word with one or two other mothers who confirmed – after a little cross-examination of their own little loved ones – that it (whatever it was exactly) was by no means confined to Ashley Oswald Ganglion. In the end she spared twenty minutes of her lunch hour (itself reduced to fifty minutes; she no longer bothered about early closing day and Mungo was always on hand to look after Wally) to consult the minister about it. She could not, of course, face Miss Pleat in person, at any rate not yet.

She told the story. He nodded. He agreed that there was nothing reprehensible about charitable giving. He confirmed, however, that this was the first case he'd ever come across of a charity – Christian or otherwise – which gave the donor such tangible returns on his generosity. He promised to 'look into it'. He accepted Grace's offer of her son's profits for the Kirk Fabric Fund. Grace felt reassured, and said nothing about it to Hamish.

Police enquiries ground slowly on, just like the better quality whodunnits say they do. There was even talk of 'jigsaw puzzles' and 'missing pieces' in the open-plan office suites of the Fairly Serious Crime Squad, the Mildly Diverting Fraud Team and the Interesting Misdemeanours Branch of Eastern Constabulary on the fifth floor of Hurd House, Dunbroath.

Gladstone Fredericks' sister was interviewed by two officers whose nerves of steel felt stressed and flaccid afterwards. Braced with a pint and a half of Elder's £4 bitter in McClure's Bar, and acting on information received ('in spades' as one of them wittily put it) they then proceeded to Haq's Universal Emporium where they arrested young Sayeed, son and heir of the Honorable Member for Mid Lummock, on a charge of defrauding Her Majesty's Inspector of Taxes by obtaining tax relief on a mortgage for a property used not as his main residence but as a source of income from rental. The following day they charged him with doing the same for seven other properties on what used to be Craigfieth's council estate. His sister Benazir obligingly furnished the authorities with documentary proof that all the mortgages

330

had been obtained from the Scottish Amiable and Providential Bank; shortly before she did this she telephoned Mr Kirk, who decamped very soon afterwards, along with Miss Huxtry, for warmer and less anti-entrepreneurial climes, leaving a clutch of similarly mortgaged properties on Lummock View behind him. The advances on these houses turned out to have been provided by Loadsahomes (Scotland) Ltd, a wholly owned subsidiary of Sayeed Haq (Holdings) Ltd, whose registered offices were discovered to be an accommodation address at the Dunbroath branch of KwikPost UK, an expanding limb of HI! Communications Inc.

There was even more talk of jigsaws in Hurd House after that.

At Boggybreck Barracks life was just fine. Water came, pure and filtered, from the taps, electricity unmetered from the sockets and every conceivable mod con – including a few even Ganglion had never thought of before – was laid on in profusion. The extensive underground apartments provided ample accommodation for the three men – and, by the operation of a handy little lever, for their car, which might otherwise have been a security problem – and a great deal more in the way of comfort and privacy than Rose Cottage ever could. They turned the upper storey (so to speak) into a dayroom-cum-conservatory. The marijuana plants flourished unseen behind the south-facing one-way blastproof windows. They shopped twice a week, at Grace's, for fresh fruit and vegetables and occasionally treated themselves to a joint of meat from Borden's, still open pending the owner's complete recovery from his car accident. These things apart, they decided to use up the vast stocks already in place – except for the nutritious chewing-gum which was saved for dire emergencies (such as civil war or nuclear attack) – rather than run the unthinkable risk of letting it go off in its tins. After three days of joy-riding on the electric lift from the ground floor to the lower ground floor, Oswald wondered what would happen if there really was a nuclear war and all the power went off. Ganglion supposed that they had thought of that when they built the place. MacGregor reminded him that the army had built it. Ganglion supposed that in that case they probably hadn't. 'But I'm not goin' ter worry about it,' he said. 'Any more than I worry where our pooh-poohs go when we flush 'em.'

They agreed that at their age they could probably afford not to worry about all sorts of things. Their shared lives proceeded happily, and they were not disturbed. Grace and Hamish knew about the shelter, of course, as did Ashley Oswald and Tammy Sproat but they could all, for various reasons, be relied on not to breathe a word. They set aside a room for Audrey in case she ever needed it, and told her so. But then Audrey was a brick, was Audrey, an old-fashioned sort of person (to use her own words) who didn't believe in telling tales. All three men, in their different ways, were very fond of her.

No one else had ever bothered about them much anyway, particularly.

For Audrey herself, however, April turned out to be a very cruel month. Landscape productions ceased to be a therapy and became instead a pain in the neck, shoulder and arm; the rest of the Craft Centre's stock was nearly exhausted. She often considered going out once more in search of dissident craftspersons, and as often rejected the idea. She felt more and more like the old Traveller; fragile, and vulnerable, and too damn tired.

One evening she gathered all her law books, statutes and commentaries around her and attempted to distil their welter of opinion into something useful and practical. At length she came up with the following unsatisfactory self-advice: either, a) her tenancy was constituted in common law for more than one year and required a written lease which ought to have been stamped under the 1891 Stamp Act, or at the very least a Notice adopted in holograph form and stamped ditto ditto, in which case she was all right, as Snotter hadn't done any of that or, b) it wasn't, and it didn't, and she wasn't, because he hadn't had to.

And the most one could say about that, she thought, was that it was no more useless than what she'd have had from a solicitor, and had not cost her several hundred pounds to acquire. She poured herself a large gin, which she didn't enjoy, and went to bed, there to muse furiously on the iniquities of a press which could, as at present, campaign with all the ink and woodpulp at its disposal for the rights of birds while at the same time allowing those of humans – or at least of one human in particular – to be trampled mutely underfoot. Not that she wasn't fond of birds, of course, other things being equal, but . . .

What was it? What was the reason? Was it that nobody thought evictions happened these days? Or was it, rather, because they were all too commonplace? Not a sparrow falls, she thought glumly, without the media making a great thing of it; but let an old woman . . . ha! Where were the headlines for her? Where was *The Times*, with its cautious upbraiding of Lord Margoyle for his 'injudicious use (if true) of pesticides'? When, for that matter, would the *Sun* call him a FILTHY MURDEROUS OLD SWINE on her account? Not in this life, Audrey old girl, she told herself. Not in this life. She drifted into unrestful sleep.

The next morning – regardless of the loss of business, which she was coming to care less and less about anyway – she drove to Duncruddie Mains, passed through the

333

shabby-genteel portals of the Mid Lummock District Council offices, and asked to see the housing manager. The receptionist smiled wistfully and suggested she see the Accommodation Liaison Officer instead.

'Is he the man to see about council housing?' Audrey asked.

The girl smiled again. 'I'll tell him you're coming up,' she said. 'Second floor, right at the end, next to the cleaner's cupboard. Mr Smellie.'

She did not think this Mr Smellie could possibly be the Mr Smellie she was thinking of. She walked to the second floor (the lift wasn't working), found his door (the cleaner's one looked rather more prestigious) and knocked upon it. A voice bade her enter. She did. He was.

He stood up. 'Mistress Pitt-Holyoake!' he exclaimed.

'Wallace Smellie! What an extraordinary thing!'

He blushed. Then he rifled through a pile of papers on his scratched and rickety desk. 'From green*grocery* to green *forms*, eh, Mistress Pitt-Holyoake?' It was evidently a well-rehearsed joke. She laughed at it.

'Well, well,' she said, sitting carefully on a wretched little chair. 'The last I heard of you, Mr Smellie, after we both lost that council election, you'd gone off somewhere to fight for Scottish independence.'

'Ah, well,' said Mr Smellie, shaking his head. 'I suppose all revolutionaries end up bureaucrats in the end; I was just a little late getting started. Now, what can I do for you? You're lucky, I only come in three mornings a week.'

She explained her predicament, succinctly and without recourse to maudlin self-pity. 'So you see, I've really no alternative but to put myself on the waiting list for a council house, Mr Smellie,' she concluded.

'Ah,' said Mr Smellie. 'Yes,' he added. 'Oh.'

'Oh I do understand, Mr Smellie – I know there is a

waiting list and of course there are others who have to take priority, young families and so on, and single parents, poor things, as if they hadn't enough to put up with – but I really shouldn't want very much, you see, I mean' – she shuddered – 'even a couple of rooms, you know, a small flat or something, would be quite adequate just for me.'

'Ah,' said Mr Smellie again. 'Yes. Yes I do see that of course . . . but.'

'"But", Mr Smellie? You mean the list is just too impossibly long already?'

'Erm, no, Mistress Pitt-Holyoake, no, not exactly. There isn't one.'

'No list? Really? Well in that case . . . I mean – I'm sorry, I don't quite understand.'

'There's no list, you see, Mistress Pitt-Holyoake,' Smellie said gently, 'because there's nothing to have a list for. No houses, you see.'

'No hou . . . but, I – I mean, surely, they're all over the place, aren't they? All those houses in Craigfieth, for example, in Fleming Way and Logie Baird Avenue, quite a lot of them are just standing empty as far as I can see . . . What is it, Mr Smellie?'

For Mr Smellie had been shaking his head throughout this protest. 'All sold,' he said.

'Sold? But – that can't be true, surely? I'm really not a nosey woman, Mr Smellie, but I do know of several people in those houses who pay rent? Craigfieth *is* a small town, as you know.'

'Oh yes, yes, right enough I do. But – erm – let me explain. You'll appreciate that quite a few were purchased by their occupants, back in the eighties, yes? And of course once that happens they're gone, I mean out of the council's control entirely.'

'Oh, yes, naturally I see that. They're usually the ones

with Georgian porches and treble-glazed lavatory windows. But that still leaves plenty more.'

'All acquired,' said Mr Smellie. 'By a private landlord. A local one in this instance in fact, Mistress Pitt-Holyoake – erm, oh dear yes, most unfortunate – the Lunie Estates Company.'

'The L – ? How,' Audrey asked, very quietly, 'did they manage that?'

'Oh, the tenants voted for it. That is to say,' he added, seeing Audrey's look of utter disbelief, 'they actually voted nearly three to one against it – those that did vote, that is. But the rest – the non-voting ones – all counted as Yes votes, you see. Under the legislation.'

'Legislation?'

'The Housing (Scotland) Act of 1988, Mistress Pitt-Holyoake. I'm, erm . . . sorry.'

'No, no,' said Audrey feebly. 'It's not your . . . So: what you are telling me is, there aren't any council houses, is that it?'

'Not as such, Mistress Pitt-Holyoake, no. Had you maybe considered B and B?'

'Bed and breakfast? For an income, you mean? Well if I had a house I might – '

'Ah, erm, no, I meant, to live in, you see.'

'To live – what, in an hotel?'

'Well, more of a hostel really, Mistress – no, I suppose not. Ah, dear dear. Of course I could help with liaison, help you with an approach to – ah. No, erm, no . . . perhaps not.'

'I think not,' said Audrey, 'no. Thank you all the same.

'Tell me, Mr Smellie,' she asked at the door. 'Is that what you do – help, I mean, to – '

'Liaise,' said Mr Smellie. 'Yes. I know. In fact they're, erm, they're making me redundant at the end of next month. Can't blame them really.'

Audrey met Mrs Spurtle in the lobby. She looked furtive and not a little put out.

'Mrs Spurtle! Fancy meeting you here.'

'Yes,' said Mrs Spurtle. 'Actually,' she continued guiltily, 'I was just checking the nominations – for the election, you know.'

'Oh, yes,' said Audrey. 'I had heard somewhere you were going to have a go. Jolly good! I hope you have better luck than I had. Who's the competition? Old Duff again, I suppose, but who else?'

Mrs Spurtle looked rapidly to left and right. 'That's just it,' she hissed. 'Today's the last day, you see, for putting them in – and there aren't any!'

'Good gracious! But I'm sure Mr Duff'll pop his in, won't he, before time's up. He must be a past master at it by now, after all.'

'I'm not so sure,' muttered Mrs Spurtle. 'He rang me up last week you know – the day after I put mine in.'

'Oh yes? And what, er – '

'He said "Thank you", Mrs Pitt-Holyoake. Just that. "Thank you".'

'Gracious!'

'Yes. I, er . . .'

'Yes, Mrs Spurtle?'

'I was just wondering you see – supposing he were to know something, that I didn't . . .'

'Yes?'

'Well, Mrs Pitt-Holyoake . . . whatever can it be?'

That night the lights burned long and sickly in Dante Cottage, and a terrible decision was taken.

Chapter Twelve

Deuda Externa, the touring Bolivian quintet, woke in their Portree guest house, the sound of the previous night's emotional applause still ringing in their ears, to a morning of miraculous and poignant beauty and the sort of traditional Scottish breakfast widely rumoured to be extinct since the passing of the steam age on British Railways.

Fuelled and refreshed they said goodbye to their host, boarded their defiantly painted minibus and drove the thirty-four miles to the Kyleakin ferry through scenery that was breath-taking even by Andean standards. Passing motorists waved to them on the way, an unconscious island habit born of an instinctive recognition of the fact that we all have to get along together somehow. They shared the ferryboat with a cattle float, a pick-up full of hens and a scattering of regretful tourists, and found themselves on the mainland at Kyle five easy minutes later.

They had a relatively easy time ahead of them: an early afternoon performance at Inverlochy Academy whose success depended largely (and in inverse proportion) on the extent to which the children might be instructed in the duties of an appreciative audience, and then nothing after that until the next night's appearance in the Dunbroath SpringFest, a feast of the performing arts instituted in 1989 as part of an attempt to prevent Glasgow's designation as the European Capital of Culture from going to its head. In between they looked forward to a free evening savouring the delights of Dunbroath's Temperance Hotel in Graft Street, a large, gloomy hostelry of the sort that is dear to the heart of a Scottish Arts Council accountant.

In the back of the bus Big Jorge and Little Carlos (one was a whole inch taller than the other) conjured wistful improvisations on their pan pipes. They cast a last look back at Skye, then set off for the Little Chef in Spean Bridge. This was their eighth year of touring Britain and they knew all about school dinners.

At about the same time as Deuda Externa took their leave of Lochalsh, Audrey Pitt-Holyoake was parking her Traveller on the little hill just outside the entrance to the Sunnyvale Private Home for the Retired, Craigfieth. Formerly the museum, the Home retained most of the external features so familiar to generations of school-children making their annual obeisance to the jealous gods of heritage. The flagpole (bare and half rotted) still rose from above the imposing entrance porch; the chimneys still boasted twenty-eight guano-stained chimney pots, though the place had long since gone over to storage heaters; the two giant sycamores flanking the drive still sighed continuously like twin souls in a genteel purgatory. Only the television aerial and the bars on the upper windows were obviously new.

Audrey took a deep breath and braced herself, rehearsing the interview to come: no, she had not got an appointment; no, she had not got a property to sell; no, she did not wish to pay anything by way of a deposit just at the moment, she just wanted to look round. Don't worry, Audrey, she told herself: you probably can't afford it anyway.

Last night's miserable resolve had, if anything, been strengthened by the morning papers: shocking photographs (one of which had the cheek to include Dante Cottage in the distance) of piteous little corpses against a backdrop of canary grass and mustard; refusals to comment on the part of Lord Margoyle, Mr Snotter, and a spokesperson for MaxProf Associates; questions to be asked by Greenish backbench MPs; speculations as to whether the Royal Patron of a leading environmental organization would cancel his annual participation in the slaughter of the Lunie game. But nothing – *but nothing* – about the threat to the world ecology posed by the imminent destruction of her own natural habitat.

She smoothed her skirt – a mid-calf grey worsted normally reserved for memorial services – walked firmly to the front entrance and rang the bell. When nothing had happened after three minutes she tried the door, found it unlocked, and went in.

Once inside, all resemblance to the old museum vanished utterly: doors had vanished, walls appeared, windows had shrunk and the ceiling, she could have sworn, was at least three feet lower than she remembered it. A most impressive mahogany reception counter, tastefully decorated with telephone, fax, VDU and brochure rack, was deserted; the silence, indeed, was positively palpable, possibly as a consequence of the thick yielding carpet, the hessian wallcoverings and the apparent absence of organic life forms. Audrey advanced on the brochures, saw they were promoting the services of financial advisers, undertakers, embalmers and dry-freeze resurrectionists, and sheered away. She started opening doors instead.

The first three revealed a sitting-room, a dining-room, and – somewhat alarmingly – a bedroom. She was forced to admit that whatever architectural indignities the place had undergone in its conversion, there seemed very little to find fault with in the way of furnishings, decoration and general ambience of the place. All three rooms were well-proportioned and generously furnished without being cluttered, and appeared both immensely comfortable and spotlessly clean. The décor was pleasing without being obviously clever, and succeeded in combining references to more than one period without committing any glaring solecisms of taste. There was even, here and there, a little touch of the Pre-Raphaelite. The facilities, in short, seemed excellent, and everything that she, as *une femme moyenne civilisée*, could desire. The fees were probably enormous.

The fourth door revealed a sort of office-cum-study, furnished with the same discreet regard for the need to combine good taste with hygiene and convenience. The fifth disclosed a sumptuously practical bathroom complete with a lavatory whose warmly inviting sculptured wooden seat (sensibly high off the ground) just cried out to be sat on. Do I dare? she wondered, and then did. Afterwards the unit did not so much flush as tactfully remove from genteel view. The air bore faint traces of jasmine. Audrey began to wonder if she could book herself in for a week's cripplingly expensive holiday. Certainly the place must be exclusive indeed if it could afford to bear the loss of having one whole floor unoccupied. She had heard that the fantastically wealthy were sometimes wont to have whole floors of luxury hotels reserved in their name, but had never imagined such goings-on not three minutes' walk from (say) the Sub-Regional Sewerage Offices in Craigfieth High Street.

Perhaps, she wondered, each upper floor reproduced the arrangement – there must be a kitchen on this one somewhere – with its own matron, or châtelaine, or whatever they were called in these places. Here, certainly, were other doors, other bedrooms perhaps. A certain amount of communal living would, she decided, be quite bearable in these surroundings. Perhaps, strictly speaking, she was trespassing. She felt a little guilty now about using their loo unbidden.

A wide staircase took off at one side of the gleaming mahogany counter; she allowed it to waft her up. At the top was a turning, and at the end of the turning was a large door. It was locked, with the key left in.

Three elderly persons were grouped in various attitudes of watchfulness behind the reflective glass of their north-facing window.

'Police?' wondered Oswald.

'Workmen?' suggested MacGregor

'Nah, military,' said Ganglion, who had the Civil Defence issue binoculars. 'Wot they used ter call Pioneers.'

'Ah,' said Oswald. 'Old moles. What for, do you think?'

Ganglion shook his head, passing Oswald the glasses. 'Dunno. They all seem ter be going that way, look, just outer sight be'ind that rise there. See the spades an' shovels?'

'Aye, very clean they are too. Been up all night polishing them no doubt. *Seo*, MacGregor.' He passed the binoculars to their tall friend. 'You'll maybe see more.'

MacGregor moved a table across to the window and climbed on it. 'Just – a wee – detail,' he said. 'Aye, I see two o' them, diggin'. Just inside what looks like a sort o' dip in the ground. But there must be dozens more further on, diggers I mean.'

'At least it's not *us* they're diggin' for, fank Gawd,' Ganglion commented, helping MacGregor off the table.

'Dear knows what it is, though,' said Oswald. 'All that part's mostly bog, as I remember it. My father said it'd take another ice age to get rid of it completely.'

'Yeah. Probly a trainin' exercise then, case there's anuvver Falklands Woar.'

'Aye, but . . .' Oswald had another look through the

342

glasses but they were out of sight now. 'If the army've sold the place to this Halleluja crowd – not that they've a right to but you know what I mean – then they shouldn't be here at all by rights, should they?'

MacGregor shrugged. 'Site clearance? Part o' the deal? Anyway, as friend Ganglion here says, nothing to do with us.'

'Well,' said Oswald. 'Maybe, aye.'

'Relax, Oz! 'Ere, come an' see wot you make of this latest loader bumf from the insurers wot I picked up at the Post Office smornin'.'

His claim having been submitted to the Norwich Royal Alliance Commercial and Accident Union Insurance Co, plc (motto: Your Choice Has To Be Us) and followed up with field enquiries and sworn statements from the police and fire brigade, a minion in the Claims Department had informed Oswald that the ground was now cleared for negotiations to proceed, and that he would be receiving a letter shortly. That had been a week ago; today the letter had arrived.

Oswald opened it and read it. 'But that's just monstrous!' he said, letting it fall in his lap.

'Don't tell me: you're not covered cos there was an r in the month? No? Um, 'ow abaht this then: as a disabled smoker they reckon the chances are tenter one you was tryin' ter top yerself?'

'No,' said Oswald. 'Worse. Listen. "Dear Mr Ochil*tree*" – get that? Buggers! – "Thank you for your", oh, blah-blahblah, the usual havers. Now then: "Your attention is drawn to the exclusions set out in Clause F[5](xi-xviii)(e), a copy of which is attached." That's – here we are – that's "Any consequences of war, invasion, act of foreign enemy, hostilities (whether war be declared or not), civil war, rebellion, revolution, terrorism, insurrection or military or usurped power." Got that, everyone? Right. They go on: "We understand police enquiries are continuing into the whereabouts of a suspect believed to be connected with the security services of a foreign power. This being the case – "'

'Blah-dee-ell! They're not suggestin' it woz an invasion are they?'

'No. Shut up and listen. "This being the case, the possibility of a terrorist connection with the incident cannot be ruled out, and therefore no payment can be made until a court or similar judicial authority rules that the incident was the result of criminal arson rather than of an act falling within the exclusions set out in your policy schedule, Yours sincerely." There! I told you it was worse, did I not?'

'Barstuds!'

'Mmnn-aye,' agreed MacGregor.

''Ere, wait a bleedin' minute!' said Ganglion, although nobody was in a rush to do anything just then. ''Old on! If this suspect is some foreign government spook, then 'e can't be the terrorist, can 'e? Oh, course I know most of 'em *are* terrorists, we all know that, look at bleedin' wossname, Nicaragua an'at, 'an all the bleedin' rest, Israel an' Iraq an' all them – but not officially, right? Well, then: if 'e isn't, then it's a bit flamin' obvious 'oo they fink *is*, init?'

Oswald started. 'Not – '

'Yeah. Us, mate.'

MacGregor seemed to find the suggestion mildly amusing. 'Children of the Mist,' he murmured happily. 'The Nameless Clan. *Ard Choille!*'

'If I woz you,' said Ganglion, being deliberately Saxon and ignoring him, 'I'd do the buggers fer libel.'

Oswald sighed. 'And who do you suggest I leave the lawsuit to in my will, Ganglion, eh?'

'Yeah, see yer point. Still,' he bridled, 'we can't jus' leave it at that, can we?'

'The omnibus man,' said MacGregor.

'You wot?'

'Ye know! There's a mannie who ye can complain to about that on-carryin'. The insurance omnibus man, they call him.'

'Aow, you mean the *ombudsman!* Yeah, worf a try, eh, Oz?'

'Mmn? Oh, aye. Worth a try, indeed. I'll do it. And I'll write back to yon buggers and tell them I'm doing it. Meanwhile . . .' He sighed again.

'Meanwhile, at least we've still gorra floor over our 'eads, eh?'

'Aye.' Oswald wheeled over to the window again. 'I'd still like to know what they're up to out there, though.'

All the muffled agonies of hell, it seemed, greeted Audrey Pitt-Holyoake when she opened the door at the top of the stairs, though it was the stench that registered first, a taste of death, and hopelessness, and damp, and filth, and faeces. Dozens of faces, some male, some female, some indeterminate, most vacant and all elderly, peered at her from the doorways that gave off either side of a long, dank, narrow corridor floored with dark brown linoleum cracked and stained and puddled. Some half-dozen or so faces resolved themselves into whole, mobile bodies, clad apparently in a twenty-four-hour compromise between night and day attire. Involuntarily she pressed herself against the wall as they surged weakly past her and down the splendid stairs, cackling and nudging each other as they went.

Audrey regrouped herself. 'Who's . . . in charge here?' she asked.

The heads shook. Some looked frightened, most suspicious. They withdrew, leaving just a few hanging bodilessly, vacuously grinning, muttering and dribbling.

'Please?' said Audrey. She glanced back down the stairs. A queue had formed inside the open bathroom door. Somebody was standing outside the sitting-room door; he, or she, was holding a red velvet cushion, stroking it and crooning. She looked back along the foul corridor. The same few faces were there, as before. She made slowly for the first door, a hand raised to steady herself against the clammy wall, and looked in.

The first thing she noticed – perhaps she was unconsciously trying not to look at what lay in between – was that the bars at the window at the far end of the room were in fact a sort of internal cage arrangement clearly intended to keep the inmates away from the window as well as preventing anyone falling out. The reasons for this extra precaution were immediately obvious: never, quite simply, had she seen such people. Once upon a time they had been old; now they were agelessly dehumanized. Rags, filthy rags, clothed the rags that clothed the bones that kept them, somehow, together in one piece. Her entry had sent them scuttling to their beds as if in some grotesque game of musical chairs; Audrey caught glimpses of grubby, shrivelled or puffy bare feet, of wet underwear, of no underwear, and realized as a physical shock that there were both men and women here. On a double bed in the corner a woman, possibly in her eighties, was attempting to suckle a toothless old man whose mouth hung slackly open as she banged it feebly against her pendulous whiteness. At the foot of their bed another man, sobbing uncontrollably, dabbed at a puddle on the floor with a corner of his dressing-gown. Most of the room's occupants were whimpering or groaning quietly to themselves; one was reciting 'Baa Baa Black Sheep' in a low monotone. It wasn't just a dormitory. There was a table with some scraps and smears of spilt food – not breakfast – on it. There were two sprung armchairs, one unsprung, the other armless. Light from three dust-shaded ceiling bulbs spilled yellowly over the scene. A door banged downstairs; the groaning ceased, but the whimpering intensified.

The other rooms, those that she had time to see, were much the same; their occupants, never fewer than eight to a room, much the same also. Particular things she remembered afterwards, or dreamed about: a bald man, tied into an apron bib, staring blankly at a bowl of cold lumpy porridge; a woman in a ball-gown dancing by herself; the man who watched her from his wheelchair, his hand masturbating in time to the silent music, his face fixed·in a smile of archiepiscopal serenity. But for the most part the occupants of the first floor of the Sunnyvale Private Home for the Retired either sat or lay in attitudes of defeat of half-querulous resignation. No one spoke to her.

She heard a strong female voice downstairs. 'What's going on here? What are you doing? Who let you out?' It said.

Guiltily, Audrey slunk behind a door; she saw a lavatory – seatless, cracked and evidently not working – and darted quickly out again. Firm footsteps were on the stair.

'But you let us out last week, Mother,' said another.

'Last week you were prepared for it! And you know, don't you, that it only happens when there are visitors! Now then, who let you out, mmm? Who did this? Who? Who did it?'

'Oh, but the door *was* open, Mother,' said another. They were nearly at the top now; Audrey dodged into another room, small, and empty save for a single chair in the middle.

'Then it shouldn't have been! Now go to your rooms if you please, all of you. I have a busy morning ahead for me. What have we here, Mr Morrison?' This from next door, the first room Audrey had been in. 'An accident? And what am I to do, do you think, about accidents like this when they – happen – every – day, mmm? Put you somewhere else, Mr Morrison, that's what I shall have to do if it goes on; this is a clean house after all, you can't expect my staff to be clearing up after your messes all day and every day. Now go and get a cloth. Now then everybody: *who – opened – that – door?*'

A chorus of 'Don't know, Mother,' 'Someone else, Mother', and 'It wasn't me, Mother'.

'Well, I see I shall just have to find out!'

The door opened slowly; Audrey stiffened, her heart pounding. An elderly lady in slightly better shape than the rest tiptoed in, backwards and gently pushed it to. 'Quick, Mrs Pitt-Holyoake!' she whispered. 'It's your only chance, my dear.'

The dress, though crumpled, might still have passed for respectable in a dim light; the hair, though unkempt, still showed traces of a blue rinse a world ago. The face, loose and toadlike, bore signs about the eyes of a struggle for reason and sentience within. A hand took her arm; its fingers shook. Audrey found herself being led to the chair.

'But I'm not an inm – . . . I'm a *visitor* here,' she whispered fiercely.

'You! Was it you?' came the voice, very close now.

'Oh, no, dear! No visitors here, it's not allowed. I thought I was one once. Now then, dear . . . that's it, sit there, now . . .' The lady began groping about the floor. 'Here we are now, dear.' She had a cord of some sort in each hand; her face worked animatedly.

'What are you – '

348

'Sssh, dear! Please! I'll tell you . . . if I can . . . later. We've got to do this, now!'

Unbelievingly, Audrey felt her hands being tied behind the chair.

'Am I hurting you, dear? Only we must make it look right, you see. Now your ankles, dear, just cross them . . . yes. There we are. You should be safe now.'

Audrey's gaoler put a finger to her lips. 'Not now!' she breathed. 'Must. Later.' She opened the door very cautiously and inched her head out. The rest of her followed, and Audrey was alone. She tried her hands and feet: they were securely tied, though not painfully. She shook her head.

Mrs Quaich! That's who it was. Mrs Quaich! Mrs Quaich who had sold her house, Mrs Quaich who was four, was it? no, five years younger than –

The door burst open. It had to be Mother: a woman in her permanent mid-forties, admitting no alternatives.

'Oh! So we've been wandering again, have we? Out of your room, hmm? Well, you know the punishment! At least we know it couldn't have been *you*, dear!' The door slammed shut. Mother was gone. Audrey was glad she'd used that bathroom.

'And remember as you, ah, pay attention to Dewed – ah . . . to these people, that it is customary not to clap until the *end* of the performance.'

Four hundred and seventy-eight blankly hostile white faces confronted five friendly Aymara-Inca ones. The first bowel-dissolving notes of *Wiracocha* filled the Academy Hall like a second creation. The concert was a remarkably successful one, considering.

'It's like my father used to say about the Great War,' Oswald observed, dropping the empty tin of Grouse Roll

Concentrate into the bin. 'The aristocracy were urged to go on eating as much game as they could stuff in, even during the big shortages near the end, because ordinary folk couldn't stomach it. This bin's full, by the way.'

'Yeah, well, I dare say the Great British Stummick's changed a lot since them days,' said Ganglion. 'Woss fer afters, Oz?'

'Tinned cabinet pudding.'

'Or?'

'Or there's some apples left, I think. I was saying, this bin's full.'

'Oo's turn is it?'

'Yours,' said Oswald and MacGregor.

'They've gone away now, Ganglion,' MacGregor added. 'So it's quite safe.'

'You sure?'

'Positive,' said MacGregor and Oswald.

'We counted them all in,' Oswald declared, 'and counted them all out.'

'Oh,' said Ganglion. 'Right then. Though wot we're goin' ter do when our rubbish 'ole's full up – '

'Find another one,' said Oswald.

'On ye go, Ganglion, it's good exercise for ye.'

'Yar,' said Ganglion, hauling his coat on. 'Gawdstrewf, Oz, you mighter tied the bag up for me.'

'Cup of tea when you get back,' Oswald placated him.

'*If* ye – '

'Har, har.'

'Don't forget to let go, old friend.'

Ganglion banged the door shut behind him; Oswald was pouring the tea when it opened again ten minutes later.

'Bleedin' chuckin' it dahn aht there!'

'Aye,' said Oswald. 'We had noticed. Tea.'

'Ta. Nah then, bet you can't guess wot Fred Karno's Army's bin up to ahtside.'

'Building latrines?'

'Officers-only-knocking-shop?' MacGregor suggested hopefully. 'Give up.'

'Well, it's odd really. They've kind of stripped all the top layer off of a big area inside the dip – all folded back neatly, it is, 'eather, bog-myrtle, the lot, an' laid neatly in its creases rahnd the edge. An' they've made this dinky little road goin' in at one side, only a few yards long, mind, but all flattened aht wiv gravel on top. An' all the way rahnd where they've bin diggin' is roped off like a sports day or somefink. Blahdy odd, I call it. This sugared is it, Oz? Good.'

'Sounds like they're preparing for a bit of a do,' Oswald commented. 'Like a ceremony or something.'

'Wot on erf would they be 'avin' a do for, way aht 'ere in the middler nowhere, though?'

'Maybe this is it, boys,' said MacGregor. 'A big Holy Joe complex, like the paper said.'

'Yeah. Or a crucifixion, p'raps. Either way, I reckon a quick trip aht 'safternoon'd be in order, get some stocks in just in case.'

'We're nearly out of rubbish bags.'

'Right, Oz.' 'Ere, 'sfunny they never fort of them when they stocked this place, innit? Wonder wot they fort they woz goin' ter put all their gash in?'

MacGregor grunted. 'Throw it over the fence for the survivors to fight over, I should say.'

'Ar! Course. Silly question.'

Audrey Pitt-Holyoake sat on in gloomy and increasingly uncomfortable solitude for over two hours – she could not see her watch, of course, but it was sometimes possible over the bedlam hum to hear a clock strike downstairs –

before Mrs Quaich returned, a greasy bowl of food hidden under her cardigan.

'I'm afraid you'll have to use fingers, dear,' she murmured apologetically. 'They count the spoons, you see.' She untied Audrey's hands.

Audrey plunged greedily in, ignoring both her finer feelings and the excruciating pain in both wrists, especially the right one. Whatever it was seemed to be mostly mashed potato, but it was still just warm.

Mrs Quaich kept up a muttered conversation while she ate. '. . . couldn't come any sooner I'm afraid, dear, because you see after that trouble this morning Mother sent a governess up to keep an eye on us all and I couldn't slip out until after lunch. They give us all pills, you see, after lunch, which I'm convinced are to quieten us all down, only I managed to push mine under my plate with my tongue – my dental plate I mean of course – and spit it out when she wasn't looking. I think I managed not to swallow anything – oh, no, let me, dear, you'll get your skirt dirty. This pocket, is it?'

Mrs Quaich found a tissue and Audrey smeared her fingers clean on it.

'Don't think I'm being rude, Mrs Quaich,' she began carefully.

'Dora, dear.'

'Dora, but what on earth are you doing in this place? I thought you had bought yourself a little flat in Dalglumph.'

'Oh . . . yes, dear.' Dora Quaich looked suddenly flustered. She poked nervously at her straggling hair. 'Yes I know, but . . . oh dear, so many things kept happening, you see! I . . . I – oh dear!'

'No, no dear,' she added as Audrey made to do something helpful. 'No, I shall be all right, really, it's just

. . . I have such difficulty sometimes remembering everything, do you find that? I never used to, you know, never,
until . . . well just lately really, since I . . .' She coughed
helplessly.

'Did you . . . go on a cruise, Dora? I did hear something about one.'

'Oh, no, I – yes, now that's it! Oh, well done, dear,
that's very helpful you see because . . . now let me get it
right: I couldn't have my little cruise, you see, because of
the money, dear.'

'Too . . . expensive?'

'Oh no, no, nothing like that. No, you see, the money
didn't come, that was the problem, and of course I had to
leave my – my house, of course, because of signing all the
documents so it was all a terrible bother, oh dear, such a
worry . . .'

'But, Dora! They couldn't make you *do* that, surely!'

Mrs Quaich looked affrightedly to the door and put a
finger to her lips.

Audrey lowered her voice again. 'They couldn't make
you, not if they hadn't paid! Surely your solicitor . . .'

'Oh, yes, but no, you see, it wasn't quite like that,
Audrey dear; *their* solicitors were doing the whole thing
for me, to save me money on fees they said, and because
I was going into this flat which they owned, anyway they
allowed me to move in without paying for that, either,
because of course you see *I* couldn't pay them until they
paid me . . . at least I – I think that's . . . anyway in the
end they suggested that since I *had* moved in they should
just draw up some new documents which would let them
pay me the difference when . . . when it was all properly
settled.'

Audrey passed her another tissue.

'Oh, thank you, dear, it's so awful having to manage

353

without one. So . . . I . . . moved, you see, into the flat, after that.'

'And was it unsuitable then, Dora, this flat?'

'Oh, no!' Mrs Quaich smiled reassuringly. 'No, not at all, dear, it was lovely, even though I was in it for only a week or two before . . . before . . . oh dear, it's gone again, I – '

'Before . . .' Audrey thought of possibilities. 'Before it . . . started leaking gas? Flooded? Fell down?'

'Oh, yes! That was it!'

'Which, Dora?'

'Fell down, dear. Well no, it didn't actually . . . oh, Dora, you *silly* – do you know I just can't, it all happened so . . . No! – no, that . . . I think. You see, there were lots, lots of flats I mean, all sort of grouped together round a sort of courtyard, you see, but all quite separate from each other because I remember insisting on my own front door. I didn't want anyone else . . . well, you know. But then I had a visit, very early in the morning. I remember that quite well because there was no milk on the step when I – when we left . . . and it was a man from the building inspectors – he *did* show me his card, Audrey, really and truly, I know what you were going to say – well anyway he did have a card, and he said there were some very dangerous cracks, you see, in the walls, the ones that held the roof up, and I would have to . . . move out until they . . . put them right.'

'And come here?'

'Yes! Yes! Only that was the awful thing, you see, they didn't show me here, upstairs I mean, that was later, after I signed the . . . other document they gave me.' She swallowed several times. 'I only saw *down*stairs, you see, and, oh, of course it was all . . . was all – lovely, you know – '

'Oh yes,' Audrey agreed. 'I saw it too, some of it.'

'Yes, well of course now I realize that's what they do to everybody when they first come! Then they said they would – would put me upstairs until my things . . . my things . . . – '

Audrey cuddled her until the sobs had fully subsided.

'Dora,' she said gently as soon as it was safe. 'Dora, you're not . . . paying for this, are you?'

'Oh n-no dear, not . . . really.'

'Not really?'

'Well they – they said . . . they'd take it off what I . . . what they . . . it's all the same people I suppose . . . it must be.'

'But, Dora – I mean, you're a . . . an able-bodied woman, I mean for goodness' sake, why not just go?'

'Oh, but you can't, Audrey, nobody can! They keep that door locked – the one you must have opened – all the time, unless they want some of us to go downstairs in our special clothes, for visitors, you see. All our meals are brought up here and . . . and everything! And I know what you're going to say, why don't those of us they do let out *do* something, well, but you don't understand, dear, it's not like that, they – they say things. I mean the woman who's in charge here does, she has us all call her Mother, about being punished afterwards if anybody . . . you know . . . says anything. And I have tried, really I have, since I've been here to . . . well, find others who would join in, perhaps, but they're all . . . well, you know. It's not their fault, poor things, they can't help it but . . . there you are, you see?'

Audrey stared helplessly at a stain on the wall.

'But now you're here, dear . . .'

She turned to look at Dora Quaich. 'I've got a plan! Only we'll have to wait until it gets darker.'

* * *

Hamish sat on after lunch until Mungo picked up his friend's aura and left the room to go back to the shop. Grace fiddled with her dessert fork. 'Aren't you . . . going back, Hamish?' she asked finally.

'Nope,' said Hamish. 'Nope. Grace, I – '

'Only Mungo's got his packing to do and I can't expect him to – '

'What?'

'I was saying, Hamish, I can't expect him to go on serving all afternoon when he's – '

'He's leaving?'

'Yes.' Grace looked up. 'Why, hasn't he told you?'

'No! When did you know?'

'Oh . . . well, this morning actually, he said he . . . well, that is I think he's a bit . : . well, afraid to.'

'Afraid? Why? What of?'

'Well of you, Hamish, of course!'

'Of m – '

'Oh come on, Hamish! Don't say you haven't realized we've all been . . . been walking on eggs for ages now, trying not to upset you because of your shop and everything, I mean even Wally goes quiet when you're in the room! And I'm sure Mungo thinks he's let you down and you'll start accusing him of betraying you or someth – '

'Hah! I – '

' – because of not being able to find out about these horrible people or do anything to put a stop to it or even get poor Oswald in the papers – he's frightened you'll, I don't know, go off your head or something. So go on, Hamish – shout at me instead!' Grace became angrily tearful. 'Well go on, Hamish! Go on! And you can tell me off while you're about it for doing well in *this* shop – as if I was only doing it to spite you or something – as if I wasn't worried too, about you, about everything, and trying to – to – do something . . . and as if that wasn't enough I'm going to – to . . .'

'Aye,' said Hamish. 'Well. Erm, Actually I've – Grace, please, don't, erm, don't – '

'Don't what?' She lifted a puffy face and sniffed hard. 'Dode wod, Habiz? Add wod hab you?'

'What have I what?'

'What have you, whatever it was you were going to say before you said please don't, Grace?'

'Oh, aye. Erm. That. Well, now Mungo's . . . I mean now I know . . . yeah, well. Anyway, it's done now. I've sold the shop.'

'Oh.'

'. . . ?' said Hamish.

'Mmm?'

'I mean – is that it? "Oh"?'

'Oh, well . . .'

'I thought . . . I mean, I think, maybe you could . . . use the money to . . . you know. What you were talking about the other . . . Expand I mean. The shop. You know?'

'To be honest, Hamish.'

'Yes?'

'Um, to be honest I thought – did think . . . was thinking, your shop, maybe . . . you see?'

'Oh.'

'If you didn't . . . well, hadn't – you know.'

'Oh. Still, but, I mean – there's always other places.'

'What, here? Where?'

'No, no' here . . . Other *places*.'

'Leave Craigfieth?'

'Well . . . aye.'

'Oh.'

'I mean I know there's a few . . . well, bills to pay, debts – no, not debts, I just mean bills, you know . . .'

Hamish laughed nervously then rapidly went on '. . . but there'd still be quite a lot left after. Well, no' just quite a lot actually. A lot a lot.'

'Oh? How . . . how much, Hamish?'

He told her how much. 'When I get it, that is,' he added. 'Which I will. I got it in writing – lawyers, everything.'

'Hamish, there's – '

'Anyway!' He got up. 'I'll have to get back now, right enough – we'll . . . talk about it, yeah?'

'Yes,' said Grace quietly. 'Yes Hamish. We must.'

Hamish bumped into Mungo on his way out.

'Erm – sorry . . .' they both began. Hamish laughed; Mungo joined in. Then they punched each other on the shoulder. 'Shit, eh!' they both agreed.

Hamish crossed the street, looked hard at Grace's shop, their own house above, the empty houses on either side. Then he shrugged and went off to Sounds Good to play Spot The Customer for the afternoon.

Haq's Universal Emporium was down to half its usual stock and the queue moved slowly with only Benazir to serve it. Oswald and Ganglion saw Hamish pass the door.

'He looks happier,' said Oswald.

'Yeah,' Hamish's father agreed. 'Good. About time, an' all. Gawd, if this bleedin' queue's not a good reason ter stop smokin' I dunno wot is!'

The bleeding queue looked sternly at Ganglion, sniffed, then turned away.

Some fifteen minutes later they passed Audrey's Traveller parked outside the Sunnyvale. 'Funny place ter leave it,' Ganglion commented. 'Considerin' there's bigger 'ills ter park on.'

'Mmm.' Oswald looked back. 'Heavens, Ganglion, you don't think she's . . . gone there, do you?'

'Wot? Where? Sunnyvale? Mrs P-H? Gawd, do us a

358

favour, Oz! Woon't be seen dead in a place like that, our Ordrey woon't! So ter speak,' he added as Craigfieth slipped out of sight behind them.

Sergeant MacEachran watched them go and shook his head sadly. He'd have to tell them the morn's morn, he decided. Sometimes it was no fun at all, being a policeman.

The M99 was closed at Pluckit Hen interchange owing to a collision between a whisky tanker, a lorry carrying ball-bearings and a coachload of English soccer hooligans on their way to Smirr Park for the European runners-Up Cup Quarter final, first leg, between Pittenweem Aca-demicals and Dynamo Tirana. Traffic to Dunbroath was diverted via Dalglumph and Duncruddie Mains on the A2001(T), itself blocked owing to flooding at Balwhiddle and a landslip at the Pass O' Slymie. Deuda Externa's minibus merged itself into a ten mph queue of traffic, the head of which was lost to view in the pouring rain. The vehicle's occupants yawned and tried to think of Skye, or La Paz, or indeed anywhere except the A2001(T) three hundred yards south of the Pluckit Hen interchange on a rainy evening.

Night, more like March than May, came dropping quickly. There were seven weeks to go before the summer solstice.

Dora Quaich and Audrey Pitt-Holyoake waited for twenty minutes after the inmates had been given their evening pill before putting Operation Matricide (as Audrey called it to herself, having added bits she hadn't told Dora about) into action.

'Right,' she hissed. 'I'm off!' Dora squeezed her arm and she picked up her chair, very quietly, and carried it down to the end of the corridor. Dora, meanwhile, stationed herself just inside the doorway of the first dormitory on the opening side of the locked door to downstairs and sanity.

Audrey put the chair down, climbed on it, and waited a few seconds in case any sound should break the gentle moaning swell of the dozing inmates. When it didn't, she cast a quick glance up the corridor to orient herself later on, turned, opened the cupboard (whose handle was just in reach) put her hand inside, found the fuse box and – standing on tip-toe, her calves complaining bitterly – pushed the switch up.

Two things happened, apart from all the lights in Sunnyvale going off. A confused and panic-stricken cackling broke out of the first floor as its occupants wondered what fresh indignities were in store for them, and there was a tremendous crash from downstairs caused by Mother tripping up and dropping a trayful of decanters.

Audrey groped her way along the noisome passage and found her ally. 'All right?' she whispered. Dora squeezed her arm again.

They had not long to wait before they heard the stairs being kicked to pieces and the key turning in the lock.

'What's going on?' barked Mother. She shone her torch down the corridor. The two escapees shrank further into the dormitory. Audrey prayed she had remembered to leave the cupboard door *obviously* open . . . She had. Mother strode off to investigate.

'Who's been – '

They did not wait to hear the rest. Dora went first. Audrey stopped before shutting the door, shouted 'Fire!' then turned the key.

'Come on!' They stumbled downstairs as quickly as they could, Audrey first. Quite near the bottom she collided with a fleshy female thing.

'You're not supp – ' began the thing, then Audrey

made a fist like Godfrey had taught her to and hit where she judged the voice to be coming from. It made a most satisfying noise, and their way was clear. The last four yards were a silent canter across the sewage-coloured carpet; from above them came the sound of distant terror.

'Oh dear, it's raining!' Dora wailed.

'Want to stay in the dry?' asked Audrey grimly. 'Come on, then!' The two ladies scuttled through the deluge, their feet squelching horribly in the gravelly morass, passed through the waterfall that was the entrance beneath the sycamores, and made it to the Traveller.

'Don't shut the door!' Audrey ordered, switching on the ignition, yanking out the choke and finding first gear. 'Put your foot on the road – like this – right – now – *push!* PUSH!' The car began to roll.

'O God,' Audrey breathed, 'if You're up there, make her start!'

The engine – not that this proves anything, mind – fired first time. They roared off to the roundabout where the Mercat Cross used to be and drove three hundred yards down the High Street and pulled up by the phone box.

'Keep your foot on the gas, Dora – here, that's right. Just going to make a call.' Audrey's face was set, her eyes shining. She looked vengeful and magnificent.

'The p-police, dear?'

'No,' said Audrey. 'Better than that. MacEachran's too good for them.'

She pulled the phone box door as far shut as it would go, lifted the receiver – thank heavens it was working – and jabbed button nine three times with a firm forefinger.

'Fire,' she said calmly, then, panting, 'Hello? This is the . . . matron of . . . Sunnyvale Home in Craigfieth . . . Suh-nee-vale, yes . . . we've got a fire . . . on the first floor . . . door jammed . . . everybody trapped . . . *please* . . . quickly . . .' She cupped her hand half over the mouthpiece. 'Aaauurgh!' she said, and hung up.

She dusted her hands together, smiled, and went back to the car.

'All right, dear?'

'Fine!'

They turned at the bottom of the street; on their way back they were overtaken by Leading Fireman Lockerbie, his slippered foot pressed firmly on the accelerator. Audrey's face in the passing street lamps was a beautiful mask of satanic glee. 'Home, Dora!' she said.

Dora began to tremble and twitter on the way, starting as they hit each puddle. Audrey patted her knee. 'Buck up, Dora dear,' she encouraged. 'Soon be over now.'

They sloshed and bumped up Audrey's track. She turned the car and parked it for punting off. 'Now, I've got a torch, Dora dear, so you just give me your arm now and we'll soon be warm and cosy and you can have a nice hot bath.'

She kept up these calming sentiments all the way to the house, where she found the lights weren't working. She could feel, in the dark, her companion begin to fall apart.

'Dear, dear!' she said brightly. 'Power cut! Not surprising, in this weather. Never mind, you come through to the kitchen and I'll put the kettle on the Rayburn and find Godfrey's old Tilly lamp, I always keep it fuelled ready.'

She led Dora into the kitchen, sat her down as gently as she could and found a candle in the drawer. 'Now then, dear, I'll just leave you with this while I – '

She saw Dora's face fall open; looked from it to where the eyes were staring; saw what they saw.

A large pile of bird corpses on the table, with a dead cat stiffly perched on top.

She had never before had occasion to find out if slapping a hysteric really worked. She slapped one now. It did. She took the candle away and instinctively went to wash her hands. The tap belched wetly, then fell silent.

'Oh, you bastards,' she said flatly. 'You vicious, vicious bastards.'

'What . . . are we going . . . to do, dear?' Dora's voice was faint, but controlled.

Audrey thought the syntax a good sign. 'Go somewhere else,' she said shortly. 'A place I know of, with good people in it. Another wet walk to the car I'm afraid, my dear.'

She helped Dora to her feet. The telephone rang.

'Ha! Missed that did you, Snotter?' She picked it up. 'Yes?'

'Mrs Audrey Pitt-Holyoake?'

'Yes!'

'Oh good, I've been trying you. My name's Clay Loan, I'm doing a press story on the bird poisonings and I understand your landlord is attempting to – '

'Yes! Yes he is so attempting, Mr Loan. And in the course of so attempting, he, or his agents, have cut my water off, cut my electricity off and dumped a pile of dead animals on my kitchen table while I was out. I'm going to stay the night somewhere else, Mr Loan, but I have touched nothing, I will leave the house unlocked since my persecutors obviously have a key anyway, and I suggest you come and get your story right away. There's a nice photographer called Campbeltown Fotheringhame who may be able to help you. Got that, Mr Loan? Oh – and it might interest you to know that my landlord's factor, Mr Snotter, is a Justice of the Peace! Good night.'

In a nice little flat in the New Town of Edinburgh, Clay Loan grinned to himself. Good old Fothers! When he promised a fresh angle, he meant just that. He scooped up his car keys, dropped the latch and went out into the fog. He could call Fothers up from the car.

* * *

363

'Come along now, Dora, off we go.' Audrey had bundled some night things for them both into a suitcase and was now gently bundling Dora Quaich into the night.

'It's a terrible world we live in, Audrey, isn't it?' She looked up at Audrey as if hoping for proof of the contrary, but not expecting it.

'Bits of it are all right,' said Audrey. 'Come along now and I'll show you one.' Oh God, she thought, I must stop saying 'come along now'. I must sound like a welfare home wardress.

'Pick your heels up, dearie,' she said instead. 'We're going to have a ball!'

'Oh dear!' sighed Mrs Quaich.

Driving through the torrential night, Audrey could not rid her mind of the thought that the Boggybreck Bunker would be flooded and that they should all have nowhere, nowhere to go. Dora had fallen mercifully asleep at her side, exhausted with age and inhumanity and lulled by the hissing tyres, the engine's monotone and the schlip-flop of the wipers as they failed to clear, flop, failed to clear, flop, failed to clear the windscreen. Audrey felt herself nodding and forced her neck into a painful position in order to concentrate. The Boggybreck entrance was hard to spot at the best of times . . .

She frowned, peered, and squeezed the ancient brakes. There was something up ahead, flashing its hazard lights; blurred figures in the headlights waving . . .

Waving her down. She stopped and opened the driver's door, the window having seized up long ago.

'Please?' said a small man outside. 'We are broken, yes, may you help?'

'Well,' Audrey began. 'I could give you a lift of course. What's happened.'

'We are breakdown,' the man informed her. 'Do you fix?'

'Well . . .' said Audrey. 'What sort of breakdown?'

'Engine something,' said the man. 'I think so.'

'Ah. Afraid I'm not much use to you then,' said Audrey, her tone implying that had it been, say the ashtray or the rubber floormat, she'd have been just the woman they needed. She squinted up the road. 'How many of you are there?'

'Five,' said the man, grinning, 'Quintet!'

'Oh dear,' said Audrey. 'My springs, you know.'

'Ah!' The man nodded. 'Springs!' The rain streamed down on him, making his black hair seem in danger of pouring off his head. Then Audrey realized where they were. She groaned, caught the man's eye, and giggled helplessly. The man grinned back, evidently quite unpuzzled. Audrey told herself not to let the side down.

'If you push your bus off the road just here' – she pointed to a muddy lay-by opposite a white gateway just visible in the Traveller's headlamps – 'and I tuck in just in front of you – yes?'

The man nodded happy understanding.

Audrey took a deep breath. 'Then,' she said, 'I know a place.'

Chapter Thirteen

'We are Deuda Externa,' said Big Jorge, passing Oswald's bath towel to Little Carlos. 'In English, Foreign Debt. We are Bolivian invisible export.'

'Only next to cocaine,' added Little Carlos from behind the towel.

Audrey picked her way through the legs in the underground communal area, or downstairs sitting-room, pushing a strand of wet hair off her face and smiling to her friends.

'How is she?' asked Oswald.

'Fine, I think. Up to her neck in your radioactive bubbles and looking a great deal more relaxed and normal. I shouldn't imagine she knows where she is, really, but I'm fairly sure it won't bother her.'

'Great fings, barfs.'

'Yes indeed. She is a little worried though, poor thing, about what she is going to wear afterwards. I think she finds my spare nightie a little too décolleté.'

'Oh, ar, well she's got that bit more ter worry abaht in that department, 'asn't she, no offence, Ordrey luv.'

'No, no of course not, Ganglion.' Audrey's nostrils flared slightly. 'She's – well, let's say I haven't quite the figure to carry that sort of thing off. I expect we can find something *long* to wrap around her.'

'Please?' Angel, the youngest and shyest of the quintet, leaned forward out of his dark corner. 'Poncho?' He produced the gorgeous thing from the large bag he'd been using as a backrest. 'And for you, Señora Ordinary, no?'

'My goodness!' Audrey hefted the weight. 'Thank you very much, er . . .'

'Angel, please.'

'And so you are! What wonderful garments, I'm surprised they've never caught on in Scotland.'

'They did,' snapped MacGregor, sucking in his cheeks. 'Sort o'. They were called plaids. We were banned from wearing them by one of your fat German kings.'

'Ah,' said Audrey. 'Oh yes.' She coughed foolishly.

'In Scotland you have had much persecution, no?' asked Little Carlos.

'Cross out the had,' MacGregor growled.

'He's a MacGregor,' Oswald explained.

'Aah!' said Little Carlos, nodding. 'Mestizo!'

'Mmnn-aye,' said MacGregor.

'It's bein' so cheerful as keeps 'im goin',' said Ganglion, struggling to his feet and kicking the old outlaw playfully in the shin. 'Come on, sunshine, gie's an' 'and wiv the grub. Oz did lunch, I did the rubbish, 'syour turn. Remember yer 'ighland 'ospitality.'

Above ground it was still raining for ever and the land, already soaked by the wettest March and April since records began, at last reached saturation point and could absorb not a drop more. A hundred thousand springs broke out, bubbling fiercely; young burns gouged their way through virgin peat, seethed over rocks, came together and swirled away insanely to join, eventually, the River Fieth, brown and frothily engorged and threatening even now to carry General Wade's bridge away with it and leave Craigfieth cut off from half the civilized world. Fields became lochans, lochans lochs. The Lunie Water, swollen and hideous with the scourings of the surrounding estate, burst the charming confines constructed for it by Capability Scrymgeour in 1792 and

dumped its nightmarish load of little corpses into the ha-
ha below the blind weeping windows of Lord Margoyle's
summer residence. Long-lost remains of sheep and cattle
worked their way to the surface of Half-a-Job's second-
best pasturage. A cardboard cat eddied out from under
the hedge of Jerusalem House, drifted, its empty sockets
gleaming in the streetlights and became involved in a
spouting storm drain two hundred yards down the road
where it capered like a ghastly piece of mobile sculpture.
That night's Community Council meeting was cancelled
when the janitor ran out of bowls and buckets. The Rev.
Gilleasbuig MacAndrew thought of Noah, his wife of
having a damp course in their next house. Sensible folk –
an overwhelming majority – stayed indoors to watch their
lights and televisions blink off and on, and thought glumly
about having to learn all over again how to re-set their
central heating timer switches. Nothing moved on the
roads, except two newspapermen in a Vauxhall Super-
nova who braved flood and landslide, detour and diver-
sion as they sped dangerously away to place their copy in
time for the late editions, and a fire engine which drove
very slowly back from the Sunnyvale Private Home for
the Retired, its crew silent, and profoundly disturbed,
and very glad to be leaving the place in the hands of their
police and ambulance colleagues.

Strange things were happening at Boggybreck. Alone
among all other depressions in a landscape pranked with
sudden pools, the scene of that morning's pioneer activity
remained relatively and curiously unflooded. Most of the
gravel, sure enough, had washed away, leaving the little
track from nowhere to nowhere a sticky gash in the
heather, and the encircling wall of clods had bled its
topsoil into the centre – but the area therein enclosed was
merely wet, rather than waterlogged. One explanation for

this strange phenomenon might have been found some fifty yards or so to the east, where a great slit mouth spewed water out of a hillside slightly lower down; another would have been the reverberant clonking, clanking, booming sound that issued from an unofficial garbage chute nearby. Taken together, these two clues might have suggested the existence of some subterranean chamber freighted with an unknown metallic cargo and drained, on this night of widespread inundation, by an accidental fault in its bedrock walls. Since nobody was daft enough to be out looking on such a night these first portents of catastrophe went uninvestigated. Meanwhile the rain poured on.

''Ow's yer crêpe suzette, Ordrey luv?'

Audrey chewed meditatively on her dessert gum. 'A little burned round the edges, perhaps, but quite palatable and not at all mean with the Cointreau. Thank you. Dora dear, you did remember not to let your water go, didn't you?'

'Oh yes, Audrey, I made sure to leave the plug in as you said, though I'm afraid it won't be very warm by now.'

'It'll do for the dishes,' said Ganglion. 'I'll go an' bung 'em in now if you've all finished, 'ave yer?'

'Oh!' said Mrs Quaich. 'Isn't that a little, er . . .'

'It's the water, Mrs Quaich,' Oswald explained. 'We're just not sure where it comes from or how much there is of it, so we kind of like to go easy – not that we don't have baths ourselves, of course!' he added so as not to embarrass her. He did not add that they all had each other's; that particular refinement could wait until she became a permanent guest, if that was what was to happen. 'Tea, everybody? Erm, Audrey, I don't suppose you . . . ?'

'Alas, no,' said Audrey. 'But I did bring this, as an after-dinner thank-you.' She rummaged in her case and produced a nightie which she unrolled to reveal a rather scruffy bottle. 'What Godfrey used to call the Last Of The Family Plate. I thought tonight might be just the occasion for it. We could drink damnation to our enemies.'

Oswald and MacGregor ogled the dusty casket of Kipplerigg Fifteen (or rather, by now, at least Thirty-five) Year Old Single Malt. 'Oh, my dear!' murmured Mac-Gregor, Audrey's earlier gaffe now evidently quite forgiven. 'I would not be wasting even a dram of this on my enemy. We must just drink it to ourselves entirely!'

'Righto then,' said Audrey breezily. 'Godfrey used to save it for wedding anniversaries.' She tittered. 'Rather a silly thing to do, really, with alcohol being what it is.'

'So expensive you mean, dear?' said Dora Quaich.

Oswald coughed. Audrey blew her nose.

MacGregor was still staring dreamily at the bottle. 'Since Ganglion is still doing the washing-up,' he said quietly, 'should we not just – '

'Give him a call,' said Oswald. 'Aye, good idea: Ganglion? Away out of there, man, and bring, erm . . . ten glasses, or whatever you can find. Audrey's brought some rather special gargle.'

Noises off, as of hearty approbation and quite a lot of crockery being left to fend for itself were followed by the appearance of the old man, looking more gnome-like than ever in his new surroundings, bearing an assortment of glasses, mugs, cups and tankards in a cardboard box. MacGregor selected a close approximation to a whisky glass and cleaned it out with his bony forefinger.

'I shall use this as a measure, ladies and gentlemen,' he said.

'An' we'll orl watch you,' Ganglion warned.

'But first,' said Big Jorge, stepping forward and arresting MacGregor's hand in mid-tilt, 'some music, yes? A little angry song for the children of persecution.'

MacGregor's bosom swelled. He replugged the cork, very carefully, and arranged his mantis limbs in a suitably receptive attitude. The others cleared their throats in a proper concert-going manner. Bolivia's invisible exports had arranged themselves, while their European friends were busy doing homage to Audrey's malt, in full performance finery of hats and ponchos, and appeared festooned with exciting-looking instruments none of which, somehow, looked quite as it ought to look.

'A song of our people who are without land,' Big Jorge announced. '*El Condor Vuelve.*'

A great plangent gale blew from the Andes through the Boggybreck Bunker, a cleansing wind carrying all stale deadliness before it with a great reviving thrill of liberty in every blow. The hearers, transported, felt their scalps tingle, their souls soar, their blood replaced with something altogether purer, livelier and more potent, the insistent, undeniable essence of beauty, true and terrible, come at long last to inherit the earth, here and now and forever –

– and then the great epiphany was past, and gone, leaving sighs and moist eyes behind it.

No one spoke. Slowly, almost reluctantly, MacGregor poured the malt and passed it round. Then he looked at Big Jorge. His hand stayed, waiting.

Big Jorge's brown eyes glittered. '*Libertad, tierra y paz!*'

MacGregor glittered back. '*An tir, an cana, 'sna daoine!*'

'Freedom and whisky,' said Audrey.

'Wha's like us?' asked Oswald.

'Millions,' said Ganglion. 'An' we ain't dead yet!'

They drank.

Later, as time slipped easily by and the tide went out in the bottle, the populous bunker was filled with storm and dance and legend; with songs of peace and cruelty, of blessing and vengeance, finally of the great Creator himself, returned at the terrible end of all things to claim his children, Wiracocha riding on the moon, singing in twining tongues of English, Gaelic, Spanish, Quechua . . .

'These Conquistadores,' muttered MacGregor at one point, shaking his head. 'They sound worse than Campbells!'

'Then we make the Third World one,' said Little Carlos, and the panpipes played with the voices and made the great music of the dispossessed of all the earth and all the ages.

Audrey and Ganglion lifted Dora Quaich, long since heavily asleep, and put her safely to bed, then retired themselves, side by side, on adjacent mattresses.

'One day,' said Ganglion, 'I should like ter do this for real, Ordrey.'

'Yes, dear,' said Audrey. 'And so should I, very much. And so we will.' She sighed happily. 'What a beautiful end,' she murmured, 'to a horrible day.'

'And termorrer?'

'Ah, tomorrow! Tomorrow, I think anything could happen.'

The rain stopped, the moon rose and the thin sour soil of Boggybreck shrugged off its load of water and let it go its ways. The booming noises ceased; above, the roped arena sagged a little, sank a little, then steadied. The stage was set. Very early next morning the slanting sun made a rainbow outside Clyde and Chylblayne's bedroom window. They took it as a sure sign and covenant, a token of God's blessing on the very special day to come.

* * *

They slept late at the bunker while all around them the dumb earth leached out its burden of water. They missed the arrival, shortly after eight o'clock of a very large earth-moving vehicle and its attendant minions who spent the next hour wiping and polishing it in readiness for the ceremony to come. They slept through two bus-loads of junior HI! executives ferried in to prepare the arena and act as stewards later on. They remained innocently unaware of the outside broadcast crew from HI! TV, of the public address riggers from Euro-Kay Electronics, of the caterers from Bread Of Heaven Ltd, of all the great work that went on in preparation for the arrival, at ten thirty, of a luxury coach from Blairlummock bearing the cream of Hosannah International's UK organization (minus Neville) and the senior management of as many of its satellite businesses as it was thought expedient to put on show. Motown P. Legover was there, and Nashville D. Hump. Klaus von Auschwitz patrolled the arena perimeter, muttering into a walkie-talkie, his elegant leather shoes skimming the astroturf which lay like a shroud over every spongy bump and soggy hollow. The Bilts arrived shortly after, pressed hands all round, then made their way on to a strip of green carpet to the gleaming mechanical shovel.

Facing the vehicle across the mud a portable worship module had been manoeuvred into place. Clyde Bilt inspected this, too, familiarizing himself with the control panel and testing the microphone with a huskily intoned 'In the Beginning was the Word, and the Word was – HI!' This piece of impromptu blasphemy brought an answering call from a hundred throats: 'HI' they echoed, and the earth itself seemed to shake in awe at it. Bilt pressed a button in the pulpit. Soft religious musak began to waft pervasively round the natural amphitheatre. Nature withdrew to a safe distance. Von Auschwitz's mutterings into the walkie-talkie grew ever more intense.

At ten forty-five a large black chauffeur-driven saloon car turned in off the road and eased itself up the track, so lately a torrent, to join the line of parked cars and coaches a hundred yards or so from the scene of this activity. Its occupant was escorted to the arena, introduced to Clyde and Chylblayne and to the two diminutive recruits from HI! Construction Corp who were crouched out of sight in the digger in readiness to operate it on the celebrity's behalf in due course. Then he was led away to press the flesh of the important personages now assembling themselves on the front row. Separated from them on the inside by the perimeter rope – newly replaced, for aesthetic reasons, on the instruction of the HI! TV director – the VIP was obliged to shuffle sideways, from one introduction to the other, on his narrow circle of artificial grass, the sunlight twinkling on his shoes and on his oiled and neatly parted toupée. Clyde Bilt, deferential in attendance, signalled discreetly for the musak to be turned up a little, to heighten the drama. Wisps of vapour rose into the warm May air from the wet earth of this charmed circle; strains of a rumba version of Bach's Toccata and Fugue rose with them until a light northeasterly breeze caught them and wafted them across the sparkling heather to the Bunker, where Sergeant Donald MacEachran stood hammering on the door.

MacGregor opened it, looked the sweating policeman slowly up and down, then turned and called, 'It's the Redcoats!' Then he faced MacEachran again. 'Do you come with Letters of Fire and Sword?' he asked.

'Who are Redcoats?' asked Angel, one floor down.

'Conquistadores,' said Oswald.

'I rarver fink our number's up,' said Ganglion.'You lot wait dahn 'ere for the moment.

'Gotcher bullet-proof sock on, Oz?' he asked as the lift

374

wheezed them up. 'An' yer copy of the European Declaration of Yuman Rights?'

'What'll you pay me no' to call you Paddy?' Oswald quipped back.

Their friend stood blocking the entrance, regaling his oppressor with a catalogue of the woes and grievances of Clan Gregor. The sergeant, most unwisely, was attempting to suggest that Rannoch Moor might not have been a very nice place to live, anyway; Ganglion and Oswald arrived just in time to save him injury.

'Well, well,' said Ganglion, gently easing the muttering MacGregor out of the doorway. 'I see you come mob-'anded, officer. Time fer us all ter fry for freedom, is it?'

'Not yet, sir, no. Not as far as I know, anyway.'

A snatch of the Hallelujah Chorus, in cha-cha time, drifted by. 'Gawd 'elp us, don't say it's all over! Where's yer scythe, Sergeant?'

MacEachran smiled, unofficially. 'I'm afraid it *is* all over, though,' he said.

'Ar,' said Ganglion. 'Want us ter come quietly, do yer?'

'Let's say I'm . . . giving you that opportunity, yes. I'm sorry. I thought it would be better coming from me, now, than from . . .' he tilted his head in the direction of the joyful noise '. . . later on.'

'Ar. I see. And, er . . .'ow long, exactly, 'ave you bin finkin' that?'

'Oh, well.' MacEachran's eyes creased a little, though it could have been the sun reflecting off the window. 'A few weeks, just. I meant to call by last night, only, what with the rain and . . . one or two other things that kept me busy, ye know. You understand there'd be . . . action taken, otherwise.'

'Yeah. Right. Well then – bung ho for the gypsy life, eh, Oz?'

MacEachran coughed. 'Catriona was saying to tell you,

375

you're welcome to use the caravan, just till you get sorted. We'll no' be needing it till August.'

'Tell your Catriona that's very kind of 'er, an' we appreciate it very much. Er, Sergeant, wot would you say – just as a f'rinstance, like – if Oswald 'ere woz ter tell you 'e 'ad a document wot says all this lot 'ere belongs to 'im?'

'Ah,' said MacEachran. 'I'd say that was a civil matter for Mr Ochilree, sir. I'm no' a lawyer, just a polisman. Thank goodness. I only deal with crimes – preventing them for preference.'

'Yeah. I see. Well, Oz: wot's it ter be, eh? Fight the good fight, or live in peace? Your choice, me ole mate.'

'Both,' said Oswald. 'For preference. But I think we'd better do as Donald says for the time being, don't you? I couldn't live much longer with this racket, anyway.' A disco arrangement of 'What A Friend We Have In Jesus' came clearly to them on the warm breeze.

'What are they doing over there, anyway?'

'I dare say it wouldn't be a criminal offence to look,' said the Sergeant. 'Not as far as I'm concerned, anyway.'

'Yer on,' said Ganglion. 'Arf a mo while I get the others.'

MacEachran stood in growing wonder at the doorway as first Oswald and MacGregor, then Mrs Pitt-Holyoake, then Mrs Quaich, then five Bolivian Indians emerged, blinking, into the blessed sunlight.

'Make that three hard-boiled eggs,' said Oswald, grinning.

Ganglion pulled the door to. 'Best leave the Dagenham Girl Pipers where they are, don't yer fink? Come on, Oz, I'll give the strong arm o' the law an 'and up the brae wiv you.'

They ascended to the strains of an electronic anthem

accompanied by a hundred or so triumphant human voices.

> Gimme that Old Time Religion!
> Gimme that Old Time Religion!
> Gimme that Old Time Religion!
> It's good enough for me!
> It was good for the Gospel Preachers . . .

'It was good for the Inquisition,' sang Audrey, 'It was good for the Ku Klux Kla-an . . .'

> It's good enough for me!
> Gimme that Old . . .

'That was rather naughty of you, Audrey,' panted Mrs Quaich.
'I *feel* naughty, Dora,' said Audrey.

> It's good enough for me!

Something was clearly approaching its climax. A pagan circle of humanity, clad variously in business suits and designer casuals and protected from the messy realities of life by a lurid ring of some synthetic stuff quite hideous to behold, leaned eagerly in to watch what appeared to be an imminent sacrifice to the greedy God of the Age of Development. A gleaming metal monster, its glittering jaws agape, seemed poised to gobble up three victims, two male and one female, transfixed before it in some sort of imprisoning altar. A lark started singing sacreligiously somewhere, then stopped abruptly. A deathly and expectant hush descended. Two prone figures lay obeisant, or already dead, inside the metal idol.

Audrey shaded her eyes and squinted. 'That's little Mr Haq,' she said. 'Isn't it? What's he doing, I wonder?'
'Praying, by the look of it,' MacGregor murmured.

377

'Really?' Mrs Quaich was scandalized. 'I thought he was a Mahommedan!'

''E's a politician these days,' Ganglion pointed out.

'True,' Audrey sighed. 'My goodness, it doesn't seem five minutes since there was all that fuss about those magazines in his emporium. I must be getting old.'

Ganglion shrugged. 'From porno mags ter snuff movies, eh?'

'Wheesht, Ganglion!' hissed Oswald, alarmed in case one of the ladies should ask what snuff movies were, and he should tell them.

'Well, woss all them cameras for, then?' his friend objected.

'They're after turning the first sod,' said MacEachran.

'Really, Sergeant!' Ganglion gasped. 'That's no way ter talk about yer elected Member of Parlyment!'

'Sssh!' hissed Mrs Quaich. 'He's going to say something!'

Mahommed Haq, MP, dark and dapper between his Aryan minders, rose to his feet on the little plastic podium. They saw his teeth flash in the sunlight and strained to catch whatever little scraps of wisdom and statesmanship the wind might bring them.

'Ladles an' jellyspoons,' Ganglion muttered.

'It is indeed a very great privilege,' the MP continued, 'to be here today and to have the honour of "taking the first scoop".' Though his words were faint the inverted commas were distinctly audible.

''Oo wrote this rubbish?' said Ganglion.

'Sssh!' said Mrs Quaich.

'. . . the opening of the Dunbroath Centre for Techno-logical Excellence you assured me then that "the best was yet to come". Indeed it was. And yesterday, thanks to you, I was able to inform the Prime Minister that Britain's first private enterprise borough – for that is what this is, my friends, nothing more nor less – was to be built right here in my own constituency of Mid Lummock. A proud moment for me, ladies and gentlemen. As indeed I know it will be for you when I tell you that the Prime Minister herself has asked me to convey to you her personal warm congratulations for paving the way to a system of local government free, at last, of all the bureaucratic restrictions of the sort of creeping socialism which her government – of whom I have the honour to be a member – was elected to stamp out!'

'Not in my country, ye weren't!' growled MacGregor, pawing the ground and glaring at the sergeant as if daring him to take him in charge.

MacEachran coughed diplomatically. 'Polismen have votes, too,' he confided.

'Sssh!' said Mrs Quaich.

'. . . the economic freedom from which all other freedoms flow! And where Hosannahville leads, the rest of Britain will follow! As a triumph for international private investment! For it is only international private investment, freed from the narrow, selfish, political interests of local and state bureaucracy, that can pave the way to prosperity and reward for enterprise in the twenty-first century. Indeed if I may, ah . . .' They saw him grin round his audience.

'Oh Gawd,' Ganglion groaned, ''e's goin' ter make a funny.'

Mrs Quaich, exasperated, kicked his ankle

'. . . could say that international private investment refreshes the parts that bureaucratic socialism doesn't even *want* to reach!'

Von Auschwitz looked up from his walkie-talkie and guffawed loudly; the others joined in, half a paroxysm behind him as Haq's plain-clothes minder in the audience nodded his thanks.

'Typical politician's joke,' Ganglion remarked. 'Ten years out of date an' not funny anyway.' He jumped clear of Mrs Quaich's scything brogue.

'. . .without further ado. But first, my good friend Mr . . .' Haq bent his ear close to Bilt's face.'Mr Bilt Clyde-Bilt, will lead us in a prayer of dedication.'

Bilt rose, head bowed, waiting for the rapturous applause to subside. The TV camera zoomed slowly in, tactfully ignoring the scuttling figure of Mid Lummock's MP as he made his way to the digger and climbed up into the cab. Audrey nudged Ganglion and pointed; they watched, intrigued, as a hand came up between Haq's legs, turned the ignition on, and disappeared again.

The ovation died away at a prearranged signal from von Auschwitz. Clyde Bilt's head came up, followed by both arms, fingers spread. A peal of electronic chords issued from the loudspeakers. The air tingled. Bilt's mouth moved, huge and fervent, a fraction in advance of the sound of his words.

'Say HI!'

'HI!'

Half a mile away a flock of sheep took flight and bolted.

'HI! to Jesus!'

'HI! TO JESUS!

'HI! to development!'

'HI! TO DEVEL'MENT!'

'HI! to Hosannahville, UK!'

'HI! TO HOS-HO-ANNAH-SANN-VILLE-AVILLE YUYU KAYAY!'

Three of the sheep had heart attacks.

'Like when they sing *Abide Wiv Me* at the Cup Final,' said Ganglion to no one in particular.

The MP's wrists were seized and his hands placed neatly at ten to two on the steering wheel.

'Mah frayunds,' bellowed Craigfieth's evangelist. 'Leddus pray!

'Awlmidey Gard, witness we beseech Thee the prayerful ennerprise of these Thy faithful bretheren of Hosannah International Inc and of this servant of Her British Majesty's Government, UK, Limited, in building to Thy Eternal Gloreagh the town of Hosannahville, Scotland, Europe, as a place of work an' worship in Thy Name and in the Name of Thy Son and Our Redeemer Lord Jesus Cryest! Guard our capital, Lord, succour our investment, protect our innerest and reap Thy dividend as we, in Christian humility, reap ours! Sanctify our endeavours, we beseech Thee, unnerwrite our assets and indemnify all actions carried out by these Thy agents here on earth we pray Thee Lord Gard Our Chairman in the Name of our Supreme Managing Director Jesus Cryest Amen.'

MacEachran looked blank; MacGregor sucked his cheeks; Oswald shook his head: Ganglion sniggered. 'Tcha!' said Audrey. Mrs Quaich looked puzzled. Deuda Externa smiled enigmatically among themselves.

'And now!' bellowed the preacher. 'Leddus sing the anthem, bretheren, composed especially for this occasion by a very talented musician well known to all of us who had the priv'lege of attending last month's Motivation day at Blairlummock.'

His right hand, unseen, pressed another button and a brass-style fanfare burst forth. The glassily smiling Honourable Member for Mid Lummock suddenly grew two extra pairs of white hands and four more feet; levers were set, pedals pressed and a plume of blue smoke shot up from the exhaust as the roar of the digger's engine was drowned beneath the triumphant inanities of Hosannahville's Dedication Anthem.

Say HI! in the Precinct
Say HI! in the Mall
Say HI! in the College
Say HI! in the Hall
Say HI! in the Nurs'ry
Say HI! in the School
Say HI! in the Moneymart
Say HI! in the Pool
Say HI! when you're workin'
Say HI! when you play:
Say HI! to Hosannahville,
Mid Lummock, UK!

Four uniformed attendants ran out and pulled the Bilts' module back to the perimeter ropes, its occupants still waving. A long drum-roll thundered from the loudspeakers, Mr Haq gripped the steering wheel tight with two hands; his other four worked the levers as the digger lumbered slowly forward on its conquering tracks, its shovel poised to ravish and plunder. The audience held its breath; the shovel flashed blindingly in the noonday sun – when HI! made a timetable it made it work – then plunged earthwards and bit hungrily into soil and rock. The digger farted black smoke, reared on its haunches, forced the shovel down. A hand, not his own, mopped the MP's glistening brow. The digger rocked to a standstill, the shovel swung back and, slowly, up . . . up, raising the momentous first scoop high into the view of man and the sight of God. A dozen employees of HI! Commemoratives (UK) Ltd stood by to preserve the contents in a hundred little pre-personalized plastic boxes. There was a clash of cymbals, a thunderous cheer, and the opening bars of *Fanfare For The Common Man*. Mr Haq removed his hard hat, bowed, still seated, to the podium, then rose, erect and sublime, to accept his accolade.

And then, swifter than thought, the earth spoke and

gaped open: digger, hat, Haq and all disappeared from view; then reappeared, memorably altered, on the shock wave of an explosion that rent the heavens and seized by its roots the very ground on which the distant watchers stood. Bits of metal and ex-junior government Minister made pretty patterns against the pitiless blue sky. The hole in the ground blew a perfect ring of coiling, liquid, pus-coloured smoke that rushed exultantly heavenwards to be followed by another, and another, and another, until all the hollow was a seething yellow cauldron and the last mangled, gravity-defying particle was lazily swallowed up.

Their spell broken, the watchers on the hill started involuntarily forward; then Oswald sniffed, and gave a cry.

'Gas!'

'Gas, boys, quick!'

And an ecstasy of stumbling as the gentle breeze, in flagrant breach of the Geneva Protocol, pursued the eleven fleeing men and women with its deadly cargo of Great War phosgene, right to the door of the Boggybreck Bunker as they set Oswald down, pulled him roughly in, and slammed it shut.

Business was brisker at the Bide-a-Wee Tearooms that morning than at any time that busy month – a month during which Mrs Spurtle found fine new specimens to add to her catalogue of human vulgarity, and Miss Phemister grew greyer, and older, and thinner, and had a terrible time with her feet. Of the welcome influx of scone-hungry clients about half, probably, came under the impression that the two gallant ladies had played a leading part in the pursuit and apprehension of a ruthless gang of international terrorists and drug-traffickers: the other half believed them to have been 'mixed up in it' in some way, and conducted various tests on the sugar before adding it to their tea. But they all munched and slurped, and paid, and that was the main thing.

This morning, however, a third wave of visitors came, clutching late editions of the morning papers. Disappointed not to find the streets of Craigfieth piled high with corpses (the cardboard cat, now lodged sideways and tail up between the bars of the storm drain opposite Borden's Family Butchers, could hardly be called a pile), they trooped instead to the Tearooms and talked of poison over the bannocks and cream slices, convinced that the locked door of the craft centre was proof positive that its owner had been done away with by gamekeepers, or worse, under cover of last night's downpour.

Clay Loan and Campbeltown Fotheringhame had played the field of Scottish newspaper offices to great effect. No two stories were exactly alike: only the *Independent*, for instance, confided to an indignant public the fact that the outrage had been perpetrated on a leading connoisseur of domestic interior design, while the *Daily Record* (thanks to Fotheringhame's memory of a remark his hostess had let fall while pouring tea) reported Audrey as 'crippled down her right side' and worked up a fine head of righteous anger about it. To the *Guardian* they imparted the fruits of the photographer's hasty torch-lit survey of her kitchen table; the paper duly published a complete list of all the affected species, not forgetting the cat – it turned out to be the Snotters' old grey tom – which it recorded as a neutered female tabby. The *Sun*, working on Loan's misinterpretation of a snap of the late Major Godfrey Pitt trying out his French on a day trip to Boulogne, wrote him up as Colonel Pitt-Holyoake, a hero of the Resistance. The *Financial Times* advised its readers to clear their portfolios, for the time being, of equity stock in Amalgamated British Agrichemicals plc.

Each journal carried its own exclusive photograph, thanks to Fotheringhame's imaginative use of lighting, angles, exposures and composition. Each was a gem of its type: the *Star* printed the heap entire, starkly flashlit; the *Express* picture was softly lit and messily focused, and showed the cat sleeping (as it were – they'd had a hell of a time jamming its jaws and eyelids shut) with a wren between its paws: 'Friends In Death', the caption said. The *Sun*'s took up a whole page; borderless, it suggested an unprintable infinity of corpses. The *Independent*'s, a grainy, long-exposure job combining two buzzards, a crow, three songbirds and a peppermill, all lit from above by a guttering candle, won three awards that year.

The public, obliged to buy all the papers that morning in order to get, as it thought, the whole istory, must presumably have thought of Dante Cottage as a sort of vast gothic mansion, full of death and kitchen tables. All the papers reproduced the snap Loan had found of the lady herself, taken on the Machrie golf course, Islay, during the exceptionally wet and windy summer of 1979. 'In Hiding' was the favoured caption, and the photograph did indeed suggest a tormented soul in full flight from some closely pursuing horror.

A spokesperson for Lord Margoyle pointed out that the peer himself was not involved in the day-to-day running of his estates; Mr Snotter, in a statement croaked down the telephone late the previous night, insisted that his function was solely to carry out the wishes of his principal – adding hastily and in a flash of inspiration provoked, perhaps, by his recent bedtime reading, that he had reason to believe that the local police were investigating a report which pointed the finger of suspicion at certain unnamed but no doubt ruthless left-wing *agents provocateurs* bent on undermining public confidence in the rule of law by smearing a Justice of the Peace and on wrecking

Lunie's contribution to the expanding Scottish economy. This report, duly typed up by a sleepy Belladonna, was hand-delivered, unsigned, through Sergeant Mac-Eachran's letter-box very early the next morning.

Mr Snotter may be forgiven for failing to foresee that certain irresponsible sections of the media would draw odious comparisons with the burning of the Reichstag in 1938. Droves of top-flight investigative reporters, meanwhile, sped north to track down the tenant of Dante Cottage and grill her with their cheque-books. They found the house unlocked and, on entering in the public interest, quite devoid of journalistic interest. The table was bare – not a feather remaining – the fuses restored, the taps in full working order. They feared a hoax and, in a heart-warming show of professional solidarity, resolved to sit it out together and beard the hoaxer in her shameful den. They put away their cheque-books and helped themselves to tea, illegal substances, and several sorts of sherry. An hour later, their efforts of fictional composition were disturbed by a distant rumble and the shaking of Audrey's best bone china.

'Wasshat?' asked the *Mail*, giggling.

'Shploshion?' suggested the *Express*.

The *Sun* was at the window in an investigative instant. 'Shmoke!' he said. 'Lotsh of pretty shmoke!'

'No shmoke without Blashe Horror,' observed the *Mirror*.'

'Or Bomb Blasht Shock,' added the *Star*, who had recently spent an indepth morning in Belfast. 'Hundredsh Maimed!'

They rushed excitedly for the door, knocking over several chairs and spilling the milk, scrambled into their cars and bumped and bored their way down Audrey's track in a heart-warming spirit of healthy professional rivalry, gabbling eye-witness reports into their dictaphones and reaching the main road just in time to get in the way of the emergency services.

'Phemmy!' hissed Mrs Spurtle, her eye at the Judas-hole. 'Duff!'

'Yes, dear, as soon as Ay've done these.'

Mrs Spurtle frowned. 'What?'

'Yes, dear, Ay know, but they'll just have to wait until Ay've served those other people.'

'Phemister,' said the widow heavily, 'what on earth are you talking about?'

'What you said, dear, only Ay must just finish what Ay'm . . . is everything all right, Joan dear?'

'I – said – Duff, Phemister. Duff. *Duff!*'

'Oh!' Miss Phemister jumped and poured at least three cups' worth (at seventy-five pence each including biscuit) over the trolley. 'Which . . . which one?' she asked, mopping it up.

'Duff the younger,' Mrs Spurtle grunted. 'Mister so-called Councillor Duff.'

'Oh! Mai guidness, dear!'

'Yes indeed! No prizes for guessing what *this* means, Phemmy dear!'

Miss Phemister blushed a little underneath her grey. It had been so long since Joan had called her that.

'Yes, dear,' she agreed. 'It's wonderful really, isn't it!'

'What?'

'His coming here, Ay mean, after all . . . well, you know – Ay must give him the nayce jam – it's so nayce, isn't it, to think that . . . Joan dear?'

'You're a fool, Phemister,' said Mrs Spurtle.

'Yes, dear,' said Miss Phemister, greyness flooding back.

Mrs Spurtle rolled her sleeves up. 'Intimidation, Phemister. Electoral malpractice! That's what this means!'

There was a sharp double knock on the kitchen door. Miss Phemister scuttled behind the trolley and seized hold of it. Twenty Bide-a-Wee elevenses shivered in sympathy. 'H-he's in the c-c-c-c-c-'

'Shut up, woman!' Mrs Spurtle planted herself in the middle of the kitchen floor. 'And let him in.'

'L-l-l-le- ?'

'And then leave us alone.'

'B-but, Joan dear,' her partner whimpered tearfully. 'Sup-p-posing Ay have to c-come back in? Ay mean – '

'Don't! Keep 'em waiting. Amuse them, I don't know, sing 'em songs, tell dirty jokes or something, only – leave me alone . . . with *him!*'

Another double knock.

'*Do it, woman!*'

Quivering, Miss Phemister opened the door and inched the trolley through, trying to keep it between herself and the legendary monster of municipal depravity. It stuck. For one panic-stricken moment she appeared to be about to crawl under it, then ex-Councillor Duff took hold of the other end and trundled it into position in the corridor.

'There we are, now!' he said. Miss Phemister moaned. Eyes rolling, she oozed round the jamb and backed off towards the tearoom door, pulling several half-empty cups and full saucers behind her.

'Is your friend all right, Mrs Spurtle?'

'Never, these days. Ignore her. Come in.' Mrs Spurtle shut the door. 'So,' she said, folding her arms across her chest like two ostrich drumsticks on a lumpy quilt. 'Mister Duff!'

'So, indeed,' Duff replied, hitching his bookmaker's tweeds and resting his bottom on the edge of the draining board. 'Mrs Spurtle!' The sunlight streaming through the window made him look less an off-duty turf accountant and more like an out-of-work violinist.

Dammit, thought the widow. Back to the light; should have thought of that. Love-fifteen. 'Well, Mr Duff?' she said, playing for time.

'Well, Mrs Spurtle!' He smiled, putting decades of political guile into it. 'I came here this morning because you seem not to have heeded my little warning the other day.'

'Hah!' cried Mrs Spurtle, uncoiling her arms and preparing to strike the first pre-emptive blow. 'Your attempted warning-off, you mean?'

'We-ell,' said Mr Duff, nodding. 'That's one way of putting it, yes.' He raised a hand in a contemptible gesture of self-defence; Mrs Spurtle remembered what her father used to say about men who wore rings on their third fingers, especially jewelled ones. 'Let me put it this way, Mrs Spurtle.' She decided to let him, just for now. 'Would I be right in thinking you do not think very highly of my, shall we say, *motives*, in being a councillor?'

'Hah!' she cried again, then shut her mouth. Her face flushed darkly, eloquent testimony of the struggle raging behind it as she fought to jettison the last dead weight of manners.

'Or, to put it another way – '

The widow exhaled like a punctured Zeppelin.

' – would you – as I'm sure you would, Mrs Spurtle – agree with me that there are, unfortunately, some among us whose sense of public duty – whose no doubt sincere sense of public duty – has, over the years perhaps, become a little obscured by a keener interest, in expenses perhaps, or in, ah, certain areas of, shall we say, self-interest?'

The widow strove to find an appropriate response; a rather feeble 'yes' was the best she could manage in the end. Then she went very red. 'You're not . . . suggesting . . . I . . . are you? That *I* would – would . . .'

389

Mr Duff laughed, a noise like a deathwatch beetle drowning in a deep fat fryer.

'No, no,' he said. 'Nonononono, Mrs Spurtle! Of course not! Any more than you would ever suggest that I . . . mmm?'

'Oh,' said Mrs Spurtle. 'Good.' She immediately wished she hadn't. Duff smiled again, and seized the first set.

'Then we understand each other, Mrs Spurtle. That's very good.' Love-six. Mrs Spurtle to serve, second set.

'I'm not sure I do,' she said. Let; fault; second service. 'Why don't you come clean for once, Mr Duff, and tell me exactly what you're here for?' A clean ace; Duff didn't bother to play it.

'Ah, well! Their days are numbered, anyway, Mrs Spurtle, you'll be glad to hear.'

'What? Whose?'

'Oh, those awful people, Mrs Spurtle – you know the ones I mean: the ones who are only in it for themselves, the ones who get their pals rehoused, their relatives appointed to nice little sinecures, the ones who are forever popping into Duncruddie for this and that bit of "urgent council business" – and having to stay the night at the Moither Arms Hotel, as often as not – the ones whose businesses seem to lose hundreds of pounds every day they're not there to run them in person because they're having to attend a meeting – all those people. They've had it, to be frank with you, Mrs Spurtle.'

'Oh,' said Mrs Spurtle. 'Really,' she added, spooning the ball feebly into the net.

'Oh, yes! And a good thing too, wouldn't you agree?'

'Oh, absolutely. Yes. Of course! But . . .'

'Yes, Mrs Spurtle?'

She attempted a late rally. 'People – I mean councillors, Mr Duff – they still have to go to meetings, though, don't they? I mean, after all – '

'Oh, yes, naturally they do, of course, yes! When there are meetings to go to, of course.'

'Yes of course,' Mrs Spurtle agreed, relaxing a little. She coughed. 'Once . . . a week, say?'

He shook his head, smiling.

'A fortnight, then? Month? Two . . . months . . .?'

'Things,' said Mr Duff, relinquishing his advantage at the sink and drawing up the only stool in the room. 'May I? Thank you . . . oh! Anno domini, Mrs Spurtle, anno domini! No, no: things are *not* what they used to be. Not in any way, at all!'

'Oh?'

'No, no. Not at all. Twice a year, Mrs Spurtle. That's the way of it now. Twice a year.'

'Tw – ?'

He nodded sadly. Then he shook his head. 'Aye, aye.' He sighed. 'That's the way of it, right enough.' He sighed again. 'So long as they haven't thrown the baby out with the bathwater, eh, Mrs Spurtle?'

'Oh quite!' She took his place at the sink, though it didn't seem to give her any sort of advantage. 'I mean of course the work of the council must go on, Mr Duff, mustn't it!'

He shook his head again, lost apparently in private reverie.

'Mustn't it?'

'And what work,' he asked carefully, adjusting his rumpled creases, 'would that be, my dear?'

The widow called up her checklist of District Council functions. 'Housing, of course, and, and parks, yes, and cemeteries, village halls and community centres, tourism, libraries, and, and – oh, planning! I mean, there's still all that!'

'Ah,' said Mr Duff. Then he sighed yet again. 'Mrs Spurtle – Joan – may I call you that? Everybody calls me

Archie, by the way. Joan.' He held up the fingers of his left hand and proceeded to number them off.

'Housing: all gone, sold or taken over by private landlords; our last part-time housing officer collects his cards next week. Old folks homes and so on, the same: taken over, or closed down like the Eventide here. Parks, leisure areas, sport centres and all the like: sold off so's they can be run at a profit; cemeteries, likewise; halls and – '

'*Cemeteries?*'

'Oh, yes: a Westminster-based firm, I believe, Rest In Peace Developments. Something to do with one of those supermarket chains, someone told me. Apparently they've given assurances. Where was I now? Oh, yes: halls and so on, they've gone out to tender now since last month; tourism's gone to a consortium of local visitor industries, naturally there's a charge if you want your own facility to be promoted otherwise it wouldn't be viable, you see? Libraries we're having to close down altogether because of a government feasibility study, except for the big towns where they're going to be organized by one of the big bookshop firms for a trial period initially. Now what does that leave us with? Ah, planning! Oh dear, yes. Well, that's all Scottish Office now, of course, seemingly we've just had one scandal too many. And of course nowadays we're finding more and more of these, whatdye-callums, Freedom Zones, you know like the new Hallelujah City or whatever it calls itself, out at Boggybreck. And Craigfieth, too. If you take my tip, Joan: buy up property while you can! We can't. We tried to put compulsory purchase orders on some of those sorry-looking places in the High Street here but, well St Andrew's House'd have none of it.

'So there we are, you see! No scope there for corrupt local politicians, eh?'

'No,' breathed Mrs Spurtle. An impatient hubbub, laced with little bleating noises, drifted through her spyhole in the hatch. She ignored it. Someone tried to force it open against the bolt. She ignored that, too. 'But . . . the meetings . . . Archie?'

'Oh, yes. I was forgetting them. Aye, indeed. Twice a year, Joan. To approve the contracts signed by our officials, in consultation with the Secretary of State's office. Half a day should see it done. They might let you claim a lunch.

'Of course,' he added thoughtfully, 'I'm not saying there won't be goings-on under the new system, you know what I mean? Corruption, hanky-panky, and all the rest of it. But that's hardly our . . . I mean – ' he coughed apologetically. 'I mean, that's a different matter entirely, isn't it? Big business, and suchlike.'

'But it's terrible!'

'In . . . what way, now?'

'Well I mean . . .' She seemed to be suddenly a little short of air. 'I mean the library closing – oh, I don't say the van was up to much, but . . . and all this profit business in everything . . . cemeteries! I can't – and no sort of local control in planning. I mean it's – it's terrible!'

'Ah, well.' Duff shrugged. 'Too late now. Unless . . . ach, well. Only I was just thinking, you see . . . ach, no. Maybe not.'

'What?'

'Well what I thought, you see, was . . . they still need councillors, don't they? That's the point, Joan, d'ye see my meaning? They have to go through the motions. Now I'm not saying I'm the right person to do that – '

'Oh no! I mean – not me, either! I don't want to!'

'Ah!' He smiled. 'Then, who, Joan! Who can you think of that you'd want to have . . . going through the motions like that?'

Mrs Spurtle, as was her custom, did not need to think. 'Nobody!' she boomed.

'Ah, aye, well, that's just it, isn't it now, Joan! I mean – supposing "Nobody" got himself, or herself, elected. Supposing "Nobody" was returned for nearly all the seats on the council! That might make the bugg – , I mean, that might make a difference, eh?'

'Is it . . . likely, do you think?'

'I know of eleven already. Eleven Nobodies.'

'Would I – or is it too . . .?'

Mr Duff consulted his watch.

'Deadline for withdrawals of nomination is one o'clock. There's just time if I drive – oh no, after you, Joan dear!'

Mrs Spurtle carved a passage for them through a scrum of dissatisfied would-be browsers and sluicers. Miss Phemister was pinned, twittering, in a corner, writing things in her notebook and tearing the sheets off. A queue, a thing unheard of since the Bide-a-Wee first allowed the common herd through its select portals, spilled out into the street.

'Hold the fort, Phemmy!' bellowed her friend and partner as they surged by. 'You can go in the kitchen now, dear!'

She cannoned into a pugnacious-looking gentleman with a wife and two children to pick quarrels for who was telling the world exactly what he thought of things in general and standards of service in provincial tearooms in particular, in no uncertain terms.

'Get her to do the patter song from *Iolanthe*,' she advised him. 'She's frightfully good at it if you can catch her in the right mood!'

She flung herself into Mr Duff's Mini and they sped lopsidedly off. They were forced to wait, fuming impatiently, at the roundabout where the Mercat Cross

394

used to be, while a procession of fire engines, ambulances and police cars tore past, hogging the middle of the road.

'They'll be next,' said Mr Duff.

'Over my dead body,' growled the widow. It took her the rest of the journey to work out why her companion found this rejoinder so amusing.

Chapter Fourteen

Sensation quickly stales. Famine overtakes earthquake, and is superseded by flood. Hurricanes come and go; wars flare up and then fizzle out as before; refugees drag themselves from one unsafe haven to another. Planes crash. Ships sink. Yesterday's disaster dissolves into tomorrow's enquiry, whose conclusions are never published. Forgotten victims surface briefly in unfashionably scheduled documentaries on minority TV channels, then sink swiftly back into oblivion where they belong. This year's balance-sheet of triumph and despair is written up, ruled off, and next year's account opened. Life goes on.

Boggybreck was no exception, unless by virtue of its banal adherence to the media guidelines on tragedy. Anticlimax, which usually sets in after twenty-four hours, was in this case clearly discernible in all the early evening news bulletins the same day. Up to three hundred men, women and children had not, it appeared, been blown to bits in the devastated barracks or vaporized as they sat in cars and coaches nearby. That advance party of Fleet Street's finest may be forgiven (may they not?) for not knowing that the lines of parked vehicles were empty to begin with, or that the eloquent piles of rubble heaped alongside were nearing their fortieth anniversary, just as the public – who had, after all, paid in honest coin and genuine sympathy for the first misleading reports – may be forgiven for feeling, well, a little cheated of its full due of shock and horror. Indeed, as the casualty figures were revised downwards through the day, those with the most stamina to waste may well have gone to bed after the late news headlines wondering whether anything had, in fact, happened at all.

Several dozen persons – insignificant employees, for the most part, of Bread of Heaven and HI! Commemoratives (UK) Ltd, who had been stationed on the less televisible, upwind side of the arena – turned out to be not dead, just concussed. Eighteen others turned up hours later – they wouldn't say where from – unscathed and apparently not in need of either tea or sympathy. They were treated for traumatic amnesia instead, to no effect. Some very pretty computer graphics on the *Nine O'Clock News* showed the poisonous cloud – already referred to, quite incorrectly, as 'mustard gas' – drifting across the empty, entailed Lunie acres, through a squat row of tied cottages (all uninhabited) bypassing the Castle itself (which was empty anyway) and dispersing harmlessly five miles or so down-wind and just short of the factor's residence (whose occupants, along with the estate's keepers and other functionaries, had gone to ground for a few days in some spare chalets at Blairlummock). An expert from the Meteorological Office explained why the wind had not been blowing any other way than the way it had been blowing, and agreed that this was a very good thing. A military expert patiently explained the difference between mustard gas and phosgene, pointed out that both were colourless, and suggested that eye-witness accounts of a 'thick yellow cloud' could be explained by rust on the shell casings, the nature of the rock and subsoil, and 'other factors'. The newsreader thanked him, and went on calling it mustard gas anyway.

The final death toll, revised and audited, was one the public could easily take in its stride: twenty-two American evangelical businessmen, a Detroit-registered lay preacher and his wife, two illegally immigrant Danish construction workers, and a little-known Scottish MP.

There was barely time for the public to attach its sympathy to the two Danes when its attentions were fully absorbed, for a day or two, by a sixty-vehicle pile-up, the worst so far that year, on the M25.

Prime Minister's Question Time in the House of Commons the following Tuesday was preceded by one minute's silence for her late Honourable Friend. Then opposition party leaders, encouraged by the latest figures for the balance of payments, inflation, homelessness and industrial unemployment, fell to the serious work of demanding an early by-election in Mid Lummock. A brace of Scottish Tory peers was roused from its hereditary slumbers and given Mr Haq's junior ministerial responsibilities.

Twenty-two pine coffins were flown to the United States; two metal ones were handed in to the Danish Embassy. An ornate casket containing various bits and pieces, some of them (such as the toupée) belonging to the deceased MP, was laid to rest in a shallow, water-logged grave in the recently privatized Duncruddie Mains Necropolis. Two Bilt-shaped lumps of vitrified plastic, fused together, were removed for post-mortem examination and discovered, eventually, to contain just enough carbon traces for a verdict of death by misadventure to be recorded. Fawn and Hall joined a heavily fortified Christian Fellowship Commune in Costa Rica, where they were said to be very happy.

Liquidators and receivers were appointed to administer the affairs of Hosannah International (Scotland) Inc, and its many and various subsidiaries and affiliates, including Eastern Sight'n'Sound, Euro-Kay Electronics, Eurocal Developments, Blacktrouser Properties, Albacorp International Estate Managers Inc, New Horizon Realty Factors, Bread of Heaven, and dozens more besides, all beginning with 'HI!', most catering for every conceivable human need and greed, some creating new demands hitherto undreamed-of and all, apparently, organized and run by the twenty-two recent victims of the war to end all wars.

It was a terrible financial and legal tangle, a complex, convoluted, intricately intertwined and richly remunerative headache and it showed, thank goodness, no sign of quick cure, especially when the battalions of lawyers and accountants assigned to the case found themselves joined by officers of the Fraud Squad, officials from the City of London and eager young persons from the United States Federal Securities and Investments Board, panting to impart the latest nuggets from the plea-bargaining of Duncan Trombo, the billionaire property tycoon now threatening to topple the régimes of three South American dictators and put yet another dent in the already battered image of US President Donald T. Ducque. The sun beat remorselessly down, all through June, on the seventeen treble-glazed floors of McRidley House, the disused office block where this investigative army was housed; inside, the fees increased and multiplied like yeast in a syrup tin. Lord Margoyle added his six penn'orth of confusion by getting Broody's to bang off a writ for compensation *in re* one thousand five hundred gassed grouse and pheasant and the utter ruination of eighteen months' hard consultancy on the part of MaxProf Associates, whose bill was outstanding.

In the stricken town of Craigfieth the after-shocks rumbled on. Dumbly its born-again citizens tuned in to Channel 423 to get the Word of God direct from HI! TV and got instead a black-edged screen wherein a photograph of Clyde and Chylblayne Bilt was displayed, interspersed with old Walt Disney nature movies. Thirty-six hours later the station closed down for ever and large quantities of video cassettes were impounded by the

Obscene Publications Squad in the interests of plot symmetry.

Hamish Ganglion tore up his blasphemy writ and wondered whether to be glad because Eastern Sight'n-'Sound had gone down the tubes, or sorry in case he didn't get his large cheque for the shop sale. To cheer himself up he stuck a notice in the shop window offering a fifty pound trade-in on any broken-down Eastern Sight'n'Sound product and, in what few gaps were afforded by the rush of custom this produced, bent his mental energies to solving the problem to the greater good of the family Ganglion.

Jerusalem House was occupied by a reformed former Inland Revenue inspector, a rather colourless little man who lived with his unmarried sister and peddled a hard line in self-denial and Godly asceticism. He spoke of all the rich men he had saved from error and demanded to know of his congregation if they were absolutely sure they weren't camels. Brethren of both sexes felt as though they had been pitched from the sunlit heights of Ararat into the very darkest November depths of Glencoe. Poor Mr Bilt had always made them feel so *good*.

Neville went to call on the new evangelist but came away disappointed. He had gone hoping to relieve his poverty, not to hear a lecture on its spiritual merits. The five hundred pounds he'd got for delivering the wretched 'Mkekwe' would not last much longer, even though Sayeed Haq, still awaiting trial in the Dunbroath Remand Centre, was hardly in a position to demand rent. Nobody spoke to him. He had a postcard from Grand Cayman – 'Great opportunities here – shame you never made it, James T. Kirk (Mrs)' – but apart from that his mail consisted of demands, final demands, and threats of disconnection. Even the Reader's Digest seemed to have forsaken him. He thought of selling his memoirs to the popular financial press, but got stuck on page two. He suffered a recurring nightmare in which hordes of hard-faced men with bowler hats and briefcases demanded to know why he wasn't wearing his trousers. He woke to the appalling realization that he was the sole surviving UK executive vice-president of Hosannah International (Say HI! to fraud, intimidation and financial irregularity). For many weeks his only point of human contact was the daily trip to check in at the police station where the sergeant gave him a cup of tea but the constable, when it was his turn, didn't. He frittered his money away on food that did not need cooking, and counted the days until the telephone bill came due.

The Craigfieth Gala Committee held an emotional emergency meeting (which Neville did not attend), co-opted Hamish, Mr Meiklejohn, Mr Borden, Mrs Spurtle and Catriona MacEachran, booted out Mr Glencairn junior and accepted the resignations of Sayeed Haq (in absentia) and Amanda Fingal, who was leaving the area because her husband had decided that Mid Lummock did not deserve the Cuisine of Tomorrow, Today. Gramps, she said (meaning her father-in-law) would be able to cope perfectly well on his own. She found it hard to keep the chagrin from her voice.

These preliminaries out of the way, it was resolved:

a) that they couldn't afford Mince'n'Tatties;

b) that they weren't really that funny, anyway, when all was said and done;

c) that this year's Gala not be called the First HI! To Christ In The Business Community Gala;

d) that it be called the Forty-Seventh Annual Craigfieth Shopping Gala instead;

e) that it be postponed, for obvious and various reasons, for eight weeks;

f) that they hoped August would not be as wet as it usually was;

g) that the WRI, the Brighter Gardens and Neater Wynds Action Group, the Stags, the Guides, the Scouts, the BBs, the Kipplerigg Distillery Pipe Band and the Craigfieth Well Women's Keep Fit and Macramé Group be asked if they could come up with something even though it was such short notice;

h) that it might not be a good idea to ask the Gospel Choir this year;

i) that someone should approach Maureen O'Rourke to see if they could get a discount;

j) that there probably wasn't much point approaching the District Council at the moment, as there didn't seem to be one for some reason;

k) that this probably didn't matter anyway, really;

l) that the Rev. MacAndrew be asked to open it as he hadn't done so since 1985;

m) that everybody ought to let bygones be bygones, for the sake of the Gala and the town generally.

This exhausting agenda completed, they sent down an order for a dozen packets of crisps (for the sake of the Ben Almond's table licence) and a reviving drink each, and three reviving drinks later they all went home under a yellow full moon and a sky of warm velvet. Mr Borden told his wife (Mr Meiklejohn his cat) that if a man was once a Craigfiethan he was always a Craigfiethan, and that he would most probably die in harness, and a good thing too. Mr Meiklejohn's cat purred and so, after a while, did Mrs Borden, though not for the same reason.

The Craigfieth Primary School Board agreed, on the casting vote of its Chairman the Rev. Gilleasbuig Mac-Andrew, to suspend Miss Pleat on full pay pending investigations of her Religious Studies syllabus and her account at Melmotte's Bank. Melmotte's Bank itself postponed its transformation into the Scot-Melmotte

One-Stop Moneyshop pending ongoing official enquiries into Trombo-related matters in London, New York and Liechtenstein. The Governor and Company of the Scottish Amiable and Providential Bank persuaded Mr McMurtry to stay on as Manager of their Craigfieth branch, and gave him a nice loyalty bonus for his success in stemming the haemorrhage of customers following the Kirk affair.

Benazir Haq won quite a lot on the Derby (so she said) and used it to revive the emporium's fortunes by stocking in to fill the gap left by the closure of Glencairn's.

Solly Chisholm patched up his old Kleinwort-Benson Offset and got ready to misprint the Gala programme as soon as someone told him what to put in it.

The *Perthshire Gazette* failed to come out two weeks running, and was then bought out by its ex-employees, using the redundancy money they would have had if the vendor had seen his way clear to paying it in the first place. Mungo's first leader was headlined: 'Say HI! To The Cashless Society'. One or two readers got the joke.

But before returning to this newly rechristened Editorial Co-Workers' Office in the Dunbroath Media Park and to his flat (now the subject of a bitter proprietorial wrangle that didn't bother him in the slightest), Mungo had one last favour to perform which he hoped would offset his signal failure to galvanize the Fourth Estate into championing the cause of the good guys. He borrowed a most professional-looking video camera from Sounds Good, blew the dust off it, decorated it with stickers left over from Perthshire Gazette Ltd's unsuccessful attempt to secure the Eastern Regional TV franchize, and drove to Dunbroath. There he called in at Jobs-U-Like where he found three of his former *Gazette* colleagues – the arts correspondent, the janitor and the girl with the amazing body and split ends who used to make the tea and check the syntax – gloomily scanning the temporary catering appointments. He took them off to the cocktail lounge of the Screen & Cursor, the purpose-built writers' pub next door to Presto's, stood them half a pint of low-alcohol heavy, and explained his plan.

At ten o'clock the following morning, armed with clipboards and propelling ball-point pens, they bluffed their way past the security guards at the West Bromwich offices of the Norwich Royal Alliance Commercial and Accident Union Insurance Company, filmed their way from reception to the penthouse office of the managing director and introduced themselves as the team from *Name that Scam*, the weekly consumers' programme on Pan-Global Television. Half an hour later they filmed their way out again, pausing only to sign autographs in the company's Circumlocution Office, and drove home.

When Oswald collected his post three days later he found a letter authorizing the rebuilding of Rose Cottage as per estimate and a fairly substantial cheque to defray his accommodation expenses in the meantime: enough, they reckoned, for a third bedroom for MacGregor with a bit left over for a holiday when supplies finally ran out in the Bunker.

At a Top Secret meeting of the National ▆▆▆▆ and ▆▆▆▆▆ Committee in ▆▆▆▆▆▆, General ▆▆▆-▆▆▆▆ suggested sending the SAS in to 'regularize' the situation at Boggybreck.

The Permanent Secretary of the Ministry of ▆▆▆▆▆▆ pointed out that the whole point of underground regional centres of government was that they should be terrorist-proof.

The Attorney-General drew the committee's attention to the tricky legal situation *in re* ownership of the site. 'It could all come out in court,' he warned.

Sir ▆▆▆▆▆ ▆▆▆▆▆▆▆, GCMG asked why the hell hadn't something been done about this privilege business, people being able to say what they damn well wanted in parliament and the courts for example?

The Home Secretary said he was working on it but could promise nothing until the next session at the earliest. It would take time to square the backbenchers, he explained.

Sir ██████ ███████████, said he'd hoped for something better after four terms of thumping majorities.

After further discussion it was agreed to remit the matter of the Boggybreck Bunker for later consideration with the committee's blind eye.

The minutes of the meeting were sealed for a hundred years, and they all went off to their clubs.

Sergeant MacEachran continued not to bother himself with matters of civil law, and saw no particular reason why the continuance of the Boggybreck squat should be likely, now that God's entrepreneurs had gone to collect their Heavenly dividend, to provoke a criminal offence. The three squatters remained out of sight until the last reporters had finished interviewing each other and gone, then carried on with their lives much as before but with fewer precautions. They parked the 2CV in the open unless it was raining (which it hardly ever was that summer, except for the occasional refreshing overnight shower) and recklessly exposed themselves, even to the extent of MacGregor taking his jacket off, to the sun's carcinogenic benison. They planted out the *Cannabis indica*, trained its vigorous growth up the south-facing wall, and had Audrey and Dora over for naughty alfresco afternoon tea. They grew beards as a filter for ultra-violet radiation, and slobbed about a lot. Sometimes they played the tapes Deuda Externa had left them as a thank-you present; sometimes they couldn't be bothered to put them on. They dozed, in the sun, like doped Galapagos lizards.

Audrey Pitt-Holyoake took Dora Quaich in until the receivers came up with a solution to her problems or Lord Margoyle sent the bailiffs in, whichever should be the sooner. The Highland Craft Centre enquired, without the least trace of apology, if Audrey still wished to take delivery of her order; she negotiated a fifteen per cent discount, and said yes. Dora had a go with the paint-roller on Audrey's production line; the results though primitive, sold steadily and Dora insisted the proceeds go straight into the till. 'By way of . . . you know, dear,' she said; thus was reached an amicable understanding over such distasteful matters as rent, bills and so on. She found the transition from retired headmistress to part-time shop assistant entirely unalarming and even enjoyable, once she got the hang of things. It was nice to twitch the reins of power again, and she flatly refused to take wages. Audrey missed her privacy, of course, though she did nothing to show it. She laid all her solitary habits, her little likings and routines, to one side for the time being and told herself how nice it was to have so much time off from the shop and so little excuse to brood alone. June 30th came, and went, and nothing happened except that Mr Snotter started sending the rent back. She put it in the building society instead.

Volunteers were out stringing bunting across the High Street as Hamish drove off, early on the morning of August 11th, through the dew-damp back roads of Mid Lummock to the Glasgow motorway. When he returned that evening the gaiety was complete and the High Street stage all set for the morrow's excitements. A passing shower at lunchtime had washed most of the dust off the bunting and saved Mr Duff (the elder) the trouble of rinsing the shampoo off the Duff Garage's Austin Princess Hearse which, with a little internal camouflage, was to serve as the Gala Queen's chariot in the parade. Someone had tactfully pinned alternate Union Jacks and Saltires over the guiltily empty windows of the Ministry of the Interior and the patch on the scorched roof of the house next to Sounds Good. The shop itself had been decorated by Ashley Oswald and Tammy Sproat who had raided forgotten corners of Ganglion's old workshop at the back and come up with a festive selection of horn gramophones, coffin-like wirelesses and an early television that looked like a cocktail cabinet with a porthole in it. Dusted and polished and unembarrassed by juxta position with aluminium and vinyl it all made, in Hamish's opinion, a most impressive display. Nice lad, Tammy, he thought; shame about the family, but a good lad, Tammy. He was in expansive and generous mood that evening.

He drove slowly down the flag-shadowed street, noting with approval how every shop and every house – every inhabited house, at least – had done its bit to ensure that the Forty-Seventh Annual Craigfieth Shopping Gala should be as much like all the others as possible. Even the Misses Urquhart had made a go of things; the corsets in Madame's window were draped and sprigged with tinsel. Tradition, Hamish decided, was a good thing. He parked the van and let himself in. He kissed Grace and congratulated Ashley Oswald on the Sounds Good display. Ashley Oswald asked if he could go and play at Tammy's and Hamish said yes before Grace could stop him. He kissed her again and helped her browbeat Wally into bed. Then he told her to forget about supper for a bit, and took her into the sitting-room where he poured them each a generous whisky and made her sit down.

'Fancy doing business with me, hen?' he asked.

Grace choked in mid-swallow. 'Hamish!' she spluttered. 'I've got all sorts of things to do and Ashley Oswald – '

407

'Oh, that as well later on now you mention it, yeah!'
He grinned. 'There's arrears to make up there, and all.
No, what I meant was, you know, go into partnership in
the shop, properly. The family firm of G.and H. Ganglion, like Mungo said.'

'Oh,' said Grace. 'You mean you've really . . .'

'Yeah!' said Hamish. 'Well – go on! Ask me!'

'Oh yes. Did you get the money for it, then?'

'Nope!' Hamish smiled and folded his arms.

'Oh. You . . . had to take a reduction then, did you?
Like it said in the papers? Sixty pence in the pound.'

'Nope!'

'Fifty?'

Hamish shook his head.

'Forty? Oh, Hamish! How much?'

'As my dad would say, nuffink. Nix. Not a bean.'

'Oh Hamish what are we going to – '

'I did a swap instead.'

'A *swap?* Wh-what for?'

'The family firm of G. and H. Ganglion, Ltd. And son.
Sons.'

'You . . . ? I don't understand, Hamish! How could
you . . . oh Hamish, how could you?'

'Easy. I had it all worked out. Okay, listen pet and I'll
tell you. First I'll fill these holes in our drinks, it's no fun
driving past pubs all day. Water, pet? Oh, there's no
room. What a shame. Now, then.' He flung himself in the
sofa – a thing they spent half their time telling Wally not
to do – took a languorous slurp at his fortified dram, and
began.

'Okay. In the beginning was the Cummingses and Mrs
Quaich, right?'

'Were, Hamish.'

'And they lived on either side of Number 33, High
Street, Craigfieth, also known as Holmlea, also known as

408

the Scottish Produce Centre, right? And then they sold up, to an outfit callin' itself Clinch McKittrick.' He took another sip.

'We know all this, Hamish.'

'Yeah: but there's knowin' . . . and knowin'. Right. So what happens next is, Number 31 has a flood and all its ceilings fall in, and Number 35 just sits there empty, right?'

'Yes,' said Grace impatiently. 'And then all those other places start getting bought up, and then there's the fire – Hamish, I know all – '

'Listen, who's tellin' this story, you or me? Eh? Okay. Time passes. The page of history turns. De-de-de-dummmm! Good whisky, this . . . sorry. Right. Then I agree to sell Sounds Good, papers signed, everything – '

'To Clinch McKittrick.' Grace's tone was reproachful.

'We-ell, to a guy who when I say "Are you Clinch McKittrick, pal?" he says, yeah, well, maybe, why not, call it that if you want to. So, yes, same thing really, given that Clinch McKittrick doesn't exist and never has done, officially.'

'Is that true? You asked the – people?'

'The Official Receiver, no less. Yup. What they call a ghost, acting for a lot of shells.'

'Shells?'

'Blueknicker Properties, Ripoff Holdings, Screw-Your-Granny Inc, all them.'

'Oh, Hamish.'

'Yeah, well, these are the nineties. Anyway: I sell it. Or agree to. Now, thing is of course all these other outfits – the shells – they're all one thing, right?'

'Mr Bilt's . . . Church?'

'Praying all the way to the bank, yeah. Hosannah International, the First Church of Christ the Con-man. All just front organizations, you see. What they wanted to do, seemingly, was to turn Craigfieth into a sort of dormitory suburb for their new town on Oswald's dad's old farm, with no shops of course, cos that'd be competition, just lots of little ticky-tacky boxes and flats in all the houses they hoped to get cheap cos by then the place'd be going down the tubes anyway. Long-term economic strategy, the guy I saw called it. He made me promise not to tell anybody, by the way, okay? Telling you's different. Right. So. It's obvious, isn't it!'

'What is, Hamish?'

'What I should do about it?'

'I don't . . . what can you do about it?'

'Do a swap, of course! See, the way I saw it was, with all the assets of HI! in America frozen cos of the scandal about, whatsisname, Donald Cornet or whatever it is, and all the Scottish end sitting on a cloud playing their electronic harps, it seemed to me the one thing the receivers wouldn't be able to come up with was money. So I did a swap instead: Sounds Good for Number 31 and Number 35. There, now!'

'You mean . . . we . . . ?'

'Yup! Well, you said you needed the extra space, didn't you? You've enough room to buy up the whole of Magic Banana now, haven't you? Or should I say . . . haven't *we*?'

'Oh, Hamish!'

'Yeah? What d'ye think then?'

'Oh, Hamish! Is it . . . I mean . . . ?'

'Oh, sure. Look.' He drew a wad of paper from his inside jacket pocket, passed it across, and loosened his tie. 'Comes to something when you have to wear one o' these to get what you want,' he commented. 'Well?'

'It all looks . . .' his wife agreed. 'Oh . . . Hamish!'

'I know!' He laughed. 'C'mon, make space for a refill, eh?'

'. . . extra bedroom,' Grace murmured.

'Yeah, well . . . if you really want one we could knock through, I suppose. But why would you want one?'

'Isn't it silly?' she added after she'd told him. 'All I could think of in the end was that Ashley Oswald's birthday was coming up and we might not have been able to afford his bike and I'd have to . . . Isn't it awful? Seeing it like that. As if we couldn't have managed. But then I was so worried, Hamish, you see, what with . . . well . . .'

'Yeah.' Hamish drained both their glasses. 'When?'

Grace blushed. 'Boxing Day,' she said. 'Probably. And Mrs MacAndrew the minister's wife's expecting about the same time, Angus Monzie says!

'Not that I want her to be christened, of course,' she added. 'I agree with your dad about that.'

'Oh, yeah,' said Hamish absently. 'Right.'

'I'm sure it *is* a she.'

'Oh . . . right. Great.'

'Um, Hamish?'

'Yeah?'

'When Mungo was here?'

'Yeah?'

'You weren't . . . I mean you didn't . . . feel . . . did you? Because I know we – '

'C'mere!' leered Hamish, avoiding the question and not giving her the option.

Later, Ashley Oswald diplomatically made himself a peanut butter sandwich and watched television. That was the great thing about being best pals with Tammy: you got to learn things.

August 12th, Gala Day, dawned bright and fair. An hour later it started to rain. Later still, the wind got up. By ten o'clock, with an hour to go, a driving gale swept up the streets of Craigfieth with a miserable, drenching broom.

411

At a quarter to eleven the rain stopped and the wind died away. The sun broke through at ten fifty-five. At eleven o'clock the Maureen O'Rourke Body Development Workshop Artistes (at one end of the High Street) and the Craigfieth Well Women's Keep Fit and Macramé Group (at the other) hoofed it up in coils of rising steam that made them look like outsize denizens of Faërie, or tramplers of some mystic harvest, or at any rate like two groups of enthusiastic females dancing to disco music in shiny stretch lurex on the warm, rain-sodden tarmac. One group made up with artistic expression what the other gained in technical expertise, and after half an hour the honours were judged about even.

Duff the elder's converted hearse added its own quota of steam to the scene as it bore the Gala Queen, Mr Borden's grand-daughter Lizzie, ponderously up the street to her makeshift dais in the middle of the round-about where the Mercat Cross used to be. In her wake came the Boys' Brigade, fluting in an Orange sort of way on their instruments, and the Scouts, the foremost of whom tried to kick the ankles of the rearmost BBs without being caught, and the Brownies all wearing their Brownie Smile: never, surely, was so much pre-sexual loathing ever gathered together in one place to celebrate community fellow-feeling.

The WRI followed, carrying a fifteen-foot plywood-and-foil abstract representing the Spirit of the Burgh and only dropping it twice. The Stags paraded in full dress aprons and Class Two Jewels. The Brighter Gardens and Neater Wynds Action Group, all six of them, came dressed as a herbaceous border and succeeded, more or less, in keeping in step. The Kipplerigg Distillery Pipe Band played the Foreshot Reel, the Low Wines Jig and the Mash Tun Rant, and set two thousand feet a-tapping, though not all at the same time. Sergeant MacEachran

412

helped the WRI to keep their effigy from falling over; Constable Simison bullied the Brownies; a hush fell over all the town as the Rev. MacAndrew rose to give the oration.

'My friends,' he said, then paused a while in thought while the public address system got itself seen to.

'My friends,' he continued. 'Today's celebrations may, I think, be summed up by a paraphrase of Dylan Thomas's great radio play, *Under Milk Wood*:

> "We are not wholly lost and done
> Who live our lives under Ben Gunn."'

Three people in the audience smiled inwardly; the rest looked at each other and shuffled. The minister was off to a bad start.

'This is the Forty-Seventh Gala,' he continued: applause: this was more like it. 'And I am sure you will agree with me when I say it richly deserves to follow the other forty-six!' Cheering: all was forgiven. 'It is, indeed, a magnificent effort! My friends, I am not going to make a long speech.' Cheers. 'But I would just like to say this.' More foot-shuffling; an outbreak of coughs; silence.

'If today's Gala shows anything, means anything, stands for anything, it is this: we are one community, united in our lives together here, in the Vale of Lummock. We stand or fall, thrive or fail, laugh or weep – together. We are one community. And our community is part of one nation, of one continent, of one world, living together under Heaven. That is what the Gala . . . means to me. We all share the same sky, my friends. It looks down on us all. And so I say to you – enjoy your Gala! Enjoy it to the full. And then – let us see if we cannot make a Gala in our hearts, and make it last – all the year round!'

He crowned Lizzie Borden in appreciative, thoughtful

silence. Then the High School Wind Band (those who hadn't gone abroad for their holidays) blew a fanfare, and amid mighty cheering the real business of Craigfieth's Carnival Day got underway in shop, hotel and tearoom as the sun shone profligately down.

Neville Wringhim, alone in his cold room, put the telephone down and frowned. He thought. He frowned again. He picked the phone up to make a call. It had gone dead. He shrugged. He had nothing to lose. He went upstairs to pack.

Audrey, Ganglion, Oswald and MacGregor rested in Grace and Hamish's sitting-room while their hosts went off to make tea.

'They seem very close!' Audrey remarked.

'She told 'im,' said Ganglion. 'An' 'e told 'er.'

'Ah,' said Audrey.

'Any news?' asked Oswald.

Audrey shook her head. 'No. Nothing. I really don't know what's going to happen. I understand from what I've read that if they don't go to court within three months of the date they gave me to quit, then the whole show's called off.'

'Oh, well!' said Ganglion. 'Only anuvver six-seven weeks ter go, then.'

'Yes. But I can't help wishing they would, you know. At least it would give me something to get my teeth into!'

'Aye,' said MacGregor. 'I know the feeling.'

'I've tried writing to his daughter, you know. Lord Margoyle's daughter, Davinia Kirkpatrick as I suppose she is now she's married our old DIY man. No good, though.'

'Oh?' said Oswald.

'Oh, well, very sympathetic you know, but she said her

father wouldn't listen to her since her marriage and until she inherited – well, "until the old man kicks the bucket" is how she put it – there was nothing she could do.'

'Ar,' said Ganglion. 'Well, 'e *is* over eighty.'

'Yes, I know. It's something of a race against the clock, isn't it? No, that's a horrible thought. Oh, I don't know. If I could just explain to him, you know? Just explain that all I really want is to die in my own home – he'd understand that, wouldn't he?'

'He's got more choice,' Oswald pointed out. 'Of homes, I mean.'

MacGregor laid a bony claw on Audrey's knee. 'He would not understand one word you were saying,' he assured her. 'Believe me. It's in the blood, that kind of ignorance.'

Audrey sighed. 'Oh well, you may be right. All the others have gone you know – all the rest. I did try to, you know, rally them round. They just seemed to accept it. Fatalism, really, I suppose, like they used to do out East when they thought they'd had the evil eye put on them. They just seemed to give up. As if – oh, I don't know – as if it was like being caught in the rain without one's umbrella, do you see? Why complain if you get wet.' She sighed again.

'They've had two hundred years of it,' MacGregor pointed out.

Audrey nodded. 'Yes, I suppose that's it. It's funny, you know, I never really thought of myself as – well different, if you see what I mean, until this happened. I always thought I belonged. Now it seems I just live here – if I even do *that* for much long – Ah! Tea! How splendid! I was just saying how much I was longing for a nice cup of tea, wasn't I, Oswald?'

'Aye! Me too, Grace ma dear. Lovely!'

Hamish grinned. 'We've agreed a name for it, Dad!'

415

'Wot? Already? Pore little bleeder, it's barely more'n a twinkle in it's – '

Oswald nudged him. 'I think he means the shop, Ganglion,' he said. 'Is that right? It's the shop?'

'Yeah, that's it.'

'Well cahm on then! Let's be 'avin' it!'

'Oswald just said it, Dad.'

'Said wot?'

'The name!' Grace passed cups round.

'Wot – just . . .'

'Yup, that's it. The Shop. Good, eh? Can't you just hear folks saying, "Let's go to The Shop"?'

'Oh, ar. Like as not it will be, too, rate you're goin'. Bloated plutocrats!'

'Oh, no!' Grace was shocked. 'We wouldn't want to put people out of business, would we, Hamish?'

'Hell, no! Just fill a few gaps like. You know.'

'Ur,' said his father dubiously.

'Well, I think it's splendid!' said Audrey, putting down her cup. 'Now you men – you promised me you'd accompany me to the clarsach recital in the Community Centre, remember? It's a shame about Mrs Thrush's poetry, but that can't be helped. Come on!'

'Poor Audrey,' said Grace as they went off.

'Aye,' said Hamish. 'Ach, she'll be all right. You'll see. Things'll work out: look at us.'

'Oh well. Maybe. Let's hope so, anyway. All right, Wally, Mummy's coming!'

Neville got a lift out of Craigfieth on the back of a lorry taking a load of Lummock Earlies to the tattie canning factory in Ballydull. His last sight of the town was of his former employer, Hamish Ganglion, apparently engaged in receiving a large sum of money – cash – in exchange for the junk in his shop window. The vision seemed, to

Neville, to sum up the cruel caprice of fate, in so far as it applied to him. Never, he thought, had market forces so deranged themselves in order to persecute one man. The sun was also too hot. He hurt himself bouncing up and down on the potatoes as the lorry careered cheerfully along the ill-patched main road. One of his suitcase catches broke. He wished he was dead.

He stood, now, as instructed, on a sort of greenish-yellow island of land surrounded by an evilly glinting, bog-pocked mire criss-crossed, in places, by lengths of sagging barbed wire and rotting fenceposts. Empty fertilizer sacks, their legends bleached by the sun and rain, stirred fitfully in a sluggish breeze that brought to the unhappy youth a whiff of nauseous sweet decay. In the distance, shimmering in the heat and haze, was the glint of machinery of some sort and the lower walls of a house, whether half-built or half-demolished it was impossible to tell. Neville peered hopefully at it for some time, but nothing moved and there were no sounds of activity. Whatever might have been there yesterday, whoever might be there tomorrow, there was nobody there today. They were probably at the Gala. Neville was alone. He sat on his suitcase and looked at his shoes. They were caked with mud. His trouser bottoms were like two filthy wicks.

The suitcase collapsed.

Not an animal stirred, not a bird sang. Half-a-Job had cleared his stock, and sold his farm, and taken a half share in a fast-food franchize in Dunbroath. The farmhouse was already half-derelict.

A dot appeared over the eastern horizon; a few seconds later Neville heard a faint angry buzzing noise. The dot grew bigger and started flashing in the sun; the buzz became a pulsing, whirring throb and all at once, it seemed, the small black bug-eyed helicopter was hovering

417

overhead, flattening the thin unhealthy grass with its rotors and making Neville cower and cover his head. The awful noise died slowly until it became a threshing, then a swishing, then a deafening silence. Neville uncovered his eyes and looked up.

A door opened. A figure stepped nimbly out, advanced towards him, then stopped, smiling and nodding its head.

'Mr . . .' Neville croaked. 'Gil . . . Martin?'

'Simeon,' said the man softly. 'Nick Simeon. But you can go on calling me The Man. Okay, Nev. Time to quit.' But he did not move.

Neville struggled messily to his feet, hugging his suitcase. The arm of a shirt had leaked out of it and he trod on the cuff and almost fell over. He recovered and stuffed the soiled thing back in. A sock fell out.

'H-how do you mean . . . quit, Mr . . . Man?'

'Hell,' said The Man irritably. 'What's quit in any language? Scram, vamoose, clear out, skedaddle. Go someplace else, yeah?'

'With . . . you?'

'Unless you're figuring to fly this little beauty yourself, Neville. But I don't think you could really handle that, do you?'

'But – ' Neville's head swam. 'I mean – what about my – my bail?'

'I reckon we get what we pay for, Neville, don't you? Those of us who can afford to buy it, that is to say. I certainly do hope so, anyway, Neville. You're not going to make me regret what I paid for you, are you?'

'*You?*'

'Sure.' The Man turned and began to stroll back to the helicopter as if unbothered whether Neville came too, or stayed and slit his throat, or anything. 'Kind of a golden hello, shall we say?'

Neville stumbled to catch him up. 'You mean you . . . I still have my job?'

'I mean we have uses for you, Neville, okay? That's all you need to know at this moment in time. I mean we think you're gonna do as you are told. I mean I'm gonna lose your bail bond in the accounting someplace, 'stead of getting it back when I deliver you up. I mean that what *you* know, Neville, and what *I* know, is gonna remain strictly between the two of us. I sure hope so, anyway. Don't you?' The Man swiped at a fly buzzing round his head. 'Jesus, this place sucks. I'm going now, Neville.'

Neville felt himself tugged forward again. 'To America?' he said.

'The US is a dud number right now, Neville. Too many windows of opportunity blocked up.' The Man's face kindled into something like animation. 'South Koh-rea, boy. That's the place; good ole South Koh-rea, got more Christian conversions per head of population than any place else on this entire planet. I'm talking Pan-Asiatic Fellowship Industries, boy. Gonna build us a Rocket to Redemption right there in that Seoul Olympic Stadium, gonna launch it, whoosh! Gonna get ourselves a little trading liquidity that way, right?' The light died. 'C'mon, punk,' he said, turning away and wiping his feet carefully on the grass.

Neville saw that he was perhaps twenty-five years younger than this man, and two stones heavier, and a foot taller. He would have liked very much to kill him and thought he could do it, too, quite easily.

Instead he followed as if on a string when The Man stepped into the helicopter.

'That's right,' said his master, strapping himself in. 'You just go right on doing that, okay? And we'll get along just fine.'

The machine rose into the forgetful air, and disappeared.

Lord Margoyle pulled to the left, discharged both barrels, and swore. Half a mile away Scrymgeour and Havers threshed about in the fodder radish trying to flush out something for the Laird to shoot at, and frowned fearfully. The Laird was not in the best of tempers this Glorious Twelfth, his game bag boasting so far only two crows, three seagulls and a brownish sort of bird that wasn't a thrush.

Lord Margoyle's moustache bristled at the passing helicopter. He reloaded and let it have both barrels; his aim this time was true but The Man was not about to become Corporate Chairman of Pan-Asiatic Fellowship Industries without having bullet-proof protection. The Laird swore again; damn upstarts, flying through *his* air! As if he hadn't enough to put up with: what with some damn fool sky-pilot digging up a lot of bombs and killing all the game; what with the gutter press sniping at him for controlling the vermin; what with Davinia – his own flesh and blood, if somewhat more pleasingly arranged than his was – yapping at him about some beastly woman, shopkeeper or something, who wouldn't leave her house like all the others had! He'd told her: dammit, yes, he'd told her. She could do what she damn well liked with the place when he was dead – that's what feudal tenure was all about, after all – except sell it! Ha! ha! The Margoyle Entail would see to that. She could turn it into a girls' school or a knocking-shop as far as he was concerned, only she'd have to make it pay, by God, she'd have to do that! And if she thought she could make it pay by pandering to a lot of scribbling lefties and bleating old crones, she had another think coming!

I might as well be damn well dead, he thought. Damn

420

nancy-boy lawyers dragging their feet over suing those American game-gassers; MaxProf's damned extortionate bill to pay; the castle to keep up, with dry rot in all eight dumb waiters; the damn tenants down in Berkshire getting uppity and calling themselves the Dottle Parva, Forelocke and Little Pander Claimants' Collective – no sense of feudal heritage there, of course – and here he was with not a grouse to aim at, shootin' vermin, and there seemed to be bugger all of them to aim at, either. Damn and blast Davinia! No sense of loyalty at all. Comes of marryin' a shopkeeper herself, he thought; can't think what she sees in him, apart from the obvious. Bad blood there somewhere, he decided, meaning his late wife's. Sister of that bloody little squirt Foutret; insisted he do his bit, as Laird, to get the little twerp elected. Bah! And what had that led to, in the end? That ridiculous little Abdul-a-Bulbul creature, or whatever he called himself, who hadn't even got the nous to stay alive! Why if he'd –

A shout of triumph from Scrymgeour and Havers alerted the peer's attention to a lazily flapping hoodie that hauled its distended guts contemptuously across his field of fire some twenty feet above the ground. Hah! Perhaps Mrs Axelrod could make a pie out of it or something, to give to the servants. He raised his gun and blasted at it. The crow folded what was left of its wings, and fell with a distant plump! somewhere in a field of sickly green stuff half a mile or so to his Lordship's right.

Rifkind, the grey-muzzled retriever, strained for permission to go seek. Lord Margoyle grunted assent, and the dog loped rheumatically off. The Laird followed, crashing through the cover crop on his all-terrain tricycle.

Scrymgeour and Havers sighed, mopped their brows, and rested on their hand-tooled 'Gamekeeper's Friend' walking sticks-cum-cudgels, a Present Frae Blairlummock.

They watched in silence as their master set off in motorized pursuit of his extinguished quarry.

'Aye,' muttered Havers. 'I tell't ye ane o' us should ha' been wi' Lordy, tae help him steer.'

'Dinna be disrespectfu',' growled Scrymgeour.

The Laird drew to a crashing halt just in time to see Rifkind, hackles up and lips curled, back away from a black something on the ground.

'Good boy, Rifkind,' he wheezed. 'Daddy knows it's not a grouse, hruargh! Pick it up then, damn yer!'

The dog growled, and backed off further still. The Laird growled at the dog, aimed a kick at it, missed, and picked the bird up himself, losing two jacket buttons in the process.

It was wet underneath, and cold, and very dead. Its insides, where Lord Margoyle's fingers met, might well have glowed, had it been dark. 'Tcha!' exclaimed the Laird, and flung the slimy thing away. Rifkind barked. 'Bugger off, damn yer!' the Laird bawled. The dog did so. He was alone. A lark sang overhead, then saw a buzzard on the horizon and stopped.

The Laird panted stertorously from his efforts, and groped with a clean hand for his handkerchief; then arrested it in mid-grope. His watery eyes had spied in the little valley below the very fount and source of some, at least, of his present woe: Dante Cottage, its kitchen chimney smoking faintly in the still summer air from Audrey's banking of the Rayburn, the clematis round the door in full ephemeral bloom. Swiftly, irrationally, the peer focussed all his frustrated anger on its absent occupant.

'Damn yer!' he breathed. 'Damn yer eyes, you hideous old hag! Why can't you be dead? Whose bloody house d'ye think it is, eh, whose land, whose property?' He grew quite purple about the chops, and stuck his little finger in his ear to calm himself down. He reamed it round a few times then drew it out to see what was on the end of it.

Something ought to be done, dammit, something *would* be done! He was here now, and while the Laird was in residence there wasn't a single bloody gutterpress reporter going to set so much as a suede toecap on *his* estate! Bulldozers, that was the only language these people understood. Cranes. Big steel bally balls! He'd show the snivelling little guttersnipes what property meant!

He stuck his finger in his mouth and nibbled it clean.

Yes, that or something like it. Smoke her out! Tell Snotter to cut off her amenities and make it look like maintenance, that was the way, these days as in days of old, nothing really changed, by God not on his land it didn't!

He smacked his lips. Amazing what you could store in an ear, sometimes. He fixed his eyes on Audrey's roof, imagined it holed and sagging, imagined the whole place wired off for fear of falling slates! – Funny, the sun seemed to have stopped giving off any heat for some reason – That was the way! Show 'em all what's what! Teach 'em all a lesson they'd never – why was he suddenly so . . .

Scrymgeour lowered his binoculars and covered his eyes. 'My God!' he choked. 'The Laird's – '

Charles Stewart Bonar Moither, Baron Margoyle, Laird of Lunie, Lord of the Manors of Dottle Parva, Forelocke and Little Pander, turned very pale. Then he flushed; then paled again, and flushed again, sweat pouring from every crater. His life, scarcely any prettier, crawled before him. He bared his fangs. He groaned. He fell over.

'Strychnine,' muttered Havers, straightening. 'From the looks o' him.'

'More likely a shooting accident, I should say,' said Scrymgeour, calmly wiping his late master's right hand and arranging it on the trigger. 'Both barrels, as he fell. Like this.'

Epilogue

It is a warm late indian summer afternoon some time in the slightly more distant near future.

Joan Spurtle, genteel caterer and co-chairperson of the People's Alternative Council of Mid Lummock, returns from a hugely successful inaugural press conference in the upper function suite of the Ben Almond Hotel to bully her autumn crocus. It is her afternoon off, after all.

At the Bide-a-Wee Tearooms Miss Phemister, resplendent in a new two-piece from Madame's Bargain Rail and an exciting pair of tights from The Shop, sings to the dishwasher as she works on her nails with an emery board. Out in the tearooms proper Mrs Dora Quaich, her true vocation found at last, puts a firm but pleasant stop to a customer's complaint and wonders, as she smiles, if she shall take two scones home with her this evening or three, as it's a Saturday. A warm, convenient flat above The Shop's furniture, gardening and toy department in what used to be her old, unmanageable home, awaits her, as does a cheque in final settlement from the Official Receiver.

Mr Fingal potters slowly about in his sun-flooded back yard and thinks about trying a few flies this evening to catch the last of the trout season on the Fieth. All sorts of visiting fishy folk come to see him these days, and nobody minds about the VAT.

Jessie MacAndrew and Grace Ganglion swell and bloom with increase. Hamish and the minister bask in the reflected glory; the former explores Eastern Region for antique wireless sets, gramophones and televisions and gives them to his father to tinker with, the latter is about to publish *Shall Brothers Be*, a collection of sermons and essays for the new century, so soon to dawn. Both have appeared on the *Perthshire Gazette*'s new local TV channel.

Aeneas Meiklejohn smiles and waves to his successor through the window of the chemist's as he sets off for a round of evening golf and gossip with Mr Glencairn senior, now a regular refugee from the Silver Threads Retirement Estate in Bonquhars. He wonders, for the hundredth time, why he never thought of renting out the shop before. The new pharmacist is such a pleasant person. He decides, again for the hundredth time, to leave the place to her in his will.

He passes the Craft Corner – closed early today and who can blame her, this lovely weather – and Sounds Good, now leased back by its former owner – where *do* young people get their energy from, these days? – where Lance Sproat, such a good lad he's turned out, polishes the charmed walnut casements and turns the little white labels price-side down. He nods to Wayne Kirkpatrick – or should one call him Lord? So confusing! – who is chatting suavely to a client in Honourable Designs the old DIY shop already quite rid of its murky past as the Ministry of the Interior.

He stops to catch his breath on the street corner and to inspect – if he can find the right glasses to inspect it through – the renovation work going on at the old museum, shortly to reopen as a hostel for homeless youth. Where would we be without charities these days? he wonders. Or charity itself, come to that. He adjusts his bow tie in the window of the Duff Brothers Motor Showroom, and makes his way to the golf course.

'Ah!' sighs Audrey Pitt-Holyoake, gently setting down her teacup and acknowledging a no-thank-you-I'm-fine

426

from her three guests. 'Autumn has o'erbrimmed my clammy cells!'

'Yeurgh!' says Ganglion.

'It's Keats,' she smiles. 'Well, mostly it is. What a wonderful autumn, though, after all the summer of our discontent, don't you think?'

The fields around them spring with winter barley and flow with tides of curly kale. Beyond, and over the horizon, the Independent University of Design, lately Lunie Castle, where Davinia, Lady Margoyle, presides as vice-chancellor over her aspiring alumni, glows in tones of gold and madder in the expiring sun. Davinia sips dry sherry as she marks some first-year Craft papers, pausing now and again to fax the better ones through to Snotter, now returned to the land of his fathers as an overseer at the Highland Craft Workshops in Blairlummock. The wonderful thing about a fax machine, she thinks, as it chatters away to itself in the corner, is not having to see people. Especially horrid old Snotter.

Audrey feels the chill and collects the cups to take them indoors and put a match to the sitting-room grate. Her guests wash and dry and put away the tea things.

'Roll on next month!' she says returning with a shawl. 'Though I daresay it isn't always hot in Bolivia either.'

'Not in the Andes certainly,' Oswald agrees. 'We'll have to buy lots of Aztec rugs and suchlike, I expect.'

'Oh, the Andes, yes! What a wonderful way to spend November, especially!'

'Wot a wonderful way ter spend back rent, come ter that,' says Ganglion.

'Or fiddled insurance money,' MacGregor wheezes, grinning.

'Don't forget to pack your *sgian dubh*, Roderick, in case we meet any conquistadoring Campbells!'

'It *wasn't* his *sgian dubh*, I keep telling ye, it was his – '

'I know,' says Audrey, squeezing his arm. 'Only teasing, my dear.'

She kisses them goodnight and waves them away back to their new improved Rose Cottage. Then she goes upstairs for her evening tub and callisthenics.

A quick mist gathers in the Vale of Lummock, obscuring the Chronicler's view as Sergeant MacEachran on his untroubled beat drops in at the Fire Station for a dram and a can or two. The good ship Craigfieth – a little leaky, much patched and lately somewhat mutinous – sails on into the uncharted waters of the twenty-first century, there to contend with who knows what reefs and shoals, doldrums, hurricanes and monsters, all no doubt too numerous and too frequent for its liking, but all too far ahead to be reliably foreseen. Night, moth-dark, falls at last.

Mrs Fotheringhame had her hip fixed. Grace had twin girls.